T0036402

THE LIGHT AFTER THE STORM

CHRIS GLATTE

SEVERN RIVER
PUBLISHING

Copyright © 2024 Chris Glatte.

All rights reserved.

No part of this book may be reproduced in any form or by any electronic or mechanical means, including information storage and retrieval systems, without written permission from the author, except for the use of brief quotations in a book review.

Severn River Publishing
www.SevernRiverBooks.com

This is a work of fiction. Names, characters, businesses, places, events and incidents are either the products of the author's imagination or used in a fictitious manner. Any resemblance to actual persons, living or dead, or actual events is purely coincidental.

ISBN: 978-1-64875-583-5 (Paperback)

ALSO BY CHRIS GLATTE

A Time to Serve Series

A Time to Serve

The Gathering Storm

The Scars of Battle

The Last Test of Courage

The Light After the Storm

Tark's Ticks Series

Tark's Ticks

Valor's Ghost

Gauntlet

Valor Bound

Dark Valley

War Point

164th Regiment Series

The Long Patrol

Bloody Bougainville

Bleeding the Sun

Operation Cakewalk (Novella)

Standalone Novel

Across the Channel

To find out more about Chris Glatte and his books, visit

severnriverbooks.com

For my Mom, Mary Glatte, her spirit and grit will always inspire.

1

Brooks Industries
Seattle, Washington
Late June, 1944

"Come on, boss, let me kill him. It'll solve everything."

Victor Brooks repulsed at the idea. He stared hard at Guy Hastings's small, wiry frame and his hate-filled eyes. *By God, he'd do it. One word from me and he wouldn't hesitate.*

"No," he stated flatly. "I've known the man since childhood. I'm not a killer!"

"Which is why I'd kill him. You can keep your hands clean."

A week had passed since Sal showed up demanding Victor turn himself into the authorities for the Trask arson. Sal remained locked in the spare room at the bottom of the stairs. He'd arranged a bed and a toilet system for him, but despite wracking his brain, he still had no idea what to do with him. Killing him actually made sense—but no. He couldn't do that even though Sal had clearly lost his mind—or was at least tipping in that direction.

"You're already on thin ice, Hastings. Your little plot to take care of the journal without my knowledge was a mistake. Sending men to Texas without my permission? Inexcusable."

Hastings's eyes went to the floor in shame, but Victor knew it was a farce.

Victor pressed. "And it didn't even work. The men you sent failed. Where are they? I want to speak with them. They must be back by now."

"I'm not sure. They should be back soon." Hastings's tone changed slightly, as though the question made him nervous.

Interesting. Sal had warned him about Hastings, telling him he'd met men like him before. Few men scared Sal Sarducci, but Hastings did somehow. Perhaps he should heed Sal's warning and keep a closer eye on him.

Hastings said, "At least let me work him over. I know I can make him talk. He'll tell me where the journal is and his new address, I guarantee it."

"The journal's not important. I asked my lawyer and it's all heresy. Anyone can write anything in a journal. Since Miles isn't able to take the stand and his accomplices are overseas, it's all meaningless drivel."

"Sal can still testify against you."

Victor wanted to throttle him. "We've been over this already. Sal stays alive."

"And what about the New York Times threat? We can't keep him under lock and key indefinitely or the story goes out."

"I just told you, Miles's journal is meaningless. If it gets sent to them, so what? It might hurt my reputation, but nothing else. My business is too important to the government right now. I doubt any self-respecting reporter would even bother pursuing it."

Hastings looked like he wanted to say something more, but Victor waved him away. "Leave me." Hastings nodded and stepped toward the door. As he stepped through, Victor added, "Have those men report to me once they arrive. I have some questions."

"You can ask me, sir. They don't know anything more than I do. They gave me a full report."

"And I heard it from you, but I still want to speak with them."

Hastings looked truly uncomfortable. "They're unsavory contract workers, sir—and none too smart. I'm afraid the war has taken most of the good men. It'll be a waste of time for you."

"Why are you being so evasive about this?" Victor asked pointedly.

"Well, it's just that I'm not sure they'll even show up here. I paid in advance, you see, and they're from out of town."

"Paid in advance? These aren't men on my payroll? You paid out of your own pocket?" Victor's interest piqued. He knew when a man was lying and Hastings was definitely lying. He doubted Hastings had the means to pay for such men, and if he did—why would he?

"Yes, sir," he said while dropping his eyes.

Victor thought about pressing the matter, but let it pass. *What is he playing at?*

"Never mind then." He shooed him away like a bothersome housefly.

After a few minutes, Victor left his office and headed downstairs to Sal's room. He knocked on the door beneath the stairs and listened with his ear pressed to it. "Sal?"

"Victor," Sal's gruff voice came back.

Victor used the key he kept in his pocket and pushed the door open. Normally he didn't enter the room without Hastings nearby holding a gun, but not this time. It was his old friend, Sal, after all.

He stepped inside and closed the door behind him. He didn't bother locking it. If Sal wanted to overpower him and take the key, he could easily do so.

Sal sat on the edge of his bed. He looked beyond Victor and said, "You didn't bring your guard dog? Or should I say lapdog?"

"Not this time. I thought we could talk like old friends." He didn't know why he didn't lie and tell Sal that Hastings stood guard on the other side of the door.

Sal harrumphed, "This is *not* how you treat a friend!"

"Yes, I know. I'm sorry, but I honestly don't know what to do with you."

"I'll bet Mr. Hastings has a few ideas."

"He wants to kill you badly. He actually wants to torture you first. I think you might be right about him."

"Being a sociopath? Of course I am. He's dangerous. You should be worried about Meredith."

"Meredith?" Victor hadn't thought of his wife in weeks. "He wouldn't hurt Meredith. He works for me, he does what I say—nothing more and nothing less."

"Nothing more? He sent men to find the journal in Sweetwater without your consent."

"He was being proactive—an admirable trait. Although he is being evasive about letting me meet them. I had some questions for them." He said it under his breath and realized he shouldn't have. Just more fodder for Sal.

"And the spying on Abby and Meredith to get that information? Is that also admirable?" Sal pressed.

Victor had forgotten that bit. It made him uncomfortable, which was probably why he'd pushed it from his mind.

"I want things to be the way they used to be, Sal. You put me in this situation. I needed to hire him because you left me. Left us."

Sal stared at him for a long couple of seconds as though confirming whether he was being sincere. Victor did his best to return his piercing gaze. Victor finally felt compelled to add, "It's all your doing."

Sal's face changed slightly. He'd failed to convince him. Why couldn't he see reason? They'd been such a good team all those years. What had changed?

Sal finally said, "Things can never be the same. I'm not who I used to be. I've grown. I've got more to live for now."

"You mean that woman and her baby in Texas? If she's so important, then why aren't you married? Have you even asked her—or did she deny you? There's quite an age difference. She's Abby's age. You'll be an old man by the time the brat graduates high school."

Sal lunged off the bed and Victor saw a flash of rage and hatred which quickly turned to just simmering anger. "I know what you're trying to do, Victor, and it won't work."

"Do? Please enlighten me."

"Maybe looking for an excuse to let that psychopath Hastings kill me. Or maybe you're just an asshole."

Victor shook his head. "Such vulgar language, Sal."

"Never talk about them that way, Victor. Keep their names off your lips."

The venom in Sal's voice made Victor's throat dry up. He had no doubt

Sal would throttle him if he continued down that path, and that wasn't his intention. "I apologize. I'm simply trying to understand what happened to you? I mean, you left us before meeting this woman and her baby, so it wasn't that."

"I left *you*, Victor. Not Meredith and not Abby—just you."

"Yes, yes, but why?"

Sal pondered the question. He finally sat down and the bed springs groaned and squeaked with the added weight. "I did it for Abby."

Victor stared at him. "Abby? She'd already left by then, too."

"Yes, and she wasn't coming back . . . ever. I could see it in her eyes at Miles's funeral. She *hated* me. All those years and she suddenly hated me. It nearly killed me—drove me mad. I had to know why. I had to find out what had happened. I left because I couldn't stand it. I went to Sweetwater to find out."

Victor stroked the tips of his silver mustache. "She looks at me that way, too." He waved his hand. "She's a child. You know how they are—she'll come around."

"She's not a child, Victor. She's married for chrissakes and she has her own career."

Victor scowled—*Clyde Cooper*. That had been the turning point. Everything collapsed as soon as that pathetic urchin entered their world. "Clyde's turned her against me—against us," he said with venom in his voice.

Sal shook his head sadly. "No Vic. You turned away from her. Hell, you tried to get the boy killed in training."

"Not killed. I just wanted him to fail—to show Abigail his true colors—he's weak. Does she know about that? Did you tell her?" The thought terrified him for some reason.

"No. I never told her. And by the way, that backfired. He made it through despite your best efforts. I think that shows he's anything but weak."

Victor felt an odd sense of relief. He asked, "I know why she's upset with me, but why you?"

"She read the journal. She knows everything. She read about my involvement in the arson and she hates me for it. She feels betrayed, like everything she thought she knew about me was a lie. In her eyes I've fallen.

Staying on with you would only make it worse. Leaving was the best decision I ever made. It led me to Beatrice and Cora—and I still have a chance with Abby."

Victor heard the unspoken accusation—the warning. Why didn't anyone understand? This wasn't personal, just business. He did what he had to do to survive in this cutthroat world of business. "She'll come around. When the war's over and Clyde comes home, she'll come home again."

Sal stood and looked him in the eyes. "She'll never forgive you until you admit what you've done. This is your last chance, Victor. You have to choose between your family . . . and *business*." He said the last word as though it tasted like feces on his tongue.

Victor scoffed at this nonsense. Sal sounded like a bleeding heart. When had he turned so weak? He almost sounded like a woman for chrissakes.

Victor took his time before speaking. This had to be delicate but firm. "I'm letting you go, Sal. Keeping you here was wrong, but I needed time to work things out. I'm sorry—truly sorry." He looked for forgiveness in Sal's gaze, but found only stony silence. He added, "And you're right about Abigail. I need to make things right with her."

"So you'll go to the authorities? Tell them what we did?"

"It's not that simple, Sal. I can't simply think of myself or even just Abigail. There's a bigger issue here. The government relies on our production staying on track. Our boys overseas rely on us—rely on Brooks Industries. Now that the war's finally turning in our favor, it's more important than ever to keep things going smoothly. The timing just isn't right. The industry, it's too important to the war effort."

Sal rolled his eyes. Victor's anger sparked deep in his belly. Perhaps he *should* let Hastings kill the ungrateful son of a bitch after all. He'd likely never get a better chance.

～

Sal could see right through Victor. At first, he thought they were actually communicating, but he soon realized that his old friend was merely giving him lip service.

They'd spoken many times over the past week, but this conversation actually had promise. He felt real depth and even understanding, but it was fleeting. He saw the change like a light switch turning off.

He'd kept himself from outright laughter at the mention of the government counting on him too much, but he hadn't been able to keep his disdain from seeping through. He realized his mistake immediately. Victor's eyes turned dangerous—reminding him of Hastings. The thought chilled him. The world didn't need more evil men.

Sal grabbed his bag as though Victor would follow through on releasing him. He faced his old friend and they stared at one another for a long moment. Sal had been here too long already. Beatrice must be pulling her hair out with worry by now. She probably thought he was dead— buried in an unmarked grave somewhere. That might still be a possibility.

"I want to get back to my family, Victor."

"Your family is here, Sal."

"No. Not anymore."

"Hastings really wants you dead."

"So you said. I know I don't work for you anymore, and to say we're friends would be a stretch, but I hope you take my advice when I tell you to get rid of that man. He's scheming behind your back—I can feel it. He's dangerous to you and everyone he touches."

Victor's eyes changed as though he suspected Hastings as well. Perhaps that might be a thread to pull on and see what unravels. But no—as soon as he left here, he never planned to return unless it was to face a court of his peers at a trial.

"What will you do?" Victor asked.

"Call Beatrice and tell her I'm alive first of all."

"I mean about us—about the arson and the journal."

"I already told you—I have to follow through or I'll never have a relationship with Abby ever again. She'll never trust me and I can't live with that. I love her like a daughter."

Victor's quick, cutting glare gave him pause. What did it mean? Did he suspect? How could he not? The similarity was uncanny. Somehow, it had never come up. Now wouldn't be the time. He might eat the barrel of Hastings's pistol before dinner.

"I urge you to reconsider," Victor finally said. "Just until the war ends."

"We might be old men by then."

"It can't last forever—and I'm sure you've noticed—we're actually turning things around."

"*We?*"

"Industry is vital to the war effort. My factory is worth an entire division of soldiers—and I'm not making that up. They told me so."

"Then we should strike while the iron's hot. Confess the to the arson now while they need us. If we wait till the end, we may end up in prison."

"The way I see it, you'll end up there, anyway. I don't see how you see yourself getting out of this without a lot of pain. You're a nobody. A disgruntled employee I was forced to fire. I'm worth an entire division!"

"So it was all bullshit? All that about making things right with Abby?"

"I do want to make things right with her, but now's not the time. Once the war's over, everything will return to normal. We just need to stay the course for now."

Sal sighed and stepped to the door. He half expected Hastings to be standing there with a gun pointed at his face—but he wasn't. "Goodbye Victor," he said without turning back.

～

GUY HASTINGS FUMED as he left Victor Brooks's office and descended the stairs. He glanced at the door beneath the stairs where Sal was incarcerated. He itched to bust it open and put a bullet between his eyes. The scenario played out in his mind, and he savored every second. If only it could be a reality. That smug son of a bitch deserved a bullet.

He rubbed his jaw, which still smarted from the blow Sal had delivered a little over a week before. *No one hits me and gets away with it.* Sure, he'd delivered many of his own hard blows afterward, but he wouldn't be satisfied until he buried Sal in an unmarked grave. No one disrespected Guy Hastings and lived to tell the tale.

He'd enjoyed his time working for Victor Brooks. The money was good and although it could be boring, he found ways to entertain himself. But now that he saw the weakness which Sal seemed to bring out in Victor, he longed to act—savagely.

The solution stared Victor in the face, but he refused to see it. Sal Sarducci needed to die. Nothing could be more obvious. Besides the two boys who'd helped Miles Burr with the arson, Sal was the only remaining eye witness. If the two boys survived the war, he'd deal with them, but Sal needed to be taken care of now.

How much longer would Victor keep him locked up in that room? The longer he did, the worse the situation. Perhaps he wanted Sal to make a move and force his hand. Hastings clicked his fingers. It suddenly all made sense. *Mr. Brooks wants me to kill him, but he wants to keep deniability.* That had to be the reason he still held him under lock and key. Simply letting him go couldn't be an option. *Mr. Brooks is too smart for that. He's waiting for me to act.*

He tapped the pistol hanging from his shoulder holster. Should he ask Mr. Brooks about his theory? No, that would force him to deny it again. *I'll just do it myself.* Mr. Brooks could keep his deniability and be rid of the problem once and for all. It also wouldn't hurt that his ability to read Victor's inner feelings and acting on them would make him an invaluable tool. *Perhaps he'll make me a partner in the business—and after that? Who knows?* Hastings Industries had a nice ring to it.

The door upstairs opened, and Hastings quickly moved away from Sal's door. He didn't have a key, anyway. He hustled to the foyer and resumed his post at the front door of the office building. One of his men sat at the desk reading a comic book. When he saw Hastings, he flung the comic into a desk drawer.

"Hey, boss. All quiet here."

"Take a break, Mel. I'll cover the entry for a while."

The guard stood, and his large frame dwarfed the desk. "Okay, boss. Whatever you say." He left through the metal doors with a quick glance back.

Hastings said, "Be back in half an hour."

"You got it, boss."

Hastings sat at the desk. The chair still held Mel's heat. He opened the drawer and pulled out the comic book. He shook his head in disgust. "Superman. Such a pussy." He tossed it into the trash and said to himself, "I've gotta find better men."

He heard footsteps coming down the stairs. It had to be Victor on his way out of the office. Perhaps this would be his chance to take care of the problem. With Victor gone, he could make it seem like Sal tried to break out and he had no other choice but to shoot him. He liked the idea more and more. Victor couldn't be mad at him, after all, he'd ordered him to make sure Sal didn't leave. *I'll make sure, alright.* He grinned to himself. It would be easy to bust into the room, and the busted door would only add to the truth of the story.

He muttered to himself, practicing his lines. "Sorry, boss, I didn't have a choice. It was him or me . . . you understand."

His plans shattered as he heard the bolt unlock from down the hall. He peaked around the corner in time to see Victor enter Sal's room.

"Shit," he whispered.

He listened for the door to shut, and when it did, he tiptoed to the door. He could hear talking, but he couldn't decipher the words. He touched the pistol, assuring himself that it still hung there, ready to kill. He had to be careful. He'd seen the displeasure in his employer's eyes when he'd told him about eavesdropping on Meredith and Abigail's conversation.

He licked his lips, thinking of the two women. He'd fantasized about what he'd like to do to each of them—especially the young one. He'd let them both participate, of course.

He shook the thought from his head. Better to think of such things later —late at night. Now was the time for stealth and violence, not perversion, although mixing them could be fun, too. He lowered himself, then pressed his ear to the edge of the door. It wasn't perfect, but he could understand most of what was being said.

He almost didn't believe his ears. Victor was going to let Sal go without so much as a broken bone. He fumed and had to stifle outraged grunts at some comments about himself. He wanted to burst in and shoot both of them dead.

But no, he needed a new plan. He couldn't shoot him with Victor standing nearby. It had to be once Sal was off the property. Deniability. He'd tail Sal and strike when he let his guard down. Perhaps he could kidnap him and take him somewhere where he could really have some fun. He'd be tough to break, but every man has a breaking point.

Fantasies abounded. Perhaps he could follow him all the way back to wherever the hell he came from and work on his woman and child, too. Excitement flooded his system. But no, that would take too long. He'd have to satisfy himself with a quick shot to the head. He promised himself that he'd shoot him in the face, not the back of the head. He wanted to see the flicker of fear just before he ended his miserable life.

2

Sal stepped into the lobby and noticed Hastings sitting at the front desk, staring at him with pure hatred. He almost looked comical.

Sal gave him a mock salute, "Good day."

"Fuck off," he almost slurred. He said it with such violent vehemence.

"You're a class act, Hastings." He wanted to throttle the little shit, but knew it might not go as he hoped. Men like Hastings were dangerous, mostly because they were unpredictable. Hastings had skills on top of his unpredictability, and that made him doubly dangerous. He risked even speaking to the man and baiting him would certainly provoke him, but he couldn't help it.

"You're a dead man," Hastings said flatly.

Sal ignored him. He heard Victor coming down the hall. He doubted Hastings would do anything brash unless Victor gave the okay, and he didn't think his old friend had fallen that far yet.

"You need to relax. All that stress will give you fits." Sal kept walking toward the door. He monitored Hastings as he passed. He could see the bulge of the pistol in his shoulder holster. If he made a move, Sal would have no choice but to react. Surely he won't do anything here, but he wished he had his own pistol nearby. Victor had taken it along with his holster when he'd first arrived.

Sal made it to the steel door and glanced back. Victor leaned on the desk with Hastings right beside him, looking like a crazed lapdog.

Victor raised his voice to Sal. "Take care of yourself, Sal."

Sal had nothing more to say. He'd said it all already. He pushed through the door and didn't look back, but he felt Hasting's eyes boring into his back.

Once the doors closed behind him, he stopped and took in a deep breath of fresh air. He hadn't been outside in a week and he missed it. This is what prison would be like. But at least prisoners had daily outside time. He'd have more freedom there than he'd had over the last week. The thought angered him, but he didn't dwell on it. He needed to get away from there before they changed their minds.

He walked three blocks before he finally hailed a cab. He enjoyed the exercise and didn't want it to end. But now that he'd put some space between himself and Brooks Industries, he needed to contact Beatrice.

He sat in the cab, and when the driver asked him where-to, Sal almost said the train station, but he hesitated. He'd missed his return ticket date by days. He did not know how many trips left Seattle station each day. The cabbie eyeballed him in the rearview mirror as he chewed on a shredded toothpick. Finally, Sal gave him an address.

The cabbie whistled and said, "You sure, pal? You got the money?"

Sal flashed him a stack of greenbacks, and the cabbie started the fare. He had no idea if she was even home, but he felt he needed to see her again. It might very well be the last time.

A half hour later, the cabbie pulled into the roundabout at the Brooks Estate. He gave another low whistle. "Must be nice," he muttered.

"I don't live here. Can you stick around for a while? I'll pay you extra."

"If you don't mind me keeping the meter running, I'll wait all damned day, pal."

"Thanks." He stepped out and took in the place. It hadn't been too long since he'd left, but he felt like a stranger. He secretly hoped Meredith wouldn't be home. Perhaps she was off with another one of her young men. But, no, it would be good to see her again.

He knocked on the massive, ornate doors. A moment later, one side opened and he saw the stunned face of Mr. Hanniger. "Sal! I mean, Mr. Sarducci! Welcome."

They shook hands, then embraced. He'd forgotten how much he admired the man. No matter what happened, Hanniger remained the rock that anchored the Brooks Estate and family. He suddenly felt better about everything. Nothing would happen to Meredith or any of the staff as long as Mr. Hanniger watched over them. He doubted even Hastings had a chance if he angered Hanniger. He knew that he'd even give himself a run for his money if all the chips were down.

"It's good to see you," Sal said.

"You too, Sal. Things haven't been the same since you left. Not by a long stretch."

Sal looked around the foyer. He didn't see anyone hanging about. He pulled closer to Mr. Hanniger. "How've you been getting along with my replacement?"

Hanniger lifted his chin imperiously. He looked down the long ski slope of his nose. "Mr. Hastings is an uncouth man. I don't get along at all, frankly."

"I fear he's more than that. He's dangerous." Hanniger nodded, but said nothing more. He rarely spoke ill of anyone. Sal continued in his lowered voice. "I worry about Meredith."

"I can assure you, I won't let anything happen to Mrs. Brooks."

"Hastings spies on her conversations."

Hanniger's face squished into utter disgust. "I suspected as much. He's always slinking about."

"Well, he's not here. I just left him at the office," Sal assured him.

"Will you be staying for dinner?"

"No, I've just come to give my regards to Mrs. Brooks. Is she around?"

"Yes. I'll fetch her if you like. She's in the library."

"No, no, that's okay. I'll find her. I can't stay long. Mr. Brooks doesn't know I'm here and I'd like to keep it that way."

Hanniger's mouth drooped, and his silver mustache followed suit. Sal said, "It's good to see you again, old friend."

"You, too. I'll announce if anyone else shows up in case you might need to make a quick getaway."

Sal tilted his head. Did Hanniger know about his confinement this past week? How could he? But he thought he must know, and he also knew or at least suspected the danger Hastings posed. The man never seemed to leave his post, but he had eyes and ears everywhere. He needed to remember that. He could be a valuable asset, but he was also completely committed to Mr. Brooks. After all, he'd employed him for generations.

"Thank you, Mr. Hanniger."

∾

ONCE HE SAT down with Meredith and talked for a few minutes, he felt relief. He wasn't sure how he'd feel about her now that he was in love with Beatrice. Would she still have power over him? Would she still make his palms sweat when she sat close? The answer was no. He felt love for her, but not as a lover, as a friend. They talked candidly about his life since leaving the estate all those months ago.

"I'm so impressed with your new life, Sal. I mean, you left so suddenly, I didn't know if you'd land on your feet, but you've found love and a new family. It's truly wonderful."

He didn't know how he felt about the praise. He couldn't really believe it himself. "I've been fortunate. I suppose fate must be real. I'm not sure I could explain it any other way."

"Well, I, for one, am happy for you. You look so healthy."

"Thank you, Meredith. It means a lot to me."

"But you still haven't told me why you came here."

"It's private business between Victor and I. I'm not at liberty to say."

"Don't tell me you're working for him again. Because if you are, I really don't . . ."

He interrupted her, "It's not that. Quite the opposite, really. I had some loose ends to tie up."

She looked around the room as though someone might be eavesdropping. Sal wondered if she knew about Hastings's nosy habits. Perhaps Hanniger had told her. She lowered her voice conspiratorially. "Is it about Miles and that journal?"

Sal nearly fell off the love seat. "You know about that?"

"Abby told me all about it. She flew here on one of her WASP trips, just a few weeks ago."

"I'm surprised she told you."

"Well, I'd already heard something about it from her friend Miss Watkins."

"Trish," Sal said, remembering she'd lost her life during Abby's visit. He'd only heard about it the day he confronted Victor a week prior. With everything he'd been through, he'd put it out of his mind.

"Yes, Trish Watkins. Tragic what happened to her. Gunned down in her own apartment. Abby was involved."

"What happened? Victor mentioned it, but I don't know the details."

"Well, I only know a little more than what the papers said. Abby flew back the next day without stopping by. She was supposed to have dinner with me, but she never showed. Mr. Hanniger got a call from her, so I didn't worry, but then I heard about the shooting."

"My God. Is—is Abby alright?"

"As far as I know, yes. The police came here looking for her, but she'd already flown out. It must have been awful for her."

"How was she involved? Is she wanted by the police?"

"No, they just wanted to speak with her. The officers said she was in the room when it happened. She was visiting Trish and for some reason, the young army driver assigned to Abigail shot Trish dead. Apparently, she was reaching for a gun and he shot her in self-defense."

"That's baffling. Was Abby in danger?"

"I do not know. But I think she might have been meeting her about that journal. It's the only thing that makes sense. Perhaps Trish threatened her and the soldier intervened. It's still under investigation."

"Will Abby be called back? Surely they must need her statement."

"She gave one, or at least, our lawyer wrote one up and got it signed. She's across the country and her job's considered vital to the war effort. I doubt they'll make her come back."

"It sounds unbelievable. It doesn't make any sense."

"What do you mean?"

"I mean, I met Trish. She was a small-time thief, not violent. This doesn't sound like her at all. I'm surprised she even had a gun."

"I heard her gun wasn't even loaded."

"I wonder how Abby's taking it. She must be torn up about it. I'm surprised she left so quickly afterward."

"I checked with the air station she flew from. She flew a pursuit aircraft along with another WASP pilot—heading for the east coast. The woman wouldn't give me specifics. She only told me that much because I'm her mother. It's all very hush-hush."

"Trish had some rough edges, but I liked her. Abby liked her, too, but I think they had a falling out," Sal said.

"Yes, I know she did. But you're right about her. She threatened me once," she added as an afterthought. Sal tensed and Meredith told him about the luncheon she had with her at the country club all those months before.

Sal remembered the luncheon, too. He didn't tell her he'd watched them the entire time. He'd spotted Trish when he'd dropped Meredith off to meet her boyfriend at the club. He'd watched Trish meet up with Meredith, then sip drinks together on the patio. After she'd met with Meredith, Sal kept following Trish back into the city, where he saw two thugs interact with her. They didn't seem to be on her side. He wondered if her death had anything to do with those two. Probably.

"Well, she wasn't the nicest person, but she didn't deserve to die," Sal said.

"I'm worried something similar might happen to Victor."

The comment tore Sal from his own thoughts. "You think he's in danger?"

"Yes, more than ever. What if it's all connected? Miles, Trish, Victor."

"Miles died in an accident. A soldier shot Trish. How could it possibly be connected to Victor? I'm not following."

"I don't know either. I'm just thinking out loud. But Miles and Trish had a thing—Abby told me that much. As you know, they both worked for Victor. Trish blamed him for Miles's death. I know their deaths don't fit, but Victor's connected to both of them and they're both dead."

Sal tried to follow the thread, but it didn't make any sense. Victor couldn't have been involved in Trish's death. The soldier was just a random army driver. He shot her when she reached for her gun. Why did Trish have a gun handy? Why did she reach for it?

He remembered Trish's apartment. He'd stood outside it while the thugs gave her a hard time. Would it still be taped off as a crime scene? He wanted to know more about the incident. Why was the driver in the apartment with them? If Abby stopped by to talk about the journal, she wouldn't want the driver with her.

"Do you have a copy of Abby's statement?"

"No. I never saw it."

He stood abruptly. "It's good to see you, Mrs. Brooks. I've got a cabbie waiting outside. I should probably get to the station and purchase a ticket."

"You don't have a return ticket?"

"I did, but I'm too late."

She looked confused, and he realized she'd have no reason not to think that he'd just arrived. She didn't know they had kept him under lock and key beneath a stairway in her husband's office building for the past week.

"I really must be going."

"When will I see you again?"

"I don't know. My life's across the country now."

She stood and extended her porcelain hand. He took it and looked into her sparkling eyes. Those eyes used to transfix him, and he remembered the passion they once held for him that night so long ago. But now he felt only friendship pass between them. Friendship and deep concern.

He smiled and he saw a flash of something else in her eyes. He'd seen the same thing in Abby's eyes, but not quite as harsh. Not as damning, but still there; disappointment. She knew of his involvement in the arson, too—she must. Abby must've told her.

"I'll make it right," he said.

She squeezed his hand. "I know you will, Sal. It's what you've always done."

～

SAL PAID the cabbie and stepped onto the sidewalk in downtown Seattle. He stretched his back while he searched for any sign of someone following him. Hastings in particular. It wouldn't surprise him if Victor put a tail on him. He'd want to keep tabs on him, perhaps hoping he'd lead them to the journal. He saw nothing obvious.

He entered the police station. He still had friends working there. He hoped old Harry hadn't retired yet. He'd made detective a few years back, he remembered. Good for him.

A heavy layer of cigarette smoke hung in the lobby. The place smelled of smoke, body odor, and bleach. A few unsavory-looking fellows sat in chairs reading tattered magazines. None gave him a second glance.

At the barred-in desk, he gave his name and asked the uninterested, middle-aged woman for Harry Gunnison. It took a few minutes, but his old friend finally poked his head into the booth behind the bars and he gave him a broad smile.

"It *is* you, you old sod." A side door opened with a loud click as the deadbolt released, and Harry stepped in and they shook hands. "I'd forgotten how big you are," Harry said while tapping Sal's broad shoulder.

Sal tapped Harry's belly. "And I'd forgotten how much you love barbecue."

Harry laughed and tapped his impressive belly. "This is new," he said, as though proud of a new child. "I've been nurturing it since making detective."

"I heard about your promotion. Congratulations."

"Ah, thanks." He invited him in and Sal followed him through a maze of desks filled with aged cops and detectives. He supposed most of the young men were overseas.

He guided him to a desk in the corner. Sal gazed out the window, looking out at the tall buildings shimmering in the afternoon sunshine.

"I forget how beautiful this place is when the sun comes out."

"I've got a pile of reports to get through, Sal. What's on your mind?"

Sal startled from the window. "Oh, sure thing. I was wondering if you know anything about a shooting that happened a couple of weeks ago downtown?"

"I'm assuming you're referring to the one involving your past employer's daughter? Or perhaps you're working for him again?"

"I'm not working for him, but that's the report I'm interested in, yes."

He rifled through a stack of folders and finally found the right one. "Here it is," he threw it and it smacked the desk in front of Sal.

"May I?"

"Be my guest. As you can see, there's not much to it."

Sal opened the folder and saw a picture of Trish Watkins. She scowled at the camera and looked much younger than he remembered. He supposed it was a mug shot from a previous arrest. He read the brief report. Gunshot wound to the chest killed her. Just one shot. Fine shooting on Private Collins's part. An unfamiliar, confined, poorly lit room at ten yards against a moving target. Was he more than just a driver?

He flipped the page and saw the young soldier's photo, obviously pulled from his service picture. He read Collins's report. It made more sense now. He'd entered the apartment because he heard shouting and came to check on Abby's welfare. That made sense. He'd noticed a gun on the table and when Trish saw him, she lunged for it. He drew and fired after warning her to stop.

He flipped the sheet and saw Abigail's smiling face. The picture must've come from her WASP graduation day. She beamed and pride burst through the photograph. She looked beautiful despite the low-quality picture.

He read her statement and immediately knew she had had nothing to do with putting it together. There was no mention of what they argued about, or any substance besides stating "meeting an old friend." No reason for the weapon, no reason for the argument—nothing helpful, except that she was there and saw Mr. Collins shoot Trish when she went for her gun.

"Pretty thin," Sal said.

"We tried to follow up, but she flew out early the next morning, apparently. She's one of them WASP pilots, but I suppose you already know that. The Collins kid's the army's responsibility."

"Know anything about him? Is he being charged?"

Gunnison shook his head. "Not as far as I know. He's pretty shaken up about the whole thing."

"I suspect Abigail is too."

"I wouldn't know. She left pretty quick. Made us a little suspicious."

"I can see why, but she's a good kid. Are you gonna pursue it any further?"

"Nothing to pursue. We didn't find anything in the victim's apartment that set any alarms off. Her landlord says she'd just paid up her rent for the next few months in advance."

Sal looked up from the report. "Really? Had she done that before?"

"The landlord said no. In fact, he normally had to pester her every month and she usually paid late."

"That's odd."

"She must've come into some money. Far as we can tell, she hasn't had a job since she worked for you folks at Brooks Industries. Doesn't matter, the case'll be closed and go down as an accidental shooting."

Sal tossed the thin report back onto the table. "Thanks for letting me have a look."

"Yeah, no problem. You owe me a lunch, though."

"Sure thing. Can I ask another favor?"

Gunnison checked the wall clock. "You've got five minutes before my next meeting."

"My old boss hired a security man by the name of Guy Hastings. I was wondering if you have anything on him."

The detective wrote the name down and tapped his pencil against the name a few times. "Doesn't ring any alarm bells for me. Is there a problem with him?"

"I just don't trust him. I've got a bad feeling about him."

"Didn't you quit that job? Why are you still involved?"

"Cause it was my job for thirty years. They're like family."

Gunnison stood and they shook hands. "I'll ask around, but I doubt Mr. Brooks would hire someone dangerous to his own family."

Sal shrugged, "That reminds me, how's Louie?"

The color drained from Gunnison's face. He suddenly looked twenty years older. "He—he died in Italy."

Sal felt like he'd been gut-punched. He'd watched the kid play baseball years ago. Harry had been so proud of him even though he wasn't a natural athlete, he tried hard. He noticed the service picture on his desk. The kid wore an Army uniform and a broad, proud smile.

"I am so sorry, Harry. I didn't know."

Gunnison sniffed and lifted his chin. "They say he died quick. Artillery shell—didn't suffer at all." He looked at the floor. "There wasn't much left of him. He's buried over there in some town I never heard of. Six months ago now—seems like yesterday."

"This fucking war," Sal cursed.

"You said it, pal—you said it."

They parted, and Sal went back out into the lobby. He noticed a phone on a table. He asked the woman behind the counter if he could use it.

"Is it local?" Her voice sounded as though she'd smoked every cigarette ever made.

"Yeah, sure," he lied.

$\approx$

GUY HASTINGS SAT in the nondescript sedan watching the front of the police station. After tailing the cab to Brook's estate, he parked and waited for almost an hour. Then he followed the cab back into town, all the way to the police station.

He wondered if he should call Mr. Brooks. If Sal planned on turning himself in to the local police, he'd probably want to know, but he hadn't been ordered to follow Sal, so he didn't make the call.

Besides, Sal didn't have the journal on him as far as he knew, unless he somehow picked it up at the estate, which he thought was unlikely. He could've sent it in the mail, but that would be risky and he would've noticed a book-sized package. Besides, most of the mail went to the office.

Nearly forty-five minutes passed before Sal exited the police station. Sal stopped in the middle of the sidewalk and looked both ways up and down the street—perhaps looking for another cab. Where would he go now? He still held the small bag with most of the possessions he had arrived with. Well, most everything.

Hastings tapped the pistol sitting on the seat beside him. He'd taken it from Sal early on and he had no intention of returning it, at least not in the way anyone suspected. His plan was foolproof—he just needed to get Sal alone. He assumed he'd head to the train station right after being released. He'd been surprised when he went to the estate instead, and now the police station.

Mr. Brooks would be furious if he found out Sal had met with Mrs. Brooks. Hastings only suspected they'd met, but he couldn't think of any other reason for him to be there. He and Meredith were old friends as far as he could tell—and he knew Mrs. Brooks's schedule. She was home.

Did Sal tell Mrs. Brooks about being held captive for the past week? If so, there'd be fireworks tonight. But soon, none of that would matter. *Poor Sal.*

Sal walked east. He didn't hail a cab and he didn't move fast—just ambled along as though pondering life. He looked more like a tourist than a dangerous security man.

Hastings waited until Sal had gone nearly a block before he pulled out into the light traffic. He didn't want to leave his vehicle and follow him on foot in case his prey suddenly hopped into a cab. Perhaps Sal had spotted him and was waiting for that exact opportunity. He'd lose him for sure.

He drove past him, forcing himself not to glance in his direction. He found him in the side mirror and kept him in sight. Sal seemed totally engrossed as he strolled along, but it might all be a ruse to lull him into making a mistake.

He pulled to the side of the road a half a block ahead and did his best not to watch him too closely. No one gave Hastings a second glance. The sun warmed the vehicle quickly. The mid-June day sparkled outside.

Most everyone smiled and looked happy, and why not? The day was warm and summery, a nice change from the endlessly dreary days of winter and early spring, and the war news was good. The allies had pushed across the English Channel and soon they'd be pushing into Paris, if the news reports were even halfway accurate. Things were almost getting back to normal.

He checked the rearview mirror. He didn't give two shits about the war's success or failure. He liked the chaos, but he hated the lack of young professionals he was used to working with. The war would produce a fresh batch of deadly killers. Nothing trained a good security man like combat, he supposed.

He'd never joined the service, but he'd grown up on the streets fighting for every little scrap, every single day. Combat would be easier but would have the same crucible effect—only the strongest survived.

He almost wished he'd gone overseas, too, but he'd seen too much opportunity right here at home. The lack of competition made getting a job easy and moving up even easier. When all those bleeding hearts returned, he'd be his own man. They'd all be working for him and then he'd shape the world more to his liking.

When Hastings looked for Sal again, he couldn't find him. He turned and scanned the crowds. He saw him slip into a doorway. Was he trying to lose him? He couldn't see the storefront well enough to know what kind of store it was. He cursed to himself. He'd lost focus for only a moment.

He looked at his face in the mirror, slicked his hair back, and sneered. "Time to end this once and for all," he muttered to his reflection. He pulled on light leather gloves, then grasped Sal's .45. He checked the action and stuffed it into his sport coat pocket.

He stepped out of the sedan and hustled across the street. He was still halfway up the block, far enough away not to attract Sal's attention, even if he were looking, which he didn't think he was. He'd picked a hell of a time for a little shopping.

Hastings wanted to do the deed at the train station. He'd already scoped out the bathrooms and the stalls would've been perfect, but at this rate, Sal may never go there. Hastings would do what he did best—adapt and overcome.

He rubbed his jaw, still feeling the slight pain from where Sal had hit him. He wanted to make Sal's death last longer, but he needed to get this done and make a clean getaway. Sometimes there wasn't time for artistry, just action.

~

SAL COULDN'T STOP THINKING about his phone call to Beatrice. She'd nearly burst into tears when the operator finally connected them. It reaffirmed to him she really loved him. He'd never been close enough to anyone to care so much. It felt good. The bright sunny day matched his mood, so he strolled along aimlessly.

Everyone smiled, made friendly greetings, and laughter floated on the warm, fresh air. Beatrice would've loved to be by his side. He couldn't wait to get back home.

It would be a long trip. He decided he needed something to read. He ducked into a bookstore. Perhaps a classic or maybe something quick, like a murder mystery—perhaps both.

The little bell over the door rang and the elderly shopkeeper lifted his head from a book, pushed his glasses up his nose, and greeted him. "Welcome. Lovely out there today."

Sal smiled, something that came more and more natural to him lately. "Yes indeed. Where are your mysteries?"

He pointed, "Back left corner near the bathroom. Everything is alphabetical by author's last name."

"Thanks." He took in the dank smell of paper, leather, and dust. Nothing smelled quite like a room full of books. He'd never been in this store. He took his time, perusing the stacks as he made his way to the back. He found the mystery section. His eyes passed over titles, some he'd read, others new. He pulled a few and read the first few sentences. Distantly, he heard the bell over the door as another customer entered. He heard the shopkeepers greeting again, but he didn't hear a reply.

He finally settled on two titles, both Agatha Christie: The Death on the Nile and a relatively new one called Five Little Pigs. He'd read her earlier works and enjoyed them.

He turned from the stacks and stopped cold. Hastings stood there with a pistol pointed at his guts.

Sal felt the blood rush to his ears. How could he have been so stupid? His call with Beatrice had distracted him. He hadn't spotted the tail. He'd forgotten all about Hastings. How ironic that love and happiness would be the death of him.

"You gonna shoot me right here?" he said loudly.

Sal didn't see the punch coming. It happened too fast. He felt the jab impact his nose though, and his eyes watered, blurring Hasting's sneering face.

"Not here." He looked beyond him, then nodded toward the bathroom door. "Bathroom. Go, but don't try anything. I'll kill the shopkeeper if I have to."

Sal raised his hands, one book in each. His mind raced. Once inside the bathroom, he'd be a dead man. The only reason he wasn't already was the presence of the shopkeeper.

He stood in front of the bathroom door, his hands over his head. Hastings stayed well back—a true professional. "Open it," he hissed.

Sal put the books in one hand and slowly reached for the copper door knob.

"Easy, nice and slow," Hastings whispered.

Sal jiggled the knob but didn't turn it. "It's locked," he said. "Must be someone inside."

"Bullshit," Hastings's voice dripped with hatred. "Open it now or I'll put one through your spine."

"But it's locked," Sal insisted. He jiggled it again to prove his point.

"Step away."

Sal stepped to the side, keeping his hands raised. He recognized the pistol Hastings held. It all made sense now. "You planning on killing me with my own piece? Try to pass it off as a suicide?"

"Doesn't matter if they buy it or not. You'll be out of the picture either way."

"Victor sign off on this or are you working on your own?"

"Better to ask forgiveness and all that," he answered. "If it's not locked, you and the old geezer both die."

Hastings stepped closer to the door, keeping the muzzle trained squarely on Sal's midsection. Sal had to make a move, but doubted he'd be able to avoid being shot. Hastings was too steady and focused to miss.

Hastings reached for the doorknob. The shopkeeper ambled around the corner. "Is the door jammed again?"

Hastings lost his concentration just for an instant. Sal hurled the books at his face and sprang low toward his feet. The pistol cracked and the bullet sizzled a track down the length of Sal's back. Before he could fire again, Sal crashed into Hastings's lower legs hard. He felt the unnatural knee bend and Hastings yelled in agony and rage.

Hastings toppled forward, and Sal kept rolling. He popped up and sprang onto the smaller man before he could turn back in his direction.

Hastings struggled to bring the pistol to bear, but Sal's body weight pinned his arm to his body. If he fired now, he'd risk shooting himself.

Sal pulled away slightly, giving himself enough room to plunge his fist into Hastings's throat. Hastings gasped, but no air came. His mouth gaped like a fish out of water and his dark eyes panned wide.

Hasting's wiry-strong body squirmed from beneath Sal and rolled away. He landed a kick into Sal's gut and pain lanced through him. Sal saw the pistol coming around. He lunged for the nearest stack of books and pulled with everything he had. The bookcase tore from the wall with an awful screech and collapsed onto both of them. The pistol cracked twice.

Sal pushed himself back from the bookcase until he felt himself break free. Books rolled off him like heavy dollops of snow. Hastings's body kept the heavy bookcase propped up. It heaved and jerked as he fought to free himself. More shots and bullets ripped through the wooden case and pulped books into tattered bits.

Sal thought about continuing the assault, but Hastings's indiscriminate shooting might connect. He turned to find the shopkeeper. The old man propped against a bookcase. His eyes stared blankly. Blood trickled from a bullet hole in his forehead. Behind him, blood and gore dripped from the books he'd alphabetized with such care.

Sal felt sick, but he didn't have time to mourn. He sprinted to the front door and burst out onto the street. Folks gave him curious looks, but no one really paid him any attention. He forced himself not to run, but he moved fast, taking the first opportunity to get off the street.

3

Camp Davis Army Airfield
North Carolina
June 1944

Abby Cooper listened to the flight briefing with feigned interest. She'd already flown the exact same route twice earlier in the week. Her route would take her up the coast all the way to New York, where she'd deliver a bright and shiny new P-51 Mustang. The only thing that changed was the weather. But summer on the east coast was smooth sailing as long as you took off before the heat—so her mind drifted as the flight ops officer droned on.

She glanced at a newspaper, war news plastered across every headline. All anyone seemed to talk about these days was the D-Day invasion of France. Abby followed the news, but she was more interested in anything happening in the Pacific, where Clyde was. These days she had to dig deep into the newspapers before she'd find them. More and more, it seemed like a sideshow to Europe. *Men are dying just as brutally, though.*

The thought made her think of Trish. She'd died brutally, but quickly at least. She'd whimpered and grunted, then gone utterly silent as her lifeblood spilled onto the floor and seeped into the shabby rug. Abby shook her head, trying to dislodge the image, but it clung like a spider's web. She hated what had happened and felt responsible. She hadn't pulled the trigger, but it wouldn't have happened if she hadn't been there. It gnawed at her constantly.

She received a letter from the Seattle Police Department requesting her to fill out another, more complete statement. She'd done so and sent it off to the Brooks family lawyer along with the letter from the police. She had heard nothing since. It was as though Trish had never existed at all, and that made it even worse.

Her head ached and she rubbed her temples, remembering the three whisky and waters she'd drank the night before. She checked her watch—just barely under the eight hours from drink to stick rule. She found the alcohol eased the pain and allowed her to sleep without dreaming of Trish's death. She needed her sleep to be sharp for flying, at least that's what she told herself.

She forced herself to think about something else. Her mind flashed to Clyde and she forgot her headache for a moment. She wondered what he was doing at that exact moment. She often had such thoughts and it sometimes drove her crazy. It had been so long since they held one another. She could feel the hollow ache in the pit of her stomach.

His letters came fairly regularly. He started the letters off with, "G'day, Sheila," which told her he was in Australia without actually saying it, keeping the censors happy and clueless. But the latest letter didn't start off that way.

He told her he'd be on a ship for the next few weeks, so she should expect a gap in the frequency of letters. She supposed he must be heading back into a combat zone. One more bit to worry about.

It was maddeningly difficult to gauge the timing of each letter, as some arrived within weeks and others in months. They'd become more consistent as the war dragged on, but she still got surprised by an occasional letter which seemed out of place, somehow. It didn't really matter. She cherished each letter and reread them countless times. Many dotted with her tear stains.

The briefing wrapped up and Abby stood and stretched her back. Her one piece flight suit fit snugly and she felt sweat dripping down the crack of her butt. She fidgeted and wished they had air-conditioning. Even this early in the morning, the place was stifling. Her head throbbed. She couldn't wait to chug a glass of water.

Mandy Flannigan came up behind her. "You ready for another milk run?"

Abby cringed at the loudness so close to her ear. "Yes, yes. Getting so we can do it blindfolded."

Mandy's grin disappeared and she leaned in closer. She sniffed Abby. Abby waved her away and huffed, "Knock it off. What're you doing?"

Mandy lowered her voice. "You better put more perfume on. I can smell alcohol on you. It's seeping from your pores."

"I had a few drinks last night, but well over eight hours ago. It's just this heat brings it out more, I guess."

"Yeah, well, it won't matter to Wanda. If she smells it on you, she'll ground you."

"Then I'll just steer clear of her," Abby said. Mandy leveled her gaze at her and crossed her arms. "I'm fine," Abby insisted. "Really. It was just a nightcap. Helps me sleep."

Mandy slung her arm through Abby's and walked her out, careful to avoid the flight briefing officer. She barely gave them a second glance.

The early morning coolness refreshed her. She closed her eyes and took in the smells of the airbase. Gasoline, oil, and the nearby sea mixed, making her feel right at home. The sun hadn't risen yet, but the distant horizon took on a yellowish glow, promising another beautiful sunrise.

Mandy pulled her close. "Can you believe we get to do this for a living?"

"They're paying you?" Abby joked.

"I'd do it for free, honestly."

Abby listened to engines coughing to life. Bursts of flame shot out from manifolds, marking the aircraft others would fly to different destinations. The past week had been unusual. The WASPs normally worked alone, ferrying aircraft to distant airfields, but this week had been a joint operation. This would be the third day in a row she'd fly with Mandy, and she relished the opportunity.

"Me, too," Abby agreed. "It's a dream come true." She was thankful to be reminded.

They strode toward their aircraft parked side by side. Mechanics and fuelers darted under and on top of the wings, making sure everything was in working order. They were mostly women.

The pair stopped in front of their aircraft and donned leather flight helmets. Abby's headache dulled as the leather cap cupped her head like an old friend. It drowned out some of the noise.

Mandy said, "I'm going to fly out over the ocean most of the way this time."

Abby asked, "Yeah? Why?"

"Sick of flying the same old route. We'll stay low off the radar so they don't keep calling."

Abby shook her head. Once Mandy got an idea in her head, she rarely changed her mind. She'd stopped trying. "I'll follow your lead, but don't get us shot down."

"We'll be miles off the coast."

"Okay, just don't accidentally buzz a destroyer out there. They might shoot first and ask questions later."

"Don't worry. It'll be fun."

Abby shook her head as Mandy sashayed to her P-51. Abby cupped her hand and called after her, "Famous last words."

Mandy flashed a wave, and a smile, then began her preflight check. Abby went to her own aircraft and started doing the same. She marveled at the smooth lines. The only word that came to mind was sexy. She blushed, but it perfectly fit this marvelous aircraft.

∽

BY THE TIME the pair of them took off, the sun had peeked up from the horizon. Rays of sunlight bathed the early morning world with promise and hope. Abby flew with the canopy open for the first few minutes to take in the fresh morning air.

She followed Mandy up the coast until they were far away from flight operations. Then Mandy arced east and descended slowly. Abby followed diligently, keeping close to Mandy's right wing.

The sun sat beneath the engine, cowling and shafts of sunlight made her propeller sparkle. She hoped they'd turn back north soon or the sun would blind her and her headache might return.

Mandy glanced back at Abby and gave her a radiant smile. Abby smiled back and gave her a thumb up signal. Mandy nodded and turned in a gradual turn back north. The sea flashed by only a few hundred feet below. A few fishing boats left white wakes which spread further and further. The Atlantic looked as smooth as a mountain lake.

The sun burned through the plexiglass windscreen but didn't heat the cockpit too uncomfortably yet. If they slowed down, she might crack the canopy again.

Mandy took them up to two thousand feet and Abby allowed herself to spread out and away from Mandy's wing, keeping a loose formation. A few clouds skittered on the distant horizon, but the day was clear and didn't look to change. Perfect flying weather.

She checked her knee map, but there'd be nothing out here but open sea. She could barely see a dark band of land to the west and endless sea to the east. She checked her watch and her speed and supposed they flew past Virginia Beach give or take a few miles. There were no landmarks over the open ocean.

The miles peeled away like a thin stack of paper in a light breeze. The droning of the aircraft and the smooth air felt like a warm bed on a cold winter night. Her eyes grew heavy and she admonished herself to stay alert and awake. She shifted until the parachute she sat on pinched her leg. The discomfort would keep her awake.

The radio crackled in her ear and she jerked and nearly banked the aircraft. She caught her breath and heard Mandy say. "What's that? Do you see it? Two o'clock low."

They weren't on strict radio silence, but they weren't supposed to be chatty either. Mandy rarely spoke other than to give directions or course corrections. Sometimes she didn't speak until she contacted the tower where they'd be landing. Flying alone more often than not had instilled a quietness in the WASP pilots. They could go for hours upon hours without speaking a word, especially when they flew over desolate sections of the country.

Abby squinted into the bright day. The Atlantic sparkled like a thousand green gems. "I don't see anything."

"I saw something down there. I'm turning into you. Watch yourself."

Abby lifted her nose slightly and banked right to anticipate the turn. Mandy's Mustang banked right. Abby cut power and let Mandy glide in front of her. She kept her nose on Mandy's tail while searching for whatever she'd seen. They sometimes spotted whales. Buzzing the enormous beasts could be exhilarating.

Mandy's aircraft suddenly shot upward in an erratic movement, catching Abby completely off guard. Mandy's harried voice came through, "Submarine. Submarine on the surface!"

Abby pulled right, not wanting to follow Mandy's sudden climb. She wanted to get far away from Mandy's erratic movements. "Are you sure? I don't . . ." but then she saw it too. It moved slowly, barely making a wake. Pencil thin, it moved parallel to their flight path. A thin tendril of black smoke burbled from the back. "I see it, too."

"Is it one of ours?" Mandy gasped.

Abby had seen submarines tied up on the piers from time to time. They were green, but this one looked jet black. As she neared it, she saw a flag whipping in the light winds which turned her insides to ice. "Oh, my God. It—it's a German U-boat."

"Get out of there, Abby!"

Without realizing it, Abby had descended. The submarine grew larger and larger and she saw figures darting around the deck. Flashes of light and yellow beads floated up at her. For an instant, she didn't know what it meant, then she remembered towing targets for the navy. She'd seen those glowing balls before—tracer rounds.

She pushed the throttle and made a climbing right turn. Tracers slashed past her wings and she waited to hear the wallop of contact. She intimately remembered how it felt when her own navy had accidentally put a twenty millimeter round through her rudder. But it didn't happen this time.

She rolled away and realized Mandy had been hailing her for a few seconds over the radio. "Abby, answer me. Are you hit? Are you alright?"

"I'm alright. They missed."

"Thank Christ!"

Abby banked, trying to get a better view of the submarine. She finally spotted it far below and out of range. "I wish I had ammunition," she murmured to herself. "I'd teach you to shoot at me." She keyed the mic. "What do we do?"

"He's diving. I've marked its approximate position. Follow me back to the mainland. We'll call it in. Maybe there's a cruiser or destroyer nearby."

"I can stay here and keep tabs on the bastard." She blushed at her language but didn't apologize. That Nazi had fired on her and scared her half to death. She wanted him to pay. She wanted that more than anything she'd ever wanted.

"Negative, he's diving. You'll lose him for sure and we might not find each other again. Stick with me."

Abby ground her teeth. She glanced at the ammo counter, hoping someone had made a mistake and given her a full load of .50-caliber machine gun ammo, but the counter read zero. She longed to dive and see how the crew liked being shot at. She pictured the cocky Nazi captain who might watch her through binoculars at that very moment. She flipped him the bird even though the submarine was already halfway submerged. She joined up on Mandy's wing. Mandy stared at her. Abby ignored her and flew straight and level.

"You alright?" Mandy's voice crackled over the radio.

"Fine. He really made me angry, though."

"We'll talk once we're on the ground. Stay with me. Once I call it in, we'll continue on the normal flight path to New York."

Abby checked her gauges automatically. They'd expended more fuel than they planned for, but they'd have plenty to complete the mission. They always carried more than they needed in case of emergencies.

After a few minutes, they came within sight of the mainland. Mandy took them close to an airfield and she called in the U-boat sighting.

The voice on the other end of the radio sounded skeptical. Abby could hear the doubt in his voice. She knew if they were male pilots, it would be different. They'd have already taken action. But as it was, he hinted that they probably saw a whale and overreacted, as women tended to do.

Abby couldn't contain herself any longer. She cut into the conversation.

"Listen here, pal. I know a Nazi flag when I see one and I sure as hell know when I'm being shot at. Have you ever been shot at?"

He stammered, "I—uh—well no—I uh . . ."

"There's a U-boat out there and I don't think he's delivering flowers," Abby finished.

Mandy cut in. "Is anyone else listening to this report?"

The voice seemed to recover. "Yes, of course. Harry and Joe are here."

"Then there are eyewitnesses to your lack of action. If that sub hurts any of our boys, they'll hold you personally responsible. I suggest you call it in, sir. Over and out."

They passed low beside the elevated tower. Abby hoped the roar of their engines made them piss their pants. She eyed the men through the glass and she fought the urge to flip them the bird, too. They gawked at them like cowed puppies. They climbed away in perfect formation until they leveled off at fifteen thousand feet. Abby still felt hot under the collar, but she'd gotten control of her rage.

Mandy broke the radio silence. "If words could kill, that man'd be a smoking pile of ash."

"I'm sorry, Mandy. I couldn't take it anymore."

"It's fine. I think we got through to them."

"What'll we tell flight ops? We weren't supposed to be out there."

"Let me worry about that." She paused, then said, "By the way, I think that qualifies you as a combat veteran. You took enemy fire. You can log your flight hours in green ink. That's what the navy does, anyway."

"What? Really?"

"Well, the infantry get combat badges. I'm not sure what flyers get, but I'll see about getting you something. You deserve it. Green ink, at the least."

"But I got too low. I was being stupid. I couldn't take my eyes off that Nazi flag—made my blood boil. They think they can operate this close to our shores?"

"Well, you did the right thing by climbing and getting out of range."

"I wanted to strafe them in the worst way."

Abby could hear the seriousness in Mandy's voice. "I did, too. God help me, I did, too."

An hour after the incident, Abby's hands shook. She made fists inside her gloves, but she couldn't stop the shaking. She felt nauseous and wondered if she might throw up. She wished she could, but there wasn't much worse than the smell of your own vomit in a confined cockpit. *Is this what combat feels like? Is this what Clyde has to deal with?* She recounted the incident step by step. It played out in perfect clarity, as though it was happening all over again. There was no denying the fear, but also the thrill. She imagined it would be tenfold if she had the means to fight back. But how awful, too.

She'd wanted those men to die. She hoped even now they were being showered with depth charges. *War turns us into animals. Those men have families.* She thought about Standish Hercules, the brave pilot who'd fathered Beatrice's daughter, Cora. The Nazis killed him. Her anger spiked. *How does the cycle end? When everyone's dead?*

The thought brought her headache back. Would she recognize Clyde when he finally returned? She yearned to rock him in her arms and tell him she understood—assure him that everything would be okay. But would it be enough, or would the scars be too deep?

～

ABBY LOUNGED on the couch and watched little Cora as she played on the floor in front of her. She and Mandy had finished their ferry mission and had a few days off before each of them would be tasked with new assignments.

Nothing much had come from their submarine incident. WASP flight operations hadn't grilled them about being off course. Quite the opposite. They'd congratulated them on the whole affair. Unfortunately, the U-boat hadn't been spotted that day, but a ship carrying fuel reported a failed attack the very next day, only forty miles from the spot. Luckily, the torpedo that struck the ship's side had been a dud.

A news report about the attack so close to the U.S. mainland made the papers, but omitted the WASP encounter. It made no difference to Abby, but Beatrice fumed and wanted to call the papers. She brought out a cup of tea and handed it to Abby. "Here you are."

"Thanks. Tea?" Abby asked. *A dollop of spirits would make the tea go down easier.* She pulled out a small silver flask and poured a healthy dollop.

Beatrice raised an eyebrow, but otherwise ignored the flask. "I'm all out of coffee, and besides, it's too late for coffee. But don't change the subject. You're a hero and they should recognize you."

"Hero? Mandy spotted it first and I goofed and nearly got shot down. I'm hardly a hero. Besides, nothing came from it. The U-boat slipped away."

"Yes, but that's not the point. You and Mandy risked your lives."

Abby shook her head. "You're making more of it than it deserves. It scared me, but also made me so mad. I know they're out there, but so close? They're a long way from the war."

"Now that the invasions happened, I suspect we'll see less and less U-boats. I suspect they'll be needed elsewhere. After all, what difference would it make to sink a ship here now? As I understand it, the German blockade kept the invasion from happening. Sinking ships here now is just wanton destruction just for the sake of it."

"It's war. I suspect everyone's a target." She changed the subject. "Have you heard from Sal?"

Beatrice beamed. "Yes. He called yesterday. I was so worried. He called while he was en route to Seattle, but then I didn't hear from him for another week and a half."

"Dear me. Why not?"

"He said he'd been too busy to call." Abby gave her a doubtful look. Beatrice said, "I didn't buy it either. He wouldn't tell me, but I think something happened that kept him from calling me."

"What do you mean?"

"I don't know. But he avoided my questions too much. He kept changing the subject. Kind of like you are with the U-boat."

Abby reached down and tickled Cora under the armpit. She erupted in giggles and squirmed away from her. Abby sat back on the couch and sipped her tea.

"When did he say he'd be back?"

"The train takes a week. He'll contact me on the way. I miss him terribly." She gazed lovingly at Cora. "She misses him, too."

Cora seemingly sensed the topic of conversation. She pouted her lower lip and said, "Papa?"

"Your Papa will be home soon, sweetie."

Abby rubbed the top of Cora's head. "He loves you so much." Cora went back to pushing her tattered doll around the floor. Abby asked, "Did he say anything about anything?"

"You mean the journal? He said he'd tell me everything when he got home. He didn't sound upset, but just . . . off somehow."

"A whole week without a word? Why didn't you tell me?"

She waved it off. "You're busy flying. Off hunting Nazi U-boats. Besides, what could you do? I worried enough for both of us, believe me."

Abby laughed. "I suppose you're right. But you must know you can call on me anytime, Bea. I'll drop everything, just say the word."

Beatrice nodded, then took a more serious tone. "Have you been getting enough sleep?"

"Me? I've had a few rough nights. But nothing like you having to . . ."

Beatrice interrupted her. "This isn't about me. What's keeping you up?"

"Nothing, I'm fine, really."

Beatrice raised an eyebrow. "I know when you're lying. Just like I know Sal's not telling me everything. Spill it."

"It's nothing. I—I just have nightmares. I'm afraid to fall asleep."

"About Trish?"

She looked directly into Beatrice's eyes and nodded. "But I've figured it out," she said.

"The bags under your eyes don't look like they've figured it out."

Abby put her hands to her cheeks. They felt hot and she had the urge to cry. She felt tired—worn out—was a better way to say it. She sipped her spiked tea. "I'm dealing with it," she finally said.

4

Moore General Hospital
Ashville, North Carolina
August 1944

Abby removed her hat as she entered the hospital. The smell of disinfectant and rubber reminded her of the time she'd spent visiting Trish after she'd been injured at her father's factory. It seemed a lifetime ago.

This hospital felt different from the one Trish had been in. For one, it was a military hospital. Instead of elderly patients and the occasional young person, this hospital only held young men who'd been wounded at the front. She couldn't take her eyes off the wounded men as they rolled by occasionally. Most were on gurneys, pushed along by nurses and orderlies. Serious looking doctors holding clipboards rushed around between patients.

She found the front desk and asked to see Gil Hicks. The nurse looked perplexed and, after rifling through her list of patients, asked if she had the correct hospital.

One of Clyde's letters told her that Gil had landed on the West Coast, but then had flown across the country in order for an eye specialist to save his eye. He'd be recovering in here in Asheville, at Moore General Hospital. She'd double checked the address.

"He was with the 503rd parachute regiment. He was based in Australia," she offered.

"Once they're in the hospital pipeline, their old units don't really mean much anymore since the men in here aren't returning to combat duty. "

Abby had only met Gil a few times, the first time at the wrong end of a gun. Gil's father was the infamous Mob boss, Julius Trambolini. Abby had been involved in an illegal gambling ring which had crossed paths with them years earlier.

She snapped her fingers. "Is there a Trambolini listed?"

The nurse flipped a page and beamed, "Yes. Giuliani Trambolini. He's in room 416. Fourth floor, turn left. The rooms are numbered in order."

The fourth floor had a more somber feel than the main floor. The hallways weren't as well lit and the nurses and orderlies didn't seem as harried. Only a few doctors prowled here and there, checking on patients, she supposed.

She held a small bouquet. They seemed an odd choice at the moment, something for a woman to enjoy, not a combat veteran. She hesitated outside the room. She hadn't seen Gil in years. Would he even recognize her? She remembered the letters they'd exchanged about Clyde's airborne training. She'd nearly forgotten all about that. He'd told her how close Clyde had come to losing his life.

She smoothed her slacks and top, then peaked her head around the corner. A man sat in bed reading a newspaper propped on pillows. She couldn't see his face, only his hands on the edges of the paper and his feet sticking out from the covers.

"Gil?" she asked.

The paper dropped abruptly and she nearly dropped the flowers. She barely recognized him. She remembered him being handsome, with thick dark hair, strong facial lines, and deep brown eyes. This man's face was crisscrossed with deep scars, some pink and puckered, others whitish-yellow. Where his left eye should be, only a deep black socket. The scarring continued up his forehead to his scalp, thinning his hair to splotches.

"Abby? Abby Cooper?"

She recovered as best she could, but knew he'd seen her shocked reaction. "Yes, Gil, it's me." She forced a smile. "Or should I be calling you Giuliani?"

"Gil," he said quickly. He smiled and she noticed his lips didn't move naturally. One side seemed to be tethered in place. "Come in, come in. I know I'm quite the sight. Sorry 'bout that," he said, as he fumbled for something on the bedside table. He held up a finger and said, "Give me a moment to make myself presentable."

"Certainly," she said and she turned toward the wall. She heard a latch and a box snapping open, then shut again.

"Okay, you can turn around now."

He'd placed a fake glass eye into the empty socket. It helped, but she still couldn't keep herself from staring. She gave him his sweetest smile. "Should I put the flowers on the table?"

"That'd be fine. Thank you. This place could use a little sprucing up. How'd you find me? Do you live around here?"

"Yes, not too far," she lied. She didn't want him to feel like she was too put out by coming her. "Clyde sent a letter. He wanted me to check in on you." She blushed. "He told me to tell you," she lowered her voice, "and these are his words, *you're a son of a bitch.*"

Gil's smile stretched as wide as the skin grafts would allow, and he roared with laughter. Abby couldn't help but join in, grateful for the break in the tension. She could hear the joy in his laughter and she felt the deep friendship he shared with her husband. It made her feel closer to Clyde than she had in a long time. This man had been through so much with Clyde, it almost made her jealous.

She went to his side, and between bouts of laughter, and she hugged him. Taken aback, he tentatively hugged her back, gently tapping her back. She couldn't keep from crying. When he felt her sobs, he pulled her tighter and stroked her back.

"Hey there, it's okay, Abby. It's okay."

She pulled away, but remained sitting on the bed. "I'm so sorry, Gil. I don't know what's come over me. I'm just so worried about him. I'm scared he'll . . ."

"Scared he'll end up looking like me?" he offered with a sideways grin. "I don't blame you."

"Don't be silly. You're alive, and that's all that matters. I—I just want him out of there. I want my husband back."

His face turned serious and he nodded his understanding. "I know. I want him out of there, too. I want them all outta there. It's—well, it isn't good."

"Will he be alright? Will he come home to me?" She knew it wasn't a fair question, but he was the closest connection she had to him. He didn't answer, just stared at the discarded newspaper. "What's it like? What's he going through?" she pressed.

Gil's eye clouded and lost focus. She saw him struggling with the questions. Perhaps it wasn't something that could be put to words. She remembered hearing stories from the First World War, unimaginable stories of death and destruction. Back then she thought they must be exaggerated, but seeing Gil's one good eye now, she knew they were probably only shadows of the reality.

He sighed deeply and looked into her eyes. "He's with good men, Abby. The airborne are the best group of guys you could ask for. They've got each other's backs all the time. The Japs—well, they're up against it." He cut himself off, as though he didn't want to talk about the enemy who'd sent his shattered body here.

Abby wiped her tears away. "I'm sorry, Gil. Here you're the one hurt and I'm blubbering like a newborn."

He touched her shoulder. "It's okay, Abby. I never really think how it must be for the people we leave behind. It's gotta be its own special kind of hell."

She focused on his face, looking at him not with pity, but with interest. "Does it still hurt?"

He touched his scarred face. "Nah, not really. The eye doctor really thought he could save my eye, but he was obviously wrong. It doesn't hurt anymore." He touched his chest and stomach region. "I still have bits of shrapnel in my chest and side, which bothers me sometimes." He raised the bedsheets and his hospital shirt, exposing white bandages crisscrossing his midsection. They looked fresh.

"The other doc said they removed the last of the dangerous pieces. The rest'll have to stay. Says the rest might work their way out on their own someday." He covered back up. "Can you imagine leaking metal?"

Abby flushed at the sight of the fresh bandages. "I didn't know they were still doing surgeries on you. Oh, Gil, I should let you rest."

"No, no, it's fine. As you can see, I don't get too many visitors."

"Your parents?"

"Across the country. I've talked on the phone with them, though. Papa's busy with work and my mama's worried I'll lose too much weight. It's hard to tell her I don't have much of an appetite left."

A silence grew. Abby had seen the Trambolini business up close and personal. They operated on the fringes of the law. Everyone knew it, but they had too much influence, so their occasional indiscretions went ignored by the authorities. The occasional kickback helped keep things level.

"I'm sure you'll gain back whatever you lost in no time. Do they have good Italian food here?"

"Hell no!" he cursed. "Oh, excuse my language."

"That's okay. The ladies I fly with say worse all the time. I'm used to it by now."

"Really?" He shook his head as though he couldn't picture it. "How's that going? Flying, I mean."

She noticed a slight hesitation in his voice, as though he didn't quite approve of women flying airplanes. She'd heard it countless times before, but it surprised her to hear it in Gil's voice. He and Clyde must've talked about her new career in the WASPs. But Gil obviously still had doubts. Did Clyde secretly feel the same way? "It's wonderful. I love it. I feel so blessed to help in any way I can."

He gave her a thin smile. "How long you think you'll have a job? I mean, I hear pilots are coming back from the front. Surely, they'll want their jobs back. And I read that the bill to make WASPs a part of the military got voted down."

She didn't know how to respond. The question seemed so out of place. But he was right, things were changing quickly. Public opinion had turned against them from one day to the next, it seemed. She'd tried to ignore it, but it was hard not to notice the disdainful looks her WASP uniform some-times evoked these days.

"As long as they need us, I suppose. I don't think of it as a career path, but more of a wartime need. It would be wonderful if the war ended tomorrow and they didn't need us anymore. I'd like nothing more. But it just keeps going and going," she said mournfully.

"Yeah, it does seem like it might last forever."

The words felt like daggers in her guts. How could Clyde survive for years upon years on the front lines?

He touched her shoulder again. "Oh, I've upset you. I'm sorry." He held up the newspaper. "There's good news in Europe, at least. The Nazis can't last much longer now that they're gettin' squeezed from both sides."

She patted his hand and stood. "How's it going in the Pacific? I mean, really? The papers don't give much detail."

He took his time. He carefully folded the paper, then stuffed it under the bedside lamp. "The Japs are a different animal, Abby. I mean, I read in the paper about Nazis surrendering by the hundreds. I see pictures of them with their hands up as they march. The Japs—well, they just don't do that. They fight to the death. I've never even seen a Jap prisoner. Not once. What's that tell you?"

Abby wrung her hands. She wanted to cry, but didn't think the tears would come. Gil didn't need to see her cry again.

Gil added, "We're winning, but it's gonna take a hell of a long time."

She closed her eyes and nodded. He didn't need to say the unspoken words, *and a hell of a lot more lives.* She forced a smile. "So, what are your plans? You must be getting out of here soon. Are you heading back to Seattle?"

He nodded, but didn't look too happy about the prospect. "Yeah, as soon as they release me, I'll hop a train back home."

"Your parents must be excited."

He shrugged as though they could take him or leave him. "I guess so. We've never been too touchy feely, if you know what I mean."

"Will you go back to work for your father?" she asked carefully. It was like asking if he planned on going back to a life of crime and she felt the discomfort between them grow.

"I dunno. My father built his business from the ground up. He expects me to take over someday, but after what I've seen . . ." he shook his head slowly. "I just dunno."

"Maybe you and Clyde could start a business together," she mused hopefully.

Gil smiled his tethered smile. "I'd like that. But what the hell do I know? I'll probably just take over the business."

"You can do whatever you want, Gil. You've earned that right more than most."

Gil worked his hands for a few seconds before he spoke again. "I know you think my family's involved in all sorts of . . ." he hesitated as he searched for the correct word, "unsavory stuff, but most of it's on the up and up, if you can believe it. If I was in charge, I could curb the unsavory stuff." He looked around the empty room as though there might be someone listening from beneath a bed. "I've never said that out loud. If my father heard, he'd cuff me upside the head."

"Well, I've only seen the one side of the business," she said as her cheeks flushed. "And it *was* unsavory, as you recall."

"I know, I know. I hope you can forgive me for that one day."

She waved it off, but the image of the gun held to her head still visited her nightmares sometimes. "I forgave you years ago, Gil. You know that." She patted his hand.

"I probably shouldn't tell you this, but I think my father still holds a grudge against your father."

The air in the room seemed to grow heavy and she suddenly had to concentrate on breathing. She tried to speak, but didn't know what to say. A threat from Julius Trambolini was serious.

"But don't worry. I won't let anything happen to your family. If he's planning something, I'll put an end to it. I give you my word."

She felt an iciness pass through her. How much influence would Gil have over his mafia boss father? Enough to change plans laid far in advance? "I—I don't know what to say. Would your father do that? What would he do?" She stared into Gil's eyes. "Kill him?"

"Your father's not a great humanitarian, you know."

She removed her hand from his and took a step back. She wanted to say something in her father's defense, but she couldn't come up with anything. She finally said in a low voice, "He doesn't deserve to die."

He raised what was left of one eyebrow at her, as though questioning her statement.

"He's done things, but he's still my father, he's . . ."

"Would it change things if you knew your father tried to get Clyde hurt in training?"

Abby felt the room spin out of control suddenly. Her vision tunneled and she only saw Gil's mangled face with the one good eye, the other fixed on her shoulder, it seemed.

She stammered, "Wh—what are you talking about?" She remembered the conversation she'd had with her father ages ago. He'd mentioned something about Clyde's training. It bothered her enough that she wrote Gil a letter asking about the training.

Gil said, "You wrote me about it, remember?"

"Of course, and you—you said it was baseless."

He squinted. "Did I? I told you Clyde had a few close calls, but I never said your father wasn't involved."

She sat heavily in the chair at the foot of the bed. "He—he was?"

"I dunno," he finally said. "But the more I think about it, the more likely someone was trying to hurt him. Clyde certainly thought so."

Abby's eyes flashed at that revelation. Clyde had said nothing about his suspicions, even when she asked about the incidents directly. He'd said they were simply training accidents. They happened all the time. Had he lied to her? "He did? He thought my father tried to sabotage his training? Is that what you're saying?"

"He didn't mention your father, but he was convinced someone messed with his parachute on that last jump. I thought he was paranoid, but when I got your letter, I wondered if maybe he was right after all. Your father has a lot of money. Perhaps he bought some instructor, paid him to do his dirty work."

Abby felt the room spin out of control again. She didn't have control of her body. She had to grip the side of the chair to keep from falling off.

Gil rose but winced at the pain and lay back down. "Hey, you okay? Take it easy. You don't look so good. Need some water?"

She rubbed her scalp, feeling a raging headache threatening. She wanted a drink, but something stiffer than water. This was too much information all at once. It wasn't what she expected from this visit.

"He—he doesn't have any contacts in the army, or even the military, besides the business side of things. How would he even go about doing something like that?"

Gil shrugged. "I didn't mean to upset you, Abby. If Clyde knew I told you, he'd likely kill me and save you the trouble."

Abby barely heard him. Her mind was reeling. She suddenly stood and clenched her fists until her knuckles turned white. "Sal," she murmured. "Sal still has contacts in the army."

~

GIL WATCHED Abby storm out of his hospital room. He'd tried to talk her down, make her think things through. Even though she nodded and promised not to act irrationally, he'd seen her eyes. He knew Sal to be a strong, hard man, but he pitied him at that moment.

How would Clyde react if he knew what he'd just said to Abby? He'd obviously kept the training accidents under wraps, at least partially, but now she knew what he'd suspected all along and it all led back to her father.

Gil ran through the conversation in his head again. Perhaps he shouldn't have said anything, but he didn't like the way Abby had looked at him when he mentioned his own father. He knew it was petty, but he felt the need to deflect his own father's guilt onto her father. He wasn't proud of it, but he couldn't take any of it back.

He made a move to sit up, but the pain from the recent surgery took his breath away and he lay back. He balled his fists and smacked the cushy bed. He hated being bedridden. He'd been a paratrooper and now he was just taking up space. Wasted space.

He'd seen Abby's shock when she first saw his face—his eyeless socket. He'd have to be more careful about having it out, but the damn thing felt odd in his head, like he had a pebble under his eyelid that he couldn't extract. He'd get used to it, but would he ever find another woman? What if they all looked at him the way Abby had? *Stop feeling sorry for yourself.*

He thought about his family, his father. What did he have planned for the Brooks family? It must be something special to ferment for so long. How long had it been since Sal gunned down his cousin? Two years now. That was a long time to hold a grudge for most people, but not a Trambolini.

It hadn't been on his mind while he was fighting the Japanese, but now it hit him full in the face. There was no way his father would let that go. Should he interfere? Perhaps he should let things play out the way his father intended. But he'd made a promise to Abby and that was the same thing as making a promise to Clyde. He'd keep that promise.

He set his jaw and leaned his head back against the pillow. He yearned for a nap. He nearly succumbed to the lull of sleep, but no. No more softness, no more coddling. He threw the pillow across the room. It tipped over the flowers Abby had brought and they scattered on the floor, immediately transforming from beauty to so much garbage. *Like my life.*

"Nurse!" he bellowed. A harried army nurse stuck her head into the room. She saw the scattered flowers and moved to clean up the mess, but he stopped her. "Leave it. I need to make a call. Bring me a phone."

5

Northern Philippines
August 1944

Frank Cooper listened to the wind blowing along the strait of water separating his small island from the main island, and Constance. He searched for any telltale signs in the darkness of her passage.

He'd sat there since midnight, hoping. He hated the soft glow coming from the east. The darkness faded steadily. She wouldn't risk a daylight crossing. She only came at night. But what kept her? Japanese soldiers? Her Uncle Mandio?

A noise behind him and he knew his old friend, Grinning Bear, approached. Just hearing his shuffle gave him away.

Grinning Bear sat beside him heavily. "She's not coming tonight."

"I know."

"She's fine. Put it out of your head."

"Put what out of my head?"

"All the shit swirling around in there. I know you too well. Stop worrying. She's fine."

"What if she's not? What if those savages have her under the knife as we speak?"

"We would've heard something. Have faith in the network."

"You sound like Gustav."

"He makes a lot of sense."

"She was supposed to come last night. She's never been two nights overdue."

"She's a smart girl. She's being careful."

Frank didn't respond, just kept staring across the ever-lightening straits.

Grinning Bear said, "We heard from HQ."

Frank spun and stared at him.

Grinning Bear continued. "They want us back in the fight. They say enough time has passed."

Frank shook his head as though dealing with slow-minded children. "They'll be ready for us this time."

"They know the score," Grinning Bear said. "It's time to shake things up. Besides, it's a small garrison. This island's a backwater."

Frank stared hard at him. "Is that you talking, or them?"

Grinning Bear spit a thin stream of spittle into the sea, then said, "Just cause you've met a girl doesn't mean we call the whole thing off. It was your idea to come here and kill more Japs. Remember?"

Frank sighed heavily. "I know. I know. I just can't stomach anything happening to her."

"You should make her stay with us. She'd be safer here."

"I've tried, but she won't do it. She's trusted and people tell her things. She knows she's too valuable. Mandio knows, too."

"Fuck Mandio."

"Antonio might be a problem, too."

"You can handle Antonio. If it came right down to it, I mean. You shouldn't worry about him. He learned his lesson. He wears the bullet wound in his forearm like a badge of honor, but I know it hurts like the devil. He fucked up and got himself shot because he let his balls do the talking."

Frank snickered, despite the awful memory. The brief firefight in town happened because Antonio wanted to make sure Constance found her way home safely, or so he said. More likely, he wanted to spend the night with her. Antonio saw his connection with her and it made him jealous. At least, that was one theory.

When Antonio stumbled into the Japanese squad, he'd opened fire and nearly got himself and others killed. He claimed he'd killed two enemy soldiers, but Constance reported no injuries on the Japanese side. He'd stirred up a hornet's nest. Now, instead of an unaware garrison unit, they faced an alert enemy.

Frank said, "Maybe Mandio's right. She might cause too much trouble if she was over here. The Japs might wonder where she went, start asking questions."

A full month had passed since the incident, but Constance still reported increased patrols and more aggressive questioning sessions of the locals. Constance had avoided questioning, but it was only a matter of time before they came knocking on her Uncle Mandio's door. She wouldn't crack, at least not right away, but what about Mandio? Frank worried about him.

Frank said, "Did HQ give any specifics?"

"They want us to move south and monitor the port area near Calaya."

Frank nearly fell off the log when he turned too quickly. "Calaya? I heard Gustav mention it, but it's far south. We'd have to cover a lot of ground, all of it heavy with enemy troops."

"Yep, but the island's small. It won't take long." he spit into the sea again.

"Does Gustav know?"

"He decoded the message."

"What'd he say?"

"You know how he is, just nodded as though it wasn't a big deal. He said he has some contacts in that area, but few. Not like here."

"The men aren't ready for something like that. Hell, I'm not ready for something like that. It'll be well guarded. Without a solid network . . ." he left the rest unsaid. "Well, monitoring isn't the same thing as attacking."

Frank stood and stretched his back as he looked across the strait to the strip of beach where Constance would've launched her outrigger canoe if she were coming. "Guess we've got some planning."

They spent the rest of the day going over rudimentary maps, which looked as though they'd been drawn during the last century. The Filipinos added to them. They added roads and towns until they had a good idea about the safest path south. The island was small, which helped, but also hurt. The Japanese garrison was relatively small here, but they also couldn't just fade into the deep jungle and disappear. There weren't enough places to hide.

Frank rubbed his chin as he studied the area. "I sure wish we had some local knowledge. There must be some connection hereabouts."

Gustav answered in his German-accented English, "I can send someone to bring a local back. They could answer our questions. It would take a few days."

"Who would you send?"

"Grace has a few cousins there."

"A woman?"

"Yes. They draw less suspicion than a traveling man."

"Can she pull it off? It's a long way to go."

"She can do it. She'll take her sister Nori. Two sisters traveling to see a long-lost cousin—they will not raise an eye."

Frank nodded. "Okay, I agree."

"I will inform them. They will leave tomorrow morning," Gustav said.

〜

WITH THE DECISION MADE, Frank retired to his hut for a midday nap. Most of them napped during this time, and he liked the tradition immensely.

He stepped onto his small porch. Before he entered the cooler insides of the thatch hut, he noticed Antonio staring at him from a dozen yards back. Frank gave him a cursory wave. Antonio lifted his chin and held up his wounded arm. Frank didn't know if he waved or just showed off his wound. The fresh white bandage shone in the midday sun. He seemed proud of his wound, even though he put everyone else at risk, including Constance, to get it. He remembered what Grinning Bear said. Antonio wore it as a badge of honor, but he saw something else in Antonio's eyes. He saw a challenge.

His thoughts went back to Constance. Her bright smile, perfectly brown skin, full lips, and sultry eyes never failed to arouse him. He longed to see her naked body laid out on his thatch bed. He longed to hold her and make love to her and hold her again until the morning. Seeing Antonio's defiant glare made him want her even more, made him want to seal the deal as soon as possible. Once he made love to her, she'd be his woman and Antonio could go to hell. *I sound like a damned caveman.*

No, he'd let things happen naturally. No need to rush things. She'd already shown an interest in him, not Antonio. She smiled at *him*, touched *him*, gazed longingly at *him*—not Antonio. Couldn't he see that? Perhaps that was why he challenged him now.

He turned from Antonio, who still held his arm up. He wondered how long he'd keep the position if he didn't turn away. Was it an open challenge or just a greeting?

He guessed Antonio to be a year or two younger than himself. He had good musculature and athleticism, but Frank had excelled at hand to hand combat training and felt confident if push came to shove, he'd prevail. He hoped it wouldn't come to that.

In the short time they had, he and Grinning Bear tried to train the Filipinos as regular army troops, including some rudimentary hand to hand combat, but they were still civilians. They couldn't expect to have the same discipline and follow the same rules and etiquette which had been drilled into them over years and years of training. They didn't have enough time for such things. Just the basics would have to do. So if a fight for domi-nance happened—even over a woman—there wasn't much he could do about it other than win. If he didn't win, the entire operation would dissolve into mayhem. No wonder the military drilled discipline into them from day one.

Perhaps Constance would come tonight. He hoped so. If not, something had happened to her. He clenched his fists. These kinds of thoughts drove him crazy. He almost wished he'd never met her. Things would be so much easier.

He lay on his bed and stared at the ceiling thatch. Spider webs reached from end to end and the hollowed out bodies of dead insects vibrated as the spiders moved along their mini-highways. Who was he in that scenario —the spider or the dead insect?

～

Darkness fell over the island like a death shroud. That's how it felt to Frank as he worried about Constance. If she didn't come tonight, she'd be three days late. He'd have to cross the strait himself and find out what happened, even though it might lead to his death or worse, capture.

Thankfully, he never had to make that decision. A dark figure approached the camp, led by an excited young man who'd been on guard duty. Frank saw the diminutive figure and immediately knew it was Constance. He wanted to run to her and take her into his arms, but he forced himself to walk. Other Filipinos trotted to the newcomer and talked excitedly in their stilted English and pidgin.

She stepped into the dim light from the hanging lantern. Her eyes sparkled and softened when she saw him approach. She held out her arms to him and he lost all control. He rushed to her and took her in his arms. She radiated heat and he felt tears form in the corners of his eyes. He didn't know why or how, but he didn't care at that moment. He held her tightly, as though she might slip away again. Everything he'd ever been through culminated in holding her and feeling her hugging him back just as fiercely.

He finally pulled away from her. He held her at arm's length and looked her up and down. He swiped at his eyes, suddenly embarrassed at his display. But no one seemed to care.

"Where have you been? What's happened?"

In her stilted English, she said, "Japs. Hold me and Mandio."

Frank felt the blood drain from his face. He felt suddenly sick as all his fears came rushing to the forefront. But he didn't see any wounds or anything suggesting torture.

"Are you okay? Did they hurt you?"

"Not me. Mandio. Took him."

"They took Mandio?" She nodded.

Frank knew what it meant. No matter how strong a person was, eventually they would talk. Pain had a way of twisting the mind, something he'd learned from years of Japanese captivity. He remembered beatings he just wanted to end. Even though they didn't ask him questions, he would've answered to make it all stop, and lying was too exhausting when pain ruled your mind. He had no illusions how long Mandio would last. He didn't hold it against him.

He exchanged a worried glance with Grinning Bear, then Gustav. He pushed Constance's hair out of her eyes. He wanted to kiss her, wanted to take her to his hut and ease her obvious anguish, but he knew it would have to wait.

"Do you know where they have him?"

Gustav stepped forward to translate, but Constance answered before he could. "Mayor's house."

"They have him at the Mayor's house?"

"Yes. Yes, Mayor's house," she repeated.

He patted her arm affectionately. "Thank you." She smiled and it broke his heart not to hug her again. He motioned for Gustav and Grinning Bear to follow as he stepped away from the main group. "We have to break him loose or the Japs'll be here before morning."

Gustav said, "I know the house. It will be difficult if they have many soldiers."

Grinning Bear added, "I agree, this whole operation dies if he talks."

"He'll talk. You know that as well as I do."

Grinning Bear just nodded, the corners of his mouth turning down like deep check marks in his face.

"We have to go in tonight," Frank persisted.

"The Nips have forced our hand," Grinning Bear said with iron in his voice.

"The men aren't ready," Frank said, almost to himself.

"They will do their duty," Gustav assured him.

Frank finally said, "I don't see any other choice. One way or another, this operation lives or dies by what happens tonight."

Grinning Bear nodded and Gustav said, "I'll tell the men to prepare for battle."

"We don't have much time. Constance can fill us in on enemy positions. Let's sketch it out and be across the strait in two hours."

~

FRANK HUNKERED alongside the road leading to town. He'd been here before on the night they hit the truck park, but he hadn't returned since that fateful night. He felt as though he were returning to the scene of a crime.

The skeletons of burned out trucks still sat where they'd burned. He knew through the network that only a few trucks had been replaced. Now the Japanese kept them on the other side of town.

He glanced back at his nine-man team. Antonio hunkered a few feet behind and he could see his sparkling eyes staring back at him. Even in the low light, he could see anger and malice there. He only hoped Antonio would push his personal feelings away for the time being. He didn't think he'd do anything brash out here, but love could make a man do strange things. He'd thought about leaving him behind, but doubted he would have listened, and besides—he needed his expertise and his leadership. The other Filipinos respected him.

Constance crouched on Frank's left. He didn't look at her, but he could sense her presence. He thought he smelled her sweat mixed with berries, but he forced himself to put it out of his mind. He had work to do so. If he survived, he planned on consummating their relationship as soon as possible.

He couldn't see Grinning Bear and his squad. He'd leapfrogged ahead a few hundred yards. Once they gave the all clear, Frank's squad would move forward and cover them as they moved into position. Once in place, Frank would take his squad to the Mayor's house and attack as soon as Grinning Bear started things off at the front.

The night noises sounded loud. He tried to filter out the buzzing of insects and the distant screeches of night animals. He listened for anything out of the ordinary. Just one sentry out taking a piss could alert the enemy to their presence and blow the whole operation sky high.

He finally heard the distant warbling of a common night bird. He recognized Grinning Bear's signal to move forward. They crossed the road in pairs. Constance stayed close to his side. He could barely hear her footfalls.

He wanted her to stay back at home base, but she'd insisted on coming along and he understood her need to help her uncle. If he forced her to stay, she'd never forgive him. He wished she'd at least stay in the rear, though.

He entered the thin jungle alongside the road. They trotted past the burned out truck park. Even now, he could still smell the burnt husks of metal. He wondered if ash from the two dead Japanese soldiers still wafted in the air.

He saw the distant lights of town, just a few specks in the blackness. He forced himself to look for movement along the edges. Most of the locals would be asleep in their beds, but there'd be enemy sentries.

He stopped on the outskirts of the tiny town. The rest of the squad slowed and spread out without a word. He searched the darkness for any signs of the enemy.

On a scratched out piece of dirt back at home base, Constance had sketched out where the sentries normally stood. He hoped they kept to the same schedule. She explained the Japanese rotated guard duty every four hours. He'd planned their assault to coincide with the third hour when they'd be at their least alert.

Frank strained to see the first guard. He thought perhaps she'd been mistaken, but he finally saw a slight movement. A darker shadow moved against the corner of a dilapidated house. The soldier leaned against the house and adjusted himself. Frank allowed himself to breathe again. Constance had been right on the money. Now he could move the squad into town, knowing where the gaps would be.

He glanced at her and saw her smiling back. He wanted to take her face in his hands and kiss her lips, but he pushed it out of his mind. *Get your head in the game, asshole.*

He waved the men off the road and pointed. The Mayor's house stood at the far edge, tucked up against the relatively thin jungle. It was a modest two-story house. The only two-story house in town. The Japanese had quickly taken it over. They allowed the mayor and his family to live in a single room on the bottom floor. Constance said they lived in fear for their lives ever since Antonio's ill-fated shootout.

The squad moved from house to house carefully. No one stirred. When they came to the middle of town, Frank leaned out from the corner of an animal stall. He saw another guard only thirty yards away. He stood in a small cone of light. The guard paced back and forth, never leaving the light.

Frank stayed put and waved the others to keep moving. He'd been worried about this guard, as he'd be the closest to their objective, but the fact that he stood beneath a light made him feel much better. The light would keep him from seeing much beyond the light. They might stroll right past without being noticed. He didn't plan on testing that theory, though.

When the last man passed, he peeled away and followed. He trotted back to the front of the column. He smiled at each man as he passed. Antonio glared back at him. *He's definitely going to be a problem.*

They finally came to the back of the mayor's house. Despite being two stories, the house looked cheap and rundown. He couldn't be sure in the darkness, but it seemed to lean to one side as though it might fall over with a strong gust of wind. Perhaps it would fall around their ears as they attacked. What then?

He crouched near the back door. It hung on old rusted hinges and looked frail. Constance said it would be locked, but he didn't think it would take much to open it. One swift kick would likely shatter it, but stealth was the order of the day.

He stiffened when he heard a scream. The sound took him by surprise with its intensity. He gripped his Springfield, thinking they'd somehow been discovered, but then realized it was a scream of agony, not surprise, and it came from inside.

Constance gripped his arm and he saw the fear in her eyes. He wanted to console her, but he felt the old fear, too. Her Uncle Mandio was being tortured—it had to be him.

"Uncle," she hissed.

He placed his hand on hers, hoping she didn't notice his shakiness. The scream shook him to his core. He'd heard similar screams from the days of his captivity, his own screams. The memory chilled him.

His fear changed to anger. The Japanese were up to their old tricks again, but this time, he'd make things right. The worst part about being tortured besides the obvious was the hopelessness and the helplessness. Helpless and hopeless, not a good combination. He longed to ease Uncle Mandio's pain. He longed to be the hope he'd always longed for when the Japanese cut on him. He wanted to go in guns blazing, but had to wait for Grinning Bear. Behind him, he felt the others wanting to kick things off, too. They wanted to stop the screams coming from the top floor as much as he did. The night sounds diminished as the screams continued with more vigor. The others itched to attack. He pressed his index finger to his lips. Any moment now.

He jumped when he heard the crack of a rifle toward the front of town. The single rifle shot became two more shots. He heard distant yelling and the screaming from the house stopped. Soft whimpers and strong Japanese voices spilled from the top floor now. It was their signal. Shadowy shapes shifted across windows. More guttural grunts as Japanese were undoubtedly pulled from their beds with the new threat coming from up the street.

Frank stood and trotted to the back door. The others followed. He hoped Constance would have the sense to stay near the back. Her small pistol would be next to useless.

He pushed against the door. He heard heavy footfalls inside as men scrambled. Would they leave anyone to guard Mandio? On one hand, he wanted to kill—wanted vengeance—on the other, he wanted stealthiness. If they took Mandio without raising the alarm, it would be better, but his torturers wouldn't pay.

He reached for the door handle and gave it a slight pull. The door flexed but held. He pulled harder and the door bent more. It wouldn't take much to break in. He caught Antonio's eye and nodded. Antonio stepped in front and kicked the door at the level of the handle. It burst open among a shower of splinters and rending wood.

Frank lunged inside, his rifle leading the way. He heard pounding footsteps, but no yells of alarm came from nearby. He slowed, not wanting to blunder into an enemy soldier. He pulled back into a darkened corner when a soldier ran past him, heading straight for the front door. The soldier had his rifle in one hand as he tried to slip on his tunic with the other.

Frank breathed a sigh of relief. If he'd taken just one more step, they would've collided. He glanced back at Antonio. He grinned evilly. Frank couldn't tell if it was relief or disappointment. He didn't dwell on it.

The stairwell loomed just ahead. He ran the few steps to the base and peered up into the dim light. The shots increased from outside. Grinning Bear had done his job and would disengage any second now. They had to make this quick. The rest of the squad watched him expectantly.

He hissed, "Some of you watch the front. Don't shoot unless you have to."

He took the stairs two at a time. They creaked and groaned with each step. If someone waited at the top, he'd have to kill them quickly. Once the soldiers heard shots coming from the house, they'd quickly reverse course. He didn't relish being caught inside without an escape route.

He crested the short stairway and saw the backside of a Japanese soldier. The soldier faced an open doorway and Frank heard moaning and curses coming from the room. His finger touched the trigger, but he didn't shoot. He ran straight at the soldier's back.

The soldier only made it halfway around before Frank slammed the butt of his rifle into his face. The crack of wood smashing bone sounded louder than a rifle shot in his ears. Blood, teeth and spittle flew from the soldier's mouth and he dropped without another sound. Frank straddled him and looked into the room just in time to see a Japanese officer holding a pistol.

Their eyes locked for an instant. Frank didn't have time to bring his rifle to bear. He lunged past the doorway just as the pistol barked. The bullet splintered the side of the doorway. Antonio burst through the door and fired his rifle from the hip. Screams of pain and fear filled the house.

Frank lunged back to the doorway. Antonio worked the bolt action and fired point blank into the wounded officer's face. A man in the corner whimpered and cowered. His hands were tied behind his back and he was naked. Blood covered his head, making what little hair he had glisten.

Constance ran to him and knelt beside him. He shook and jolted with her touch, but she finally got through to him and he calmed down. His bloodshot eyes focused, and he looked at his rescuers in confusion and fear. Tears mixed with the blood dripping from his slashed head.

Constance cooed and cajoled until Mandio finally stood. She pulled a vicious-looking knife from her belt and slashed the bonds. He sighed in relief and rubbed his swollen, cut wrists. She helped him walk as he staggered.

"We have to go, now!" Frank barked.

Not everyone understood his words, but the intent was clear. Constance held her uncle and helped him along. She spit on the dead officer as she passed. Frank followed her out. Antonio smiled grimly at him. He clearly enjoyed killing the officer.

Frank's skin crawled as he stepped in front of him. It would be easy for Antonio to shoot him in the back. He could say it was an accidental discharge, or say a Japanese soldier shot him. His men might back up his claim.

The soldier he'd clubbed moaned as he stepped over him. Frank glanced down at him. He felt sick at the damage he'd caused, but he also knew the Japanese had doled out far worse.

Antonio lunged, and Frank thought his fears had come true, but instead of attacking him, Antonio descended onto the wounded soldier. A knife flashed and he buried it in the soldier's neck. Blood spurted onto his hand as he twisted, then pulled it with a vicious slash. The soldier's mouth opened in a ghastly attempt to breathe, then he lay still.

Frank couldn't take his eyes off the spectacle. Antonio wiped the blade on the dead soldier's tunic and strode past as though nothing had happened. Frank took one last look at the soldier before following him down the hall. His burning hatred for the enemy didn't burn as brightly.

The squad descended the stairs in a thundering stampede. Frank wondered if they'd collapse under the strain. Surely they weren't meant for so many feet all at once. He made it to the bottom floor. He hesitated. Yelling Japanese voices came from out front. He could see shapes darting this way and that. The occasional rifle cracked, but Grinning Bear and Gustav would already be halfway to the beach by now.

Frank pushed the men along. "Come on—keep moving! Keep moving!"

He saw Constance and her harried uncle dart through the back door. More squad members squeezed through, some being pushed into the doorway. A shot erupted from outside and he felt a bullet pass close and smack into the wall with a thwack. Where had it come from?

He spun back to the front of the house. A Japanese soldier worked the bolt action of his rifle. Frank dropped to a knee, aimed, and fired. The roar of his rifle surprised him. The soldier twisted as though an invisible force punched him. He screamed, dropped his rifle, and clutched at the wound.

Frank ran toward the back door. He worked the bolt and slammed another round in. He didn't look back, but waited to feel the bullet he knew would come. He threw himself headlong out the door and did a half roll. He popped up and ran into the thin jungle, chasing the backs of his men. They sprinted away from the sounds of yelling and rifle fire. None seemed to be aimed their way.

He felt panic rise in his guts. The others ran with abandon, and he joined them. It reminded him of a dream where a monster chased him and he couldn't run fast enough, but this time he could and he took full advantage.

A Filipino slammed into a tree at full speed. The sound and the painful grunt pulled Frank to his senses. He yelled, "Stop! Stop running!" He knelt beside the injured man. He shook the cobwebs from his rung bell. Frank touched his shoulder and saw it was Antonio.

"Easy does it," he cooed, but knew his words meant nothing to him. The squad ignored his pleas and they evaporated into the night, still running. The only sound was their stampeding feet and crushed brush. Hopefully, they'd come to their senses soon and head to the beach. If they ran into a patrol, or the Japanese reacted quickly, they'd be easy pickings. He had to get control of them.

He looked around and was relieved to see Constance. She panted heavily and held her uncle close. He looked ready to drop. How had she kept up with him in his headlong sprint?

"We have to get control of the others," he hissed.

Antonio tried to stand on his own when he saw Constance, but he nearly fell over and Frank gripped his shoulder again. Antonio shook him off and grunted a guttural curse.

Frank said to Constance. "Tell Antonio to get control of the others."

Constance's voice changed and she spoke quickly. Antonio winced as though she'd slapped him. He nodded and, with a last look at Frank, he staggered into the darkness, calling out to the others.

"Thank you," Frank said.

She beamed at him. Mandio leaned heavily on her. Even in the darkness, his nakedness was obvious. Frank went to his side and helped. They staggered away from town.

6

Once reassembled, Frank and the others quickly paddled across the strait. He leaped onto shore and helped pull the outrigger canoes up and out of sight. Despite the long night, he felt energized. He wanted to whoop. They'd done it. They'd actually pulled it off.

He helped Mandio off the canoe. He couldn't help noticing the way Constance kept sneaking peaks at him. He glanced back at her, hoping he wasn't imagining things. He fought the urge to take her in his arms. It would be the perfect ending to a successful operation.

They passed Mandio off to others, waiting to help along the straits. Mandio seemed to have recovered. He talked expressively, obviously ecstatic to be out of the Japanese clutches. He had cuts and bruises but he didn't seem to have any lasting effects, besides a few obviously broken fingers. Someone had given him a smock to cover himself with.

Constance leaned into Frank's side. His arm went around her instinctively, and he gazed down at her. She said in her stilted English, "Uncle tell nothing. No tell."

"That's great," Frank said. He felt he should say more. Should he believe him? What if he had broken and told them everything? Surely they'd be on their way here right now. He looked across the water. He could barely see the other side. Perhaps he should've left a few men over there as an early warning system.

"He must be very brave."

She smiled at him, and her arms wrapped around his waist. He squeezed her into him and felt her curves and soft skin. She smelled of sweat, and a hint of something more feminine and heady. He desperately wanted to explore every crevice of her body.

They walked a few feet behind the last man. The starlight gave off just enough light to see the pathway leading back up the hill. She tugged at his side and he turned to her. She tilted her chin and he grasped it between his finger and thumb. Her eyes sparkled, reflecting the starlight. He cupped her face, and her cheeks radiated heat as he leaned down. He hesitated for a moment, inches from her lips. She pulled him into her until their mouths found each other. She tasted exotic. He'd never felt such soft lips, far beyond what he'd ever imagined.

He kissed her softly at first, but quickly gave in to the rising excitement. She matched his intensity and their tongues danced and twisted together with unbound passion. His hands went to her buttocks and his erection felt as though it would burst from his pants. Her hand went there and he gasped as she gripped him through the pants.

He lifted her and she wrapped her legs around his waist. He regretted the loss of her touch, but the heat from her center radiated to his manhood. He'd never wanted anyone more than he did at that moment.

Never letting his lips leave hers, he walked to the edge of the water, where the sand turned from dry to wet. He set her down gently. She reached for his shirt. It came off quickly. He reached for hers, but she pulled it over her head before he had time to do it himself. He took in her surprisingly full breasts.

She smiled and pulled him down to her. She worked his pants with her hands and her feet like a contortionist until they lay in a heap in the sand. She quickly shed her own pants and her mound glistened in the cooling air.

They hesitated for an instant, then fell into one another. Her body accepted him and he gasped in a pleasure he never thought possible. She moved under him, and her fingers dug into his back and she nibbled his neck and earlobes. He felt the wave of ecstasy crashing toward him. He thrust and she arched and whimpered as both their waves crashed onto shore.

They finally collapsed against one another, gasping. Frank kept holding her and rolled onto his back, pulling her with, trying to catch his breath. She giggled and willingly rode him. She lay on his heaving chest and he kissed the top of her head. The stars shimmered and twinkled overhead. He didn't remember ever seeing them so bright, even on the endless nights as they crossed the ocean on their way to this island. He'd never felt such contentment. *Is this love?*

He squeezed her shoulder and she giggled and snuggled ever closer. He wouldn't have minded if she'd peeled his skin back and crawled inside. He didn't want the moment to end. He felt his passion rising again.

She noticed too. But she raised an eyebrow, then pushed up and said, "No. We must go."

∾

THEY PULLED themselves off the sand, dressed, and made their way up the dim path. She walked behind him, but her hands linked with his. He couldn't stop turning back to see if she hadn't been some cruel figment of his imagination. Each time, she smiled back at him.

They crested the hill and entered the camp. Grinning Bear stared at him. He whispered in Frank's ear, "Jesus, Frank. Can you be more obvious?"

Frank didn't care. He shrugged. "I can't help it."

Grinning Bear said, "Well, wipe the silly grin off your face." He glanced toward Antonio. "Look at Antonio."

Frank saw the burning hatred there. He pulled Constance even closer and she willingly clutched tightly to his side. "I don't care about Antonio. She's my girl now. She always has been."

"Yeah, maybe, but he looks ready to pull his knife and skin you," Grinning Bear pointed out.

"Nonsense. He won't do it. Not like this."

Antonio's gaze went to Constance. A flash of hurt was quickly replaced with a burning rage. He cursed and said something to her. She stiffened at Frank's side and retorted in fast pidgin.

Antonio's fists turned white as he clasped his fists. Frank didn't know what either of them said, but he could guess. "Tell him not to disrespect you, or there'll be trouble," he growled.

She didn't understand everything he said, but she squeezed him tighter. Frank glared at Antonio, willing him to start something. Teaching him a lesson would be a perfect end to such a day. He felt invincible.

"Easy now," Grinning Bear extolled. "We need him on our side, Frank."

"No, we don't. If he wants to go, he won't hurt my feelings. Let him go."

"He'll take half the men with him. Might even give us up to the Nips."

Frank cringed at the notion. "No way. He might hate me now, but it's nothing compared to the Japs. He won't do that. His own people would skin him alive."

"You willing to bet your life on that?"

Frank gently pushed Constance away from his side. She resisted a moment, then moved away. Frank addressed Gustav, who stood in the darkness, just outside the main circle. "Tell him we're in love, Gustav. Tell him there are no hard feelings."

Gustav stepped closer, but instead of addressing Antonio, he addressed Frank. "His pride is hurt. He's angry."

"I know, but it can't be helped. Constance and I are together. He'll just have to deal with it."

Gustav addressed Antonio. With each word, Antonio's face reddened. Instead of placating the young man, the words seemed to enrage him even more. In fast pidgin, he answered Gustav. Gustav nodded, then addressed Frank again. "He agrees to a fight."

"Wait, what? A fight? Who said anything about a fight? What'd you tell him?"

"I told him what you told me to tell him."

"I didn't say nothin' about a fight."

"He agrees to a fight."

Frank blew out a long breath of air. He glanced at Constance. She had her arms crossed and she glared at Antonio, but she also seemed excited to watch two men fight over her.

"This is ridiculous," Frank uttered.

Grinning Bear said, "You brought it on yourself. You can take him."

Frank stripped off his shirt, crumpled it, and threw it on the ground. He held up his fists and said, "Well, alright then. Let's get it over with. Unless he wants to wait till we can see better."

Gustav looked as excited as anyone to see the spectacle. He gazed up at the sky. "The stars are enough." He spoke to Antonio and he stripped off his own shirt and came at Frank like a charging bull seeing a red cape.

Frank barely had time to step aside. Antonio rushed past him, barely missing with a haymaker. Frank moved his feet the way they'd taught him in the ring back in the barracks. He'd never been the best boxer, but he could hold his own most of the time.

Antonio spun back to him. He charged again. This time, Frank stepped aside and punched him as he went past. His fist connected with Antonio's cheek. The blow made him stop and shake his head. Frank wondered if the tree he'd run into earlier that evening still had him addled. Perhaps he should take it easy on him.

Antonio roared. He charged again, but this time, he pulled up when Frank stepped aside. He changed course and slammed into him. They went to the ground in a heap. Antonio punched Frank's ribs and belly incessantly. Frank did all he could to cover up, but Antonio had the advantage and his fists felt like iron anvils. He struggled to break free, but couldn't. *Strong son of a bitch!*

Frank mustered all his strength and rolled. Now he straddled Antonio, but he held tight, not letting Frank pull away where he could use his fists to pummel him. They strained against one another and Frank heard the spectators yelling and egging them on. How would Constance take it if he lost? He didn't plan on finding out.

He lurched away from Antonio's grasp and freed his fists. He wasted no time pummeling Antonio's face over and over again. His hands hurt, but he knew how to punch. It only took one good punch to take a man out of a fight, but he couldn't quite line it up. His blows kept glancing off his him.

Antonio pulled his arms up to protect his face, but at the same time, he blinded himself to Frank's next move. Frank saw his opportunity. He clutched the front of Antonio's hair and pushed his head back, raising his chin. Frank leaned back enough to deliver an uppercut to his jaw. He felt the snap and crunch as teeth shattered.

The fight went out of Antonio like a plug had been pulled on a pool of water. His body went limp, his arms fell from his face and his eyes rolled crazily. For one terrifying moment, Frank thought he'd hit him too hard and broken his neck. But Antonio's focus soon returned.

Frank heaved himself off his chest and staggered away a few feet. He struggled to catch his breath. Antonio moaned, and a few of his friends went to his side, but he pushed them away angrily. Sweat, blood, and dirt glistened on his battered body.

Constance ran to Frank's side with a delighted squeal. He cringed as she slammed into his side, where Antonio had landed too many punches. She touched him lightly, then stroked the dirt off his sides. He draped an arm over her shoulder.

Antonio glared at them. He eased himself to his feet and rubbed his jaw. Blood dripped and he looked where his hand had touched it. He cursed and spit, then spoke to Frank.

Gustav translated, "He says you bested him. He won't bother you again."

Antonio turned from the group. Frank said, "Wait. Is he leaving? He can stay. We need him. Tell him we need him to stay. We'll kill more Japs."

Gustav spoke, and Antonio stopped. He slowly turned back toward Frank. He spoke through Gustav. "You will still have me? I've caused nothing but trouble. First in town and now this."

"You're a fighter. We need fighters," Frank answered. "We'll kill many Japanese together."

Grinning Bear stepped forward and stood beside Frank, showing solidarity. Frank raised his voice so they could all hear him clearly. "The enemy will look for us now. We must stick together if we hope to survive. We must fight them on our terms."

Most understood, but Gustav translated, and a murmur of agreement sifted through the crowd.

Frank continued. "Tonight was just a taste. The Japs will make it hard on the civilians after this. They may kill them in retribution for our attack. I hate this, but we must harden our hearts and keep killing them and sabotaging them. We must make them fear us. It is time to strike back."

A roar of approval rose, and the men pumped their rifles overhead. Frank hoped none fired off rounds. They'd need every single bullet in the coming weeks.

Neil sidled up beside them. He'd been monitoring the radio all night. His eyes popped wide at the spectacle. "Jesus, Frank. What'd I miss?"

Grinning Bear laughed, "Most everything."

Frank let out a long breath. His ribs hurt and his fists were cut and bleeding. He felt the weight of the past twenty-four hours come crashing down upon him. He leaned on Constance and she gladly took his weight.

She said, "Come. You need sleep. Rest."

Despite the pain and fatigue, Frank felt aroused all over again with just her touch. How did she do that? He followed her to her thatch hut and let her take care of him.

∽

FRANK WOKE FROM A DEEP SLEEP. He never remembered sleeping this hard. He stared at the ceiling and remembered the night before. Even lying still, his body ached. It would be torture once he stood. He felt the heavy breaths of Constance tucked close beside him. He didn't want to disturb her, but nature pushed on his bladder and he had to answer the call.

He slowly slid to the side of the little raised thatch bed. They'd made love before falling asleep. Their efforts had collapsed one side of the platform, but they hadn't the energy to fix it. It hadn't made a difference in the sleep quality. He felt as though someone had drugged him.

He stood and his ribs and stomach screamed at him. His legs ached and his fists throbbed. He checked on Constance. She still slept soundly. Her little snore made him smile. Her body lit up in the early morning light, shafts streaming through the front door, made him think of a golden goddess.

He stepped outside. A few men and women moved around on various errands, but the camp seemed to still be recovering from the long night. He wondered about Mandio. He must be four times more sore than himself.

He saw Grinning Bear. He sat on a stump, sharpening a bolo knife.

They used the shaped knives for cutting cane and such, but the Filipinos found them useful on Japanese soldier's heads, too.

He nudged him as he passed. "Good morning."

Grinning Bear grunted. "It is morning. Wondering if you were gonna wake up or not."

Frank glanced back at the hut where Constance still slumbered. "I don't remember ever sleeping that well."

"You kept half the camp up last night."

Frank reddened. "Oh, sorry 'bout that." He couldn't keep the grin off his face. "I've gotta take a leak."

"No doubt." Grinning Bear sheathed the bolo and followed Frank to the edge of the jungle. Frank relieved himself while leaning against a tree.

Grinning Bear said, "I put out security last night. The Nips didn't cross the straits. They must not know where we went."

Frank said, "I shoulda made that order. Thanks for covering me." Grinning Bear only shrugged. They covered one another in such instances. Frank outranked him, but for such day-to-day decisions, they trusted one another to do the right thing.

"What's our next move?" Grinning Bear asked.

"I suppose we need to follow orders and head south."

Grinning Bear took a moment before answering. "I don't know about that. Seems we could do more good around here."

Frank finished pissing. "How do you mean?"

"Well, the Filipinos already know the area. If we move south, we'll have to start all over. Gustav has connections down there, but not as many as here. Also, where would we set up shop?"

"But that's where the harbor is. That's what they want us to hit."

"If we hit their garrison hard enough up here, they'll have to send reinforcements up here to deal with us."

Frank saw the sense of it. "Weakening them down south."

"Exactly."

"None of it will be easy. I wish we had more ammunition."

"That's another reason to stay here. The Nips must have a store of ammo somewhere nearby. Even a small amount would be a boon for us."

Frank stroked his chin. "Gustav has said nothing about it, but if they do, the locals must have some idea where it is."

He glanced back at the hut as Constance emerged. Her hair looked disheveled and she wore only a thin sarong. He thought her the most beautiful thing he'd ever seen. She waved and smiled.

Grinning Bear said, "You're getting too attached to that girl."

"I love her."

"Love? Jesus, Joseph, and Mary. You don't even speak the same language. How can you love someone you can't even talk to?"

"I—I dunno, but it just feels right. We have a deep connection."

"Oh, for crying out loud. You're skating on thin ice, Frank."

"What d'ya mean?"

"The Nips are gonna know Mandio and his niece are a part of this whole thing. Why else would she disappear? It's only a matter of time before they come across the water to check out our little slice of heaven and when they do, things are gonna get hairy."

"What's that have to do with us?"

"You won't make rational decisions. What if the Japs take her? What if she gets hit? You'll be next to useless. You'll put everyone at risk."

"Are you saying you wanna take over? Cause that's fine. I trust you and so do the others."

"No, I'm not the leader type. I'm just sayin' you need to keep your head on straight, even if it endangers her. Think of the greater good."

Frank couldn't imagine anything happening to Constance. It made his guts roil to even think about. He knew his old friend was right; if he had to make a decision like that, he might make the wrong one. Her life meant far more even than his own at this point.

He lowered his voice. "Maybe we should just hunker down and wait for liberation. It'll keep everyone out of harm's way."

"It's too late for that now. The Nips won't rest until they find those responsible for last night. They lost an officer and a prisoner right under their noses. They won't let that stand. Besides, your little speech last night really fired everyone up."

Frank sighed heavily. He'd spoken in the heat of the moment. He'd let his adrenaline get the best of him. "You're right." He squared on Grinning Bear. "You need to make sure I don't do anything stupid, Larry."

Grinning Bear shook his head as though it was a ridiculous notion.

"I mean it. If I give an order, you don't think is in the best interest of the group, I want you to stop me. Knock my teeth out if you have to. Understand?"

Grinning Bear said, "You won't, but if you do, I'll set you straight."

Frank slapped him on the back. "Good. Now let's ask Gustav what he knows about any ammo dumps."

7

Burma
August 1944

Shawn Cooper picked a scab on his knee until it peeled away and bled again. He looked out over the distant valley. The huge sweeping Irrawaddy river sparkled in the midday sun. He could see the edge of the Myitkyina Airfield poking from the valley, ending at the river's edge.

He noted a Japanese aircraft lifting off—make that two. Two Zeros lifted off side by side. Their wings sparkled in the sun as they climbed steadily away.

He noted the time and counted four more sets of two take off behind the first pair. Right on time. He wondered what it must be like for the pilots. Every time they went up, they faced dangerous conditions, not only from the ever-increasing presence of Allied aircraft but also from the unrelenting weather these Burmese mountains produced. More often than not, the returning numbers didn't match. Far different from when they'd enjoyed air superiority only months before.

He watched for more aircraft, but didn't expect any. He stood and stretched his back. Henry Calligan touched his shoulder and Shawn nearly fell off the cliff. "Jesus, Calligan. How many times have I told you not to sneak up on me?"

"A better question is, why do you continually allow it? I wasn't even sneaking—I never do unless I'm killing Japs. Just the ten again?"

"Yeah, Zeros."

"You'd think they might at least alter the timelines."

Shawn looked at his notes. "They're ten minutes early today."

"Hmm. Well, someday they'll pay for their predictability."

Shawn raised his eyebrows. "Yeah? When?"

Calligan kept his hand on his shoulder. "I know you're bored stiff lately. You and the others expected more action by now."

Shawn shrugged. They'd left the Marauders nearly three months before and set up with Calligan and the two other OSS men, Guthrie and O'Donnelly. The Bellevue men had thought they'd be taking the fight to the enemy, but so far all they'd done was watch and report enemy movements into and out of the airfield.

"Well, now that you mention it, yeah. When do we get the green light?"

"Soon, Shawn my boy, soon."

"You've been saying that for weeks now. At least let us go out and set up some booby traps—something to keep us occupied."

"This time I mean it. Didi has returned."

Shawn looked beyond Calligan. He didn't see the diminutive Kachin warrior. He normally didn't stray too far from Calligan when he was around. He hadn't been around for a few months now. Calligan said he had urgent family business to attend to, but Shawn knew that was probably bullshit.

"Yeah, where is he? I don't see him."

"He's sleeping at the moment. He had a rough time."

Despite the man's stature, he still scared Shawn on some level. He'd never met a more brutal killing machine. He savored killing Japanese as much as any man he'd ever met. He must've killed hundreds by now. What would such a man do after the war ended? Could he simply settle down and raise a family? He had a hard time imagining it.

"I thought his family died early on?"

"They did, but the Kachin think of any Kachin as family."

"So what does that have to do with us?"

"He brought back information for us." Calligan held up a binder. "The Japanese have been on the move. They're desperate to stop the Chinese and Americans before they link the Ledo road with the old Burma road. If they don't, India will once again be able to directly supply Chiang Kai Shek's men in China—a devastating blow. It might very well turn the tide in China."

"So we'll be hitting targets? Is that what you're saying?"

"Yes. There are many weak points."

"Well, hot damn. Let's get on with it, then. Me and the boys are itching for some action."

Calligan beamed his winning smile. Even through his thick, long beard, his teeth shone through. He could've been a movie star. "Yes, our days of waiting and watching are over. We'll hit their supply routes starting tomorrow. Gather the others and meet in the clearing in a half hour. I'll lay out our first mission."

Shawn watched him go. He'd been one of the first OSS men he'd met out here. Calligan had been an original member of Detachment 101. He'd been in Burma since the early days. He'd scared him at first with his nonchalant attitude toward killing. He vowed never to become like him, but now here he was champing at the bit for action.

He took off the baseball cap he wore and spun it in his hands. It had been his friend Clem's hat. The Japanese had butchered him along with the rest of the air crew after they hauled them from their downed C-47. The image flashed in his head and he shut his eyes hard, trying to expel the memory. But he knew he never would. He no longer felt remorse or pity for the Japanese who'd die by his hand. They'd earned their fate. He replaced the hat on his head and went to find the others.

~

THE DARKNESS PRESSED in around Shawn like a physical entity. He'd wedged himself between two rocks and the overhang created a sort of half-cave. He listened to the Japanese soldiers speaking in low tones only yards away. They'd moved into the area after the OSS men had stopped for a brief rest. Instead of moving on, the Japanese seemed intent on staying the night.

Shawn felt the weight of his knife in his hand. It felt solid and deadly. In his other hand, he held his carbine. But this would be wet work. They were too close to other Japanese units to tip their hand with gunshots. These Japanese soldiers would die silently.

As the night lengthened, the silence between their stilted conversations grew longer. Shawn imagined them rolling out their makeshift beds, searching for dry areas without obvious anthills or rocks. Perhaps they had hammocks. Despite the darkness, he could see shadowy shapes he imagined being enemy soldiers.

Finally, the conversations stopped completely, and he heard only the sounds of buzzing and clicking insects. How long before the other OSS men moved in? JoJo and O'Keefe were on the other side of the enemy bivouac site. They'd opted out of this one, choosing to watch for more enemy troops.

Shawn sensed more than saw movement from his right. A barely discernible shadow crept forward. Not enough time had passed. The soldiers might still be awake. But that wasn't his concern. His concern was the single man standing guard duty somewhere close.

Shawn silently pulled himself to his feet. He left his carbine leaning against the rock, careful not to let it slip and give away his position. He concentrated on his peripheral vision. That's where he'd see movement or the shape of a human. He took a careful step. The shadow to his right moved with him, and he knew it had to be Didi. Of course, he'd be the one to move before the enemy was properly asleep—eager for the kill.

Shawn's senses worked in overdrive. He ignored the sweat dripping off the tip of his nose. He took another careful step, making sure nothing snapped beneath his sandaled feet. The world seemed to come into focus during times like these. He felt he could see better, smell better, sense better, and move better.

The sentry was less than fifteen yards away. Which way would he be looking? Movement to his left made him freeze in mid-stride. He balanced on one foot. The scraping of fabric against a tree pinpointed his target, and he slowly placed his foot on the spongy ground.

A brief surge of panic touched the corner of his mind. He quickly shunted it away. He didn't have time for such nonsense. He stood stock still. The shape of a man slowly formed, leaning against a large tree. He saw more slight movements as the soldier fidgeted. His mind thought logically about the situation. The Japanese in these parts hadn't been harassed in months. It surprised him they had any guards out at all. He might simply walk up on him without trouble, but he couldn't risk a rifle shot in the night, so he crept slowly.

It took him nearly ten minutes to cover ten yards. He could clearly see the outline of the soldier now as his eyes adjusted to the darkness like a nocturnal predator. The soldier hummed a song and Shawn heard the breathiness of it. It sent a chill up his spine—a thrilling chill. His prey suspected nothing.

Shawn bent to a low crouch and watched from the corner of his eye. The guard continued to hum and shift his weight from side to side, foot to foot. Trying to stay awake, no doubt. His struggles would be over soon enough.

Shawn focused all his thoughts on the next few moments. He imagined how he'd do it, imagined how it would feel when he sank the blade deep into the soldier's neck, just behind his ear. He'd scramble the brains and ease him to the ground without a sound—easy peasy. The queasy feeling he used to feel simply didn't happen anymore.

The humming stopped but the soldier didn't tense as though he'd seen his approaching doom. Shawn still didn't stare at him. Staring always brought attention, and in the dark, his peripheral vision worked far better.

The soldier arched his back and let out a long sigh. Shawn moved like a striking viper. He covered the remaining few yards in a heartbeat. The sentry stiffened as Shawn's free hand pushed his head back and away. He thrust the blade into the soft neck tissue beneath his ear and he felt the snick and scrape as the blade pushed beneath the skull and into the brain. He rotated the blade, scrambling the brains.

The soldier spasmed and Shawn eased him down to the ground with barely a whisper. The rifle slipped from the dead man's hand and Shawn thrust his foot out, keeping it from clattering against the tree trunk. Warm blood covered his hand. He withdrew the knife and silently wiped the blade on the dead man's tunic, while he watched for any movement from the other sleeping men. No one stirred.

He strained to see Didi, Calligan, Killigrew, and Guthrie, but he saw nothing but shadows and darkness. He glanced down at the man he'd killed. He couldn't see much, but he imagined his open eyes glassing over as the life seeped from his body. He felt no remorse—only the satisfaction of a job well done.

He looked back up in time to see shadows come alive in the small clearing. He tried to guess who was who, but could only be sure of Didi because of his small stature and his fluid, almost ghost-like movements. The stalking shadows hesitated for a moment, then, like striking snakes, they leaped onto their sleeping prey. Shawn heard the sounds of slashing and expulsions of air, but nothing louder than a loud sigh escaped the doomed soldiers. The shadows stayed motionless atop the twitching men, making sure no sounds escaped their dying lips.

Shawn went to them. The nearest man, Guthrie, turned as though he might be a threat, but he quickly relaxed when he recognized him. Shawn went close to his side and tapped his shoulder, signaling that the deed was done. They spoke no words as they silently slipped back into the night. Shawn found his carbine where he'd left it. The small group moved off deeper into the vast jungles of Burma. When they'd left the dead far behind, they slowed.

Shawn moved beside Calligan and said the first words he'd spoken all night. "Think we'll find any more pockets like that?"

Calligan didn't take his eyes from the jungle. He moved nearly as silently as Didi. "I hope so," he said.

"Me too," Shawn answered, and he meant it. The killing made him feel alive. *What would mother think?* Thoughts of home tried to crowd into his mind as though a lifeline from a past life was being hurled at him. He pushed it out of his mind—shunning that life. He didn't need saving. The Japanese needed saving and he'd be the one to send them to their savior, whoever that might be. *Buddha? Nah, the emperor himself.*

He itched his nose and smelled the iron smell of dried blood. He held his hand close to his face and saw the streaks of blood. At one point in his life, he might've been disturbed by such a sight, but not now. Now he savored the sight and even the smell. The smell of a vanquished enemy.

~

SHAWN WOKE WITH A START, but immediately controlled himself. He'd been dreaming something about fire, but it slipped away. Sunlight streamed through the tops of the dense jungle canopy. They'd moved all night, covering miles upon miles. At dawn, they found a secure area and slept. Based on the slanting sunbeam angles, he figured it was mid-morning.

He rolled to his knees and saw JoJo and Guthrie sitting nearby, eating. He went to them. He stretched and yawned, working the kinks out.

"You get your beauty rest?" JoJo asked.

"All two hours of it," Shawn responded.

Guthrie handed him a can. "You want some?"

"What is it?"

"Supposed to be some kind of meat."

Shawn took it without remark. He pulled out a spoon, which had been with him since he left India, and dug in, slurping and gulping it down with abandon.

"I always forget what a chow-hound you are. You'll eat anything."

JoJo said, "Yeah, keep your hands and feet away or you're liable to lose 'em."

"Y'all hear the good news?" Guthrie asked in his Texas drawl as he strode into the space.

"News? What news? I haven't been asleep long enough for news," Shawn said between mouthfuls.

Guthrie continued. "We're meeting up with the rest of Calligan's Kachin. Gonna hit something big."

Shawn exchanged a quick glance with JoJo, who confirmed it with a nod. Shawn asked, "Calligan's Kachin? I thought most of them were still up with the marauders."

"Most are, but Calligan's been culling out the most gifted ones for himself. He and Didi, that is."

"The gifted ones?" Shawn asked.

Guthrie explained. "You know, the most brutal ones. He's been doing it ever since we set up that outpost outside Myitkyina. Just kinda keeping tabs and having private discussions with certain men."

"That's the first I've heard of it," Shawn said.

JoJo said, "Doesn't surprise you though, does it?"

"No. So now he has his own little private army of evil sons of bitches?"

Guthrie said, "Exactly right."

"How many?" Shawn asked.

"Twenty."

"So few? Not much of an army."

Guthrie grinned, and Shawn saw his cowboy charm for a moment. "You know how they are. One well-trained Kachin's worth ten Nips. Hell, ten marauders, for that matter."

"So, what's the big target?"

He lowered his voice as though giving away state secrets. "Jap artillery unit."

"Interesting," Shawn said.

Guthrie continued. "The Nips are pushing Indaw, where the Brits are holed up, and their artillery is causing a lot of problems. We're gonna take out one of their batteries."

"And the Kachin know where they are?"

"You're pretty smart for a Yankee."

"How far we gotta travel?" Shawn pressed.

Guthrie shrugged. "I dunno. I told you everything I know. Calligan'll fill in the blanks, I suppose."

"Well, that is good news. I suppose the Nips don't just leave their big guns unguarded, though."

JoJo chimed in. "Yeah, I think we can expect at least a weapons platoon."

"Guess we'll know when we get there," Shawn said.

The rest of the OSS men filtered into their position. A few looked like they'd just woken, too. Shawn felt well rested despite only copping two hours. His body had adjusted to the lack of sleep a long time ago—they all had. He wondered if he'd ever sleep normally again. He brushed the thought from his mind—his future was here.

Calligan wore his usual broad smile. With his carbine slung over his shoulder and his long beard and shabby clothes, he looked more like an armed beggar than a high ranking OSS man.

He clapped Shawn on the back like a long-lost friend. He always greeted him the same way. "Glad to see you up and about, Shawny."

It never ceased to amaze him how he could make him feel bad about sleeping. To his credit, though, Shawn rarely saw the man sleep. He always seemed to work on something important—no time for sleep. Sleep was for lesser men.

"The boys have been telling me about our mission."

Calligan glanced at Guthrie who spread his hands as though apologizing. "Have they now? Well, good." The group of Kachin stood off a bit and Calligan addressed only the OSS men. "My friends tell me our target's some seven miles from here. The Japs use the roads, so they'll be easy to find, even if they've moved by the time we get there." Calligan squatted onto his heels, a pose he often used while addressing his men. It made him look even more like a Kachin. He was more Kachin than the Kachin. "We're supposed to coordinate with a group of Chindits on the way."

A murmur went up. Shawn had heard about the Chindits. They were a conglomeration of British, Burmese, and Ghurka soldiers, led by a British commander. He knew little about them except that they'd been doing long-range operations out of India since the early days. They had an excellent reputation.

Killigrew asked, "Chindits? Sounds like something you contract at a brothel house."

JoJo guffawed and said, "Well, you should know. You're a walking Petri dish."

Calligan said, "They've been doing good work around Indaw. From everything I've heard, they're almost as good as our Kachin."

O'Keefe guffawed, "Fucking Brits, always going on about themselves. We have to meet up with 'em? Operate together?"

"They'll provide support in case we run into more than we can handle.

They're kind of a hybrid unit, kinda like the Marauders. In fact, they helped old Vinegar Joe form the Marauders. They're in the area and command mentioned we should coordinate with them, since they have a much larger force."

Shawn had nothing against the Brits. The ones he'd met had been solid soldiers, although a bit stiff sometimes. They held their own against the Japanese, and that was enough for him.

Shawn punched O'Keefe's arm, "They'll have you eating tea and crumpets in no time, O'Keefe."

"That's what I'm afraid of," he muttered.

JoJo asked, "What about the Kachin? What do they think of these Chindits?"

Calligan stroked his beard. "I'm not entirely sure. I've heard them praised and I've heard them disparaged. We'll have to see what happens. Should be interesting." Calligan finished. "We'll move out in an hour. Be sure to eat and fill up canteens, we'll be moving fast. I'd like to hit their guns tonight." He stepped away toward the Kachin.

Shawn felt his heart rate quicken. He wondered how Calligan planned to meet up with the Chindits. Did they have radio contact? He doubted their radios spoke to one another, but perhaps Calligan had their frequencies and vice versa.

JoJo said, "I hear those Chindits are something else."

Shawn said, "Me too, but they can't be any better than the Kachin at killing Japs. I mean, can they?"

O'Keefe said, "I've never heard of them."

"You call yourself an OSS man? We're supposed to be smart and well informed, for chrissakes," JoJo said. "They've been kicking the snot out of the Japs before we even got here. They've had a lot of success. Wingate? Does that name mean anything to you?" O'Keefe shook his head and JoJo continued. "He died in a plane crash back in March. I don't know who leads 'em now, but Wingate was a damned hero."

"Well, okay," O'Keefe said, making no attempt to hide his disinterest in the Chindits.

Shawn said, "I just hope the Kachin don't start something with them. You know how they can be about other Burmese."

"I suppose it's probably like the way Texan's think of New Yorkers, huh, Guthrie?" O'Donnelly asked.

Guthrie turned from packing his pack. "I don't mind New Yorkers specifically. I mean, not really. I dislike Yankees, pretty much all of 'em equally."

"You're surrounded by them, hoss," JoJo said.

"Don't I know it? If y'all were Texans, this war'd be over long ago."

O'Donnelly shook his head as though he'd never heard such drivel. "You can barely tie your own boots, Guthrie. Hell, without us, you'd probably be sucking on Tojo's cock by now."

Guthrie pointed at his compatriot. "See, that's the difference. You Yankees are nasty. You kiss your mama with that mouth?"

"Just yours," O'Donnelly teased. "When I can get her away from her cousin, that is."

Guthrie went after him in a flash. He tackled him to the ground and they rolled back and forth, trying to get the best of one another. Shawn and the others hooted and laughed as the men struggled in the dirt. Men gathered quickly and cheered them on and soon it was a full-fledged wrestling match. O'Donnelly was a fireplug of a man, and Guthrie was long and lean but strong as an ox. They were evenly matched.

Money passed hands quickly as they thrashed back and forth. One would get the advantage, then lose it a second later. Guthrie finally pinned O'Donnelly in a painful pose, which made O'Donnelly seem more pretzel than man.

O'Donnelly struggled to find relief, but his struggles only made Guthrie squeeze harder. Finally, O'Donnelly said through gritted teeth, "Uncle."

Guthrie taunted him. "What? I couldn't quite hear you," and he put the screws to him even more.

"Uncle, uncle, uncle, you cocksucker," O'Donnelly pleaded.

"Say it nicely."

O'Donnelly nearly gagged with the added pressure. He finally uttered, "Uncle. You win . . ."

Guthrie released him and sprang to his feet. He danced around his friend with his hands up as though he'd knocked out the heavyweight champion of the world. He started singing a cowboy tune that none of them had ever heard. Money passed to those who'd bet on Guthrie. Shawn lost on the deal. "Dammit, O'Donnelly, you owe me fifteen bucks," he said.

O'Donnelly flipped him the bird. "Here's the first one," he spit and dusted himself off.

Calligan had come to see what the ruckus was all about. He shook his head. "Alright, you silly sons of bitches, let's get on with it."

8

The Kachin Calligan had recruited looked no different from other Kachin's although most were older. They had hard eyes but still sported broad smiles. Instead of U.S. Army issued uniforms, they wore regular civilian clothes. They had carbines, M1s, or Thompson submachine guns, and bolo knives lashed to their sides.

They led the OSS men along faint jungle trails, which the Kachin found effortlessly. Shawn doubted he'd be able to find them again if pressed. That wasn't uncommon. He wondered how they'd get along in the forests of the Pacific Northwest.

They trotted along at a steady, mile-consuming pace, only slowing to bypass a village or the occasional Japanese position. The Kachin seemed able to sniff these out long before the OSS men had a hint. Despite being in Burma for what seemed like a lifetime, Shawn still felt like a newcomer compared to the Kachin.

Occasionally they veered close to roads. Once they heard engines and saw plumes of dust. They watched a convoy of Japanese pass by—the trucks full of men and supplies heading to the front. In daylight, they seemed a ripe target for an airstrike, but the skies remained empty of aircraft from either side.

Shawn commented on the lack of aircraft to Calligan. Calligan explained, "The Japs are on the move. I suspect our flyboys are busy hitting the frontline positions. They're not going to waste their time searching for targets way back here." He grinned. "That's where we come in."

They moved steadily despite the incessant heat. Shawn and the others were well acclimated to both the heat and the pace, but by evening, and many miles, Shawn felt a deep fatigue setting into his legs. He kept pushing, using Calligan's seemingly endless energy reserves as a model. They'd been through far longer days. Shawn tried to keep his situational awareness focused, but the Kachin moved with such speed and confidence, he let himself slip into a bit of a trance. He trusted the Kachin not to lead them into an ambush.

The Kachin finally stopped and hunkered nearly simultaneously. Shawn almost bumped into JoJo, who scowled at him. Shawn gave him an apologetic shrug and mouthed, "sorry."

He strained to hear anything out of the ordinary, but heard nothing to cause the sudden stop. The air felt suddenly charged with a tension that wasn't there a moment ago. He tensed, wondering if they'd stumbled into a large Japanese position. A full minute passed before he saw movement. He relaxed slightly when Calligan rose and walked forward with his rifle slung —a good sign. The Kachin followed him automatically. Shawn exchanged glances with JoJo and O'Keefe.

Shawn leaned forward. "They're like his own personal bodyguards."

"I don't think you're too far off. You've seen the way they look at him. They *revere* him."

Shawn muttered under his breath, "Not sure that's a good thing or not."

"Loyalty?" O'Keefe asked.

"*Blind* loyalty," Shawn said.

O'Donnelly and Guthrie moved forward. Guthrie slapped Shawn's back as he passed. Shawn and the others followed. Shawn tensed when he saw men he didn't recognize. Some wore shorts and were obviously Caucasian, while others wore lightweight uniforms and had dark skin. They carried an assortment of weapons including, Lee Enfield rifles, Sten submachine guns, Thompson submachine guns, and even Bren heavy machine guns. They held them in various postures of readiness. Shawn noticed the faded yellowish insignia on their shoulders. The Changue, a mythical creature which guarded the entrances to sacred and holy places. The heavily faded insignia barely looked recognizable as such.

They'd found the Chindits.

Calligan conversed with a British officer. They laughed and joked as though they'd known each other for years. The other Chindits looked on with mild interest. They had a hardness that was only found in combat veterans.

"They look dangerous," Shawn whispered to JoJo.

"Hopefully just to the Nips," he said back.

The two forces looked one another up and down, as though assessing a threat. A few Chindits spread out as though the meeting might turn violent. The Kachin eyeballed them with outright hostility.

Calligan motioned the OSS men forward. "Come, come. I want you to meet Leftenant Roger Burberry."

They made introductions all around. Shawn winced at the man's crushing handshake. He felt thick callouses on his hands. Despite being a British officer, he obviously worked for a living. His broad shoulders gave him the look of an athlete. His high cheekbones, made more distinct by sallow cheeks, gave him an austere look, but his crooked and somewhat flattened nose ruined the effect.

"He and his men will lead us to the rest of the company," Calligan said. "Then to the Nip artillery."

"Just so," Burberry said with a smile which didn't travel to his sky-blue eyes.

"He doesn't seem too pleased to find us," O'Keefe whispered.

"Don't worry about it," JoJo said. "All Brits look like they have a stick shoved up their asses."

"Arses," Shawn quipped. JoJo's nose crinkled in confusion. "The Brits say arses, not asses," Shawn explained.

"Whatever," JoJo shook his head. "Just hope he's not an *arse*-hole."

Shawn couldn't keep from laughing. He drew a scowl from a few of the Chindits. Shawn covered his mouth and tried to keep quiet, but it only made it worse.

Guthrie came up beside him. "What's so damned funny, Cooper?"

"Sorry, nothing. I'm just tired."

"The way those fellers are looking at you . . . I'd watch your back."

"You won't watch it for me?" Shawn stuck out his butt and sashayed from side to side.

"Damned Yankee," Guthrie muttered with a shake of his head.

They walked in silence for another mile. The Chindits led them out of the valley and up a steep hillside, using cutback trails hacked from the jungle. When they finally crested, they made their way along the ridge's backbone. It narrowed until they walked along a spine no wider than a few feet. Before too long, hundreds of feet fell away nearly straight down along both sides. To trip and fall would be fatal.

The Kachin moved as though they walked along normal flat ground, but everyone else took careful steps. The Chindits had obviously been this way before. They moved with more confidence, but Shawn and the OSS men took their time, although Calligan conversed with Burberry as though on a Sunday stroll. The wind kicked up, making Shawn want to get on his hands and knees and crawl. He wasn't scared of high places, but he didn't seek them out either. He slowed noticeably.

O'Keefe put a hand on his shoulder. "One step after the other. That's all it is."

"I don't like this damned wind."

"You and me both," O'Keefe said. "But the slower you go, the longer we have to be up here in the wind."

From up ahead JoJo said, "You're making us look bad in front of the Chindits."

Shawn didn't give two shits about what the Chindits thought of him. Many expletives crossed his mind, but he kept his mouth shut. Before too long, the trail widened and descended.

Shawn looked back the way they'd come. The knife-edged ridge flowed in and out of view as a thin mist moved across it. It was beautiful but also made him wonder if they had to leave the same way they'd come.

He took a swig of water from his canteen as the others walked on by. He kept his eyes on the ridge. Something caught his eye, making him pause mid-slurp. He squinted, concentrating. He'd seen something, but what? A flash of movement far up the trail. He never took his eyes off the ridge as he screwed the lid back on the canteen and secured it on his belt.

The others had disappeared into the jungle. He could hear their fading footsteps. An eeriness took hold of him. The mists flowing across added to the feeling. No more movement. Perhaps he'd imagined it. He shook his head and pinched the bridge of his nose hard, then took one last look.

He stopped breathing. An animal moved in and out of the shadows and mist. It moved with deadly grace, tracking them—tracking him—a tiger.

Despite holding a rifle, Shawn felt wholly inadequate. The beast was still a hundred yards off, but he felt his yellow eyes boring into him, tapping into a deep fear embedded in his soul. Predator and prey the way it had always been.

Shawn's brain screamed to run—to catch up with the others. Safety in numbers. The big cat wouldn't dare attack such a large group of humans. But something kept him there, standing stock still as death stalked him. It wasn't fear, although he felt that nibbling at the edges, but something else —something less tangible. He saw the challenge in the Tiger's yellow eyes. To run would be cowardice. Even though justified self-preservation, he couldn't bring himself to leave.

He slowly dropped the carbine and unsheathed the curved bolo knife with a soft snick sound. The tiger kept coming, never taking his yellow eyes off Shawn—never blinking, never wavering.

Only yards away now, the immense cat's muscles rippled with each careful step. The thick whiskers twitched and the long tail swished side to side stiffly. The massive pads made no sound as the beast approached. Would he see the sharp claws before they tore into him?

He gripped the bolo knife, knowing he'd only get one chance at this. A deep guttural sound, like a rattle snakes buzz slowed down a thousand times, emanated from somewhere deep in the tiger's chest. The magnificent beast took one more step, then stopped and lowered his chest and hovered only inches from the ground. His fur rippled as his muscles tensed and flexed beneath the skin, preparing to pounce.

The world came into sharp focus. Nothing else existed but the tiger and himself. The war with the Japanese suddenly felt trivial—for this war between man and beast—the war for survival—had been waging for millennia.

The thought calmed his mind. He relaxed his grip on the bolo knife. He kept his eyes firmly locked on the tiger's as he stood up straight and dropped his hands to his sides. The side of the tiger's mouth twitched up and his gleaming teeth flashed momentarily.

Shawn shut his eyes slowly. The tiger would surely kill him, but it didn't matter. It would be far more natural to die this way than at the hands of a Japanese soldier or from a scything piece of shrapnel from an artillery shell hurled from an unseen gun miles away. At least this might benefit this glorious beast—this king of the jungle. Perhaps his body would sustain a family of cubs waiting and watching just out of sight.

But nothing happened.

He opened his eyes—the tiger was gone—vanished. He blinked in the burning sunlight, searching, but there was no sign of him. He couldn't have imagined the whole thing. It was far too real.

He stepped to where the tiger had been standing—checking for footprints, but the hard ground didn't reveal a track. He searched frantically. If he'd imagined the whole thing, he was surely losing his mind. Impossible.

"What the hell are you doing back here, Coop?"

Shawn spun and saw JoJo and O'Keefe standing there staring at him. He shook his head, as though ridding himself of cobwebs. "I—I'm just admiring the view," he finally replied. They'd never believe him if he told them and they might send him to the loony bin.

"Well, pick up your weapon. We've got a Jap artillery unit to hit."

Shawn scooped up his carbine and waved them away. "Okay, okay, I'm coming." He turned back to the ridge and thought he saw a flash of orange and black moving away, just as the mists swept across and blotted out the view. "Not today, friend," he said under his breath.

～

SHAWN LISTENED as the Chindit company commander, Captain Sparks, spoke with Calligan. He had an imperious, yet affable way about him, which made Shawn immediately trust and like him. He and Calligan carried on as though they'd known each other for years.

The rest of the Chindits kept to themselves. They mostly ignored the Kachin, but acknowledged the OSS men with nods. The Kachin kept their distance from the Chindits, but didn't hide their cutting glances and wary glares.

Shawn approached a group of Chindit soldiers. "Hello," he waved. They looked up from various tasks but mostly ignored him. "How long you been out here?" he asked awkwardly.

A soldier took pity on him and responded in broken English. "Long time. You?"

The accent threw him at first before he realized it was a combination of British and Tibetan. "Yeah, me too." He extended his hand and they shook. "I'm Shawn Cooper, OSS."

"I'm Raj Alakar, Chengue, First Battalion."

"Chengue?"

"What you call Chindits," he said with some distaste.

"We've been pronouncing it wrong? But everyone calls you Chindits."

"Major General Wingate mispronounced it first and he didn't bother to correct it. I suppose it rolls off the tongue better."

Shawn had heard about the famous leader of the Chindits. His success in Burma had filtered through the ranks and he was well regarded for his work in helping with the formation of the Marauders.

"The man who created the name mispronounced it himself?" Shawn couldn't help but laugh.

"That's right," Raj said without a hint of a smile.

Shawn took the hint and did his best to turn his face neutral. He steered away from the subject. "Are you Tibetan?"

"Yes. I was in the Ghurka Regiments."

Ghurkas may as well have been mythical creatures for all the incredible stories he'd heard about them. "I never thought I'd meet a Ghurka in a million years."

Raj clearly didn't know how to take the comment. He glanced at his fellow soldiers and a few stopped sharpening their curved kukri knives to stare. "I mean, I heard about Ghurka soldiers way before the war. You guys are like meeting something out of a storybook or something. You're legends."

Raj's chest puffed out and he smiled, then said something to his fellow soldiers in his own language. and they grinned and went back to their tasks.

"You OSS men are also legendary," Raj said. "We hear many good things about your operations."

"Well, that's good to hear, but I'd hardly call us legendary. We're the new kids on the block around here."

Raj tilted his head, clearly not understanding what he meant.

"I mean, we've only existed a few years. You guys have been around a long time."

"Ah, I understand. Yes, we have fought in many campaigns before this one."

"Is this *your* first?"

Raj shook his head and simply said, "No." His eyes dropped as though remembering.

The silence lingered until Shawn said, "Well, it's my first."

"Yes, you are young." He locked eyes with Shawn and asked, "Do you like it?"

Shawn rubbed his chin as he thought about the question. At first he'd hated it, hated the killing and the butchery. But now? "Yeah, I like it all right." The answer surprised him. "There's no place I'd rather be."

Raj nodded his understanding. "The Japanese are easy to kill."

Shawn didn't quite know how to take that. "Easy?"

"They need to die. They deserve to die. It makes the killing easier."

Shawn agreed. He supposed Raj had been involved in other campaigns that didn't have such cut and dried lines of right and wrong. He didn't know if it was true, but the Ghurkas hovered between being soldiers and mercenaries. He thought about asking for clarification, but a Chindit junior officer's voice cut him off.

"Form up, men."

Shawn parted ways with Raj with a quick nod and found the other OSS men. He guessed eighty men gathered in the small clearing with more around the edges. Each man looked lethal, as though they'd been hand-picked from a vat of veteran soldiers. If not for their uniforms, they could easily be mistaken for a huge gang or perhaps a powerful cadre of pirates.

Captain Sparks raised his voice. "Men, our scouts have found the Jap artillery." A murmur of approval went through the group. "They're only a few kilometers from here. As luck would have it, they are on their way to their final firing positions, so they're vulnerable to attack. We will move into position tonight and hit them in the wee hours."

Shawn exchanged glances with the others. If they'd been in any other unit, the prep work would've lasted for at least another day. He was glad to see the Chindits understood the need for aggressive, fast action as much as the OSS did.

"We can expect to encounter a company-sized force. Our scouts say they are fresh troops, but they're experienced. They're a part of the 11th Regiment, under General Miroshi. They've fought campaigns in China before coming here, but our scouts say they don't seem concerned this far behind the lines."

Shawn wondered about the fate of the poor devil who'd divulged such delicate unit information. It must have been extracted while under the knife. He doubted he still breathed. He could almost picture Raj or one of his cohorts going to work on the captive Japanese soldier with their razor sharp Kukri blades. It sent invisible shivers up his spine.

"We have the advantage of surprise. Once we kill them, we'll spike the weapons, blow their ammunition, then rally back here." He motioned toward Calligan, who stood ramrod straight a few feet away. "Captain Calligan and his OSS and Kachin Rangers will join us. They are skilled soldiers who need no introduction. I urge you to give them every consideration. Now, get some food and water, kit up, and be ready to move in an hour."

A junior Chindit officer released them formally and clots of men faded into the surrounding jungle.

"Well, he gets straight to the point," O'Keefe said.

"Not much meat to the plan. Just kill 'em all and destroy their equipment," Shawn said.

Calligan approached. He'd heard their comments. "Sparks and his men have been doing this stuff for a while now. They know what they're doing."

"And what about us? What's our part?" JoJo asked with an edge to his voice. "I thought this was our operation. I hope we're not just here to observe."

"Far from it. We'll go in with the second wave and secure any documents we find. They're hoping to capture some officers, but you know how they are."

"We'll miss all the action," Killigrew complained. "We're errand boys."

"Can that shit" Calligan said with uncharacteristic anger. "You know how it is. The Chindits are the larger force and they've been fighting together a long time. It's like us and the Kachin. If the roles were reversed, I'd have the Chindits stay back while we led the way. This is the way it has to be this time." He grinned. "But don't worry, I'm sure we'll run into a few live ones."

～

SHAWN COULD SMELL COOKING fires even this far back from where the enemy artillery unit languished. Even though his eyes had adjusted to the darkness, he couldn't see more than a few yards. The Chindits had advanced past them an hour before. He expected to hear the initial clash any second. He hissed to JoJo, "I hate waiting."

"Me too. What's taking them so long?"

Fifteen minutes passed before the peaceful night was suddenly infused with fire. Shawn instinctively closed his eyes to the flash of an explosion, but too late. He saw spots. He rubbed his eyes in a vain attempt to clear them.

The rumble rolled past their position, making the leaves sway from the concussion. He felt it deep in his chest. Small arms fire erupted and muzzle flashes winked in the darkness. It reminded him of distant lightning.

"That must've been their ammo truck," O'Keefe suggested.

Guthrie said in his Texas drawl, "Hell of a way to kick things off."

The small arms fire rose to a crescendo. For almost a full minute, there was no break in the noise as the Chindits poured rounds into the position. A flickering glow filtered through the trees from a burning vehicle. The noise dissipated quickly, reduced to single shots and short bursts from Thompsons and Brens. A few answering rifle shots came from the Japanese, but not many.

They looked toward Calligan. He crouched facing the action, his broad back barely visible in the low light. Two long minutes passed before he finally stood to his full height and waved them forward.

Shawn relished moving. He'd been crouching for so long, his legs cramped. It took a few steps before he felt the blood rush back into them. He scanned the darkness and flinched at the more and more infrequent sounds of gunfire. A few bullets zinged through the treetops, but he felt sure they were stray bullets and not aimed at the OSS men. *A stray bullet can kill you just as dead*, he thought.

His mind went back to the tiger. He'd willingly left himself open to attack. The magnificent beast could've ripped his throat out in a mighty flash of fur and fang, but he hadn't feared dying. He'd almost welcomed it, but now he didn't feel that way at all. He wanted to live—or at least die fighting. What was the difference?

They stepped into a clearing. Flames licked the sides and top of a Japanese truck, hungrily devouring anything that would burn. In the glow from the fire, enemy soldiers sprawled facedown, unmoving. Small fires crackled on their singed clothing.

Shawn gripped his carbine as he stepped past the grisly scene. Gunshots and yelling came from the Chindits, still engaged with the remnants of the enemy. He cringed at the sound of a harsh metallic clang.

"They're already spiking the big guns," Calligan said.

The glow from the burning truck lit up a tent, which had survived the initial attack. A few shredded soldiers lay around the perimeter. Few had weapons and some were mostly undressed.

"Looks like they woke 'em up," O'Donnelly said.

Calligan pointed at the tent. "Get in there and search for anything that looks useful."

Shawn went in first, sweeping his carbine side to side. Smoke lingered in the air, burning his nostrils and making his eyes water. "Smells chemical," he said.

"Yeah, unnatural," JoJo agreed.

Shawn pulled his shirt over his nose and mouth and pushed forward. He poked a soldier lying face down with his gun barrel. The soldier didn't move, but Shawn felt a wave of warning sweep over him. Something didn't feel right. He stepped away a few feet, keeping his weapon trained on the soldier's back.

"Get up!" He yelled. Nothing happened, but he got the attention of JoJo and O'Keefe.

"Put a round in him, if you're not sure," O'Keefe said.

Shawn stepped forward and stomped the body hard in the side. He felt the crunch of ribs through the soles of his sandal.

The Japanese soldier screamed and rolled while swiping his legs out. Shawn fell hard onto his back, unable to keep his carbine on target. Shawn gasped for breath, but he'd lost his wind. He'd felt the sensation plenty of times when he'd wrestled with his friends and cousin and more than a few times in airborne training, but he never got used to the helpless, panicky feeling. And now there was an enemy soldier only inches away.

He pushed himself away as he tried unsuccessfully to fill his shocked lungs with air. His eyes widened as the enemy soldier rolled to his feet. He held a gleaming sword and his face dripped blood from a grisly gash on his forehead. He looked like death itself come to claim him.

He raised the sword high over his head and took a step toward him. Shawn raised an arm to fend off the blade and locked eyes with him. The seething hatred he saw there nearly turned his bowels to liquid.

O'Keefe and JoJo slammed into the soldier simultaneously. JoJo went high and O'Keefe went low from the opposite direction. The soldier went down hard and he lost his grip on the sword. It clattered away and sunk into the side of a small desk.

JoJo straddled his chest. He pounded his fists into the soldier's face over and over. With each blow, blood spattered until JoJo's fists and face were sticky and dripping.

Calligan stepped forward and grabbed JoJo's fist just before he landed another punishing blow. "That's enough!" he yelled. "We want him alive."

JoJo kept trying to attack, but Calligan kept his fist in an iron grip. JoJo screamed his frustration into the stunned Japanese soldier's face. He finally stepped off him and shook out his cut, bloody fists.

Shawn staggered to his feet. O'Keefe released the soldier's legs and stepped to Shawn's side. "You okay?"

Shawn had his breath back. "Yeah, I thought he had me. I really did."

Calligan pulled the stunned soldier to his feet. The soldier's eyes shifted crazily from side to side as he tried to focus. JoJo's fists had opened up more cuts on his face, adding to the blood from the gash in his head.

Calligan spoke to him in Japanese. When he didn't get an answer, he shook him hard and repeated more insistently. The soldier swayed, but he murmured something back.

A few minutes later, Calligan pushed him to the ground. "Get his hands tied behind his back." JoJo pulled his knife. Calligan pointed a finger at JoJo, "Don't kill him. He's an officer. We need him alive."

"Got it," JoJo said as he cut a span of rope, helping to hold the tent up. "You want me to make him a cup of tea, too?"

Calligan ignored the comment. "Alright, let's see what else we can find here."

9

Mindanao Sea
Aboard *LCI 970*, en route to Mindoro Island, Philippines
December 13, 1944

Corporal Clyde Cooper sat on the deck of LCI 970 and watched the skies for suicidal enemy pilots. Before leaving Leyte that morning, bound for Mindoro Island to the northwest, they briefed them about the terrifying new tactic being used by the Japanese. Although Clyde hadn't seen it first-hand, the word was that Japanese airmen dove their perfectly good aircraft into ships to assure damage and death.

"You believe what the navy pukes are telling us? I mean about the Kamikaze's?" PFC Oliver asked Clyde.

Clyde kept his eyes on the skies. "I wouldn't put it past them. You've seen their banzai charges—those are suicidal, too. It makes sense that their flyboys are just as crazed."

"Yeah, but having an officer with a pistol at your head right behind you, that's one thing, but flying an airplane into a ship? Why don't they just ditch at sea and wait out the war? Or land at another airstrip and act like nothing happened?"

"Cause they're Japs. Haven't you been paying attention? They don't like us much."

"Think they'll come after us?"

Clyde opened his arms to take in all the islands they passed in the distance. "Every one of these islands is filled with Japs. We must be in range of hundreds of airfields. They barely hafta use binoculars to see our Task Force. We're a ripe target. They'd be fools not to hit us, especially in this narrow strait. The ships don't have room to maneuver."

"Wish we had some carrier support. That'd make 'em think twice, at least."

"Once we get around the horn and through these straits to the other side, we're supposed to have aircraft carrier coverage all the way to San Jose."

"San Jose—sounds like we're invading California," Oliver scoffed.

"I wish," Clyde said.

"Sure will be strange doing an amphibious landing instead of a drop."

"Should be a lot easier than jumping in, but I agree, it'll be strange. It feels like we spend more time at sea than in the air these days."

"Think the Japs are waiting for us?"

"You know what the reports say as much as I do. They don't expect much, but Noemfoor was supposed to be a cakewalk, too."

Suddenly, a destroyer seven hundred yards off their starboard side opened fire. Other warships joined in until the sky overhead pocked with black and white plumes where ack-ack shells exploded. Tracer rounds sprayed the sky in between.

Oliver pointed. "There they are."

Clyde squinted and finally saw the tiny black specks of aircraft. "Looks like bombers."

The line of LCIs continued on course, undeterred by the chaos happening overhead.

"Shouldn't we be zigzagging or something?" Oliver asked.

"We're in the strait. Faster we get through, the better." Clyde gripped the handrail and whooped as he saw a distant dot flare and fall trailing a graceful arc of smoke. "They got one!"

"Nice shooting!" Oliver whooped.

A shattering explosion tore their attention from the skies to the sea. A ship further back belched flame and smoke from the bow. It immediately listed and slowed, sending up a white wake.

"What the hell? That wasn't a bomb. They're still too far away."

A naval officer with a pair of binoculars hanging from his neck yelled to whoever would listen from his perch above them. "Kamikaze! Jap kamikaze hit the Nashville. She's on fire and listing."

They had to duck as enemy bombs whistled down toward them. Clyde cringed, thinking how ironic it would be for a paratrooper to die on a ship steaming toward an amphibious landing. The whomps from the bombs exploding in the water reverberated through the steel sides of the ship. He saw white plumes of water in the distance.

"At least the bombers didn't hit anything."

Oliver peeked over the side. "Sneaky bastards used the bombers to draw their attention high while the kamikaze flew in low, I'll bet."

"You're probably right."

They watched the injured ship slowing in the distance. The droning of more aircraft overhead drew more ack-ack fire from the naval gunners. There were even more dots this time. Streaks of smoke high in the sky marred the perfectly blue sky. But the streaks were far behind the puffs from the ack-ack.

"Looks like our flyboys are getting into the act," Clyde surmised.

"About time. Wonder what those fellas think of the damned suicide pilots?"

"I don't give a shit, as long as they kill 'em before they fly into us."

The show lasted another thirty minutes. No more kamikazes made it through and no bombs hit their marks. Clyde didn't know how many enemy aircraft had gone down, but it had been a costly raid. The injured Nashville faded to the back of the convoy and eventually turned back toward Leyte. A swarm of friendly P-38s kept a close vigil on her.

"I sure hope she makes it back okay," Clyde said.

"Wonder how many sailors bought the farm?"

"I dunno, but I'm glad I've got a foxhole to hide inside when the Nips send their bombers. These poor bastards just have to sweat it out."

As night descended on the Task Force, Clyde and the rest of the company stayed topside and watched the stars slip by overhead. Tomorrow, they'd disembark like regular infantry troops and hit the beaches of an enemy-held island. Despite the fear gnawing at his gut, Clyde's eyes grew heavy and he fell asleep with the gentle rocking of the sea.

~

CLYDE TOOK in the extraordinary sunrise. He hadn't slept well—the coming assault made that all but impossible.

"Another fabulous sunrise in paradise," Private Butler said from close by.

Clyde hadn't heard him approach. He spit over the edge of the ship's rail. "Something I can help you with, Butler?" he said with a barely contained sneer.

"Nah, just wondering if you've heard anything else about Hicks? I mean, besides that he's alive."

Clyde tapped his front pocket. "Just got a letter from him before we shipped out."

"Well, how is he? What'd he say?"

Clyde looked at him sideways. He'd written Butler off after he'd shot and nearly killed First Lieutenant Milkins back in the arid outback of Australia months before, but Butler had performed well at Noemfoor and almost certainly saved him from being skewered by a Japanese bayonet, but his voice still grated on him.

"Why you so interested in PFC Hicks?"

"No reason. I know you two are close."

"He lost an eye." Clyde gave a slight shudder as he remembered shoving the orb back into his best friend's skull after a mortar round exploded in his foxhole. The delicate organ had felt like a big marble in his filthy hand.

Butler made an audible gulp before saying, "that's a shame."

"Small price to pay for getting out of this place."

"You really think so?"

"They saved his legs and he's still got his balls . . ." he shrugged. "He's got another eye that works just fine. I'd call that a fair trade." Clyde tapped out a crinkled cigarette from his diminishing pack. "Why the hell you up so early?"

"I couldn't sleep," he muttered.

"Me either."

Butler stared at Mindoro Island, shimmering in the early morning light. "They say it's gonna be easy. All the Japs are gone."

Clyde took a deep drag from his cigarette. "You seem more concerned with Hicks than the landing."

"I've been wondering about Hicks for a while. Just haven't had a chance to ask you."

"Well, put him out of your mind. He's fine. He should already be back in the states by now." *Unless they torpedoed his ship.* He flicked the rest of his cigarette over the side. "You ready? Know where you're supposed to be?"

"Yep. No problem. All we gotta do is walk off the ramp. This'll be much easier than jumping."

"Guess that's why they pay us the extra fifty bucks a month."

"Is that why you joined the paratroopers? For the extra pay?"

"Not really, but it certainly doesn't hurt."

"Why did you join?" Butler pressed.

Clyde considered brushing him off. After all, they were about to assault an enemy island. There were more pressing matters to attend to, but things wouldn't kick off for at least another hour, and the son of a bitch *had* saved his life.

"I thought with all that extra training, the war might be over by the time I was through." Clyde wished he hadn't been honest as soon as he said it. But instead of being disgusted or even surprised, Butler simply nodded and showed very little reaction.

"That doesn't surprise you?" Clyde asked.

"A little, but everyone has things going on in their lives that we can't really fathom."

"How 'bout you? Why'd you join the paratroopers?"

"You mean, why didn't I let my father get me some cushy job back in the states?"

"Well, yeah. I guess that is what I'm asking."

"I did it to spite the son of a bitch. Pure and simple. He didn't think I'd have the balls."

"I guess being rich isn't all it's cracked up to be—huh? I married into a rich family." He saw the surprise on Butler's face. He let it hang there—he knew he didn't come off as the rich type. "My wife Abby's father is a bigwig businessman in Seattle. Biggest prick I've ever met. It galls him to see his daughter with the likes of me."

"Is that why she did it? To make him mad?"

Clyde felt a wave of anger wash over him. He pushed his chest into Butler's and they stood nose to nose. "Fuck off, Butler."

Butler backed up a step and held up both hands. "Easy does it, Cooper. I didn't mean anything by it."

"Just drop it."

Clyde wondered for the hundredth time if letting him back into Second Platoon had been such a great idea. He'd performed well in combat on Noemfoor, but he still seemed to think his shit didn't stink.

"Get the hell outta here before I wring your neck, private."

Butler jolted as though offended. Clyde stifled the urge to punch him in the face. Maybe he'd get him transferred out of the unit. Huss would give the okay if he asked him nicely.

Clyde turned back to the rising sun and searched for another cigarette. He heard Butler's steps fading away. He didn't look, but figured he'd either have the kicked puppy-dog face or the irreverent sneer.

Clyde pushed Butler from his mind and thought about Abby. Her letters had caught up to him on Leyte and he'd devoured them during their brief stay. The old familiar ache grew in his gut and he pulled the picture she'd sent to him from his front pocket. He smoothed it out and blew the dust off. She wore her WASP uniform and he appreciated the way it fit her hips. Her loving, lighthearted gaze filled his heart with joy, but just like always, he stared at her perfectly shaped hips. He longed to grasp them as he hugged her, then later as they made love.

"Don't do this to yourself, dammit," he muttered to himself. The picture never failed to get him worked up, which was why the corners were already frayed. He kissed the image, wiped it clean and carefully shoved it into his pants pocket. He tried to focus on the here and now, but how could he? He hadn't seen her in years. He could hardly remember how she felt in his arms.

Her letters remained upbeat and full of love. She still gushed how much she missed him, and what they'd do when he finally returned home, but he thought he noticed something else sometimes. He couldn't put his finger on it, but he sometimes wondered if she'd grown out of him—moved beyond him with her new pilot career. When his imagination got the best of him, the urge to get home by any means possible grew strong and made him irritable.

Perhaps Gil had been right—maybe he should put his foot down and make her quit the WASPs. But that would only make her resent him. Besides, once the war ended, she'd stop flying and things would return to normal—just the way her letters spelled it out.

He realized with a start that he was thinking as if he might actually survive this thing—something he'd been careful to keep close to hand. Hope led to crippling fear, and crippling fear led to death. The men who survived battles always seemed surprised. They did their jobs despite the fear because, in their minds, their deaths were a foregone conclusion. Accepting death didn't get rid of the fear, but it did dull the edges a bit and made it possible to function under seemingly impossible circumstances.

But there was no denying the Japanese were reeling from one defeat after another. With the Allie's successful invasion of Europe last summer, the feeling that the war might actually be winding down formed in the back of his mind. But this wasn't Europe. The Japanese weren't Nazis. The Japanese would fight to the last man. He'd seen it firsthand many times. They wouldn't give up until every last one of them had been killed, and the closer they came to their homeland, the harder they'd fight. He couldn't imagine what it would be like to land on Japan itself.

They were still thousands of miles from Japan, with hundreds of thousands of seasoned soldiers between them and Tokyo. Even if Hitler surrendered, Japan never would. They might hang on for years after the war in Europe ended. What would it be like to fight on the streets of Tokyo? Even the smallest child would try to kill them. The thought chilled him, despite the growing morning heat. He muttered to himself, "You did it right, Gil. You lucky bastard."

~

THE ROAR OF THE DESTROYERS, cruisers, and other assorted naval vessel's deck guns firing seemingly all at once, made Clyde plug his ears. Great plumes of smoke curled out over the sea as the low angled barrels spewed shells of all calibers toward Mindoro Island. Gouts of black and white explosions soon marred the landing beach and the sparse jungle beyond.

So far, there had been no return shore battery fire, but a few desultory air raid attempts had been beaten back by the antiaircraft batteries and the swarm of Hellcat fighters from the four aircraft carriers helped deter any significant attacks.

LCI 970 churned in slow circles, along with four other LCIs, each holding a company of paratroopers. Another line of LCIs circled farther west, carrying 19th Regimental Combat Team soldiers. Both sets of LCIs would head to the beach at the same moment in a coordinated beach assault.

Overhead, aircraft loaded with bombs streaked inland and dropped their explosive eggs on suspected enemy positions. A few smudges of black ack-ack fire followed them, but they flew away unscathed. Large plumes of smoke and fire rose from their targets.

A bell rang overhead and their ship turned toward shore and increased speed. Time to get below and standby the massive ramps. Half the company would leave through the port side ramp and half through the starboard side ramp.

He hefted his pack onto his back and felt the relatively light weight. Filled mostly with food and ammunition, they weren't nearly as heavy as what they jumped with.

PFC Gutiérrez grinned at him and said, "Like carrying a cloud."

Oliver stood beside him—he agreed. "These legs have got it easy."

Lieutenant Palinsky, Second Platoon's CO, raised his voice. "When the ramp drops, get your asses in gear and get up the beach. Let's show them how paratroopers assault a beach!"

There was a smattering of hurrahs, but mostly the men kept quiet and concentrated on getting the job done. Clyde checked his Thompson submachine gun. He'd swapped out his M1 carbine for the harder hitting

.45 caliber. The Thompson wasn't as accurate, but in close jungle fighting, he could suppress the enemy better. The city of San Jose, six miles inland, was their main objective, and having the Thompson would help there, too.

The hold of LCI 970 reeked of sweat, oil, and gas. The lights overhead bathed the entire area in red and yellow as they spun and flashed. The loudspeaker blared, but Clyde couldn't decipher a single word.

The sound of squeaking cables combined with the ship slowing down told him they were close. To keep the LCIs from grounding, the navy threw an anchor off the back connected to a large winch, which unwound a few hundred yards of thick cable. When they reached the end of the cable, the ship lurched to a halt.

Sweat dripped down Clyde's face as the men recovered from the abrupt stop. A strange silence followed, where all he could hear was his own heartbeat. Then both ramps lurched and opened with a metallic whine. They dropped slow at first but picked up speed, finally splashing into the sea, sending out undulating waves. Daylight streamed into the hold, blinding them momentarily.

Someone yelled, "Go! Go! Go!"

The paratroopers pushed forward as though rushing out of the side of a C-47. Clyde leaped off the ramp's end and landed in knee deep water. He felt a sandy bottom. He squinted, looking for enemy muzzle flashes, but saw only bright sun and smoking craters on the beach. Further inland, the navy's smoke screen hung thickly. They must've fired that off after he'd gone into the hold. He waded forward, keeping track of Third Squad.

The water deepened and came to Clyde's chest. He stopped and made sure the shorter men had help to get over the deep section. It didn't last long before the sand angled up steeply and he waded onto the beach, dripping wet.

Paratroopers streamed from the sea and hustled up the beach to the sloping grasses beyond. The Bugsanga River flowed in from the right and the murky color mixed with the greenish blue of the sea.

It didn't take long for Second Platoon to form up and move inland. So far, there hadn't been a single shot fired. Everywhere he looked, he saw smiles. Not only did they not have to risk injury from a jump, but there didn't appear to be any enemy resistance—a cakewalk.

Palinsky yelled, "Keep alert. Once we secure the railroad tracks, we'll help push into San Jose. Push the scouts out."

Clyde hunkered and watched the four scouts hustle forward. Instead of jungle, they pushed through cane fields. Mindoro had been a sugar producer before the war. The fields were overgrown but still relatively flat and easy to walk through, even with the sweltering heat.

They made good time, although they had to skirt a few swampy sections, which slowed them down a little. The scouts stopped when they came upon a huge building, which had obviously been some kind of sugar processing plant.

They moved forward cautiously. Clyde didn't like the look of the place. Too many windows for snipers to shoot from. He pictured his head in an enemy sniper's scope. He felt the fear rise. He shook his head, *if it happens that way at least it'll be quick.* His fear subsided and he could breathe again.

Palinsky conferred with the NCOs, then radioed back to the growing beachhead. He finally made contact. He looked as relieved as Clyde felt when he ordered them to bypass the factory. Another platoon would clear it. Command wanted nothing keeping them from their objective.

As they left the sugar processing plant behind, the sky overhead came alive with the buzzing of aircraft. Clyde saw at least ten enemy aircraft. They flew low, heading straight for the beachhead. He wondered if they were kamikazes or just run-of-the-mill zeros on a strafing run. A few men raised their rifles and submachine guns, but Huss barked, "Save your ammo! Let the flyboys take care of 'em."

The scouts pushed ahead and soon the processing plant disappeared behind them, leaving only fields of hip high grass and sparse trees. They moved slowly, but the longer they went without opposition, the harder it was to maintain their slow speed.

Huss barked, "Watch your intervals."

Finally, the scouts stopped again and this time they waved them forward. Clyde saw the train tracks cutting through the fields. Grass grew over them as though they hadn't seen an engine in at least a week, maybe more. Lieutenant Palinsky hunkered and called into HQ.

Oliver hunched nearby. "So this leads to San Jose?"

"That's how the map reads. Figure it's four miles west," Clyde answered while pointing.

"What'll we do if a train comes along?"

Clyde shrugged but didn't answer. Palinsky would have to make that call.

Palinsky handed the handset back to Erickson, the radioman. He raised his voice. "We'll follow this to the outskirts of the city, but command wants us to wait for the rest of the company before we move in. Keep your eyes peeled. I know we haven't seen anything yet, but this is still enemy territory. You know how sneaky these bastards can be. Stay sharp."

The train tracks ran straight and true into the far distance. Thin jungle crept in from each side, but the flat terrain made for easy walking.

They'd moved a mile when the sounds of aircraft increased, making them hunker and watch the skies. "Get ready to move into the trees. If the Nips find us exposed like this . . ." Palinsky didn't need to finish the thought. One strafing run would cut them to ribbons.

Rogerson, the lead scout, pointed and yelled back to the others. "Zeros!"

Clyde saw them an instant later. Two Zeros darted back and forth, jerkily. They followed the train tracks, but they were high and he doubted they'd be able to spot them as they darted back and forth.

"What the hell are they doing?" he asked no one in particular.

"Our boys are right on their tails!" Rogerson yelled.

Sure enough, two twin tailed P-38s followed the zeros as they desperately tried to shake them off their tails. The zeros dove and pulled up only a few hundred feet off the deck. They came straight at Second Platoon, but they were only concerned about losing the P-38s.

Clyde hunkered and stared at the spectacle along with everyone else. The dance of death was mesmerizing. He saw a flicker of light on the nose of the leading P-38. Tracers flowed past the zero and slammed into the metal railroad rails and wooden ties, splintering and sparking with an awful sound.

Everyone dove to the ground. Clyde flung himself off the tracks and rolled as far as he could into the sparse jungle cover. He waited to feel the impact of a heavy caliber bullet plowing into him, but it never came. The ground erupted in fountains of dirt as the stray bullets tore into the soft dirt. The deafening sound of machine guns and the roar of rotary engines overhead took his breath away. He curled into a ball, making himself as small as possible.

It was over as fast as it started. The dueling aircraft flashed past and were out of sight within seconds. A tinkling sound replaced the engines' roar.

"What the hell?" Gutiérrez said. "What's that noise?"

Clyde saw shell casings bounce off the metal rails. "It's spent brass."

Huss stepped out from the brush and swatted at his dirt spattered pants. "Anyone hit?" Everyone seemed more stunned than injured.

Palinsky's face was a deathly white. He'd done well on Noemfoor, but he was relatively new to leading the platoon. He looked like he might throw up.

Sergeant Plumly, the platoon sergeant, slapped him on the back. "Imagine coming all the way out here, just to get shot up by our own flyboys, sir."

Palinsky glanced back the way the fighter had gone. There was no sign of them now, but the smell of burnt gunpowder and churned up soil still hung heavy.

He said, "Sure hope they got those bastards." He focused back on the task at hand. "Let's move it out."

They made it to the outskirts of the city an hour later with no more trouble. The city looked more like a town, but out here it ranked as a city.

They kept out of sight, not wanting to draw attention. A few Filipinos walked the streets, but they didn't see any sign of the enemy. The sun beat down on their backs and Huss reminded the squad to go easy on their water. Each soldier carried two canteens. Clyde had already drained one and most of his second. Once the rest of Able Company arrived, they'd be resupplied. At least, that was the plan.

"This is almost too easy," Clyde whispered to Huss.

Huss grunted, not taking his eyes off San Jose. He said, "The Filipinos have a resistance cell in San Jose. I wonder if they've already taken care of the Nips for us?"

"Hadn't thought of that. I doubt they take prisoners."

Huss focused on something over Clyde's shoulder. "Well, I'll be damned. Here comes the rest of the company. They're early."

Clyde's chest swelled with pride as he watched them come. They moved like a well-oiled machine—a deadly—well-oiled machine. Second Platoon came out from the brush and handshakes and backslaps went around as they reunited. It had been a remarkably easy day, and everything seemed to work out just the way they'd planned.

After conferring with Captain Stallsworthy and the other officers and senior NCOs, Palinsky informed Second Platoon. "Baker Company met up with the Filipino resistance, and they say the Japs have moved north. The city's wide open."

Clyde hurrahed along with everyone else. He hoped their good fortune would continue, but doubted it could last for long. His experience told him to remain wary, but for now, it was time to enter the city as conquering heroes. A throng of Filipinos approached them along the railroad tracks. They hooted and hollered and when the two groups came together, there was more backslapping and even hugging. The women wept openly and the men smiled broadly.

"How long they been under the Japs' boots?" Oliver wondered.

"Long enough, by the looks of things," Clyde answered as a young Filipino woman kissed his cheek and squeezed his hand.

Huss slung his submachine gun and hefted two children into his burly arms. He walked with them as they chittered excitedly into his ear as though he were their long-lost uncle.

10

Over a week passed and the paratroopers found themselves without a proper mission. The distant sounds of combat sometimes floated on the fetid jungle air, but it could've been thunderstorms if Clyde didn't know better. After liberating San Jose without firing a shot, they'd moved inland and helped secure the vital airfields which would allow the flyboys to strike Luzon directly.

At the moment, they guarded Australian construction workers as they scraped out a new airfield along the banks of the Bugsanga River. The Australians genuinely seemed to appreciate their presence, but Clyde heard the paratrooper's disgruntled complaints and felt their morale slipping. They wanted back into the fight.

Sergeant Huss pulled him aside. The gruff veteran still scared him a little, even though both men had chewed the same dirt and came through unscathed—at least physically. "Just heard from Lieutenant Palinsky. There's a group of Nips on the northern tip of the island being a pain in the ass. The brass wants us to put an end to them."

Clyde's cheeks flushed with both fear and relief. "Thank God! This guard duty's driving the men crazy."

"Yeah, I know. It's like using a hammer on a hangnail."

"I get the feeling the brass doesn't quite know what to do with us."

"Well, that's about to change. Able and Baker are heading north to root 'em out."

"Any idea what we'll be facing?"

"Not really. They say it's just a token force of fanatics, but you know how those intelligence types are . . ."

"Next to useless," Clyde finished for him.

"Exactly. It could be a troop of girl scouts or a division of the Emperor's finest. We'll just hafta wait an' see."

"When do we leave?"

"They want us to celebrate Christmas Day properly, so we'll go the day after."

Despite the efforts to decorate the place in holiday cheer, the tinsel and various homemade—mostly vulgar—ornaments hanging from palm trees did little more than make Clyde yearn for home. This would be the third Christmas he'd spend away from his wife and family. How many more would he miss?

"Don't mention any of this to the men. Let them enjoy their Christmas Eve dinner tonight. The CO wants to tell 'em tomorrow afternoon."

Clyde glanced at the sky. Despite the encroaching evening, the day remained hot and humid. Somewhere, snow fell in the world. He could hardly remember what that felt like. Back home, he'd loved visiting his Aunt's cabin in the Cascade mountain range around this time of year. There was always snow, but not so much that you couldn't walk around without sinking up to your eyeballs. Frank and his cousin Shawn had the most epic snowball fights and would set speed records—by their own accounts—on sleds, toboggans, and huge inner tubes. Sometimes they'd combine the snowball fights with the sledding. That trip always signaled the beginning of winter and Christmas time. It felt like a lifetime since those days.

"Doesn't feel much like Christmas," he uttered.

"Just another day, far as I'm concerned," Huss said.

"You're not a believer?"

"It's easy during peacetime, not so much out here."

"I know what you mean." The pause lengthened between them as they both pondered God, war, and mosquitos.

Sergeant Huss finally said, "The CO wants us shaved and cleaned up for dinner. Wants to make a good impression on the Aussies, I guess."

"I'll pass it along."

A few hours later, Clyde joined the raucous scene in the mess hall. The windows had blackout curtains drawn, turning the confined space into a stifling oven. But that didn't deter the men from devouring everything they could stack on their plates.

Christmas songs blared from an old record player. Between mouthfuls of turkey and canned yams, the men sang together. The paratroopers and Australians joined arms and swayed back and forth until the long tables threatened to collapse under the strain. Someone spiked the punch turning it into true jungle juice, but even without the added alcohol, the men were happy for a hot meal and could put the war behind them for a while.

Clyde wondered how his brother Frank fared that Christmas Eve. Last month, he'd received a letter from his parents with the almost unbelievable news that his brother had somehow escaped the Japanese POW camp and was somewhere in the Philippines. His parents didn't know much more than that.

It raised more questions than answers. Why wasn't Frank being shipped back home? Where in the Philippines? After all, *Clyde* was in the Philippines, too. He couldn't tell his parents that, but he'd enquired about Frank's whereabouts during his brief stay on Leyte and again as soon as he they'd secured Mindoro, but no one seemed to know anything. He wondered if it might be some cruel joke by the Japanese. He wouldn't put it past them. Perhaps they'd send a lopped off finger to his parents wrapped in Christmas paper.

His thoughts came to a crushing end when two soldiers burst into the mess hall, nearly tearing the door off the hinges. Through a bullhorn, one of them yelled, "Attention! Jap naval convoy sighted nearby. Take cover!"

The raucous singing from the men stopped, but the blaring speaker kept banging out "Jingle Bells." Someone pushed the needle and it squeaked loudly. Then all hell broke loose. Clyde pushed back from the table along with every other soldier. It tipped toward him and spilled men off the side. Plates and trays crashed to the floor and utensils pinged and spun crazily through the air.

Just like everyone else, Clyde had left his weapon outside. It wouldn't do much good against an enemy naval armada, but he yearned to feel the weight of it in his hands. Was this an amphibious landing or just a shelling?

Men streamed toward the two exits at opposite ends of the mess hall. A glut of green and brown uniforms stacked and pushed as the men struggled to get out and find cover in the various slit trenches, dug for that reason. Beyond the door, he saw the darkness of late night. He'd lost track of time. Was it already Christmas Day?

Clyde fought the urge to push into the crowd. It would only make things worse. He yelled, "Take it easy! No pushing!" But the longer it took to get out, the more frenzied the pushing and yelling.

He finally made it outside. Men scattered and ran in every direction. He briefly forgot where the slit trenches were. He took a deep breath, trying to focus. Perhaps this whole thing was just a false alarm. It was something he could see his old pal Gil pulling off. That thought evaporated when he saw a flash of light, followed immediately by the screeching roar of an incoming shell.

He threw himself to the ground and covered his head with his arms. Despite the fear, he could feel the uncomfortable lump of food in his belly pushing against the ground. The shell slammed into the airfield a couple hundred yards away. The ground shook beneath him and he held on as though the hammerhead ride operator at the county fair had forgotten to strap him into the seat.

Someone clutched the back of his shirt and yanked him off the ground. "Come on! Get to cover!"

Clyde's feet didn't seem to want to work, but the signals from his brain finally kicked in and he sprinted. He followed the dark silhouette of the soldier, who seemed to know where he was going.

Another shell landed and burst into magnificent white light. The soldier seemed to freeze in the intense light, but it was Clyde's eyes shutting down. He blinked and his eyes watered, but he could only see bright spots. He stumbled ahead, barely slowing down. He glimpsed only flashes of movement now. He hoped he didn't run headlong into anything hard.

The ground suddenly disappeared beneath his feet and he felt himself falling. He instinctively curled into a ball. He slammed into a dirt wall and lost his breath. He rolled onto his back and gasped and struggled to breathe, but nothing came. His ears rang, his vision spotted, and he couldn't breathe. Direct hit? Was he dead?

His lungs finally refilled and he took in a raspy breath full of dust. He hacked and coughed and barely made it to his side before he threw up his turkey dinner with heaving convulsions. He couldn't be dead—too painful.

The ground continued to shake with each exploding shell. He curled into a ball and noticed other men curled against his backside and his front. He couldn't see them, but felt them shuddering all around him. *I'm in a trench,* he decided. The realization didn't ease his mind.

The shells felt as though they were coming closer. Between impossibly loud thunderclaps, he heard men whimpering and screaming. His throat felt raspy and raw from his own screaming. His body didn't feel like his own anymore. His soul had been shaken out somehow. He welcomed the calmness, but it didn't last more than a second before excruciating pain gripped every nerve.

His throat felt as though he'd swallowed glass and dust. He tasted blood and once again wondered if he'd died and his mind hadn't quite caught up yet. How much more could he take? The shelling never let up and lasted for twelve lifetimes. How could they still have this much ammunition?

Finally, calmness settled over the trench. The air sparkled with bits of light as fire reflected off bits of crazily descending debris. He thought it was fireflies at first, but they knew better than to live on this merciless island. He felt a hand on his shoulder and pain shot down his arm like a lightning bolt.

"Hey, you okay? You okay?"

He could see a vaguely familiar soldier's mouth moving, but he could barely hear him. "What?" he yelled. "Who?"

"It's me, Guti."

Clyde shook his head to clear the fuzz. He gripped his forehead, feeling the worst headache he'd ever felt. He focused on the soldier in front of him. His dark eyes sparkled with the reflection of the burning palm trees overhead.

"Guti? Is that you?"

PFC Gutiérrez said, "Holy shit! Those bastards really know how to light up our Christmas Eve!"

Long minutes passed. Clyde's hearing came back and his eyesight, too, but he still sat with his back against the wall, staring at Gutiérrez. Private Oliver joined them. His eyes darted crazily as though the shelling might resume again at any moment.

Clyde scraped the grime from the face of his watch. The hands had stopped moving. He put it to his ear, but heard nothing. It was asking a lot from his abused ears. In the dim light, he could see his watch had stopped at ten minutes past midnight. "Merry Christmas," he uttered.

Oliver gave a low whistle. "Those bastards shelled us for a half hour straight."

"They can't have any more ammunition after that," Gutiérrez said.

"I dunno." Clyde pushed himself to his feet, using the wall for support. He had to get himself together and get a headcount—try to make himself useful, but he could hardly stand on his own two feet. He swayed, despite leaning on the wall. He put his hands on his knees and leaned over. He wanted to throw up, but there was nothing left in his sore belly. "Those sons of bitches must really hate us."

$\sim$

CLYDE and the rest of Able Company piled out of the troop trucks. He landed hard and took a moment to stretch his aching back. The jungle road hadn't been made for trucks and the holes and divots along the way pushed the truck's springs to the absolute limit, not to mention the men hanging on for dear life in the back.

"I feel like I got run over by one of them trucks," Oliver snorted as he rubbed his buttocks.

"Better'n walking," Clyde said.

"I guess so, but at least I'd only be tired—not beat to shit."

Huss barked, "Alright you apes. Unload and get your asses in gear. Move up the line. It's time to earn your pay."

"You're gettin' paid?" Gutiérrez teased.

Huss ignored him, but scowled at Clyde as though he should rein in a child making a scene. Clyde ignored him. If Huss wanted to chew out a veteran like Gutiérrez, he'd have to do it himself.

An hour later, Able Company joined an undersized platoon from the 19th at their forward HQ and set up shop. Captain Stallsworthy laid out how they'd go about pushing into the suspected enemy outpost.

As the morning passed through noon, Second Platoon pushed forward. They moved slowly, despite the easy walking. Each man had his weapon ready—trigger finger resting on the trigger guard.

Oliver moved closer to Clyde. "Why are we always out front?"

Clyde didn't take his eyes off the thin jungle, paying close attention to the tops of the trees. "What're you talking about?"

"I mean, we're always out front. Always. I thought it might change without Milkins, but even with Palinsky, nothing's changed. Why is that?"

Clyde missed his friend Gil Hicks more than ever. He always had a quick quip for this kind of bellyaching. Without him keeping it in check, it seemed to get worse. As much as he wanted to deny it though, Oliver had a point.

"I'm a corporal, Ollie. You might've noticed my sleeve?"

"I'm just sayin' it ain't fair."

"Well, stow it or file a complaint with Stallsworthy."

"He's right, you know," Private Raley chimed in.

Clyde glanced back at the big man carrying the BAR just a few yards behind him. The weapon looked huge, even in Raley's mitts.

"You just concentrate on your job, Raley. We need you in the fight when me make contact."

"I know my job," he huffed.

"Then why you so damned close? Spread out and keep your intervals, dammit. No more talking."

Raley spit into the dirt and faded back a few steps, but he looked ready to put a round through Clyde's backside. He focused on the terrain to his front and the damned treetops. He almost hoped they found the enemy just to give the men something to take their minds off things.

The heat rising from the sun-scorched ground and the sun beating down made Clyde yearn for a quick drink of water, but he fought the urge. If he stopped to drink, everyone would. Surely Lieutenant Palinsky must be thirsty, too. Why hadn't they stopped? He remembered how dehydration led to pour decisions back in Australia. They'd lost a good officer.

The men in front finally stopped and hunkered. Clyde did too, hoping for a quick water break, but instead a scout scooted back and conferred with Palinsky. Clyde took a sip from his canteen. He noticed other men doing the same. He quickly screwed the lid on and tucked the canteen back into place. Even the short sip sent a shock of energy through his system, but he wanted more.

The scout finally left Palinsky's side and the officer turned back to the rest of them and signaled. Huss passed it along and soon Third Squad moved left and forward.

Clyde slowed as he passed Sergeant Huss. Huss hissed, "They spotted movement. We're moving up to contact on their flank. Don't fire unless you have to. We're going for surprise."

Clyde felt the old familiar knot form in his stomach. He passed the orders onto the others, trying to maintain a stoic, business as usual air. He doubted he succeeded—the crack in his voice gave him away.

He made eye contact with Raley, the BAR man. He gave him a grim nod back. Clyde wracked his brain for anything else he should do, but the men knew their jobs.

The air suddenly felt too still. The heat radiated off everything, but it felt muted. Sweat still dripped down his backside and into the crack of his ass, but he barely noticed. His crushing thirst still tugged at the corners of his brain, but he focused on the enemy somewhere up ahead.

They moved fifty yards into a thicker portion of jungle. The smell of the sea and the hint of something he couldn't quite place wafted on a welcome breeze. Then it hit him; wood smoke. Someone cooked up ahead. Campfire smoke could travel long distances, but this smelled close.

He froze when he heard the unmistakable sounds of voices—Japanese voices. The squad had decent cover, but he wished they had more. The grass and anemic jungle trees wouldn't do much to stop bullets. Digging in would make too much noise.

His heartbeat sounded loud in his ears. He gingerly brought his Thompson to his shoulder, but kept the muzzle pointed at the ground. It felt solid in his hands, like an old reliable walking stick on a difficult creek crossing, but far more deadly.

Commotion behind pulled his attention. Palinsky positioned the mortar teams to support them. A machine gun crew hustled to the right flank and loaded their .30 caliber. It didn't take long. Palinsky waved to get Huss's attention, then waved him forward. Huss's eyes met Clyde's for an instant, then Huss stood to a crouch and waved the men forward. Clyde licked his dry lips. The next few moments might be his last—particularly if the enemy saw them first. None of the other squads moved forward. Why were they the only ones?

Clyde waved his team forward. They crept. He stayed as low as possible. His helmet threatened to push over his eyebrows. He wanted to push it up but didn't dare take his hands off the Thompson.

The enemy conversation continued in spurts and halts just ahead. At least they still had the element of surprise, but they were closing in quickly. Any moment someone would notice them. They should stop and find targets, but they kept going closer and closer.

He bit back a yelp when he saw movement through the trees and bushes. He hunkered and brought the Thompson to his shoulder. The greenish uniform of the enemy filled his sight picture, and he put his finger on the trigger. More blurs of uniforms through the trees were only thirty yards ahead. From the corner of his eye, he saw the others stop and aim.

He could clearly see his target's face. The soldier cleared off the ground with his boot, then sat while holding a small bowl. He lay his rifle alongside and shoveled rice into his mouth, as though he hadn't had a decent meal in months. *Sorry to interrupt your lunch, fella!*

The Thompson swayed with his pounding heartbeat as he held the sights on his target. *What the hell are we waiting for, New Year's Eve?*

The quiet scene erupted when a startled Japanese soldier yelled in alarm. The soldier in his sights stopped mid-scoop and stared into the jungle with wide eyes. For an instant, their eyes met. He squeezed the trigger a half second after Sergeant Huss did. The hammering of submachine guns and rifles filled the air. His target bowled over backward, his bowl of rice thrown up in the air as the heavy caliber bullets rode up his body like powerful hammer blows.

He shifted his aim to the next man, but he was already falling from multiple gunshot wounds. Clyde fired anyway, adding to the carnage. The intensity of fire continued for twenty seconds before Huss yelled, "Cease fire! Cease fire!"

Clyde quickly reloaded. His breathing came in quick gasps as he walked forward, his eyes still on the gun sights overlooking the smoking barrel. He swept side to side, but no one moved. Blood and spilled food mixed on the hard ground. The small cooking fire smoked heavily—the pot of rice had fallen into the flames, partially dousing it.

Clyde walked up to the man he'd shot. He swept the muzzle over him, but it was obvious by the man's glazed eyes and pale color that he wasn't a threat. He kneeled beside the body, keeping his muzzle trained on the sparse jungle beyond the small camp. He saw six other enemy soldiers, all dead or dying. Could this be the entire force they'd been sent to eliminate? They looked emaciated even in death. Their uniforms hung off them. He had the urge to pick the man up to test his body weight.

Palinsky strode into the circle of death along with First and Second Squads. He took in the death and destruction with excited, almost hungry eyes. "Great job, men. Well done."

Huss asked, "Is this all of 'em?"

Palinsky never got the chance to answer. First rifle fire, then concentrated machine gun fire came from the jungle ahead, cutting a large swath. Clyde dove behind the man he'd killed and he felt sickening thumps as bullets impacted the body. He scooted back until he could roll behind a downed tree trunk. Bullets zipped over his head and tore up the ground to his right, sending dirt spouting onto his back.

He heard Huss yell, "Palinsky's hit! Medic! Medic!"

Clyde risked a look. Palinsky was on his back, clutching at his neck as gouts of thick blood oozed out from between his fingers. His mouth worked as though trying to give orders, but he only gurgled. His legs soon stopped pushing against the ground and his blood-soaked hands fell away from his neck, revealing torn flesh, blood, and bone.

Clyde saw Janikowski running in a half crouch, ignoring the bullets whizzing past him. The medics only focus on getting aid to his fallen leader.

Clyde waved him to get down. "Forget it! He's gone, Doc! He's gone!"

Janikowski ignored him and kept coming. Clyde cursed under his breath, but rolled out and fired his entire magazine into the jungle. Janikowski dove into Palinsky's inert body. He felt for a pulse in his pulped neck and came to the same conclusion Clyde had. He was gone.

Bullets stitched the space between Clyde and the medic. Janikowski rolled into a ball and clutched his helmet to his head. Clyde reloaded and fired, trying to draw the gunner's attention. After half a mag, he yelled, "Get the damned mortars working!"

He heard Huss taking up the call and soon the distinct thumps of outgoing mortar rounds arcing overhead added to the chaos. The rounds erupted in the trees and gave a brief respite from the overwhelming enemy firepower.

Huss yelled, "Fall back! Fall back!"

Clyde knew it was the right call. They didn't have enough cover, and they had no idea how many enemy soldiers they faced. Let the mortars work them over, then call in the artillery.

He rolled to one knee and fired the rest of his magazine toward the unseen enemy. He sprinted to Janikowski's side and lifted him by the back of his shirt. "Come on! Move out!" Now both on their feet, they sprinted back the way they'd come. Clyde ran until he saw Huss and the rest of Third Squad. They watched the jungle with wide eyes.

He skidded in beside Huss, his breath coming in short gasps. "Palinksy's dead. Shot in the neck."

Huss looked at Janikowski, who nodded his agreement. Huss slapped the butt of the Thompson. "Damned shame. He was shaping up nicely." He pointed to the tree line. "Keep watch while I check in with the C.O."

The mortar crews called out, "Rounds complete!" The rhythmic thumping of outgoing mortar rounds ceased. The Japanese didn't start up their fire again and the jungle took on a surreal quiet.

Huss hissed into the radio as Private Erickson looked nervously on. Clyde reloaded and checked in with the rest of the squad. No one had been hit besides Palinsky. The brief high from killing the enemy had quickly vanished with the loss of their platoon leader.

Huss waved him over. "The C.O. wants us to fall back and dig in while he figures out what he wants to do."

"What about Palinsky? We can't just leave him there, the Japs'll mutilate him."

Huss spit, then nodded. "Yeah. We'll get him back. Take your team and get back here fast."

Clyde waved his Team Two men to him. "We're going to get Palinsky." He pointed at Raley, the BAR man from Team One. "You're coming with us, Raley." Raley grinned, eager to join them.

They moved forward slowly. When they came to the edge of the camp, it felt different, even though it had only been minutes since the initial attack. The jungle beyond still smoked from the high explosive mortar rounds. Nothing moved. Palinsky lay on his back, his eyes wide open and his mouth open to the sky. Besides the ghastly gash in his neck, he appeared to be frozen in mid-sentence, as though trying to describe something wonderful he saw in the sky, but having trouble finding the right words.

"Alright. Butler, Wallace, and Hellam. Get out there and get Palinsky. Don't dawdle. If you see anything, take cover. We'll cover you."

The three men exchanged nervous glances. They moved from the edge, keeping low and moving fast. Clyde expected a hail of bullets at any moment. He had his Thompson at his shoulder and Raley had the BAR propped on a boulder, ready to send heavy slugs downrange. The rest of them had weapons to shoulders and eyes wide open.

Butler and the others got to Palinsky. They slung their weapons and each positioned themselves to carry the dead weight. But before they did, Butler low crawled his way to the enemy soldier Clyde had killed, then he moved back to Palinsky. They hefted him and half carried—half dragged his body.

When they were halfway, the Japanese opened fire again. Instinctively, the three of them dropped and took cover. Raley opened fire, almost drowning out the less powerful weapons of the rest of the squad.

Clyde swept the distant trees with fire, then yelled, "Come on! Keep coming!"

The three men rose and hauled the body as fast as they could over the uneven ground. They fell exhausted into the relative safety of the trees. Bullets whacked into tree trunks and shook them, knocking leaves and branches onto their heads.

"Cease fire!" Clyde barked.

The enemy fire kept coming for another few seconds but without a target and no return fire, it soon tapered off.

"What the hell were you doing out there, Butler?" Clyde asked.

"I left a little surprise for them." He touched his harness and Clyde noticed he had one less grenade.

Clyde wanted to lay into him, but he didn't have the energy. Besides, if it took out another enemy soldier—good riddance. "Come on, let's get back to the rest of the platoon."

~

"How long we gonna sit on our asses?" Oliver asked no one in particular.

Since Clyde sat the closest, he answered. "Until the navy hits the Nips with the big guns."

"How long does it take to sail a few miles?"

Sergeant Huss, who still chafed from losing Lieutenant Palinsky, growled. "Be glad they're not sending us in there without the bombardment. We don't know what they've got there, but it's more'n they thought."

"Yeah, I guess so. Just wished they'd hurry the hell up. Say, are we gettin' a replacement for Palinsky?"

"Not yet. They folded us into First Platoon. We'll be taking orders from Lieutenant Bregger."

Everyone had heard of about Bregger, a hard-charging officer who cared more about the mission than the men. That could be good and bad.

Gutiérrez murmured, "Hope he doesn't get us all killed."

Despite his low voice, Huss heard him. "We'll likely be in reserve on this one. Bregger doesn't know us well enough."

Orders came down the line. Huss hustled off to get the scoop. He came back a few minutes later, looking even more grim than before.

Clyde sidled up to him and asked, "What's the matter?"

Huss ignored him and raised his voice for everyone to hear. He cut his eyes at Oliver. "You got your wish, Ollie. Naval bombardment's canceled—the shallow reefs make it too risky and there might be enemy subs waiting for them, so Able's going to kick those Jap sons of bitches off the island, personally. We'll dig in tonight and attack in the morning." A smattering of voices—approval from the new guys and grumbles from the veterans—sifted through the ranks.

Clyde felt the familiar fluttering of butterflies in his stomach. An image of Palinsky's pallid face and gasping mouth filled his thoughts. He likely didn't know what hit him, but his last moments were certainly filled with pain and fear. A sniper shot to the head would be better. Never know what hit you. One moment you're alive, the next you're not—end of story.

He shook off the thought and concentrated on the matter at hand. The men knew what to do, but he still made the rounds to make sure. Everyone had finished digging temporary foxholes, but now that they'd be spending the night, they'd dig them deeper.

He found Huss and gave his report. The men were dug in for the night. Huss grunted and said something Clyde couldn't make out. He seemed deeply affected by Palinsky's death.

"You okay, Huss?"

Huss gave him a sideways glance and a dark scowl. "I don't need any inspirational words from you, corporal."

Clyde shrugged and turned back to his own foxhole. If Huss wanted to talk, he'd talk.

Fatigue set in as he put the finishing touches on his foxhole. The long day, heightened by the short but intense firefight, felt like a thousand pound weight on his shoulders. He thought about the enemy soldier he'd killed. *How many is that now?* The soldier had felt no pain. The heavy slugs ended his life before his brain knew what had happened.

He hadn't heard Butler's booby trap go off, but he wondered if the enemy had collected their dead yet. Would he have to see the body in the morning as they marched toward the enemy stronghold? He thought he could just make out a hint of rotting meat smell in the air. By morning, it would be suffocating. He settled into his foxhole and pushed his nose close to the freshly dug dirt. It would mask the smell of rot, at least for a little while. He didn't mean to, but he fell asleep within seconds.

He startled awake. The darkness surrounding him made him wonder if he'd opened his eyes or if they were still shut. He rubbed at them and saw stars. He shook his head and pushed himself upright. He'd fallen asleep awkwardly and both legs had lost blood flow. He staggered and kicked, trying to get the feeling back to them.

He hadn't meant to fall asleep at all. How long had it been? Why hadn't anyone woken him for security rotation? Panic cut through his guts like a frozen knife's edge. Was he all alone? Had they pulled back while he slept?

He squinted to his right and could make out the pile of dirt from a hole ten yards away. He thought it was Butler's hole. He whispered as loudly as he dared, "Butler. Hey, Butler."

No response. He fought the urge to leave his hole and crawl to Butler's. Stupid idea. Never get out of your hole at night while the enemy is nearby unless you wanted to be shot by your own guys. He'd seen it happen and heard about it more than once.

"Butler," he hissed again with more urgency.

Movement and a groggy voice. "What the hell? What's the big idea? What's wrong?"

Relief flooded him. His legs warmed as the blood flow returned. He suddenly had to take a leak. Judging by the darkness and the feel of things, it must be the middle of the night. He didn't even know the unit's disposition. Who was on duty? Where the hell was Huss? As assistant squad leader, Clyde had duties and he hadn't performed them. Huss would tear him apart in the morning.

"Nothing. Go back to sleep."

"Jesus, Cooper—that's what I was doing," Butler hissed.

Clyde watched the darkness where the enemy likely waited. The urgency of his bladder increased, but he didn't do anything about it—he deserved the pain and misery for his leadership failure.

The sun finally lightened the eastern sky to his right. With each passing minute, he spotted the other holes and the occasional top of a helmet or rifle muzzle. He wondered which one Huss sat in. Deciding it was light enough, he hopped out of his hole and made his way back to the rear until he found a place to piss. The relief made him moan in pleasure. Had any other piss ever felt as good?

He checked on the men and eventually found Huss back at HQ, receiving final orders for the morning's attack. He regarded him as though nothing odd had happened. He seemed just as ornery as usual.

With his gravelly voice, he said, "Just like I thought—we'll be in reserve for First Platoon. Bregger looks ready to kill someone." He lit a cigarette but didn't take a puff, just held it in his grimy, beat to shit hands.

He continued, "Make sure the men eat and are ready to move within the hour."

Clyde said, "Hopefully, this'll be wrapped up before lunch. We didn't bring more'n two days' rations."

"Well, we'll see soon enough. Where the hell were you last night?" He pointed the cigarette at him accusingly.

"In my hole—why?"

Huss dropped his gaze and grumbled, "Couldn't find you. You usually come find me, but you didn't last night . . ."

"Got dark quicker'n I thought it would. Ran out of time."

Huss gave him a knowing grin. "You fell asleep."

Clyde stiffened, as though failing an inspection back at Fort Benning. "By the time I woke up, it was already dark," he admitted with a lowered voice.

Huss waved it off. "It turned out alright this time, but don't let it happen again."

Clyde just nodded. If the enemy had attacked, the chaos of combat would've been exacerbated by his inattentiveness. It could've gotten men killed. Huss didn't need to remind him of that fact.

11

"For once Second Platoon's not leading the charge," Oliver said.

Gutiérrez guffawed, "Yeah, it only took Palinsky getting killed to make it happen."

"Stow it, you two," Sergeant Huss grumbled. "Just cause we're in reserve this time, doesn't mean they won't need us."

Clyde didn't know how he felt about not being at the front of the assault. The fear that came with impending combat was a double-edged sword. He hated it, but had to admit that a little part of him yearned for it. Nothing compared to the focus and intensity that combat brought out. Sitting back here in the rear twiddling his thumbs felt wrong somehow.

He stiffened when he heard the first rifle shots in the distance. The thin jungle allowed sound to travel much farther and he instinctively ducked into the foxhole. Soon he heard .30 caliber machine guns open fire, then the thumps of mortars. Japanese fire sounded weak and ineffective compared to the onslaught from Able Company.

Butler yelled into the early morning air, "Give 'em hell, boys!"

So far, everything sounded the way Clyde expected. Once the company found the edge of the enemy holdouts, they'd hit it hard with overwhelming firepower, then sweep up the dregs. The firepower was supposed to be a heavy naval bombardment, but the 60mm mortars and machine guns would have to be enough this time around.

He flicked out a cigarette and shoved it unlit into his mouth as he watched the flashes erupt in the trees. He could just make out green clad paratroopers hunched behind cover, waiting out the mortar barrage.

All four mortar teams would send one full complement of mortar rounds each. After the twenty high explosives and five smoke rounds had been expended, the rest of the company would move forward and mop up what was left.

Clyde unconsciously counted the outgoing rounds. After twenty-five, he tightened his grip on his Thompson and strained to see First Platoon troopers some fifty yards ahead. The machine guns stopped with the last mortar round.

"Wish we had some armor up here," Huss said.

"Armor? When have we ever used armor?" Clyde said.

"I don't like this."

Long minutes passed before the relative silence ended in a mishmash of enemy heavy machine gun and rifle fire. The onslaught of enemy fire sounded much more intense than what they'd faced the day before.

Clyde kept watching the trees. The occasional ping of a stray bullet whizzing past, or caroming into the air, kept their heads down.

"They're catching hell up there," Oliver said.

"Knew it wouldn't be easy," Huss muttered.

A base of friendly return fire, led by the heavy machine gun crews, made it sound like a full scale battle unfolding. Yelling and the bone chilling call for a medic turned Clyde's stomach. Who'd been hit? He hated not knowing, not being a part of the action.

He lit the cigarette with a shaky hand. He inhaled but the smoke tasted like cow dung, so he spit it out and crushed it beneath his jump boots.

His heartbeat sounded loud in his chest. He picked his fingernails until they bled. If he could pace in the small hole, he would. He wanted to leap out and join the fight, run to the hurt soldier's aid, do something, anything except sit here on his ass watching. He cut glances at Huss, but his expression still held the same heavy scowl that never seemed to change. How did he stay so calm?

Private Erickson, the radioman, shared the hole with Huss. He'd been at Palinsky's side for months and months, like a loyal dog. How did he feel about him dying right beside him? It must be tough.

The chaos continued. The machine guns from both sides dueled back and forth. The .30 calibers would get the upper hand, then the Nambu's took over as ammunition ran low and the crews changed out barrels. The cracks of rifles and the thumping of exploding grenades filled the gaps.

Finally, the mortars opened fire again. Smoke rounds mixed with high explosive rounds lofted into the jungle. The volume of outgoing small arms fire increased, then tapered quickly, then increased again.

Huss yelled, "They're falling back! Hold your fire!"

"Hold your fire!" Clyde mimicked to the men nearby.

Gutiérrez in the hole to Clyde's left yelled to him, "Are they being overrun?"

"They're falling back. Stay alert."

Clyde didn't like it. Paratroopers didn't fall back. The objective must be a tough nut to crack. He expected Second Platoon to be committed long before a general fallback order, but here they still sat and here came First Platoon, angling back to their original position.

One squad moved while the other covered, and vice versa. They weren't retreating, just withdrawing, which made Clyde feel better. For a moment he wondered if they'd been routed—but no—it was orderly. He heard Huss answering a radio call. He strained, but couldn't decipher what was being said.

A few stretcher bearers hustled past their position, taking wounded men back to the waiting jeeps and trucks. The last wounded man sat upright with a pained look on his face. Clyde recognized him.

He hopped out of his hole and trotted alongside for a few yards. "Hey, how you doing, Rawlins?"

"I'm alright. Nips just clipped me."

"What's it like up there? How many Nips?"

"I never saw a single one of 'em, Coop. Bunkers and tunnels."

Clyde squeezed his shoulder, "See ya 'round," then moved to Huss's hole. He was just finishing his call. "What's the scoop?"

Huss looked annoyed. "Stallsworthy's calling in the flyboys. They ran into some kind of bunker system up there. Nips are dug in tighter'n a tick."

Clyde thumbed back toward the stretcher bearers. "Rawlins from First said he didn't even see who hit him."

Huss ignored the comment, but added, "Since First took casualties, the CO wants us to give it a go after the fly boys get finished."

Clyde felt a lump in his throat and a burning ember in his belly. Now that he'd be getting what he wished for—he didn't want it.

Huss added, "Move the men out of the foxholes. First'll take 'em over. Make sure they've eaten and have plenty of ammo. The flyboys are due here in an hour, we'll attack soon as they finish."

"Will Lieutenant Bregger be leading us in?"

"He's in command, but Sergeant Plumly will be the joining us directly."

Clyde nodded his understanding. The no nonsense Platoon Sergeant could be a pain in the ass, but the men respected him and he made good decisions. "I'll pass it along to the men."

"One more thing. Since we're dealing with bunkers and tunnels, satchel charges are on the way. Be sure the right men get 'em." He pondered for a moment. "Wallace and Butler."

Clyde nodded and slunk back toward the rest of the team. Wallace was a grenadier and the natural choice for handling explosives, but Butler was a rifleman. Every paratrooper knew how to use the heavy explosive devices, but he wondered if Butler was a good choice. Hopefully, they wouldn't need them at all, if the flyboys did their jobs.

～

THE ROAR of aircraft overhead made Clyde cringe despite expecting them. Ever since the kamikaze attacks on their ships, any aircraft engine sounds gave him fits.

Oliver, sitting beside him, slapped him on the back. "Relax, Coop. They're ours."

Clyde shaded his eyes and caught the glint of aircraft overhead. The familiar gull-shaped wings were unmistakable. The corsairs had arrived.

"Guess it's time to sit back and enjoy the show," Butler said excitedly.

"Find some cover first," Sergeant Huss barked. "Those stupid sons of bitches have been known to drop their eggs on friendlies."

The relatively light overhead cover gave them a perfect view as the deep blue painted aircraft buzzed overhead. Thick smoke plumed from the front of their position, marking friendly lines for the pilots overhead.

The graceful airplanes met at altitude, then one peeled from the flock and made a shallow dive. Every few seconds, another peeled and dove toward the target. The first corsair came fast. The engine made a throaty growl and wind whistled over the airframe. Two bombs pickled off the wings and the pilot immediately pulled up and away. The bombs floated down gracefully and impacted. An eruption of flame, smoke, and debris from the enemy held bunker line rose into the sky. A concussive wave rolled over their position, but by then it had lost most of its power.

With each pass, their confidence grew. Even bunkers wouldn't be able to withstand that kind of beating—as long as they were on target.

With bombs expended, they made another pass with rockets. The white trails shot out from the wings and slammed into the enemy positions, adding to the carnage. Clyde cheered along with everyone else. In the final pass, the corsairs ventured even lower and fired their machine guns. The six .50 caliber M2 machine guns firing all at once sounded like ripping fabric. The odd tracer ricocheted into the morning sky like an afterthought.

The last corsair finished strafing and arced away in pursuit of his squadron mates. The sudden absence of roaring engines, bombs, rockets, and heavy machine guns made Clyde's ears pop. Smoke rose from the enemy position. He'd seen no return fire since the show started.

Lieutenant Bregger stood behind Second Platoon. He raised his voice and ordered, "Okay, Second Platoon . . . move out!"

Clyde wondered if Bregger planned to join them or lead from the rear. They encouraged paratrooper officers to lead from the front, but some had uncanny knacks to stay just behind the action. Bregger didn't mind sending his men into the fray, but he didn't have the reputation of leading from the front.

Clyde exchanged a glance with Plumly. He'd seen him eyeballing Bregger. The platoon sergeant rolled his eyes. Seems he didn't have a high opinion of the man, either.

Second Platoon moved forward slowly. With each step, the smell of cordite, burnt gunpowder, and phosphorous grew stronger. Clyde clutched his Thompson and watched for any movement.

Smoke and small fires dotted the jungle. Palm trees with pulped trunks where bullets and shrapnel had hit became more frequent. A few had been cut in half and debris still drifted down through the shattered palm fronds. Besides the crackling and hissing of flames, an uncanny silence grew.

He moved slowly, making sure of each step. Plumly veered right and conferred with Huss for a moment. Huss nodded and signaled for the others to spread out. This must be where the rest of the company had come into contact the day before.

Clyde walked to the edge of a deep smoking bomb crater. A pool of blood with drag marks caught his attention. He hunkered and realized body parts carpeted the base of the hole. Some of the scattered logs had been cut with saws, not scythed by shrapnel. His heart skipped a beat. He stood in the middle of a destroyed bunker. The flyboys had scored a direct hit and this was all that remained.

He frantically signaled a halt. The trenches and tunnels must connect nearby. A few men stopped, but they were spread too far. Huss didn't notice his signal and kept moving one careful step at a time.

A Nambu machine gun opened fire and Clyde saw the winking flashes from a dark slit near the ground only thirty yards ahead. He threw himself into the hole and couldn't keep himself from rolling to the bottom. A second machine gun joined the first and fire crisscrossed over his head.

A chunk of red-pulped meat with a hand attached lay only inches from his face. He clearly saw the still ticking wrist watch firmly attached. The charred skin was torn and peeling like burnt paper around the watch, which seemed unscathed.

He lurched away and crawled up the side of the hole toward the fire, but away from the gore. The smell of putrefied death mixed with gunpowder and the taste of fear in the back of his throat nearly made him gag.

The nearer he got to the lip of the hole, the more he heard his men yelling and the more urgent the whizzing bullets became. At least three of his men had been in front of him when the Nambu's opened up. Had they found cover or been cut in half? Where were Wallace and Butler with the satchel charges?

Someone came flying into the hole from behind, rolling down the opposite side and into the blood and gore. Clyde spun, bringing his Thompson to bear, but it was Oliver.

Oliver repulsed when his hand landed in a pile of grey coils and blood. "Ah, shit! Goddamn cesspool!"

"Get your ass up here, Ollie."

Oliver wiped his blood-covered hand on his pants and scrambled up the side to join him. Oliver couldn't tear his eyes from the bottom of the hole. Clyde thumped him on the back of the helmet to get his attention. "There's a bunker thirty yards directly ahead. You seen Wallace or Butler?"

"I dunno about Wallace, but Butler was behind me when this shit show kicked off."

"Go get him. I need his satchel."

Oliver cringed as another volley of bullets passed overhead.

"I'll cover you. Go."

Oliver didn't hesitate. He skirted the bottom of the hole and crawled up the way he'd come down. Clyde made eye contact and they exchanged a nod. Clyde crawled forward until he just cleared the lip and could see the bunker. The machine gun had stopped firing, but he could see the smoke pouring from the dark firing port. Maybe he'd caught them between reloading. He rose to a knee and fired his entire magazine toward the bunker slit.

He dropped back down and saw that Oliver had gone. How long did it take a Nambu to reload? He pulled a grenade from his harness, pulled the pin and went to his knees again. Perhaps he'd get lucky and throw a strike. He hurled the grenade as hard as he could muster from the awkward position. It landed a few yards in front of the bunker, rolled toward the slit, then exploded.

An instant later, the Nambu opened up and laced the ground where he'd just been. He lay on his back, reloaded the Thompson while trying to get control of his breathing. That'd been too close. *Now the bastards know where I am.*

More and more friendly fire added to the growing crescendo of sound.

The rest of the company was getting involved. The second Nambu stopped firing, but the first still stitched the lip of the hole.

Clyde searched for Oliver. He hoped he hadn't been hit and lay bleeding to death only feet away. He moved around the hole, avoiding the cesspool at the bottom. Perhaps he could see more from the backside.

He noticed a gap in the crater's wall. Cut logs were still intact and he realized it must be a section of the bunker that had survived the airstrike. He slowed and brought his Thompson to the ready position, concentrating on the corner the gap created.

The steep sides and the freshly churned dirt made the going tough. He glanced at the bloody pool, which had already drawn hundreds of flies. The last thing he wanted was to trip and roll back down there.

He made the corner and hunkered. Now that he was close, he could tell it was likely an entry and exit point. Had any enemy soldiers escaped, or were they on their way here to see what had happened?

He wistfully glanced at where Oliver would come from, but still nothing. The hammering of the .30 caliber machine guns and the Nambus battled overhead. The smart move was to wait for help. But for how long? *I won't go far, just around the corner.*

He glanced at the sky and said a quick prayer to whoever might be listening, then he leaned and peered around the corner. The trench had sturdy logs lining the sides and even a wood lined floor, but he saw no enemy soldiers alive or dead in the short ten yard section to the next turn.

He stepped into the trench and took a few steps, sweeping his Thompson's muzzle from side to side. It felt strange to be in an enemy made trench, as though he were trespassing. A voice in the back of his head urged him to wait for help, but he ignored it. They'd be along shortly, and perhaps this trench would lead to the next bunker. Butler and Wallace could waltz right in and hurl the satchels with ease.

The trench ran straight for ten yards, then turned to the left. Another corner. He hunkered and listened, but couldn't hear anything over the din of machine guns, rifles, and now mortars. He glanced back the way he'd come. Still no sign of Oliver and the others.

He leaned around the next corner slowly and immediately pulled back. An enemy soldier with his back to him was only feet away. If he'd faced him, he surely would've seen him. He fought the urge to run back to the crater. Perhaps a grenade around the corner would take care of the problem.

He steeled his nerves, made sure his Thompson was ready to fire, and leaned around the corner. He fired a short burst nearly point blank into the soldier's back. The body shook and slowly tipped over like a half sawn through tree, but the soldier was already dead—a victim of the bombing, no doubt.

Clyde stepped over the body, wishing he hadn't fired in the first place. Anyone close would've surely heard the Thompson's distinct burp. Another corner loomed twenty yards ahead.

A soldier carrying a long rifle lunged around the corner. His eyes went wide when he saw Clyde's smoking muzzle pointed directly at his chest. Clyde pulled the trigger, firing from the hip and his bullets stitched the soldier from low to high. The final bullet snapped his head back in a spray of blood. The soldier flopped backward, the top half of his body around the corner and out of sight.

Clyde crouched there, waiting for another soldier to round the corner. Quick movement, a hand, then the hiss of a grenade. It bounced off the wood-lined wall and caromed toward him. He turned and dove back the way he'd come.

The grenade exploded. The concussion took his breath away, but the blast and shrapnel must've been blunted by the body. He sprang to his feet and ran the other direction for a few yards, then turned and hurled a grenade back the way he'd come. He watched it smack the wall and bounce around the corner, a perfect throw. He didn't wait to see the results. He ran back to the relative safety of the crater, breathing hard. He surprised Oliver and Butler, who had their carbines leveled at his chest—their eyes big as dinner plates.

Oliver said, "Jesus Christ, Coop! Where'd you come from?"

"Japs in the trench. Get ready!" He aimed the Thompson, not wanting to take the time to reload. Indiscriminate yelling emanated from the trench —they were coming.

Oliver blurted, "How many? Sounds like a lot!"

Clyde didn't have time to answer. A screaming soldier flew at them, firing a pistol. A bullet narrowly missed Clyde's head. Two more carrying rifles came behind the first, also screaming. He emptied the rest of his magazine into them. Oliver and Butler emptied their carbines and the enemy soldiers dropped, adding their blood to that of their comrades.

Clyde stepped aside and quickly reloaded. Oliver and Butler did the same. No more screaming Japanese and no more grenades rolled from the trench. They stayed down, ready for whatever came next.

Clyde hissed, "There's more down there. Throw a grenade."

Oliver quickly dug into his bag of grenades. He stepped forward cautiously until he stood beside Clyde. Clyde nodded, then lunged around the corner and fired a short burst. He stepped back into cover and Oliver hurled the grenade. "Eat shit!" he yelled.

The grenade exploded with a dull thump. They waited, but no more enemy soldiers came.

Oliver said, "You went in there alone?"

"Not far, but yeah. I think it links to the other bunkers." He made a quick decision. "You got the satchel?"

Butler shifted the pack on his back to his front, showing him the explosive charge. "Right here."

"This is our way in. I'm gonna get the rest of the squad."

Oliver nodded, but touched his shoulder. "I was just there. I know the way. I'll get 'em."

Clyde hated sending him into the fire zone again, but it made the most sense. "Okay—go. But hurry—if the Nips rush us, we won't have enough ammo between us to stop 'em."

Oliver didn't wait. He hustled up the side of the hole like a crazed monkey. He hurled himself out and rolled out of sight. Clyde watched him disappear.

Butler focused on the trench, trying to ignore the bloody gore at his feet. "He'll be alright. He's too fast—Nips can't touch him."

Clyde repositioned himself partially in front of the trench. If anyone came around the corner, he'd have a perfect view. "What's going on up there?" he asked, motioning toward the battle.

"Second's pinned down, but the rest of the company is pushing their flanks. It's hairy up there."

"Anyone hit?"

Butler gulped. "I think so, but I don't know who."

Clyde felt a pit in his stomach. What friends had he lost today? He wished Gil was with him, but quickly admonished himself for the thought. *Gil's regaling nurses in the states by now and I'm sitting in a pile of Jap guts waiting to die.* Gil was far better off, but Clyde knew he'd switch positions with him if he could—with or without his eyeball.

~

WHAT SEEMED like an eternity passed before the rest of Third Squad arrived in the bomb crater. No more Japanese had come barreling down the trench, but bullets continued to snap and carom overhead.

He decided the greater danger came from the trench and not a frontal attack from the bunkers. The Japanese were too well dug in for that. If he was wrong and they came over the top, he and Butler wouldn't have a chance.

"Bout time you got here," Butler said to no one in particular.

Huss ignored him and addressed Clyde. "Ollie says you found a way into the bunkers."

Clyde motioned toward the trench with the muzzle of his Thompson. "I think so. It must connect, but I haven't gone more than a few corners. At the very least, it'll get us closer."

Huss stepped in front of the trench with his Thompson ready. He kicked at the enemy soldier, still seeping blood at his feet. He seemed to decide whether to risk it.

"Alright," he finally said, "let's see where this leads. Anything's better than up there."

Clyde stepped in front of him. "I'll lead." He stepped into the trench before Huss could protest. If it led to a death trap, he didn't want to be responsible for Huss's death.

He retraced his steps until he came to the second corner. He peered around and saw nothing but the grenade-shredded body of the soldier he'd first shot in the back. The soldier at the far end of the trench no longer sprawled there. He'd either dragged himself away, or more likely been dragged. Smoke curled up from the recent grenade exchange.

He stepped over the body and concentrated on the far corner. His senses worked overtime. He heard nothing but small arms fire and the sounds of nearby combat, but nothing in front.

He hunkered near the corner and listened. Men stacked up behind him. He signaled the closest man to throw a grenade. Private Hallon quickly did the job. Clyde waited for the blast, then went around fast.

He saw movement through the smoke and dust—a fleeing soldier. He fired and his rounds knocked the soldier down flat. Clyde ran forward, leaping over the body. Ahead, he saw another corner. This one turned to the left. They had to be close to the next bunker entrance.

He hunkered and again signaled for a grenade. This time, Hallon and Butler both threw grenades. Startled screams, then the crash of the grenades. He rose, but before he could round the corner, Gutiérrez pushed him back and took the lead. He recovered in time to be pushed again, this time by Oliver.

"Dammit!" he cursed. He finally made it around the corner in time to see Gutiérrez and Oliver finishing already mortally wounded soldiers. The trench was becoming crowded with bodies, both alive and dead.

The Nambu sounded loud nearby. Oliver and Gutiérrez pushed forward. The trench widened and empty ammunition crates were stacked neatly along the walls. A few more yards exposed the entrance to the bunker. A thin trail of smoke ran out the top and the Nambu chattered from the darkness.

Huss ran past him and quietly gave orders. "Grenades first, then the satchel." He pushed Butler forward. "Throw the charge as far as you can." He raised his voice for the rest to hear. "When he does, run like hell."

Gutiérrez and Oliver pulled grenades and held them at the ready. Huss stepped into the gaping entrance and fired his full magazine from the hip, then stepped back. The grenades went next, each man throwing them as though pitching fastballs at a baseball game.

The dual crump and billowing smoke rolled out, choking them. Butler pulled the detonation cord and stepped into the entrance, but instead of throwing the hissing charge, he ran into the gloom and disappeared.

Clyde lunged forward, but Huss grabbed his shirt and held him back. "Get the hell outta here!" His powerful arms hurled him back despite Clyde's best efforts to follow Butler.

"Butler!" Clyde screamed into the smoke.

A second later, Butler sprinted from the gloom and slammed into the far wall, knocking over the stacked ammunition crates. Clyde helped him get his feet and pushed him hard. They sprinted past dead bodies and around blind corners right on the heels of the rest of Third Squad.

They skidded into the bomb crater and nearly slipped into the gore. Huss finally came, and Clyde caught him and pulled him around the corner. The blast shook the ground and partially collapsed the trench walls onto themselves. Smoke poured from the trench and soon, every man hacked and coughed.

Light turned to dusk for nearly a minute as the smoke blotted out the sun. Wallace skidded into the crater from behind. He carried the second satchel. He found his way to Huss and held out the charge.

"I've got the satchel," he hacked.

"You're a little late, asshole," Huss said.

Wallace slumped to the ground and lay his head against the crater, breathing hard. "Carrying this thing around for nothing," he mumbled to himself.

"Don't worry, cowboy. You can set it off and get a ticket straight back to those mountains you're always going on about," Gutiérrez said as he slapped his shoulder.

Clyde carefully climbed the side of the crater and peered out. He pushed his helmet back and said, "Jeesuuus Christ!"

Where the bunker had been, only a smoking hole remained. No sign of the enemy. No shots rang out. Paratroopers popped up like gophers and stared at the carnage. Palm fronds flitted down all around him. A slight breezed blew inland from the sea and, for a brief instant, he smelled the sea instead of smoke and death.

Huss stood beside him. "Well, I guess that's that."

12

Virginia airspace
September 1944

Abby leaned toward the cockpit plexiglass and the view almost brought tears to her eyes. The different colors and patterns of autumn laid out from this elevation was truly awe-inspiring. It almost made her forget her problems.

Since visiting Gil Hicks in the hospital and learning the jarring news about her father's possible interference in Clyde's training, she hadn't had a single day off.

With the war in Europe going so well, and the slow death of the WASP program, she thought her flying might taper off, but it seemed to have the opposite effect. The need for airplanes across the Atlantic had only increased and with it the need to ferry aircraft back and forth all across the country. And despite the returning male pilots' complaints about the WASPs still flying, there was a shortage. That was fine with her. Having to work quelled her anger a little. She simply pushed it to the back of her mind to let it simmer.

She leaned away from the window of the P-51 and checked her instruments. Everything looked to be in order. She checked the flight map strapped to her knee and matched it with the small body of water shaped like a tadpole off her left wingtip. Right on course.

She rubbed the back of her neck and felt the knots there. Flying for endless hours across the country sounded romantic, but the toll it took on her body was real enough.

She adjusted herself in the seat, careful to keep her feet off the rudder pedals. She instantly regretted the move as it reminded her of her full bladder. It pressed on her painfully, screaming for attention. She wished she had the portable potty system that some of the women used, but she'd forgotten it on this flight, which meant she had to monitor every drop of water she drank. She could usually make it until she needed gas, but this time she wasn't so sure.

She checked the map, searching for the nearest airport. She wasn't near any big cities, but there were a few towns scattered here and there. Perhaps one might have an airfield where she could fuel up and pee. Maybe they'd even have a barbecue with a burger or some other delicious foods. She often found small town airports to be very accommodating. Some even treated her like royalty after the shock of finding out she was a woman.

She traced her finger along her intended flight path. The next scheduled stop was still two hours away. No way she could hold her bladder that long. The mere thought made it even worse.

No obvious airfields popped up, so she scanned the map further south, then further north. There had to be something nearby. There, a small town with an airfield symbol on the map. She did a quick calculation, drew a pencil line on the map, diverting just sixty miles from her flight path. At her airspeed and elevation, she could be there in minutes.

She scanned the skies and when she didn't see any other aircraft; she banked left, cut her power, and descended. She kept a close watch on her map, marking and passing landmarks leading to the airfield. She'd have to find her way back to her original flight path or she'd be hopelessly lost. This aircraft didn't have the Vario installed, a radio beacon receiver, although there was an empty slot for it.

By the time she finally saw the airfield, she was still five thousand feet above ground level. She didn't see any kind of tower. She keyed the radio, but doubted anyone would monitor the radio, even if they had one, and the frequency would be a complete guess. She tried a few different frequencies before switching the radio off. She'd do this the old-fashioned way.

She descended to two thousand feet and checked her surroundings again. The town was just a few buildings in the distance. The airfield had an old windsock which hung down limply at the far end. A single large hangar stood nearby with a big tank nearby, which she hoped held fuel. If not, she had plenty to reach her original airfield, even with the fuel expenditure required to takeoff and regain altitude. She eyeballed the dirt airstrip, making sure it was long enough to allow for an easy takeoff. More than one pilot had been stranded after making that error.

Satisfied, she made a low and slow pass over the field, hoping to see some signs of life. No one darted out from the hangar to see who was about to drop in on them. She usually caused quite a stir in such situations, but not this time.

She lined up on the runway, checked the windsock one more time, then lowered the gear. The P-51's engine purred and the big propeller blades cut through the heavy air with ease. She barely felt the wheels touch. In the rearview mirror, she saw the massive dust storm her arrival caused. She taxied as close to the hangar and the fuel pod as she could, then shut down the engine going through her engine shutdown checklist.

The dust slowly faded and still no one emerged to greet her. She noticed an old truck on the far side of the fuel pod, but it could've been there for years or minutes as far as she could tell.

She unlatched the cockpit canopy, then unstrapped herself from the seat and parachute harness. Now that she was so close to relief, her bladder was even more insistent. She wondered if she'd make it out of the cockpit in time.

She hopped onto the wing, and her legs nearly collapsed with the newfound movement. She slid onto her butt, then slid off the wing and onto the dirt strip. That's when she saw the three grease monkeys staring at her from the hangar door.

She beamed her best smile and waved. They looked at one another but didn't otherwise react. It wasn't every day a mechanic saw a real live P-51, particularly in a backwoods place like this, but these three barely gave it a second glance. They only had eyes for her. She felt as though they'd never seen another human being, let alone a woman, before.

Their stares made her nervous, but she had to find a bathroom or risk wetting herself. She threw caution to the wind and ignored her internal alarm bells. "Hiya, fellas. Sorry to just drop in like this, but I really need to use your ladies' room. Could you point me in the right direction?" She hoped her levity and beaming smile would make them smile, but no.

One of them spit a long stream of red tobacco juice onto the dusty ground. It skipped and formed a dirty little ball near an anthill. She doubted even the ants would find a use for such vile stuff.

"Who the hell're you?" the middle one asked.

"Oh sorry. My name's Abigail Brooks. I fly for the WASPs." When she only saw blank stares, she added, "I fly for the US government. I'm a ferry pilot." She hoped that bit would give them pause, make them think twice if they had evil intentions.

"We don't got much use for the government round here. What you doing here?" The three of them stepped from the hangar door and spread out a few feet as they approached. She didn't like the looks in their eyes one bit.

She pointed to the fuel pod. "I need fuel. I can pay." She thought it best not to mention her need for the toilet again. At the moment, her need seemed to have taken a backseat to self-preservation.

One of the others leaned in closer to the talker and said something, which made him sneer and chuckle. It made her cringe and take a step back toward the aircraft.

"Tanks been dry for years now. We ain't got no fuel for you. But maybe something else." He grinned and now she had no doubt of his intentions.

"Oh, well then, I'll just be going." She hustled to the side of the aircraft.

"Now just wait a minute, will you? No need to run off. You just got here."

She didn't turn, but shoved her foot into the notch step, but her boot failed to open it properly and slipped back to the ground. She heard them coming. She whirled to face them. They were only feet away, and their leering confirmed what she already knew.

"Stay away from me." she reached into her flight suit and pulled a .38 from the shoulder holster.

The men stopped in their tracks and held up their greasy hands. The talker gave her a grimy toothed smile. "Easy, darling. We just wanna talk with ya. Isn't that right, boys?"

Both of them nodded and said, "Uh huh."

"You said you needed a toilet, well there's one inside the hangar." He honeyed his voice as much as he could, but he wasn't fooling anyone. "I wouldn't call it a ladies' room though. It's pretty rough, even for us. Isn't that right, boys?"

"Uh huh."

Abby kept the muzzle pointed straight at his head. She hoped her hand didn't shake too much. "Go on back to the hangar door," she demanded. When none of them made a move, she added, "Now!"

"You got it all wrong, lady. How 'bout I help you up onto the wing? I can do that for you."

"Move!" she bellowed and was happy to see them jump with her outburst. "Or I'll put a bullet through your worthless pea brain."

The talker took one step back and the others followed his lead, but his slimy smile only grew. "You know how to use that thing? Is it even loaded, darling? Come on, we haven't seen a woman like you in a long time. You're like something outta Life magazine. All's we wanna do is talk."

She could see the hunger in their eyes. It made her stomach turn. "Don't test me!" she barked. "Get back to the hangar doors or I swear I'll shoot you. Nobody'd miss the likes of you."

She saw anger flash in the talker's eyes. He was used to getting his way and didn't like being talked down to, particularly by a woman.

"All right, all right," his voice took on a soothing tone and he took a step back. But then he lunged straight at her. The quickness and surprise nearly worked, but she pulled the trigger when he was only a foot from her.

His heavy body slammed into her, pushing her against the fuselage. She hit her head and saw stars. She fell and found herself looking at the underside of the P-51. Warmth spread across her lap as her bladder finally gave out. She scrambled backward. The man clawed at her from the ground, but she kicked his hands away. The other two only stared, stunned into inaction.

She sprang to her feet on the other side of the aircraft now. The pistol wavered in her hand, a wisp of smoke seeped from the barrel. The man still lay on the ground, groaning and cursing her while his head bled buckets of blood. "You shot me, you bitch! You she-devil!"

He tried to get up and his agonized scream nearly made Abby forget his evil intentions. She'd never heard so much pain in a man's voice. She'd shot him in the head, or so it seemed, but how could he still be alive?

She hurled herself onto the wing, nearly dropping the pistol. She leaned across the cockpit and aimed at the other two men. They raised their hands high as though in competition with one another. Their ringleader's screaming took on a more guttural sound, like a growling dog.

She glanced down at him. He pushed himself to his knees and gazed up at her. His eyes spewed hatred, but also intense pain. Blood trailed down both sides of his nose and into his mouth. His filthy coveralls and greasy off-white shirt turned dark where the blood met the fabric.

Rage and fear overcame Abby. She screamed at him, "What's wrong with you? All I wanted was a little gas and a rest. What the hell's the matter with you? We're in a war and you're attacking *me?*"

She kept the pistol aimed at the other two as she wiggled back into the cockpit. She felt the urine squish into the seat of her pants. The smell of fear and ammonia was overpowering.

She yelled at the other two. "Get him outta the way or the prop'll chop his damned head off. But you make a move toward me and I'll shoot you dead."

They only stared at her, their hands still raised high overhead. She didn't wait, and she didn't go through her normal checklist for the engine start. She knew it by heart and it came to her automatically. The still-warm engine came to life with a sputter of smoke and fire. She clamped the cockpit shut and stowed her pistol back in the shoulder holster. She didn't bother strapping in. She'd do so once she was far away from here.

She taxied back to the little dirt strip as quickly as she could. She saw the two men pulling their wounded friend toward the hangar and the truck, but the wounded man struggled and flailed until one of them ran for the hangar door and disappeared inside.

He emerged holding a hunting rifle. "Shit, shit, shit," she cursed and pushed the throttles to full. The P-51 shot down the runway like a bull out of the chute at a rodeo. It bounced along but seemed much too slow to her as the rifle came to the man's shoulder and the muzzle seemed to center on her. She ducked as low as she could, praying the aircraft didn't swing off the strip and crash into the ditch.

She didn't hear the blast, but she saw the kick against his shoulder and heard the clang as the bullet slammed into the airframe. "Oh my God!" She finally reached rotation speed and pulled the stick back. Despite whatever damage from the bullet, the P-51 lifted off the runway and into the dusky sky.

She turned to watch the airfield grow smaller. She thought she saw another shot fired, but felt nothing this time. She wished she had ammunition for the guns. She pictured herself strafing the simple sons of bitches. That'd serve 'em right. She screamed at them, but knew they were too far away to hear.

She leveled off at six thousand feet and trimmed the aircraft until it could nearly fly itself. She checked her engine gauges. Nothing looked out of whack, although her oil pressure was down a little and the temperature was above normal, but that could've been from the hasty takeoff and steep climb out.

A wave of emotion suddenly overtook her. She ripped off her leather helmet and rocked back and forth, trying to wrap her head around what had just happened. She'd shot a man. He deserved it, but still. Would he live? Would he file a police report? Surely he'd have to be taken to a hospital and questions would be asked. The other two would probably say whatever he told them to say if he lived. She might find herself in handcuffs when she arrived back at home base.

She patted the pistol, thankful she had it. It was against regulations, but Mandy had convinced her it might be necessary. She thought it might come in handy in case they were ever stranded in the boonies, but they both knew the real reason. She'd just lived it.

She pulled it out gingerly, not sure if she should reload it or fling it out the window. It might become evidence in a case against her. No one would find it in a million years, way out here in the vastness of the wilderness.

The engine made a slight hiccup sound. She replaced the pistol in the holster and scanned the gauges. She tapped the oil pressure and heat. Both were out of sorts. She adjusted the throttle and propeller pitch, bringing the RPMs down slowly. Another hiccup and her stomach dropped.

She scanned outside, found the map beneath her wet butt and spread it out on her lap. The smell of ammonia was nearly overpowering. Nothing looked the way it should. "Crap, I'm lost."

~

ABBY TRIED to forget what had happened on the ground and concentrated on the here and now. She turned the radio back on and sent out an emergency call to anyone who might be listening. She heard only static in response. She tried a few more times before she had to focus on getting the airplane on the ground safely.

She'd drifted off course and inadvertently flown into a mountainous region chock full of deciduous trees in full fall plumage. She checked her altitude. With the engine overheating quickly, she knew she had to find a place to land soon or risk a fire. She saw no roads, and no fields. Panic nipped at the corners of her mind. She could feel it welling in the pit of her stomach.

She shook her head hard and uttered, "No! I can do this." She scanned the ground carefully. There had to be somewhere she could land, but she saw only endless forest and steep sloping hills leading to moderately sized mountains.

She studied her sodden knee map for a few moments but didn't see any mountains. She hastily unfolded the map and gasped when she found her likely position. She'd drifted at least a hundred miles off course. The timing didn't seem right, but winds could help carry an aircraft much farther than anticipated and she hadn't been in her head for the past twenty minutes.

She berated herself for the error, but what was done was done. She couldn't change that, no matter how hard on herself she was, so she stuffed her anger into the back of her mind.

She turned back south, hoping to get closer to civilization. Perhaps the engine would settle out long enough for her to find somewhere safe to land. She thought about her parachute strapped to her back. She didn't want to use it, but she may be forced to soon. She didn't relish having to crash through all those trees while dangling from a few shroud lines and silk. She knew how to use the contraption, but she'd never actually practiced. It wasn't something that was done routinely. *Unlike Clyde.*

She checked and rechecked her gauges. Nothing changed for long minutes, although the hiccup continued and she thought she smelled something burning.

She gasped when acrid smoke seeped into the cockpit and swirled and hung like cigarette smoke around her boots. Her throat burned and she coughed uncontrollably. She fumbled with the canopy and finally managed to unlock it and slid it open. The relief of fresh air had her taking huge thankful breaths.

Smoke poured into the cockpit faster and faster. Would fire be next? Undoubtedly. She had to do something now, before it was too late. She looked at the ground flashing by six thousand feet below. Still forest and rolling hills. She had no choice.

She cinched the parachute harness as tight as she could manage. Her urine had dried somewhat, but she could still feel the clammy mugginess of it in her pants. But that was the least of her worries.

She unlatched her seat restraints, careful to keep her parachute harness tightly strapped. The smoke thickened despite the open cockpit. She could hardly see her instruments. She wanted one last look at her altitude, but there was no time.

She hated to abandon the aircraft that had been entrusted to her care. Would they fire her? Could they forgive such a thing? She'd heard of other WASP pilots damaging aircraft, but no one had been forced to bail out. How would they ever find her? Perhaps it would be better to ride it down? There had to be some meadow somewhere down there. Perhaps she'd see it better if she were lower.

Fire licked into the cockpit. She felt the heat on her shins. She forgot her fear of the WASPs ire. She pulled up and felt the P-51 rise. She flipped it onto its back. She felt herself coming off the seat. She held onto the stick as though it might keep her there a little longer. She was reminded a time on a rope swing around a lake when she must let go and fall to the water or risk smacking the tree she'd leaped from. She'd hesitated, but then let go. This felt the same.

She released her grip on the stick and she fell out of the cockpit as easily as falling out of bed. That sensation changed a moment later when the wind hit her like a wall of bricks. She lost her breath as she tumbled and rolled. She glimpsed the aircraft lancing into the sky, a black smudge of smoke marking its path. How far would it go? What if it hit a house or caused a forest fire?

She marveled at her thoughts. She pushed them to the back of her mind and reached for the tab, which would deploy her parachute. She grasped at it and finally found it. For an instant, she only clasped it. Perhaps it would be better to simply fall to the ground. It would be quick, painless.

A scene erupted in her mind, almost like a movie. She saw Clyde dressed in civilian clothes. He smiled and looked the very epitome of health. Between his legs, he helped a little girl waddle side to side. She wore a new bright dress dotted with red and yellow flowers. She had curly brown hair and her chubby hands barely fit around Clyde's fingers.

She pulled the cord an instant later. The happy scene extinguished with a violent snap. She gasped, feeling herself being pulled apart momentarily. But it quickly subsided and she floated. She drifted side to side and the sensation made her smile. The sound of the wind and her own heartbeat mixed with the hum of the shroud lines.

Her elation only lasted a moment. She looked down between her feet and saw only thick forest. She grasped the shroud lines and held on tight. Despite the feeling of floating, the forest came up quickly. How long before she crashed through? What if she broke her leg or a branch skewered her and she died a slow, agonizing death? Would anyone ever find her body? Clyde would never know what happened to his bride. Perhaps the image she'd seen had been someone else's reality—perhaps another woman's child.

The thought angered her. No, she wouldn't die out here. She had too much to live for. This damned war had already wasted too much time. She and Clyde would have their chance to finally live—really live.

She remembered to cross her legs as the trees closed quickly. Now that she was closer, they didn't seem so dense. She saw tendrils of sunlight penetrating through to the forest floor in spots. Most of the leaves hadn't fallen yet.

Before she was ready, she smashed through the top of a giant tree. Branches snapped and she closed her eyes as the shroud lines caught and shook and jolted her body violently. She felt scrapes and gouges every-where. For one terrifying moment, she thought she was being torn to shreds, as though her body was falling through a meat processing plant, being turned to ground beef.

She finally stopped with a quick jolt, which snapped her harness tightly around her waist and legs. She gasped and gingerly opened her eyes. She saw the ground only ten feet below her swaying feet. The massive tree's trunk was inches to her right. The gnarled bark reminded her of an old man's skin who'd spent most of his days outside—deeply dark and mottled.

She finally caught her breath. She assessed her body. She felt pain everywhere, but nothing screamed for more attention than any other. She looked up and saw the parachute tangled and snagged hopelessly in the branches. It looked impossible to ever come unraveled. The tree and the shrouds and silk would live out the rest of their lives intertwined forever.

She felt wetness drip off her nose. She touched it and her hand came away bloody—very bloody. She panicked momentarily. Perhaps she didn't feel intense pain because she was in shock. She'd heard of such things happening. The body simply shut down when things became too much to bear. *Am I dying? Is this tree the last thing I see?* It wouldn't be too bad. The worst was past.

She hung there a few minutes. The sounds of singing birds and the light wind through the trees made her feel at peace. Perhaps she'd slip into unconsciousness and simply not wake up. A calm came over her, not exactly comfort, but calm. She closed her eyes. *Just for a moment.*

"No! Wake up!" she heard a vaguely familiar voice yell.

She opened her eyes, searching frantically for whoever the voice belonged to—they were so close. Right in her ear, but there was nothing and no one there. "Who's there? Is someone there? Trish?" Only the birds chirped in reply.

13

Abby sat on the ground beneath her shredded parachute, still tangled in the tree above her. The silk and shroud lines waved in the breeze, becoming even more a part of the tree. The silk seemed to wave at her.

It had taken all her strength to swing herself to the tree trunk, then with one hand clutching the tree and the other hitting the quick release in the center of her chest harness, she'd dropped to a thick branch. After catching her breath, she'd climbed down as close as she could get. She had to jump the final six feet. The short fall had crumpled her legs and she hadn't moved since.

Blood continued to drip from a scalp wound, but it had lessened. She probed the wound with her hands. A flap of skin covered a deeper cut. Her touch didn't cause pain, and that worried her in a distant sort of way.

She looked for the person attached to the voice she'd heard so clearly, but there was nothing but forest and bird song now. It must have been in her head, but it had sounded so real.

She suddenly had an overwhelming desire to drink. She touched her flight suit, hoping to find a forgotten water flask she'd placed in one of the many pockets, but all she found was a stick of chewing gum and a scrawled note she could no longer make out. Distantly, she realized she'd lost the pistol. The shoulder harness remained, but the .38 must've been lost during the jump. *Good riddance.* The thought made her giggle. If the authorities wanted to charge her with murder, they'd have to find her first, and that might be a feat beyond anyone's abilities.

The light shifted. She looked through the interlocked tree canopy and saw the evening quickly approaching. Soon it would be dark. Summer had recently passed, but the nights would be cold without shelter. She wore lightweight long johns beneath her flight suit. It had been more than enough in the comfort of the cockpit, but she doubted it would be enough to keep her warm through the night.

She forced herself to her feet. Her head spun and she leaned against the tree trunk. The bark felt coarse and dry, but she felt a subtle warmth there, as though the tree wished her luck. She patted it gratefully and took one last look up its impressive trunk. She'd broken many branches, scraped and scarred it, and even left it covered in tattered fabric and shroud lines, but she couldn't shake the thought that it had somehow protected her as best it could.

She leaned into it and hugged it like an old friend. She pushed away and shook her head. "I'm losing it." But she gave it one last pat. "Thank you," she uttered.

It didn't answer, which she took as a good sign.

The sun was setting, so she had a good feeling of direction. She angled south. How would she keep her bearings once night fell? Would it matter? If she didn't find help soon, she'd either die of exposure or of thirst. There had to be a stream nearby. Forests had streams. She'd seen countless in her many hours of flight. Surely she couldn't help running into one, eventually. But her southerly course moved her uphill. She could feel it in her knees. Streams and rivers would be in the bottom of the dips and ravines, not uphill. Perhaps she'd find a precipice and be able to see more of the land. She continued trudging along.

The going was relatively easy. The forest floor had brambles and thick sections, but for the most part, she found open spaces between. She weaved through trees and brush. Her flight suit caught on thorn bushes, but she pulled through. Sometimes the snags gripped and tore the fabric, but she paid little mind to such things. She concentrated on putting one foot in front of the other.

With each step, her thirst grew more urgent. It hadn't been that long since her last drink, but her tongue felt thick and gummy. She couldn't remember ever being so thirsty. She envisioned the thousands upon thousands of mud puddles she'd seen in wet Seattle, and the dirtiest and foulest cesspools made her crazy with lust. She imagined dipping her head into them as passersby watched her gulp great mouthfuls.

She didn't know when it happened, but suddenly it was dark. Had she fallen asleep on her feet? Fallen asleep as she walked? It didn't seem possible, but what else could've happened? Where had the light gone?

She checked her wristwatch in the dimness before remembering it hadn't survived her bailout. The frozen hands still marked the time it stopped performing its one and only function. Had she stopped functioning, too? Not yet.

She thought of the flashlight she always took on each flight. She wished she'd thought to shove it into her flight suit before bailing out, but then remembered the fire and the smoke. She'd barely gotten out of there unscathed as it was. Even if she had remembered it, there wouldn't have been enough time.

She frantically took in her surroundings. The light hadn't fled altogether just yet. She could still see well enough to find cover. Soon her most pressing need wouldn't be thirst, but warmth.

She stumbled a few more yards into the forest. She hoped for a cave or even a copse of rocks with overhead cover, but found only trees and brush. She came to a tree that had lost most of its leaves already. The ground surrounding what she thought might be an elm was covered in an inch of leaves. She went to her knees and piled them. She pushed them toward the base of the elm's trunk until she had a large pile. She hoped it would be enough.

She stepped into the mess and scrunched herself as deep as she could go, then pulled the leaves over her body. She stuffed some inside her flight suit and zipped it up tight to her neck. She thought of the bugs she'd invited close to her body. She wondered if she could eat them if it came right down to it, but she wasn't hungry enough yet—thirsty enough to drink from a mud puddle, but not hungry enough to eat bugs—not yet.

She settled her back into a fold in the trunk. The hard wood pressed deeply into her back, but she doubted it would matter. Fatigue overtook her body. Sleep would come no matter the discomfort—at least she hoped so.

She wasn't warm, but she wasn't cold either. She closed her eyes and felt herself relax. Would she wake up? She hoped so. She desperately wanted to see and hold Clyde again, but did she deserve to live? She'd as good as killed Trish and now that disgusting hick. *I'm a killer,* was her last thought before her body shut down.

$\sim$

SHE AWOKE with a start and did not know where she was or even who she was for a moment. She shook her head and pain met her like an old enemy. The darkness made her wonder if her eyes were open or not. She touched her eyelids to make sure, and the movement made her wince. But what had woken her? Something had made a sound nearby. Or had it? She had no sense of it other than it was close. Was it a deer? A rabbit? A bear?

Her mouth couldn't produce any saliva despite her best efforts. She shivered, causing little leaf avalanches. The tree trunk pressed into her back. The need to move was overpowering, but what if whatever she may or may not of heard found her out and devoured her. Fear fought for absolute stillness, but physical need finally won out. She leaned forward slowly from the tree trunk, relieving her back.

Her body had melded to the tree and moving felt as though her body reshaped itself. It felt awful and amazing all at the same time. How could that be? She felt a rush as blood coursed into the spots where the tree had tried to assimilate her body.

How long had she been asleep? It felt like a long time. The forest was absolutely silent. Not a bird or a cricket. The only sound came from her breathing and the soft papery vibration of leaves tumbling down her body.

Cold seeped into her backside where the leaves hadn't protected her. The cold tree trunk had done a poor job. She shivered, but willed herself to stop when she heard a step. It sounded close, just on the backside of the tree. But what kind of step? She couldn't place it, but it sounded bigger than a deer. Would she hear a bear's step? Surely their thick pads would dim the sound to nothing.

She imagined the man she'd shot coming for her. Perhaps it was his rotten apparition coming to take its revenge for killing him. Fitting end for a murderer.

The tree suddenly shook as though something had smacked into it from the other side. A smell of rot and corruption swept over her. She stopped breathing, all her senses focused on the night. What could it possibly be?

Long minutes passed, and nothing happened, although the smell diminished. Had she really smelled it or imagined it? Despite her alertness, she felt on the edge of sleep.

She hadn't heard footsteps leaving or approaching, and the tree remained stoic and still. She took breaths as quietly as possible, but her heart thudded in her chest like a crescendo orchestral piece with an inordinately large drum section.

She had no sense of time now. She supposed an hour passed, but it could just as easily been four hours or even a week. She slowly forced her tense body to relax ever so slightly.

Whatever it had been, it had gone. Perhaps she should investigate. But what good would it do in this inky blackness? A polar bear may sit there and she wouldn't see it. The thought almost made her smile. She yearned for daylight almost as much as a sip of water. But would a bear care if it ate her at night or during the day? Probably not.

The darkness felt deep, as though it might never end. Had she slipped into an alternate universe where only darkness thrived? A cricket chirped. It sounded louder than normal. The sound she always took for granted gave her hope. She was still here and at least crickets still lived. More joined the first until the night's grasp seemed to lessen.

She pictured the black insects stroking their legs, making the sound they'd made for endless epochs of time. She'd never been more thankful for sharing this world with them. She promised to never take them for granted again, for they vanquished whatever corruption had been lurking on the other side of the tree.

She adjusted her body flat on the ground and pulled more leaves around her, leaving her eyes free to gaze at the branches overhead. She could see spots of stars peeking through the treetops—another reminder of normalcy.

She fell asleep a moment later.

She opened her eyes what seemed only a moment later, but must've been longer. The all-encompassing darkness had given way slightly. She felt predawn in her bones. She shivered uncontrollably. The leaves had allowed her to fall asleep, but they could only do so much. The predawn chill, for that's what she convinced herself she felt, had seeped into her bones.

She curled into a ball, feeling her muscles ache and protest, but unable to do anything else. She tried to sleep more, but it wouldn't come. Her shivers kept her awake. If she could just fall asleep, everything would be alright if she just slept a few more hours.

"Get up! Move your body, Abby!"

She sat up as though a bolt of lightning had struck her. "Mother? Trish?" she stammered.

No response and no one loomed over her, but the words sounded so real and close. It couldn't be her imagination . . . could it?

She didn't want to, but she pushed herself to her feet. Her muscles screamed and she felt every scrape and bump she'd received from her ill-fated crash through the tree.

She felt her head and winced when the pain momentarily screamed louder than every other painful part. The flap of skin felt hard and the deep cut was lumpy with clotted blood. She must look quite the sight. She supposed any wild animal would consider her a wounded animal to be killed and eaten at their leisure.

She stepped around the tree, half expecting to find a bear or wolf waiting to devour her. She couldn't see much in the darkness, but she didn't see any sign of whatever had been there—if anything ever had been. She remembered the smell. It hadn't been her imagination. She'd never imagined smells before. Sounds—even sights—but never smells, and certainly nothing so rank. But whatever it had or hadn't been, it was gone now.

She couldn't see much, only the outlines of endless trees, but she sensed she should move before her body froze up and demanded sleep again. If she succumbed, she may never wake up again. She knew all about hypothermia's siren call to simply sleep. The WASP program had covered survival training to some degree. "I've nearly made it through the night. No need to sleep now," she muttered to herself.

"Atta girl."

She thought she saw a figure in the darkness just ahead. It disappeared behind a tree an instant later. "Trish? Trish, is that you?" But the figure was gone, making her wonder once again if she was losing her mind.

She went to the tree where she'd seen the figure and searched but only found darkness and more trees. She may as well go this way. She'd know more about direction once the sun rose.

"Okay, Trish, I'm coming."

Her throat clenched with thirst, and she choked when she tried to swallow. No moisture wetted her mouth. She croaked, "Could use some water, though." She hugged herself against the cold and kept walking. The leaves in her flight suit crunched against the thin thermal underwear. She wished she'd worn the heavier set, but it was still summer, mostly. "How can summer be so cold?" she whispered.

Dawn broke over her shoulder and she realized she moved west instead of south. She stopped and swayed on her feet. She turned to face the sun, hoping the distant rays would warm her face, but the dense forest kept the ground dark and cold.

"We're going the wrong way, Trish." She felt foolish, but she heard the reply clearly.

"Trust me, Abby."

She saw her then, glowing in the early morning light that wasn't quite there yet. She seemed to have her own glow, only no warmth emanated from her.

She reached for her, "Trish. Trish, that's west. We need to go south." She didn't know if she was actually speaking or communicating through her thoughts. Her throat didn't hurt or rasp, so maybe it was all in her head.

"Trust me, Abby."

The glowing Trish moved off west. Abby tried to catch up. She would've liked to have held her old friend's hand again, but when she looked again, Trish wasn't there, just early morning mists rising from the dew-wet ground.

Dew! She ran to the spot and dropped to her stomach, ignoring the pain. She swept her hand over the wet blades of grass and leaves and licked her fingers as though they were sticky with homemade ice cream. But this was so much better than anything she'd ever tasted. She licked blades of grass, but it wasn't enough to slake her thirst. She crawled along, working for each tiny lick of wetness. She finally collapsed and rolled onto her back.

"Time to go," Trish said.

Trish stood directly above her, her face just the way she remembered it. She even wore the old dock worker hat and she had that same crooked smile full of mischief.

"I don't wanna get up. I wanna rest here."

The face turned angry, but still glowed. "Now, Abby!" The voice blared in her head as though someone bellowed in a cave. Her voice bounced around like an echo chamber.

"Okay, Trish. Okay." She pushed herself to her feet and put one foot in front of the other. Trish stayed just out of reach and disappeared occasionally, but just when Abby thought she lost her, she'd reappear and wave her forward.

"Are you leading me astray again, Trish? I wouldn't blame you. I got you killed."

She shut her eyes but kept walking. If she hit a tree, well, so be it. She was so tired. She only wanted to rest, to slip into oblivion.

Right next to her ear, "Open your eyes, Abby."

She startled, but Trish wasn't there. It took her a moment for the world to come back into focus. But when it did, she thought she must be dreaming. A little stream of clear water burbled along a low cut in the forest. Massive trees with intricate tree roots hugged the banks greedily.

She staggered to the edge of the stream and fell to her knees. If it turned out to be a dream and she only sipped the air, it would kill her. But no, it was real. She drank deeply, feeling the water infuse her body with life. She'd never tasted anything even close.

She lifted her sopping head from the creek and saw Trish standing there in that low glow. "Thank you, Trish."

She smiled her wry, aw shucks smile, then faded and became not Trish but a stout tree. Abby bowed her head and drank deeply again.

~

ABBY DIDN'T STRAY FAR from the water. When the day warmed sufficiently, she stripped off her coverall, letting the leaves spill out like dried entrails. Careful to keep the clothing dry, she gingerly slipped into the cold water. She'd found a deeper pool able to accommodate her entire body. It was ice cold, but once she got used to it, she felt the water soothe her aching muscles. She washed the many cuts as best she could. Her head wound took more aggressive scrubbing, but by the end, she felt immensely better about things.

She stayed beside the creek until the sun shone directly overhead, or as near as it would get this time of year. She dressed and followed the creek wherever it led. She didn't have any way to carry water, so it would be better to keep it close. As near as she could tell, it ran mostly south.

Animals, including humans, lived near water. She did not know how to catch an animal and no way to start a fire to cook it, but perhaps she'd get lucky and come across a homestead. The thought of food made her stomach rumble.

She hadn't spotted Trish or heard or smelled anything out of the ordinary since before the creek. She'd almost convinced herself that it was all a figment of her thirst-addled mind.

She walked through beautiful, pristine deciduous forest for miles upon miles. She had hiked occasionally on well-marked and well-used trails near her home, but this was far different. She couldn't simply shut off her brain and know the trail would lead her in the correct direction. She had to stay vigilant. The only marker was the burble of the creek off her left shoulder.

Occasionally, the brambles near the creek became too thick to stay close. In those instances, she was forced to veer away, sometimes out of earshot. As soon as she found a break, she'd reestablish the creek before continuing her trek. When she became thirsty, she simply dipped her hand and drank deeply.

The creek grew steadily the further she followed it downstream. It would soon become a river if it didn't join one soon. She thought of it as her traveling companion, always there and always willing to slake her thirst.

She saw wildlife, but only darting shapes of deer and the skittering and complaining squirrels in the trees. She watched the squirrels running through the treetops like high-flying circus dancers. She could eat them if she could figure out how to kill them. But it seemed utterly impossible.

Despite her growing hunger, the thought of gnawing into raw flesh turned her stomach, even if she somehow managed to bring one down with a lucky rock throw. It didn't keep her from trying, though. It only made them titter at her more, as though laughing.

As the sun sank lower, she came to the edge of a field of solid grass. The meadow spread out like a green carpet. A light wind moved through, swaying the grass like undulating ocean waves. The creek meandered through lazily. She'd seen many such meadows and creeks from her airplane. They always looked accommodatingly pleasant.

Coming from the forest and into the wide open space felt like entering a new world. The sun felt warm on her face and she took a moment to simply face it with her eyes shut. The sweet scent of flowers added to the pleasure.

She scanned the skies, hoping to see or hear the dot of a passing airplane. Nothing, only wind and a mostly clear sky. Would anyone be looking for her yet? She'd be overdue by now, but it wasn't uncommon for WASP pilots to run into trouble and be stranded at some far-flung airfield. No alarms would sound just yet, unless they found the wreckage of the P-51.

Panic briefly coursed through her veins as she pictured rescue crews searching for her around where the aircraft wrecked. Perhaps she should've stayed with her parachute. What would signal rescuers better than a big white parachute? She might already have been rescued if she'd just stayed put. But no, she wouldn't have found the creek. She might be dead by now. Besides that, she didn't know how far the P-51 had flown before it finally pitched into the ground. Had it exploded on impact? Probably simply broke up in the trees. Without smoke, no one would ever see it. She suddenly felt lonely.

She stared up at the sky. The sun warmed her face and the meadow's swaying grasses sounded like mute conversation, as though it was trying to tell her something, but she couldn't quite decipher it.

She needed to find cover for the night. Something more than a tree trunk this time. She stepped into the meadow. Perhaps she'd find something on the other side.

At first, the buzz of mosquitos in her ears was a minor annoyance, but soon the little beasts assaulted her the way she imagined Japanese soldiers' banzai attacked. She slapped at them but soon gave up. There were simply too many. She moved faster, trying to get across the meadow before every drop of blood had been sucked from her body. It didn't seem like a far-fetched scenario.

About halfway across, her feet sank into mud. She tried to find dryer ground, but every step except backward turned wetter and sloppier. The mosquitos kept up their suicidal attacks. She veered away from the creek, her steps dictated by the dryness. Soon she found herself on the edge of the woods again. The mosquitos still buzzed, but they'd lessened the further from the creek she'd gone.

She sat on a log, untied her boots, and wrung out her wet socks. She did her best to dry them in the fading sunlight. She itched her neck and scalp like a crazy person. Some of the little bastards had even bitten her through her coveralls. Did they have iron proboscises?

In the distance, she saw a band of rocks sticking up from the forest canopy. She hadn't seen any distinct land masses except endless forest for the past two days. The sight made her giddy. Perhaps she could see something from there. She imagined seeing a town in the distance.

Her stomach rumbled and she felt a gnawing pain in her guts. But she'd have to leave the creek, at least for a little while. It would be worth it if it helped her situation, but her thirst would become an issue quickly. She desperately wished she had some way to carry water. She thought about returning to the water one last time for a drink, but didn't relish the thought of fighting endless swarms of mosquitos to do it.

She veered toward the rock outcropping and away from the water and the meadow. The forest wrapped its dark arms around her once again, as though welcoming her home after a brief time away.

She lost sight of the outcropping almost immediately, but she knew if she kept the sun on her left, she couldn't help running into it. Distances were hard out here, but she decided she could make it before dark.

She briefly wondered if she'd see Trish again . . . or something much worse. She shivered as she thought of the fetid smell of rot that first night.

~

ABBY DIDN'T KNOW how much time had passed, but she thought she should've found the rock outcropping by now. Long since, actually. But the only constant was the endless forest and the dying light.

She hurried her steps. It had to be close. She didn't relish another chilly night in the forest. The outcropping wouldn't be much better, but it would at least be under the wide open sky and not quite so crushingly close. Perhaps she'd find some cozy cave, perhaps an old hunting cabin with a wood stove and matches—some canned food.

The thought didn't help her hunger, but it kept her moving, despite her growing fatigue. She tried to ignore it, but her legs felt weak and her breathing seemed short, as though she'd been running instead of trudging.

She finally came to a large boulder. It seemed so out of place after the endless forest that at first she didn't know what it meant. A smattering of other boulders led upward through a scree field and above that, a large band of rocks spread out in a long cliff line.

She stepped out from the forest. She looked back at it and it seemed to want to hold onto her a little longer, as though she were betraying it in some way.

With each step, the day brightened as the forest canopy gave way to wide open skies streaked with wispy clouds, just coloring from the low sun. It felt as though an hour or two had been added to the day just by stepping from the cloying closeness of the forest.

She made her way through the boulders. She touched the gray behemoths as she passed, hoping to feel some leftover warmth, but they felt cold and unforgiving. She lost her footing a few times in the scree field but finally made the scramble to the cliff base. Now it was just a matter of finding her way to the top.

She searched for a route, but saw nothing obvious. It had looked so inviting from the meadow, like she could simply step up to the top without a problem, but from here, it looked impossible.

She moved laterally across the top of the scree field. She finally found a smaller boulder she could use to start her ascent. The first boulder led to another and another until she saw the route she'd take to the top. Her legs ached as she strained with each upward step. She raced the sun now, but she couldn't afford to fall and break her leg or even twist her ankle, so she concentrated on each step.

Finally, there were no more steps to take. She crested the top. Only then did she take the time to look around. The view would've stunned her during normal times. The sun hung over the horizon to the west, coloring the wispy clouds in red and orange. She could see in every direction. There were too many colors and combinations of colors to count. But the beauty didn't register fully, for she saw no signs of humanity. Nothing but the tops of trees.

She found the green meadow in the distance, but she couldn't make out the creek from here. It looked much closer than it actually was. She desperately wanted to drink from those waters once again. She collapsed onto the cold rock. Instead of hope, the endlessly gorgeous view held only despair. Nothing but endless forest in every direction.

Something skittered nearby and she saw a lizard doing mini-pushups as it studied her. Her stomach somersaulted, and she realized she'd eat the thing whole if she could only catch it. Would it poison her? She'd be willing to take that chance at the moment.

She forced herself to her feet. The lizard made quick darting movements, his escape route into the rock cracks never far away. "Don't worry, little fella. I won't eat you," but of course she lied. "May as well explore my new home," she uttered to the wind.

She walked around the front part of the rim. In spots, the cliff face dove straight to the scree field more than two hundred feet below. She wondered if the outcropping had a name. Surely it would be on her flight map, but the map was scattered somewhere in the forest's vastness. The thought lifted her spirits, though. At least she stood atop a named piece of ground, not just stuck in the middle of the massive expanse of forest.

Perhaps someone would think to look for her here once they realized she'd gone missing. It must be in the scope of the search. How could she signal someone? She wished for the hundredth time that she had grabbed her small survival pack before hurling herself from the P-51. The matches would've gone a long way toward her survival and even discoverability.

Smoke would draw rescuers like mosquitos to exposed skin. No use wishing for what she didn't have.

She soon found a small cleft in the rock. Beyond, she saw a small flat outcropping with sand and good cover from the wind. She carefully made her way through the cleft, then plopped onto the strip of sand. An ancient tree had tried to grow there sometime in the last millennium and left only a stout dead trunk jutting up from the rock. It looked like a twisted wizard's staff.

She grasped it and pulled. It moved a little, but it did enough to let her know it would come with a little more coaxing. Too bad about those matches. The wood would've burned through the night. She gave one hard yank and it finally gave up the tug of war and she hefted the stout staff in both hands. At the very least, it would make a fine walking stick, and if the bear, or the spirit, returned, at least she wouldn't be defenseless.

She sat on the sand. She ran her hands through it. It was nearly as fine as dust. It would be softer than lying on the bare rock and the tight walls would keep the wind off and perhaps unwanted critters. She sat with the stick across her knees and watched the color show as the sun set. It would be a long cold night, but at least she'd have the stars as company. Perhaps tomorrow she'd see about catching that lizard.

14

Despite the chill in the air, Abby slept on and off for a few hours. The sand molded to her body and she used a smooth rock as a pillow. It wasn't perfect, but she fell asleep quickly and only woke when her body shivered uncontrollably. She curled into a ball and tucked her back as far into the gap formed where the sand and a boulder met.

A few hours before dawn, she decided she'd had enough. She hadn't seen or heard Trish. She took that as a good sign; she only seemed to come out when she needed a kick in the pants. The bear, or spirit or whatever, hadn't come either.

She slithered her way out through the rock cleft and onto the top again. The wind cut through her thin layers of clothing. She wrapped her arms around herself and thought about going back into her sleeping spot, but she noticed the moon just coming up and she stared, transfixed.

She walked to the edge of the cliff and crouched with her arms wrapped across her knees. The wind lessened and she watched the world bathe itself in moonshine. The stars faded, leaving only the brightest visible. She supposed they must be planets.

She sat there, rocking back and forth until her legs went numb. She was cold, but comfortable somehow. The world seemed at peace. She only wished it were true. How many people gazed upon this same moon across the globe? How many struggled to survive or died violently in the past few minutes?

"Stay safe, my darling," she murmured into the night. She pictured Clyde in his paratrooper uniform, just before he shipped out. He looked so handsome, yet unassuming and modest. His arms full of hard new muscle wrapped around her body and held her so tightly she could hardly breathe. She closed her eyes and could almost feel his warmth.

She must've dozed off, for when she opened her eyes again, the sun had risen, turning the moon papery white, almost transparent, against the light blue sky.

The sun's rays felt good against her body. She slowly stood, unwinding from her crouched position. Her legs screamed in protest and she felt the blood rushing to them with pins and needles. Normally, the painful sensation was unpleasant, but out here, it reminded her she was still alive. She'd made it through another night.

Her thirst and hunger had been forgotten for a moment, but her stretched body reminded her. She had to find water today or she'd be in trouble. She looked longingly back to the meadow where the meandering streams crystal clear water flowed. Perhaps she should return and continue her trek along its lush banks. But then she wouldn't be able to see if someone searched for her. They must be searching for her by now. But what if they weren't? Could she afford to stay here in the hopes of being discovered? Or should she be proactive?

Her mind reeled with indecision. She felt fuzzy, as though she couldn't quite wake up from a nap which had lasted too long. She shook her head and the pain in her neck and the cut in her head cleared her vision momentarily, but it made little difference. She still didn't know what to do next.

She remembered the lizard. Soon it would come out to absorb the sun's warmth. Perhaps she could surprise it. At least it would give her something to do for a while.

She found the spot where he'd come from, a small boulder with a dark shadowy underside. She found a sizable rock and placed it on the lip of the boulder, then placed herself behind the rock in a crouch. She faced the sun and watched the crevice for any movement.

Clouds built on the horizon and soon a carpet of thin gray clouds threatened to encroach across the sky. Since becoming a pilot, she'd learned to estimate cloud cover height. The thin stratus sat at around ten thousand feet and wouldn't cause any problems for pilots searching for her, at least not yet.

She closed her eyes, allowing the sun's rays to hit her square in the face. It allowed little warmth, but some. It would tempt the lizard. Or perhaps he'd simply come out from another crevice.

She watched the shadows near the rock diminish second by long second. She grew more intent on her purpose. Then, the lizard appeared. It poked its head out gingerly, looking all around with its disproportionately large eyes. She sat hunched like a gargoyle. Would it notice her or think she was simply part of the landscape?

It took another furtive step out from the crevice and stopped. She could see its fine little feet just on the edge of the sunlight. It skittered forward a few inches and stopped in the full sun. Its belly stuck out from the sides and she could see it moving as though with each tiny breath. Its dark backside rippled slightly as the sun warmed it and she thought its eyelids lowered as though relishing the sunlight like a delicious food.

Her hands already rested on the brick-sized stone in front of her. All she had to do was push the stone and it would fall directly onto the basking lizard. She thought about eating it. She couldn't cook it, but she supposed it wouldn't matter. At least it would be something.

She edged the stone forward in microscopically slight movements until it only needed one more slight nudge. The lizard's head turned sideways. It looked at her, but it didn't move, simply stared. She pushed and the stone fell. The lizard skittered back toward the shadows, but not in time. The stone landed squarely on its back and rolled off, leaving behind a crushed lizard. Half the innards had come out its split side and its tongue stuck from the pallid mouth.

She'd done it! She'd killed her breakfast. She grasped the little corpse and held it up for closer inspection. The guts and blood left a little discoloration on the rock, but most of it came with the body.

She sniffed it. Thankfully, it had no discernible smell. Her stomach rumbled painfully. She inspected it carefully, not sure what she was looking for, perhaps a good place for her first bite. Perhaps it would be better to simply swallow it whole. It fit in the palm of her hand. It would be a mouthful, but if she was careful, she wouldn't choke.

Perhaps she should gut the thing, just eat the meat, but no, there wasn't much as it was. The organs would provide much needed calories. Despite her hunger, she still couldn't imagine eating it whole. The thought nauseated her. Perhaps cutting it in half would make it go down easier. Smaller bites, that's how she used to eat broccoli when her mother forced her to. At the moment, even broccoli looked more appealing than a raw lizard.

She held it by the tail and upended it so it hung over her open mouth. She hoped the guts wouldn't drip into her mouth before she was ready. *Just drop it into your mouth.* She closed her eyes, willing herself to do it, but every time she tried, the nausea grew. It would do no good if she simply vomited —in fact—she'd be worse off.

She cursed and stuffed the corpse into the shoulder holster deep inside her jumper. "I'll save it for later. As a last resort," she told herself as she buttoned her coverall.

Her stomach cramped and she bent over painfully. The pain made her writhe on the ground. It felt as though her guts were being torn out, just like the rock had done to the lizard. The cramps finally passed, but she stayed crouched and breathless, nervous to move too fast and cause them to return.

She unwound herself and stood on shaky legs. The sun dimmed as the cloud cover slowly took over the sky. A wild thought hit her—perhaps it would rain! The thought energized her and she explored the rocky top, looking for a place where rainwater would pool. She found a couple of likely spots, even noticing rings where moisture had dried in the past.

In her wanderings, she came across other interesting features. She found old scat from small beasts, likely rabbits and mice. Some was fresh, but most long since dried. A rabbit. Now that would be much easier to eat raw, and she knew it was safe to eat. But how to go about killing or trapping one of those?

She patted where the dead lizard sat in her coverall. She couldn't feel it through the shoulder holster, but just knowing it was there made her feel better. Perhaps she could use the lizard as bait for some other, more palatable animal. Did rabbits eat lizards? No, of course not, but perhaps they'd investigate a corpse? It was worth a try, but how would she kill a rabbit? They were far too skittish to use the same method.

Perhaps she could build some kind of trap. She thought back to her childhood. She'd trapped her cat in a trap once, but she'd used string, a box, and a stick. Well, the stick wouldn't be a problem, but everything else would need to be improvised. She remembered the stick she'd torn out of the soil where she'd slept. It would be powerful enough to kill most anything if she swung it hard enough.

She set about making plans.

~

ABBY LEANED down alongside the pool of rainwater and drank. Drinking this way always reminded her of how animals drank from pools, leaning on their haunches, bellies scraping the ground. It was fitting. She'd become more like an animal than she ever thought she'd be.

She wiped her mouth, savoring every last drop. It had rained for two days, filling the rocks with water wherever it could pool, but that supply was dwindling as the sun came back out and slowly dried things out.

Her hunger never left her. She'd long since abandoned her fear of eating lizard. She'd killed a few more and found them easier to eat in parts. She sawed their legs off and cut them in half with the edge of stones. It was messy work, but it made consuming them easier and slightly more palatable.

She'd also successfully cornered a rabbit, which had wandered into her sleeping area. At first, she thought she must be dreaming. It hopped in and simply stared at her with its incessantly twitching nose.

She slowly stepped in front of the cleft, blocking its only escape route, then whacked it to death with her walking stick. It had been brutal and taken a few whacks before it finally died. The human-like shrieks nearly made her stop, but her hunger won out.

She'd peeled the skin off and eaten the raw meat down to the bones. She even broke those and sucked the marrow from them. The heart she ate in a single gulp, but the rest of the guts she put out as bait for other animals, but they only seemed to attract bugs.

She'd killed three more rabbits in the same sort of way, but forced herself to parse out the meat to make it last longer. She used the soft furs to help soften the rock she used for a pillow.

All the days seemed to run together in her mind. She used a rock to etch the number of times the sun rose. She'd recorded 6 sunrises. She wondered how many more she'd have to endure before her luck finally ran out. The rain water would be gone soon, leaving her in an impossible situation. She couldn't stay here much longer, but she may never find her way out of the forest if she left, not to mention her chances of rescue would plummet in the forest. But it would be better than dying of thirst on this rock.

She sat on the edge of the cliff, looking out over the carpet of colors. She pulled a rabbit leg from her shoulder holster. It had become her food repository. The meat had dried and shriveled, but that made it easier to choke down. She devoured it, tearing off chunks, savoring every morsel.

She'd have to kill more beasts soon. How many could be left on this barren hilltop? She sucked the bones, then stuffed them back inside her filthy coverall. She figured she could use the sharpened bits of bone for something, perhaps a hook for fishing. Her shoelaces had already been used for setting snares, one successfully. She supposed the laces could tie to a bone-hook and the stockpile of rabbit guts would be good bait, but that would mean leaving the rocks outcropping and finding the creek again. Something she wasn't quite prepared to do yet.

She sensed something coming up behind her. She remained as still as the stones, listening for footsteps. But there was nothing but the wispy sound of wind over rock and brush. The feeling was unmistakable, though. Something approached.

She gripped the heavy stick next to her side. She turned quickly, bringing the stick up like a sword or bludgeon. Trish stood there with the sun at her back.

"Hiya, Abby."

"Oh, it's you. I thought it might be the bear again."

Trish had been visiting her on and off since her ordeal began. It no longer seemed strange to her. She turned from her friend and looked out over the forest again. A flight of crows rose from the treetops all at once, making a racket. Trish sat beside her without a sound.

"Wonder what's got them so worried," Abby said.

"Coming for you, Abby."

Abby faced her old friend, horrified. "What? Who, the bear?"

Trish didn't answer, only gazed at the startled crows.

Abby strained to see through the canopy of fall leaves. A tree shook some way off as though something large pushed past. Another, closer this time, shivered in the same way, dislodging more startled birds.

Abby gripped the stout staff. "Well, it won't take me without a fight," she said.

She felt the small bit of food hit her system and infuse her with energy. She could almost feel each calorie being processed, as though she stood on a factory floor watching skilled workers make widgets. The thought reminded her of Miles.

"I'm sorry what happened to Miles, Trish."

Trish didn't speak, only sat silently watching the forest in that soft glow.

Abby reached for her hand and felt an energy, but not flesh and bone. "I'm sorry I got you killed, Trish. I'm sorry I wasn't a good friend to you." If she had moisture to spare, she would've shed a tear, but nothing came. "I wish you weren't dead. But I'm glad you're here now, at the end."

Trish turned to her and smiled. "It wasn't your fault, Abby. You didn't kill me. It wasn't your fault."

Abby closed her eyes. The words she heard or the thoughts she heard in her head—she couldn't quite decide—hit her hard. She gasped and sobbed, but no tears would come. Her mouth felt gummy and dry.

She felt a heat in the pit of her stomach. It burned like fire and in her mind's eye, she pictured a tiny sun slowly burning its way through her guts. It rose and pushed to her spine. She convulsed in agony, dropping the staff and reaching for her back. She stifled a scream as the burning mass singed through her skin, hesitated a moment, then exited her body.

As soon as it left, she felt a lightness return to her body. The burning mass of guilt and shame had left a scorched path, but it mended quickly and she immediately felt better about everything.

Beads of sweat formed on her forehead. She looked at Trish, whose feral gaze turned back to something she recognized and loved. "Ah, Trish," she gasped. "Don't go."

"I have to, Abby."

"But the bear's coming."

Trish faded and the warmth Abby felt dissipated like evaporating water. She grasped for her, but it was no use. Her friend was gone and this time she knew it was forever.

She startled when the bear roared. Trees swayed and shook as it passed them quickly, beelining straight for the cliff face beneath her. She couldn't see it, but she saw its path as the trees shook wildly. Would it be able to scramble straight up the side?

She stood on shaky legs and gripped the staff. The bits of blood and fur from the slaughtered rabbits still clung to the heavy end. She'd killed before and she'd kill again. She thought about the man she'd shot as though in a dream. It seemed so long ago, like something from someone else's reality. What had become of him?

She spread her legs into a more balanced and ready position. The trees trembled with the coming tornado of claws and teeth. "Come on!" she roared. "Come on, you coward! I'm ready for you!"

The roar grew and grew like something not born of this world. She stood her ground, determined to fight to the death. She'd give no quarter and expected none.

A blue flash streaked through the air, seemingly only feet away. She ripped her gaze from the forest and tried to come to terms with this great blue albatross streaking through the sky.

∾

MANDY FLANNIGAN PEERED from the backseat of the Stearman trainer with binoculars glued to her face. She scanned the ground for anything which might give her a clue to where in the world her friend and fellow WASP pilot could be. *Where are you, Abby?*

She keyed the mic without taking her eyes from the binoculars. "No sign of her. Let's get to the next grid."

Wanda Uster, the pilot and WASP instructor, answered. "Roger, I'll head northwest to sector 6A."

Mandy checked the map strapped to her leg. "Confirmed, 6A is the next grid on our list." She sighed and mumbled to herself, "Show yourself, Abby."

As though she'd heard Mandy's lament, Wanda said, "Don't worry, we'll find our girl. 6A's approximately forty miles from the wreckage."

Mandy keyed the mic. "Think it's a long shot?"

"Not at all. It's been seven days since she went down and who knows how far the mustang flew before it went in. We've checked the obvious spots. This could be it."

Mandy scanned the thick forest below. "If she's down there, it'd be a miracle to find her. It's thick forest as far as I can see."

"I know, but . . . we'll find her somehow."

Mandy said, "Yeah, we'll find her." To herself she murmured, "If she even survived the bail out."

A hunter had spotted the aircraft wreckage while he was searching for a buck to shoot. He'd cut his trip short and reported the downed aircraft as soon as he could. A few hours later, the identity of the missing pilot was confirmed. The fact that she wasn't with the shattered aircraft led them to believe, or at least hope, that she'd bailed out. The P-51 had broken up on impact, but it hadn't burned, leaving the cockpit relatively intact, although scorched.

As soon as Mandy and the other WASPs not already out on missions heard about their missing sister, they dropped everything and started searching. It had taken a few hours to set up search grids and other logistics, but now no less than ten aircraft were out looking for her.

But looking down through the impenetrable forest canopy turned Mandy's guts cold. She couldn't imagine having to parachute into that mess. There was a good chance she'd bailed out over bare ground, but they'd covered that area extensively all along her flight path and they hadn't found anything.

"What would you be doing way out here?" she pondered to herself.

They'd found the aircraft wreckage way off course, but figured it had sailed after she bailed out. But the lack of any signs of her in the obvious areas made them broaden their search sectors. If she'd bailed out over this area, she might be dead, still hanging from a tree. They might never find her.

"Take us lower. If she's in this mess, I won't see her unless we're low."

Wanda nodded and pushed the nose down slightly. The Stearman dropped to six hundred feet and leveled off. "How's that? Better?"

"Yes, at least I can see bits of the ground now. Maybe she'll hear us and signal."

"Or maybe we'll see her parachute."

Mandy let the binoculars hang from her neck. From this lower elevation, they weren't helpful.

An hour passed. Mandy's eyes burned. She took a moment to rub the bridge of her nose. She checked the map again. They were nearly done with this sector.

As though reading her mind, Wanda keyed the mic and said, "Coming to the end of 6A. Just that bit of rock ahead, then we'll be onto 7B."

Mandy leaned over and looked ahead. She saw the large rock feature sticking out from the colorful forest floor. Despite the circumstances, she couldn't help appreciating the awe-inspiring autumn views—truly spectacular.

She checked her map. "I don't see that on the map."

"Me either, but I think it's called Cathedral Rock, or something like that."

"That's fitting. Take us around it so it's off the right wing."

"Roger."

Cathedral Rock grew in the windscreen as they approached. Wanda went lower, nearly the same height as the band of rocks. It was larger than she first thought. It would be a lovely place to hike to and have a picnic, if it wasn't in the middle of nowhere.

Mandy caught movement near the edge of the rock. She brought the binoculars up, scanned, and stopped. She could hardly believe her eyes. A figure stood on the edge of the precipice, holding a large stick as though readying for an attack. She couldn't hear words, but she had the feeling the figure was yelling into the forest below.

"There—there she is! Oh my God, that has to be her."

Wanda screeched, "What? Where?"

"On the edge. See her? She's holding a stick!"

Wanda edged closer and tilted the aircraft. They roared past the lone figure, who startled as though seeing them for the first time. The figure gaped at them as Wanda turned sharply back toward her.

Mandy nearly fell out of the aircraft she leaned so far out. "Abby! Abby! Abby!" she screamed and waved wildly.

Abby stared up at them with her mouth wide open. She turned slowly as they flew in circles around her. She didn't seem to recognize them. Wanda radioed in, barely able to contain herself. The airwaves lit up and soon a small squadron flew around Cathedral Rock.

Mandy studied the large flat rock. "I think we can land down there. We can pick her up."

"No way, Mandy. Too risky. Let the Moth do it."

"Give me the aircraft, then. I can do it." She reached for the controls.

"No, Mandy. We're too big and heavy. Don't be stupid. We'd only add to the problem."

Mandy knew she was right, but she desperately wanted to get down there and help her friend. Something seemed off with her. She still hadn't waved back at them, just kept watching and holding the stick like a swordsman. She must be delirious.

"The Moth's only a few minutes out."

"Then get higher and I'll parachute to her," Mandy insisted.

Wanda spun around in the cockpit and yelled over the din of the engine. "No way! Sit tight! She's fine!"

Long minutes passed. The small, lightweight Moth joined the mass of aircraft. The pilot made a few low and slow passes over the rock before finally deciding on the best place to land.

The pilot lined up and seemed to hover as it came down with full flaps, the airspeed just above a stall. It set down with a kiss, bounced a few times, rolled less than a hundred feet, then came to an abrupt stop.

The side door opened and a woman in coveralls ran to Abby. Only then did Mandy see Abby drop the stick and fall to her knees.

Mandy watched as Eberdeen Huss wrapped Abby in a hug. They remained like that for long minutes, before Abby finally stood and with

Eberdeen's help, staggered to the Moth. The pilot stepped out and ran to help.

Wanda's voice came over the radio, choked with emotion. "Eberdeen and Margie have her. She's okay, she's okay."

Mandy couldn't keep the flood of tears from streaking her cheeks. Minutes later, the Moth rose into the sky and the entire search party of aircraft escorted them back to the nearest airfield.

~

ABBY SAT in the back of the tiny Moth aircraft. She wore headphones and heard a flurry of women talking over one another. She could barely wrap her head around what had happened. One moment she was about to do battle with a bear that may or may not have been a figment of her imagination, and the next she sat in an airplane surrounded by old friends.

The voices coming over the radio vied for her attention, but she couldn't take it. She pushed the headphones off her head and put her face in her hands and rocked slowly back and forth.

Eberdeen put her arm over her shoulder and pulled her tightly to her side. The human warmth felt good, but she still didn't know if it was real or not. Trish had felt real enough, but she'd faded away like an apparition. Perhaps the bear had killed her and this was just a cruel joke.

Eberdeen pushed something against her side. Abby saw it was a canteen. She took it with shaky hands. Eberdeen helped her unscrew the lid and kept her hands steady as she raised it to her mouth. Abby felt the coolness course down her throat. She gripped the canteen as though it might be taken away. She emptied it quickly. Eberdeen provided another and she emptied that one too. She leaned back and wiped her mouth. If it was a dream, it was a good one. The water tasted as she imagined elixir from the gods would.

Eberdeen held out a chocolate bar with the wrapper already peeled back. Abby looked at Eberdeen, then back at the chocolate. Her mouth filled with saliva and she took a bite. She couldn't keep herself from quickly shoving the rest into her mouth. She closed her eyes in sheer ecstasy. Her stomach convulsed and she nearly vomited, but she kept it down. She looked out the side window. The vastness of the forest spread out beneath her like a multicolored carpet. She wondered if the foul smelling bear still sought her out. But that couldn't be real. This was real. The sweetness of the chocolate bar in her mouth was real, this aircraft was real, and her friends who'd rescued her were real.

The Moth touched down and taxied to a stop. The other aircraft followed them in. Abby stepped out from the Moth. Her legs felt unsteady at first, but she could feel the energy from the water and chocolate coursing through her like a freight train without brakes.

Margie and Eberdeen helped her walk, although she didn't feel she needed it. Soon she was swept off her feet in an enormous bear hug. Mandy swung her in a circle like a child. Abby laughed and finally felt like a halfway normal human again.

"Oh, Abby!" Mandy said. "We thought we'd lost you."

She finally released her and Abby let them all have a hug. Tears which wouldn't come before flowed freely now. Her friends had come for her. They'd dropped everything and come for her. She put her hand to her mouth and fell to one knee, unable to keep from sobbing.

15

Northern Philippines
November 1944

Frank Cooper crouched in the deep shadows cast by the jungle. A Japanese convoy trundled past. The armored car leading and the five trucks following passed only yards away from his hiding place. Filipinos holding rifles surrounded him. He cursed at the timing. His group was running late.

Grinning Bear crouched nearby. He spat a stream of spit onto the jungle floor. Once the last vehicle passed, Grinning Bear looked at Frank and raised an eyebrow.

Frank nodded. If the informant's information was correct, this convoy would turn into the fueling station soon. The informant's cousin worked at the refueling station, so he deemed the information solid. The only problem was, they were already supposed to be there when the convoy arrived.

He spoke with Grinning Bear, "We're behind schedule and they're ahead of schedule. We have to move fast."

"Yep," Grinning Bear replied.

They moved onto the road and trotted. The sound of the vehicles faded in the distance, but dust still floated in the midday sun. Frank pointed to three men. "Watch our backs." They slowed and held back. They didn't expect another convoy, but you couldn't be too careful. Ever since they'd rescued Constance's Uncle Mandio from beneath the Japanese's noses, the enemy had been more unpredictable. More patrols in bigger groups sometimes showed up at inopportune times. They'd had some close calls.

Frank double-timed and the others did the same. They didn't look like much, but Frank was proud of each and every one of them. They'd sacrificed safety and easy for danger and hard. No one had any doubts what would happen if the Japanese caught them holding rifles. If they were lucky, they'd be shot on the spot. If they were unlucky, they'd be tortured first.

It was only a matter of time before one of them was picked up by the enemy. That was the reason they were out here now. They needed more weapons and ammo. They needed to be ready when the Japanese finally came for them. None of them thought they'd be safe for much longer on their little island refuge. Eventually, the Japanese would come.

The twenty-man squad of Filipinos, including Frank, Gustav, and Grinning Bear had left their home base a few days before. They'd moved mostly at night. They'd seen increased enemy activity, but had been able to avoid them by sticking to the thick jungle. Because of the increased patrols, they'd lost some time.

It felt odd being out in the open in broad daylight, running down the middle of a dirt road—far too exposed. But what choice did they have?

Baredo, the one with the cousin at the fueling station, spoke with Gustav. Gustav nodded and relayed the information to Frank. "He says the station is just up ahead. It usually takes about an hour to fill all the trucks."

"Good, we'll have plenty of time to get into position," Frank said.

They trotted along the road in single file, Grinning Bear in the lead. Frank kept glancing back. If another convoy, or even just a single command car came barreling around the corner, they wouldn't have much time to get to cover. They'd have to engage and the whole operation would fail. They only had one thing going for them, surprise.

Grinning Bear slowed, then held up a fist and went to a knee. He signaled for them to stay put. He crept forward to a curve in the road. He disappeared around the corner for a couple of agonizing minutes. He returned and signaled them toward the jungle and cover.

Frank signaled and they moved off the road. He'd chosen the best men for this mission and they seemed to know what they were doing.

Once again in cover, Grinning Bear whispered, "I saw the station. It's just ahead, around the corner. Most of 'em are stretching their legs. They're spread out all over the place."

It's how they figured it would be based on Baredo's cousin's description of how things went during these fill ups. "We'll have to be careful getting into position, but we should have enough time."

Frank smelled the station before he saw it. Gas and diesel fumes wafted through the jungle. He heard voices and laughter. The two big fueling tanks loomed large. He crouched and took it all in. The station was laid out exactly the way it had been drawn up on the sand table.

Two trucks at a time fueled up. On top of the big gas tanks, a Filipino cranked a hand pump. It was slow, but steady. Frank wondered which man was Baredo's cousin. He supposed the cousin must wonder where the hell they were. He knew they planned to hit the convoy, but that was all.

The others streamed past him. A trail just inside the thick jungle kept them hidden. They could see the trucks and enemy soldiers easily, but they wouldn't see them unless they came into the jungle. Frank counted thirteen Japanese soldiers. Two per truck, plus the three in the armored car with the mounted machine gun. He really wanted that machine gun.

The last Filipino passed, it was Antonio. Since they'd fought, there hadn't been any more trouble between them, although Frank still didn't entirely trust him. He followed Antonio along the path. They moved slowly and in absolute silence. He could feel the tension in the air. They'd trained the Filipinos as best they could, but they were still just regular folks, not military men. Being this close to the enemy would make even the most salty veteran nervous. He just hoped and prayed no one accidentally placed too much pressure on a trigger. That machine gun would chew them up.

Grinning Bear led the way. He finally stopped and crouched. The fuel tanks stood on stilts only yards from their position. Frank could smell the sweat from the Filipinos working the hand pumps mixed with the fuel. Japanese soldiers hung in groups, some smoking cigarettes, others keeping to themselves. The officer from the armored car watched the refueling process with his arms crossed. He scowled at the Filipinos as though it might make the process go quicker. He'd be the first to die.

Frank didn't like being this close, but he didn't have a choice. A solid wall of jungle at his back kept him on the trail. Baredo assured him the trail was well hidden, and he was right. It just felt wholly unnerving to be this close.

The Filipinos pulled the hoses from the trucks and held them ready for the next two trucks. The officer barked and two soldiers leaped into the fueled trucks. The engines roared to life and spit bouts of white smoke from the exhaust pipes. The noise would cover any sounds of their movements.

The trucks rolled forward and around the armored car until there was room for the next two. They parked and shut down the engines. The soldiers sprang out and quickly moved away from the officer, rejoining their comrades.

The Filipinos began fueling the next two trucks, but not before the nearest man turned and stared into the jungle, no doubt looking for his wayward cousin. Frank cursed to himself. The fueler stared way too long for his liking. Had he seen them? It didn't matter, he just wanted him to turn back to his job before the officer noticed.

Frank nearly choked when Baredo waved. The Filipino beside him jabbed him hard in the side and he stopped. The cousin grinned and turned back to his task. Frank watched the officer. He didn't appear to have noticed anything. The officer tore his eyes from the fuelers and picked at his cuticles. Frank breathed again. He exchanged a harried glance with Grinning Bear.

Twenty minutes later, the two trucks finished fueling. When the engines started, Frank stood and waved the men forward. Like they'd planned, the officer and the men in the armored car would need the most attention, so they needed to move forward and the engine noise provided the best opportunity.

The final truck moved to the forward-most tank. Baredo's cousin called to the other Filipino fueler to take over. He looked annoyed, but he scampered to the forward tank and took over the pumping. Baredo's cousin hopped from the tank and absorbed the landing with a deep knee bend. He smiled broadly at the Japanese officer. The officer scowled back in disgust.

To Frank's horror, the cousin stepped into the jungle where they hid. He stood there only yards away and took a leak. Baredo went to him and they exchanged quick words. Baredo smiled broadly, as though it was the greatest lark ever.

Frank watched the officer closely, barely breathing. At first, the officer watched the Filipino with interest, but when his intent was obvious, he shook his head and muttered to himself, obviously disgusted with the Filipino's crass behavior.

The cousin looked up and down the line of resistance soldiers. His smile only grew. He finally finished his impressive stream of urine. He shook and tucked things back into his pants. He turned back to the fuel tanks.

Frank nearly choked when the officer barked at him and strode with purpose to him. He unlatched the snap, keeping his pistol in place. He didn't draw, but the meaning was crystal clear. Baredo's cousin lifted his hands as though in surrender. He spoke quickly in pidgin. The officer's voice rose over him and soon he was yelling into the Filipino's face. The cousin lowered his head, but didn't go to his knees, which was clearly what the officer wanted.

The other Japanese soldiers watched the scene unfolding. Most grinned, relishing the cruelty, but a few looked as though they were just happy it wasn't them being abused. The officer smacked the Filipino across the face with an open palm. The harsh smack reverberated through the ranks.

Frank wanted to wait until the soldiers were back in their trucks before attacking, but things were getting out of hand quickly. He could feel the anger and hatred growing in his men. No one wanted to standby while one of their own was beaten, not while they held the means to end it in their hands.

Frank stood, bringing his rifle up. The altercation was happening right in front of him. The others followed his lead. He doubted they would've waited more than a few more seconds, anyway.

He quickly pushed through the thick wall of jungle where the cousin had pissed. The officer reared back when he saw the jungle suddenly come alive. When he saw the barrel aimed at his face, his mouth opened in disbelief.

Frank gave him a wry grin before he shot him through the head. He dropped like a sack of rice. For an instant, only the echo of the shot and the sound of the officer collapsing filled the space. Then the rest of the squad stepped into the space and opened fire.

Frank reloaded a round and ran to the armored car. The young soldier standing near the mounted machine gun had just turned the weapon onto them when Frank shot him in the chest from only a few feet away. The soldier spun off the gun and fell on the other side of the car.

The element of surprise quickly vanished as the Japanese soldiers not hit in the initial onslaught, which was most of them, came to their senses and found cover.

Grinning Bear crouched beside the armored car. He rose and fired, dropping a soldier who'd stuck his head out too far from beside the truck.

Frank launched himself into the back of the car and swung the machine gun around. He felt desperately exposed. Four enemy soldiers could see him clearly as they hunkered beside the truck on the opposite side from the Filipinos.

Frank leveled the machine gun and pulled the trigger. Nothing happened. The Japanese brought their rifles to bear. Grinning Bear lunged into the car. He racked the top bolt of the machine gun. "Now! Fire!"

Frank pulled the trigger and the machine gun spewed hot metal into the Japanese soldiers. They spun and reeled as bullets shredded their bodies. Frank kept firing until the small box of ammunition emptied.

"Don't hit the trucks," Grinning Bear was yelling into his ear.

"Empty!" Frank yelled back.

The remaining Japanese soldiers scrambled for cover from the machine gun, but it did them little good. The Filipinos swept around the trucks and fired point blank into them.

Grinning Bear reloaded the machine gun and slapped Frank's back. "You're back up."

Frank looked over the smoking barrel, but only saw downed soldiers and his own men.

Grinning Bear tapped his shoulder and pointed. "There! They're making a break for it."

Frank shifted the barrel to two fleeing men. They'd dropped their rifles and sprinted like Olympic athletes, or men running for their lives. Frank lined them up and fired a short burst. The men tumbled forward in the dust and didn't move. It was over. Frank felt exhilaration sweep over him. He thought they had a fifty percent chance of success, but they'd done it without sustaining a single casualty. "Holy shit, we did it!" he exclaimed.

Grinning Bear said, "You sound surprised."

"Aren't you?"

"A little."

The Filipinos realized they'd won. They raised their rifles over their heads and cheered as though their favorite team had just scored the winning goal. Frank couldn't keep from smiling. He let it go on for a few seconds before he yelled, "Okay, okay! Get the bodies off the road. We leave in five minutes."

Gustav repeated the orders for those non-English speakers. The frivolity died down and soon the squad was hard at work, although most of them still smiled and congratulated one another, no doubt talking about the parts they'd played.

Baredo and his cousin approached. Baredo said in broken English, "This is Luisito, my cousin."

Frank held his hand out to him. "Thank you for your help." Baredo slapped his cousin's back, pride exuded from his broad smile.

The cousin shook Frank's hand with both his own. "We help win," he said.

"Yes," Frank nodded. "Will you be okay? You must leave the area. The Japs might come for you."

Baredo and Luisito turned serious. Luisito said, "Yes. I join."

Frank's smile faded. He needed men like Luisito to keep feeding him information about targets, not by his side as resistance fighters. He had enough of those. "No," Frank said.

Luisito's face dropped. He looked confused.

Frank continued. "You stay and find out more about the Japs. We'll kill more that way."

Baredo looked crestfallen as well. He squeezed his cousin's back. They spoke in lowered tones, their heads pressed to one another. Luisito's smile returned. He looked Frank in the eye and nodded. "Okay," he said.

Frank broke away. He raised his voice to his men. "Okay, turn these trucks around and mount up."

Gustav translated. It didn't take long before they led the convoy in the opposite direction. Frank rode in the passenger seat with his rifle at the ready, while Gustav drove, and Grinning Bear manned the machine gun.

~

THE STOLEN convoy of trucks driven by the Filipinos, trundled down the dirt road at a fast clip.

Gustav drove the small lead vehicle too fast for Frank's liking. Every sharp curve that Gustav took too fast made Frank grip the seat harder. He nearly told him to slow on a number of occasions, but he understood the need for speed. The longer they stayed on the main road, the greater their chances of running headlong into more Japanese.

Grinning Bear held onto the machine gun handle and swung side to side with each turn. He flexed his legs when the car bounced over potholes with jarring regularity. Frank worried he'd be thrown at any moment.

"How much further?" Frank asked on a rare straight stretch with few potholes.

"A few more miles. It's a narrow road to the left. It will take us to the village," Gustav replied.

Everything was happening according to plan—well, almost. The ambush hadn't gone off the way he'd imagined. But a win was a win.

They'd stashed the vehicles in an out of the way village. They chose it for its remote location and little to no Japanese presence. The Japanese had only visited the village a few times. Even before the invasion, the village was considered somewhat backward, but the residents hated the Japanese as much as the next Filipino, and were overjoyed to help in any way possible. The trick was getting there before they discovered the theft.

Frank checked his watch, but there was no need. There wasn't a set schedule, just a vague timeline. He concentrated on hanging on as Gustav nearly went up on two wheels.

Frank glanced back. The trucks were out of sight. They'd have trouble keeping up with the smaller vehicle. He didn't like all the dust they put up, but it couldn't be helped.

As they approached a corner, Grinning Bear and Gustav both exclaimed simultaneously, "Shit!"

Gustav slammed the brakes, sending them into a hard skid. Frank saw himself careening straight toward the grill of a troop truck. He thought he'd be smashed between the car and the grill, but Gustav corrected and the car fishtailed around the vehicle, missing it by scant inches.

Grinning Bear had dropped and held onto the stout metal pole bolted to the floor, which the machine gun rested upon. When Gustav brought the car to a halt in a cloud of dust, it faced the back of the troop truck. Grinning Bear rose and primed the weapon with a solid clunk.

The truck they'd narrowly missed slowly came back into view as the dust settled. The canvas top had been pulled off, making the truck look as though it had ribs.

A few Japanese soldiers who'd been sitting in the back now sprawled on the floor. The soldiers gingerly came to their feet. They didn't instantly react when they saw the armored car. For a moment, the two parties stared at one another. One Japanese soldier raised his hand in greeting, but his face changed to horror when, instead of other Japanese soldiers, he saw Caucasian faces and the machine gun muzzle.

Grinning Bear opened fire. Frank cringed and threw himself out the side of the car and hugged the ground. Spent shell casings rained down on his back, and a few found their way under his shirt. He rolled away, batting at the burning pieces of metal.

Grinning Bear kept the hammer down for what seemed like a long time, but was less than thirty seconds. Frank gazed at the truck. It had multiple bullet holes. Bodies were strewn everywhere, tangled up with one another. A stream of blood ran down the open tailgate and dripped to the dusty ground.

"Jesus Christ," Frank exclaimed.

The truck driver's side door opened with a rusty squeak. Grinning Bear adjusted his aim, ready to mow down whomever showed himself. A bloody soldier staggered out. He fell to his knees and gagged. He glanced back at them and the fear and anguish on his face gave Frank pause. Grinning Bear didn't fire. Frank was glad about that. He seemed more like a scared kid than a soldier of Imperial Japan.

The rest of the convoy rounded the corner. The lead truck ground to a halt, sending up another cloud of dust. Three Filipinos burst from the passenger side door. They ran forward a few feet until they cleared the dust. They saw the staggering soldier. All three raised their rifles, took aim, and fired.

The bullets passed through the driver, and he dropped without another sound. The killing bullets slammed the ground around the armored car. One ricocheted and tore the back tire to shreds. The armored car slumped to the side.

Grinning Bear barked, "Cease fire, dammit! Cease fire!"

Gustav stepped from the stricken vehicle and yelled in pidgin. The Filipinos looked at one another as though being scolded by the headmaster from primary school.

Gustav kneeled beside the blown-out tire. "We have to change the tire." He went to retrieve the spare mounted on the back. He cursed in German, "Schiesse, it took a hit, too."

Frank dusted himself off. "Well, that's it for this one, then."

Grinning Bear was already dismantling the machine gun from the mount with tools he'd found in the glove compartment. "I'll have this bitch off in a jiffy."

"I'll grab the ammo," Frank said.

The Filipinos sorted through the dead soldiers in the back of the truck. They took their weapons and ammo and anything else of value they found. A Filipino tried starting the truck, but it only whined, then stopped making any noise at all. They left the bodies in the back and, with the help of the armored car, pushed it as far off the road as they could manage. The bare metal wheel from the armored car left deep gouges in the road.

After pushing the truck, Gustav drove it into the jungle as far as it would go before it lurched to a stop. The Filipinos went to work, camou-flaging the two vehicles the best they could.

Frank hurried them along. "Come on, come on. It'll have to do. We gotta go."

They crammed into the trucks. Frank eyed the stowed vehicles as they drove away. They stuck out like sore thumbs, impossible to miss. "The next Jap patrol will find 'em for sure."

Grinning Bear nodded. "They woulda found the Jap bodies back at the fuel depot, anyway. Just a matter of time."

"Yeah, just hope the village is far enough away from it all, otherwise they'll be in for some trouble. Japs won't leave any stone unturned after this."

Gustav had taken over the driving duties of the lead truck. He seemed to enjoy driving, even though he did it like a maniac. He said, "You're worried about them?"

"Of course I am."

"They can take care of themselves. I have told you this before. They know sacrifice and are willing to pay the cost for their freedom."

"I know, I just don't like it."

Grinning Bear added, "We can't save 'em all, Frank. We're gonna lose a few."

Frank's thoughts went to Constance. She'd be waiting for him at the village. She and her uncle Mandio had friends there. They'd been the ones who mentioned it as a possible spot to stash the vehicles. He looked forward to seeing her, but wished she'd remained back on the island with Neil and the radio.

He thought about sending her back, but doubted she'd listen. He didn't blame her; she wanted to fight the Japanese as much as the next Filipino. Even if she'd listen, he couldn't deny her the chance to take her revenge. It would be the same for him if this was happening in the U.S.

The terrified eyes of the Japanese soldier who'd been driving the truck suddenly filled his mind. He'd looked so young. How would Constance react if she saw such butchery? He thought about American women. They'd be repulsed by it all, but the more he thought about Constance, the more he doubted her response would be much different from the men who'd gunned him down. If she'd been in the situation, would she have added her own bullet? Probably.

Far too soon, they came to the road leading toward the village. Gustav yanked the wheel, barely slowing down. Frank barely saw it before Gustav cranked the wheel. He wondered how the men in the back of the truck fared. Even sitting in front where there were plenty of handholds was difficult. Riding in the back would be murder.

He looked back and saw the other trucks following. This road was much narrower than the main one. Vines and brush scraped along the side of the trucks, making an awful squeaking racket, but Gustav barely slowed. The truck bounced even more as the road turned more into a trail than a road.

Gustav finally slowed when the road climbed steeply and became a series of hairy switchbacks. The final switchback was so severe, the men jumped out of the trucks for fear of tipping off the cliff edge. The big trucks barely had enough room, but they all made it.

"The village is another half mile," Gustav stated. "No more switchbacks."

"Thank Christ," Frank murmured.

16

Frank finally relaxed. The trucks had been stashed and camouflaged sufficiently. The villagers had carved out recesses a couple hundred yards from the village near a band of cliffs. The jungle wasn't excessively thick, but the cutouts reminded Frank of a large garage. The trucks would be invisible from the air and the only way enemy troops would find them would be if someone led them directly to them.

Frank had little fear of that happening. The Filipinos here were poor, but he sensed their commitment to the cause immediately. They greeted them like conquering heroes, showering them with food and drink. Frank accepted their kindness, but knew they must be pushing the village stores to the limit.

Children of all ages flocked around them, particularly Frank and Grinning Bear. They couldn't get enough of the Americans. They'd dart in and touch their leg or hand, then dart away giggling like crazy people. Soon, they lost their shyness and stayed close to them wherever they went. It reminded Frank of a group of ungainly puppies, always in the way.

The parents finally shooed them away, but a few lingered on. One little boy, in particular, took an immediate liking to Frank. He smiled up at him and even saluted like a proper soldier. Frank saluted him back and the boy hugged his leg fiercely.

The trucks proved to be a boon of ammunition and even weapons. A crate of Japanese Arisaka rifles and many boxes of ammunition for them would keep them in business for the foreseeable future. There was also another Nambu heavy machine gun and two light machine guns, both with enough ammunition for a sustained firefight. Two boxes of grenades filled out the stash.

He hadn't seen Constance yet. He didn't inquire to her whereabouts because he didn't deem it appropriate. Mandio finally took mercy on him and told him she would be back shortly. She was off with other resistance members, making sure no enemy had followed them. Frank acted aloof, but he doubted he fooled anyone.

With the trucks stowed and their bellies full, the squad members were ecstatic that only a close brush with death can bring. Frank worried about Constance. He wouldn't be able to relax until she returned, but everyone else was ready to celebrate their success.

Grinning Bear stood beside him. "The men are waiting for you."

"What? What do you mean?"

"They did a good job. They're ready for their commander to tell 'em so. Look at 'em, Frank."

They milled about, stealing furtive glances at him. Frank had never seen them this way. They normally did whatever they wanted once they were off mission. "Well, I'll be damned. They're acting like soldiers more and more."

Grinning Bear agreed, "Yep, and they're ready to celebrate."

"Well, what the hell am I supposed to do? Make a speech? They did what we asked of them. They're not all gonna work out that well. You know that as well as I do, Larry."

Grinning Bear shrugged. Frank's shoulders slumped. "Okay, okay."

He put two fingers in his mouth and gave a sharp whistle. The squad gathered around, with the villagers filling in the gaps. Gustav stood with his arms crossed, ready to translate, but many would pick up on his words without his help.

"Men, we had a successful mission. We hit the Japs without losing a single man. I'm honored to fight alongside each and every one of you. The ammo we stole will help us kill many more Japs." Gustav spoke after each pause. Frank continued. "You've all earned the right to celebrate."

Gustav's voice rose with the last bit, and a raucous yell erupted. Rifles raised and pumped up and down in jubilation. Some were brand new Arisaka rifles. Frank was happy to see that no one fired off any rounds.

Frank looked at Grinning Bear. "How was that? Good enough for you?"

"Good enough," he said in his signature growl. "Real inspiring," he added. Frank noted the sarcasm. The men whooped and congratulated one another. Frank couldn't help smiling. A group of Filipinos emerged on the road. He saw Constance's slight frame. The rifle she had slung over her shoulder was almost as tall as she was.

A group of celebrating Filipinos noticed them. They surrounded them, slapping backs and laughing. Antonio went to Constance and lifted her off her feet in a hug. She laughed and threw her head back. Frank immediately felt a surge of jealousy. It was ridiculous. She'd told him over and over that she considered Frank her man. Frank knew Antonio meant nothing to her, but it still made him uncomfortable.

He rushed through the throngs of Filipinos. Some slapped his back as he passed, praising his leadership, but he ignored them, his only focus on Constance and Antonio.

After a full spin, Antonio put her down. She stepped away from him, somewhat breathless. Her hands lingered on his muscular arms a few seconds longer than Frank liked. Did her eyes have a hint of desire? He couldn't decide.

He suddenly felt awkward. It made him angry. Why should he feel this way, after everything he'd already been through? He crushed the urge to pummel Antonio again. This wasn't the way he'd pictured being reunited with her. He should be the one hoisting her and hugging her.

He stopped a few feet from her. He crossed his arms and raised his voice to Bartholomew standing next to her, an older Filipino who'd led the group. "Did you see any Japs?"

Bartholomew snapped to attention. He shook his head. "No sir. Nothing."

Frank pursed his lips. "Good, good. Get you and your men settled." He gave Constance a sidelong look.

"Yes, sir," Bartholomew answered.

Constance's eyes lit up, and her smile broadened when she saw him. He desperately wanted to hug her, but his emotions wouldn't get out of the way. He'd long since given up trying to hide their relationship, but he couldn't shake the image of her grasping Antonio's arms.

She ran to him and wrapped her arms around him. Her body felt warm and soft. She looked up at him with her simmering eyes. She hadn't looked at Antonio that way. He finally gave into her charms. He hugged her back.

"My warrior," she cooed.

How did women do that? How could they hurt you one instant, then make you feel like the only man in the world that mattered the next?

"Were you careful?" he asked slowly. She'd become much better at English in the weeks since their meeting.

"No," she said, and her eyes sparkled with mischief. "I want to kill Japs. No careful."

He slung his arm around her shoulders, and they walked into a shady spot. The rest of the squad carried on as though it was the most normal thing in the world for their commander to be intimately involved with one of his soldiers. Antonio let his gaze linger a few seconds longer than the others.

She drank water from the canteen he offered. She gulped it down hungrily. The little sounds of her swallowing made him relish her even more. Was it just a wartime infatuation? He had little experience in such things, but it seemed like more than that. It seemed real and deep. But did she feel the same way? Part of him eschewed the question. *Just enjoy it while you can.* But another, more practical side said, *she'll break your heart one way or another.*

Gustav approached and pulled him from his musings. Constance draped over Frank's arm and stroked his back, sending shivers up his spine.

Gustav gave her a nod, then addressed Frank. "I need to return to the island."

Frank gave Constance an apologetic look and pushed her off him gently. She stuck out her lower lip, but unwound herself from him. She kissed his cheek and left him with one last sultry look before joining the others in celebrating.

"She's a fine woman, Frank."

"I know," he said as he watched her little butt swing side to side for his benefit.

"I am overdue for checking in with HQ. They'll want to know of our progress."

"You can finally report something positive."

"Yes, I'm sure they will be pleased."

"It wasn't the dock, but anything helps, I suppose."

Gustav said, "It was not what they intended, but now that we have more weapons and ammo, we will be more effective. We can achieve the mission easier now."

"I still don't like it, though. I felt safer on our little island."

"We are halfway between the island and the harbor. It will make a good staging area."

"I just wish we had a radio."

"We have the next best thing . . . runners. I will keep you informed."

"I know, I know. I'll send a few men back with you as escort."

"No need. I know the routes better than most Filipinos. I will be better off alone. Remember, Baredo and Bartholomew know this area and have many connections. Family connections."

"The best kind," Frank said.

"Yes. I do not fear treachery. I will send word when I receive orders for you." He waved at Grinning Bear as he approached.

Grinning Bear sidled up and spit a string of tobacco juice. "You heading north, Gustav?"

"Yes, old friend."

"Well, keep your head down and your powder dry." Gustav gave him a confused look. Grinning Bear cleared things up. "Be vigilant, Gustav."

"Yes, of course. You do the same."

∽

FRANK HEARD the loud footsteps on the stairs leading to the hut he shared with Constance. It was still pitch dark outside. It had to be at least 2A.M. Constance's soft breath tickled his chest hairs. He relished her warm body tangled up with his own. They'd made love before falling into a deep sleep, but now something was happening.

He sat up and Constance gave a slight whimper of protest before her breathing returned, steady and deep. He couldn't remember the last time he'd slept as deeply as Constance seemed to do routinely. She was a marvel in more ways than one.

He went to the door and picked up his rifle, where it leaned against the wall. He stepped out and Antonio stood there with a few others from his squad. At first Frank thought it might be something about Constance and it spiked his adrenaline.

But that quickly faded when Antonio said, "Japs are on the road."

"Shit. How far out?"

Antonio's younger brother, Elano, said, "A few miles. They approach the first big turns."

Frank understood what he meant, the first switchbacks. Frank cursed to himself as he quickly thought things through. "How many?"

"About fifteen on foot."

"Okay, wake everybody up. Assemble in the center of town ready to go."

The four of them hustled away to do his bidding. He glanced back to where Constance still slept. He thought about waking her, but decided he'd let her sleep as long as possible.

Grinning Bear came out of the night like a ghost. "What's going on?"

"A squad of Japs are at the start of the hill."

"On foot?" Frank nodded. Grinning Bear asked, "What d'you wanna do?"

Frank knew the Japanese would come eventually, but he'd hoped they'd have more time. He hadn't had time to fully come to terms with how he'd react. He squeezed the bridge of his nose. "We hafta leave long before they get here. If we stay and fight, they'll send more troops and crush us." He hated the thought of leaving the villagers on their own, but if they stayed, it would only make it worse for them.

"The Nips won't find the trucks. They'll bust a few heads like they always do, then leave."

"And report back to their superiors that there's nothing but poor villagers here." Frank rubbed his chin and mused, "Maybe everybody should leave. They'll just find a deserted village. No one gets hurt."

"Not enough time. Even if we had days, the Nips would know they recently abandoned it and then they'd wonder why. It's the right call to leave them here. You know it is."

"We'll melt into the jungle and wait 'em out while the villagers pay for our actions, possibly with their lives." Grinning Bear shook his head, but didn't respond. He hustled into the darkness to help rouse the others.

Frank knew Grinning Bear was right. They couldn't evacuate everyone in time. They had to let things play out or risk losing everything. The Japanese wouldn't find the trucks unless they did an extra thorough search and they wouldn't do that unless they had a reason.

A half an hour later, the resistance group moved toward the jungle. Most of the villagers stood near their houses and huts watching them go, stoically. Frank wanted to run back and get them out of harm's way. He hated leaving them like this. He followed the last man into the jungle. Just before he plunged into the darkness, he looked back. One villager raised his hand with his fingers in a V for victory sign and a broad grin. Frank returned the signal, then joined the others. He wished he shared their confidence.

They moved through the darkness carefully. The fewer signs of their passing they left, the better. They climbed a grass and moss covered hill. It would give them a view of the village once it was light enough. It was far enough away that the Japanese wouldn't see them as long as they stayed hidden, but close enough to see any goings on in town, particularly the town center. Frank didn't know if he wanted to see anything, but he wouldn't have it any other way. If the townspeople were about to suffer, he wanted to at least witness their pain and suffering. After all, he brought it upon them.

Grinning Bear lay down beside him. "Everyone's out of sight and in a good position."

Frank nodded, but didn't tear his eyes away from the sleeping town, which was hardly more than a dark spot against the black night.

Grinning Bear added, "Whatever happens, it's not your fault, Frank."

Frank rubbed the back of his neck. His old friend had an uncanny knack for reading his mind. "I know," he murmured back. "I don't know that I've ever dreaded a sunrise more than this one." He meant it, even though every new day as a POW had been hellish. But worrying about himself was a damn sight easier than worrying about an entire village.

"That's because you're a good man."

Frank clutched Grinning Bear's arm. His voice was low and hard. "If they do anything really bad, don't let me make a bad decision."

"You won't make . . ."

Frank squeezed his arm. "I mean it, Larry. No matter what."

Grinning Bear's face turned to stone and he nodded. "We'll see how things play out."

~

THE JAPANESE SOLDIERS didn't wait until the sun rose to enter the village. Just as it became light enough to see, they stepped from the jungle, holding their long Arisaka rifles at the ready. Frank counted fourteen soldiers led by an officer. Like every other Japanese officer he'd ever encountered, he seemed hellbent on doling out punishment to whoever got in his way.

A few villagers milled about, stoking cooking fires and making trips to and from one of the four wells. They stopped what they were doing when they noticed the soldiers.

He couldn't hear them from this far away, but they could see well enough. The officer barked orders and the soldiers hustled into houses and huts, kicking the residents onto the dingy streets. When a Filipino didn't move fast enough, or did anything not to the soldier's liking, they were smacked by fists and rifle butts. Frank gritted his teeth, but kept calm. Everyone hated watching this, but he needed to be the example for his men —calm.

Soon, the center of the town filled with villagers. Most had their heads down in vain attempts not to provoke their tormentors. The officer paced as the roundup finally ended. He faced the villagers while his men surrounded them with their rifles ready.

The officer addressed them. Even from here, his voice came through, but muffled enough that he couldn't understand the words. He and Grinning Bear had learned Japanese pretty well during their internment, but it didn't help them here. Frank wondered if he should get closer, but nothing the officer said would be useful and would only act to inflame his rage.

The officer paced again. He still talked loudly, even though the villagers would have little understanding of his words. After a few minute tirade, the officer finally stopped.

Half the soldiers moved away. They entered houses and shacks in pairs, obviously searching for any stragglers. The villagers stood by with their heads bowed.

Soon, they separated children from mothers and fathers. This caused obvious anguish. Villagers tried to hold on to their children and even from here, they could hear terrified children's screams as they tore them from their families.

They gathered the children into a smaller group surrounded by riflemen. Mothers wailed and fathers tried to console them. The separated family members still called to one another in heart-rending screams.

Frank exchanged a worried glance with Grinning Bear. Both of them were all too familiar with Japanese terror tactics. He hoped no one would give up their position, but if they did, he wouldn't blame them. The family bond was often much deeper than anything else.

"They're just trying to scare 'em," Frank said, more to himself than anyone else. "Trying to get someone to talk."

The Filipinos shifted and glanced nervously at one another. They knew those people down there. They'd shared their food and shelter just hours before. They were more than just fellow Filipinos, which was enough most days. If Frank was wrong and they started shooting, his men may enter the fray with or without his blessing. Perhaps it had been a mistake to watch.

The full contingent of soldiers returned and reported their findings to the officer. The officer continued his pacing, then suddenly went to the closest child, pulled him from the group and held him by the collar in front of the adults. He pulled his pistol from his holster and held it to the child's head. He yelled and screamed at the villagers.

A mother screamed and pushed to the front of the group. She tried to hurl herself past the soldiers, but a soldier grabbed her by the hair and yanked her to the ground. The soldier held her tight, the bayonet on the end of his rifle inches from her neck, but that didn't stop her from screaming and writhing.

A man, probably her husband, went to her side, trying to control her, but she shoved him away and continued screaming. The soldier gripped her hair as she shook and shrieked.

The officer kept threatening, the pistol pushing against the back of the boy's head. Even from here, they could see the stark terror on the boy's face. Frank thought it might be the boy who'd taken such an intense liking to him the day before. He'd barely been able to escape the child.

"Don't do it," Frank pleaded. "Don't you fucking do it, you son of a bitch." The scene felt familiar to him. Instead of children, the Japanese often threatened fellow prisoners with harm in order to eke out confessions. It didn't matter if the confession was true or not, if it kept a prisoner alive for another day or just another hour, it was worth it. But this was someone's child. Surely they'd crack. *I would.*

If they started killing kids, things up here would disintegrate quickly. He wouldn't be able to stop it, even if he wanted to. His men would take their revenge on the enemy. That would be fine in the short term, but then the full force of the Japanese garrison would come down on the village. No one would survive.

He wished he'd thought this through better. They should never have used the village. It would have been much better to simply burn the vehicles in place and take what they could carry on their backs. No one expected the Japanese to react so quickly. He'd been so high from their success, he'd forgotten how brutal they could be.

The woman stopped shrieking. Her voice had probably given out. The officer kicked the boy in the back and he sprawled. He went to another child, this time a girl. He yanked her in front of the villagers and pushed her down hard. He removed his belt and, for a stunned instant, Frank thought he may witness her rape. That would have the same effect as a killing, maybe even worse.

The officer folded the belt and used it like a whip against the girl's bare back. Her screams echoed through the forest, making birds alight from the tops of trees in alarm. Another mother and father pushed forward and wailed for their daughter. Two soldiers kept them from helping her, their bayonets gleaming in the morning sun.

A young teen burst from the group like a shot. He smashed into the nearest soldier, knocking him to the ground. He rolled past him and came to his feet. He ran straight at the officer. He came within a few yards, but the officer was ready. He pulled his pistol, aimed, and fired three shots. The boy staggered and took a few steps before his legs gave out and he crumpled and rolled into his sister.

For a moment there was only the echoes of the gunshots. Then the sister saw her dying brother writhing in the dirt. The shriek that rose from her throat and through the trees tore Frank's heart out. The mother and father broke free from the soldiers and went to their fallen son's side. They pawed at him and the mother pulled him onto her lap, stroking his head and rocking him like a newborn babe. The father clutched his daughter to his chest and soon they all wailed together.

Frank's knuckles ached from gripping his rifle too hard. He looked to Grinning Bear. The situation had gotten out of hand and they both knew it. He looked behind and saw every Filipino staring back at him, but the one he paid attention to the most was Constance. Her eyes were wide and full of a mixture of fear and seething hatred. She wanted revenge and she wasn't alone.

Would the carnage continue? Attacking would do no good if the Japanese were about to leave. Perhaps they would sense how outnumbered they were by the irate villagers. They'd kill many, but if the villagers attacked, eventually the soldiers would be brought down and hacked to death, unless they left now.

Frank had a decision to make. He stayed on his belly and watched the Japanese. They decided for him. The officer went to the little boy he'd first threatened and shot him through the ear. The boy slouched onto his haunches as the life drained from his head.

The shrieks and screams that rose from the village would haunt him for the rest of his days, but for now, they pushed him off the hill and down into the jungle with reckless abandon.

He didn't look back, but sensed the others surging to keep up with him.

No one yelled or war whooped, they were too incensed for anything but getting at the Japanese as quickly as possible.

It only took a few minutes to cover the ground, which had taken them a half hour to cover in the darkness. Grinning Bear ran up beside him. Frank half expected him to talk him out of it, but no, his old friend simply said between breaths, "Don't forget to take off your safety."

Frank made it to the edge of the jungle. He considered setting something up, some basic attack plan, but the sound of another pistol shot and a smattering of rifle fire told him there was no time. The hated enemy was killing defenseless Filipinos. It had to stop.

He darted from the dimness of the jungle and into the light of day. He wove his way through the maze of shacks and houses toward the center of town. His finger hovered just off the trigger. He'd remembered to take the safety off. His men followed and spread out.

Frank came to the edge of the town's center. Chaos reigned supreme. The villagers were attacking the soldiers with their bare hands. The soldiers slashed with their bayonets and fired as fast as they could work their bolt action rifles. It was a bloodbath. A few soldiers fell and were swarmed with fists and whatever else the Filipinos could use as weapons.

Frank's eyes went to the Japanese officer. He wielded his pistol expertly, shooting anyone close. Frank pulled his rifle to his shoulder, but couldn't pull the trigger before a shape darted in front of him, blocking his shot. Constance ran straight at the officer, her rifle held low at her side. The officer's eyes widened as he saw the new threat, thirty well-armed resistance fighters coming at his men like unleashed tigers from hell.

Constance fired, and her bullet grazed the officer's cheek, cutting across his ear. The officer yelped and clutched his face for a moment, but he quickly recovered. He brought his pistol up and centered it on Constance's chest. Frank steadied his aim. He'd either hit Constance or the officer. He fired and his bullet smashed the smug look off the officer's face in a gush of blood and bone.

Constance never stopped her mad rush, even though his own bullet nearly took her head off. She slammed into the crumpling officer's chest. She planted the barrel of her brand new Arisaka rifle into his neck and rode him to the ground. She rolled off him and came to her feet. She lurched for her rifle, which still stuck from the officer's neck, ponderously.

Frank ran to her side. He gripped her arm. "Are you alright?"

The feral look on her face made him rear back. She seemed more animal than human. She sprang away and he lost his grip. She worked the bolt action, pressed her barrel against the back of an enemy soldier desperately trying to defend himself against a mass of angry Filipinos. She fired into his spine and he stiffened, then collapsed at her feet.

Frank thought sure her bullet must've also hit one of the Filipinos beyond, but it miraculously missed. She didn't hesitate to load another bullet and seek another target. He lost sight of her as she threw herself into the melee. He tried to stay with her, but an enemy soldier thrust his bayonet at his guts. Frank sidestepped and the soldier lost his balance and fell. Four villagers descended onto him, pinning the rifle. They pummeled him with fists and clubs until his face was a caved-in, bloody mess.

The Japanese didn't stand long against the enraged Filipinos. Frank still looked for Constance, but the scene was mass confusion. Bodies flew everywhere.

Two soldiers tried to surrender. They dropped their rifles and held their hands up. They were cut down, shot in the belly to prolong their suffering. The screams of the children had been replaced with the screams of the dying Japanese.

By the time it was finally over, Frank felt sick to his stomach. Death surrounded him. He had little pity for the Japanese, but many Filipinos had died, mostly civilians. The bodies of children affected him the most. The boy who'd gripped his leg the day before lay in a puddle of his own blood. His parents both cried over his body, even though both had grievous wounds of their own.

17

Shawn Cooper sat with Henry Calligan and the other OSS men overlooking a river. A few days had passed since the attack on the Japanese artillery unit, and they were getting antsy.

The Japanese had responded quickly to the attack, however, the Chindits and OSS contingent were long gone by the time they arrived. The gun battery had been destroyed and they'd left plenty of devious booby traps.

Shawn chucked a stone and watched it slice into the river with barely a ripple. He spoke to them all, but mostly to Calligan, the ranking officer. "So, what are we gonna do about the prisoner?"

Calligan tossed his own stone. "Nothing. We'll leave him for the Chindits to deal with."

"I mean, what're we gonna do about the information?"

Calligan's mouth turned down. He finally said, "Our British friends sent an encrypted message, but they haven't heard back yet."

"We found him. If anything comes from it, we should be the ones to act on it," Shawn said hopefully.

"I can't imagine nothing coming from it," Calligan said. "But how and who they send to check it out is out of my hands."

"It's a perfect mission for us. It's almost tailored made for us. You know that as well as anyone."

"You're right, but that still doesn't mean the higher ups will see it that way. It might be more political for them."

JoJo piped up, "Horseshit! If we don't act soon, it won't matter anyway. The date's quickly approaching."

Calligan looked around, then motioned them closer. "If I have heard nothing by the end of today, we'll move out."

Shawn looked around the group. "You mean we'll act on it without orders?"

"No orders doesn't mean we don't have things to do. Our orders before the artillery mission was to harass the enemy supply lines. We'll just go back to doing that, only we'll do it up north a little bit . . . say around Lashio."

Shawn pushed for more. "And what happens if the mission goes to the Chindits?"

"It won't. But if it does, we'll tag along. Either way, we'll do something about it."

"How can you be so sure?"

"Cause they need the Chindits to keep the Japs in a pincer. The priority is to squeeze them between the Chinese, the Chindits, the Marauders, and all the other units involved from India and even Africa, and crush them in place. Then the Ledo road can connect to the Burma road and the war here shifts dramatically in our favor. One little general dying in his whore house mansion won't fluster too many feathers. Won't matter who did it as long as it gets done."

"It's better to ask forgiveness than permission. Is that what you're saying?" Shawn asked.

"Exactly."

The day passed slowly for them. They'd run out of busy work the day before. They resupplied, cleaned their weapons to a high glossy sheen, and gotten plenty of rest. Now all they needed was a mission.

As they scrounged their dinner of half C-rations and half bully beef from the Chindits, Calligan sauntered out from the command tent. He rubbed his chin and stared at the ground as he walked, as though thinking something through. They watched him carefully.

He came within a few feet, still thinking hard. Guthrie asked, "What's the word boss?"

Calligan startled, as though he didn't know they were there. He looked around the ring of eager faces. "I spoke with Captain Sparks. There hasn't been any word since they sent the message out. I told him we are returning to our previous duties in supply interdiction and harassment."

Shawn felt a surge of excitement. "So we're going after the general?"

Calligan put his hand out for quiet. "Don't shout it to the whole world, Shawny. As far as they know, we're just heading to their supply lines."

The OSS men dug into their meals with abandon. Knowing Calligan, they'd be leaving sooner rather than later.

"I'll tell the Kachin. Gather your things. We leave in an hour." Calligan stalked off, still thinking earnestly about something.

"I've never seen Calligan so . . . I don't know, I guess worried's the word," Shawn mused.

"As long as it gets us moving, I don't care if he's a nervous Nelly. He probably picked up something from one of the local gals," JoJo said.

"I can't picture Calligan with VD," Shawn said.

"I can't picture him with a woman," O'Keefe chimed in.

"I hear he was quite the ladies' man before the war," Shawn said.

"Really? I just can't see it."

"Well, not out here. He's doing a job. We all are."

"You don't think he'd partake if the opportunity presented itself?" JoJo asked. "You think he's a Quaker or something?"

"I know he's not a Quaker. He's too good at killing for that. I'll follow him anywhere," Shawn said and realized he really meant it. He'd been horrified when he first met the man, but a lot had changed since he first entered Burma. Calligan had earned his respect and admiration.

∼

FOUR DAYS HAD PASSED since they left the Chindits in the south. They stayed off the roads mostly, keeping to the jungle, letting the Kachin lead them along rivers and tiny paths only they could find. By the time they neared Lashio, Shawn thought they might have traveled as far up and down as they had in a straight line. The paths the Kachin used often meandered up steep slopes and descended to the other side before going up again.

Now they lingered on the outskirts of Lashio, a town just southeast of Myitkyina. It was mid-afternoon and even from their elevated position nearly a mile away, they could easily see the Japanese were in control of the entire area. Japanese patrols moved along the roads, some on foot, but most in vehicles. Lashio itself was a bustling place. Shawn couldn't tell if it was always that way or if it had something to do with its proximity to the front lines and the influx of Japanese troops.

Calligan scanned the town with his binoculars. He'd been at it for most of the day. The Kachin watched their backs for Japanese while the OSS men watched the town.

Finally, Calligan waved them closer. He handed the binoculars to Shawn. He pointed. "See that building to the right of the long single story with the shingled roof?"

Shawn found the building and focused the binoculars. "Got it."

"I think that's our target, but I can't be sure."

"I see what you mean. I just saw a few officers enter. Ladies met them at the door."

"I've seen that happen a few times."

Shawn kept the binoculars pressed to his eyes. "Would the general share a building with his officers or have his own?"

"Without actually seeing him, we can't know for sure," Calligan said.

O'Donnelly said, "So we send a few Kachin in there to watch."

Calligan shook his head. "Lashio isn't like most of the rest of the country. They don't have a Kachin presence there. That's why we don't have much intelligence about Lashio in general."

"They're sympathizers?" Shawn asked incredulously. He'd never heard of such a thing.

"Not exactly. But they're not friendly to the Kachin. Didi can barely speak of them. He doesn't know why it's that way, it just is, and has been for generations. They'd spot a Kachin easily."

"Well, we can't very well hit the building if we don't know if it's the right one. It's not worth the risk."

"Exactly," Calligan said. "Which is why we'll have to go in ourselves."

Shawn dropped the binoculars off his eyes and stared at Calligan. "In case you haven't noticed, we're not Burmese, boss."

"Nonsense. We know the language and most of us are dark enough to pass for locals." He paused and stroked his chin again in the way that had worried Shawn before. "Shawn, JoJo, O'Keefe, and I will do it."

Everyone else tried to voice their opposition to being left out, but Calligan nipped it in the bud. "Rest of you will watch our backs from those foothills." He pointed to a set of low hills only a couple hundred yards from the town. Trails crisscrossed the hills and were obviously used often.

"Looks like a high traffic area," Killigrew said.

"It's the best spot for entering the town without being noticed—likewise, leaving. We'll set up at night. There's enough cover for you if you're careful. We might leave in a big damned hurry and your rifles will help immensely. That's what I've got, unless you boys see anything I'm missing."

"A hit in a city isn't our normal forte," JoJo said. "But I'm all for it, if it bags us a general."

"How do we do it? A rifle from a window, or is it gonna be more personal?" Shawn asked.

"We can't bring rifles, too conspicuous. Pistols and knives only. Preferably knives. If we can make the hit without anyone the wiser, that'd be optimal."

"Slip into his room while he's debasing himself. I like it," JoJo said.

Calligan shook his head. "I doubt we'll have the opportunity to enter the building, but we'll see. This isn't a suicide mission. If it doesn't look right, we abort. No general is worth a single OSS man. Hitler or Tojo maybe, but not this joker. Any other concerns?"

Shawn raised a finger. "Just one. Your beard's gonna stick out like a sore thumb. Burmese don't have beards and if they do, it's nothing like yours." Calligan stroked his beard as though noticing it for the first time. Shawn pointed at O'Keefe. "And O'Keefe's complexion doesn't really work either."

O'Keefe shot razors from his eyes, leveling them at Shawn. "I'll keep my head down," he growled.

Calligan thought about it for nearly a full minute before he finally said, "Okay, Shawn, JoJo, and Guthrie."

O'Keefe's face reddened. "Dammit, Cooper. You're light skinned, too."

But it was obvious that Shawn could pass for a Burmese much more easily, particularly with his light beard.

"Nothing personal, old buddy. Just trying to optimize mission success."

O'Keefe sighed and let it go. They were professionals, and it was the right call. That's how they operated. Everyone had a say. If someone disagreed with his assessment, they would've spoken up, but the changes made sense, so everyone kept quiet.

Calligan said, "Okay, then. We'll continue watching them. Maybe we'll get lucky and see his horny ass."

⁓

THE REST of the day on the overlook produced no more leads about the general's whereabouts, but they noted times and routes of a few enemy patrols. The enemy was wary, but not overly so.

The OSS men waited until midnight before they left their perch and made their way to the low hills. The Kachin led them slowly through the light jungle. This close to town, there were signs of human habitation everywhere. Crisscrossing trails, domestic animal shelters, and watering holes dotted the area. They had to move around two different homesteads before they made their way onto the hills.

From the first overlook, they'd seen several places they could hole up and move into the town. The heavier brush and rock would be easier to hide in during the day, although the heavily trafficked area made everyone nervous. If someone came upon them, they'd have a hard time passing themselves off as locals.

They discussed what they'd do in such a case, but hadn't come to a solution. No one wanted to kill an innocent civilian just for the sake of a mission. It would be up to them at the moment. Shawn was glad he wouldn't have to make that decision—or perhaps he would. The same thing could happen in town.

Calligan and O'Keefe opted to be the ones who would stay on the low hills and give them cover if they needed it. The rest would stay on the overlook and if they saw something they didn't like, they'd send runners to Calligan and O'Keefe. It would be up to them how to proceed from there.

Shawn, JoJo and Guthrie broke off from Calligan and O'Keefe. Nothing was said, but Shawn thought he could feel O'Keefe's eyes burning into the back as he moved off. He didn't feel bad about altering the plan. O'Keefe was just too Irish looking for his own good.

They stayed low and moved slowly until they reached the outskirts of town. They had seen no one. The occasional sound of farm animals and dogs broke the silence of the night, but nothing alarming.

The three of them hunched and watched the town. The enemy patrols were nowhere to be seen. It felt like the most unnatural thing in the world to Shawn when they simply stood up and waltzed into town as though they owned the place.

He walked with a mild hunch, trying to portray a diminutive, unassuming posture. Just an old man in from the fields. They wore tattered hats low over their eyes and they hoped their civilian clothes matched those of the villagers. He could feel the pistol tucked deep into his waistband. The knife, which he strapped to his ankle, felt natural to him by now.

The streets were mostly empty. The Japanese likely had a curfew set, so they stuck to the darkest parts of the street. They veered toward smaller, more out of the way streets as much as possible. They passed a few bars which still held patrons. Shawn noted one was obviously a bar catering to the Japanese occupiers. It would be good intelligence when they made it out of there.

They finally made it deep enough into town to recognize buildings. The suspected brothel house was deep in the city, but with a slightly more upscale feel. Many of the buildings were two and three stories, much different from the rest of town.

They exchanged glances. They had decided that they'd split until they found the correct building. There were three likely options. They came to a corner. Shawn stopped and the others pressed in beside him. There was barely any light seeping from the streets, but this felt right. "I think this is the first one," Shawn hissed in Burmese.

Guthrie nodded. He'd blend into the alley and hunker in amongst the other street people sleeping in the filth. This would be the tricky part. If the Burmese noticed something out of place, they might sound an alarm. But after watching them all day through binoculars, they doubted they'd care.

But just in case, Shawn and JoJo waited while Guthrie disappeared into the alley and joined the riff-raff.

They waited long minutes. When nothing untoward happened, they moved off to their own locations. In the dark, it was difficult to discern one area from the next. It was mostly guesswork. They'd know more when the sun rose.

JoJo was the next to peel off. Shawn waited fifteen minutes before moving even deeper into the city. He'd drawn the short straw and would be the deepest man.

He ambled along the street, keeping to the darkest shadows. More people were out and about, both soldiers and civilians, but the civilians walked taller and were dressed nicer, when he glimpsed them in the low lamplight. This area was more affluent, which would make him stick out more.

He heard raucous laughter spilling from a building and guessed it was another bar open late to accommodate the Japanese. He watched a group of soldiers leave all at once—obviously officers. He thought it would be another prime target for a little plastic explosive, but that wasn't why he was here tonight. He made a mental note of the location, then moved off.

He found an alleyway just around the corner from the bar that would fit his needs. He saw a few lumps of humanity he could slip in beside. The smell was atrocious, but the entire city stank, so his nose had already adjusted.

He pulled the smelly blanket he'd brought from inside his shirt. He sat down heavily. None of the nearby lumps glanced at him. He wondered if they breathed. Perhaps he'd chosen the alley of the dead.

He pressed himself into the wall and draped the blanket over himself so only his eyes were exposed. He kept his eyes open but feigned sleep in every other manner. He could hear the heavy wheezing breaths of the people around him. He wondered how they'd come to such a sorry state. He supposed street people had it rough no matter what, but it must be worse with occupiers to worry about. Did they ship them off to work camps? Did they need to hide during the day?

Despite being deep inside an occupied city, undertaking a dangerous mission to find and hopefully kill a general, his eyes grew heavy and he slept. He jolted once, then decided it would be better to simply fall asleep like everyone else. He certainly could use an hour or two.

~

SHAWN SLEPT for two hours under his filthy blanket in the Lashio slum. He peeled his eyes open slowly. The scene hadn't changed all that much, but he sensed the morning approaching. A few lumps moved and stood on shaky legs. Guttural complaints about pissing, shitting, and the hard ground passed between a few of them. One ambled past him and kicked Shawn's foot.

Shawn didn't know if it was intentional or not. He feigned sleep and murmured indistinctly. The man passed without further incident, but Shawn observed him. Surely, the man wouldn't recognize him as an outsider in the darkness. But he couldn't be too careful.

More and more of them rose and ambled around. Shawn thought there must be a reason, so he pushed himself to his feet as well. He moved slowly, like they did. He cursed and spat like they did, and complained about the hard ground and general abyss of life.

Most moved toward the main streets out of the alley. He moved deeper into the darkest parts of the alley, hoping to find an outlet. Instead, he found a wall and a form pissing against the wall.

Shawn mimicked his actions, and soon they pissed in unison. They're streams adding to the stench of countless other pisses and probably shits, too.

"Who the hell're you?" the form said with a voice that sounded as though he gargled water. Shawn just grunted and spit. But the man didn't let it go. "I asked a question."

"What's it to you?" Shawn said in his most slurred Burmese. He tried to sound drunk or demented, someone to keep your distance from.

The man didn't respond right away. He finished pissing before Shawn, but he didn't move off. When Shawn finished, the man finally said, "American?"

Shawn reacted in an instant. Before he knew what he was doing, he'd brought the knife from his ankle and had it at the man's throat. He could see his eyes bulge with fear. His hands went out and his voice barely changed from before. "I'm not the enemy."

Shawn pressed the tip of the razor-sharp blade to the where the man's carotid artery pulsed with lifeblood. "Who the hell're you?" Shawn asked him back.

"A friend."

Shawn let the blade relax slightly, but he kept it close. He glanced down the alley. No one remained. Had they fled when they saw what happened, or was it simply time to leave?

"How can I trust you?"

The man shrugged. "If you kill me, you'll never know, and I doubt you'll make it out of Lashio alive."

"You're threatening me? All I have to do is push and you're a dead man."

"Yes, but you will die soon after."

Shawn looked around as though there must be men ready to leap out or possibly shoot him, but the alley was empty.

"You wouldn't last the day as you are. They would see you as an outsider and report you before noon. The Japanese will torture you by dinner."

Shawn hissed, "How do I know you're not a sympathizer?"

"Because I wouldn't help you. I wouldn't warn you."

Shawn relaxed his grip on the man's arm. He kept the knife in his hand, but lowered it. "You have a point there."

"Come, I will take you somewhere safe."

Shawn bit his lower lip. He wanted to trust him, but could he? He had a decision to make and it might kill or save the others. He struggled only for a moment. "Wait, there's more of us."

The man's voice changed to concern. He nodded and pushed Shawn toward the front of the alley. "Take me to them quickly."

"If you betray me, I'll kill you before they take me."

The man smiled and, even through the darkness and grime, he saw his rotting teeth. "Yes, then I won't betray you. We must hurry, though. It'll be light in a half hour. They won't last long after that."

Shawn slipped the knife back into place. He hustled to keep up with the man. When they came to the alley entrance, the man said, "Stay close to me and try to blend in."

"Wait, what's your name?"

"Rogan. Now which way."

Shawn pointed the way they'd come. "The first one's two blocks and the next is two after that. In the alleys with the bums . . . I mean street people."

Rogan didn't react to his slip. He kept his head down and shambled along the road. Shawn kept his head down as much as possible, but kept alert. The streets came alive with each passing minute. Doors opened and shit and piss pots poured into alleys. He suddenly realized why they left the alleys when they did, to avoid being showered in piss and shit. Apparently, sleeping in it was acceptable, but not showering in it.

A few Japanese soldiers walked along the streets. One group had obviously been out partying all night. They held one another up and stumbled along, using the walls to help support them. The Burmese gave them a wide berth.

They came to the first alley. Shawn couldn't be sure if it was the same one. "Here," he said and pointed.

Rogan nodded quickly and pushed him into the alley a few yards. "Stay here. I will check."

Shawn nodded and considered pulling his knife. If Rogan betrayed him and brought the Japanese instead of JoJo, he'd put the knife through his eye.

He watched the street instead. More and more people moved about. It made him feel safer, but also nervous. If he stuck out to Rogan in low light conditions, he'd stick out even more in broad daylight. He pulled his hat lower and tried to act bored. The OSS had covered such things in their courses, but none of it seemed to work in real life.

He saw Rogan hustling along with a few men in tow. Shawn stiffened. The son of a bitch had betrayed him. He reached for the knife, then saw JoJo and Guthrie were the two others. He relaxed and gave them a smile while tipping his hat back slightly.

Both men's faces relaxed noticeably. They'd undoubtedly been as suspicious as Shawn had been. Shawn had only been away from them for a few hours, but it felt much longer. He wanted to hug them, but he said, "You alright?" They nodded. "I see you've met my new friend." They looked from Shawn to Rogan, clearly still unconvinced. "I guess we have to trust him."

Rogan looked at him with dark eyes. Shawn hadn't gotten a good look at him in the dark alley, but now he saw he sported an almost flat nose and heavy scarring along both cheeks, as though he'd been cut by a knife, or perhaps shrapnel. He'd clearly had a rough time. He had no idea about his age. He might be twenty or one hundred and twenty. No matter, he'd decided to trust him and his gut still told him it was the correct decision.

"How was your night?"

Rogan's voice came out angry. "There's no time for that. They have been discovered."

Shawn looked around in near panic. "What? How do you know?"

"Must you Americans question everything? We must leave now. Follow me closely. Do not leave my side for any reason."

Shawn exchanged glances with the others. He'd have to question them as to why they were in the same alley at a later time. He could see and hear real fear in Rogan's voice. "Okay, then go."

Rogan moved quickly along the road. Despite his situation, he seemed like a man on a mission. Was this some elaborate ruse to make them give up more OSS men? His gut told him no, but he could be fooled.

They passed a few Japanese soldiers. They hadn't been partying the night before, but moved with supreme confidence. The Burmese bowed to them when they passed close. The Japanese didn't seem to notice the bows, but they probably would if they didn't bow. He'd seen it before. Failure to show proper respect earned a beating, at the very least.

Rogan finally ducked into an alley. He strode to a small door and knocked. The door opened almost immediately, raising the hairs on the back of Shawn's neck. Had they been waiting for them?

An old man held the door. A young man stood behind him. He held a pistol. He glared at the OSS men as though they'd rolled in shit. Shawn hesitated a moment before Rogan pushed on his back. "Go!" he hissed.

Shawn led the way, with Guthrie and JoJo close behind. JoJo said under his breath, "I don't like this."

The door shut behind them, and a deadbolt locked in place. Shawn put his hand close to his pistol. If it came down to it, a gunshot in the indoor location wouldn't alert anyone outside. He sensed JoJo and Guthrie had similar plans.

Rogan spoke in low tones to both men. The younger one never took his eyes off them and he looked angry. The older man simply listened and finally nodded.

Rogan raised his voice to them, "This is Dachen," he indicated the older man, "and this is Cetan. They are friends. Not sympathizers. You are safe here."

Cetan's scowl grew deeper. "You are not safe. You have made us all unsafe."

Dachen touched the young man's shoulder. "Please control yourself. We will deal with the problem and the Japanese will lose even more face in front of the enemy."

Shawn didn't know what he meant, but he extended his hand. "I'm Coop and this is JoJo and Cowboy," he thought it best to keep things vague until he knew more.

"Come in and make yourself comfortable. You must be tired and hungry."

Shawn smiled, but he didn't let his guard down. This could all still be an elaborate ploy. They followed them through the labyrinthine interior. He took in everything. If they had to break out of here, recalling the layout could save their lives. The OSS had beaten such things into their heads in training, and now it was automatic.

They finally brought them to a large room. A few Burmese lingered, but it was mostly empty. They drew stares from the unfamiliar faces. No one seemed to be taken in by their ruse to fit into the general population.

Dachen gestured to a long dining room table. "Sit down. I will have food brought."

The OSS men exchanged glances. Their mission didn't involve breakfast, at least not in this manner. How could they continue their mission now that they'd been found out. Could he trust them enough to ask for their help? It was probably his only option. If not, they'd have to scrub the mission, and he hated failing.

18

Their Burmese hosts fed them and kept their questions to a minimum, but it couldn't last. They knew they had to be there for some purpose. So far, the OSS men hadn't told them more than their nationalities, which they'd guessed anyway, and their nicknames.

Once they finished eating and thanked their hosts, an awkward silence filled the room. Dachen had men stationed at the doorways. Shawn couldn't decide if they were guarding against the Japanese or keeping them from leaving—a combination of the two, perhaps.

Dachen finally said, "Rogan said he found you in the gutters with the other street people, yet I doubt your purpose here is to become a street person."

Shawn exchanged glances with the others, then he smiled. "No, you're correct. We have other business here."

Dachen waited for more, but when it didn't come, he said, "I wonder if it has to do with a visiting general?"

Despite all their training, each man couldn't keep the surprise off their faces. Shawn figured there was no use lying. If this was an elaborate ruse, they wouldn't get out of here alive. They may as well toss the dice and see where they landed.

"You know him?"

Dachen shook his head slowly. "No, I only know he is here. I don't suppose you are here to simply observe him."

They'd already come this far, they may as well go all the way. "No, we came here to kill him," the smiling, fun-loving ruse left his face and he looked hard at Dachen. "If you have information that could help us, we'd be much appreciated."

"You think I seek appreciation?"

"I don't know what you seek. Perhaps you should tell us and we can help you get it—if we can."

"But only if we tell you where the general is—is that it?"

"The Japanese are losing this war. The tides are shifting. It would be wise for you to be on the correct side of things when this war ends."

"Now you are threatening me? I could have you killed with a snap of my fingers, or I could simply turn you in. The Japanese would pay handsomely for OSS soldiers."

Shawn did his damndest to keep the surprise off his face. "OSS? I'm airborne. US 501st Airborne."

"Impressive, but also horseshit, as you Americans say. It would surprise you how much I know about Allied operations in my country. There are no American airborne troops in Burma—only marauders and OSS. You don't strike me as a marauder. And you're certainly not a Chindit since you're definitely Americans."

"And how do you know so much about the Allies?"

"Let us just say that before the war, we were not in such seemingly sparse circumstance." He gestured around the room.

Shawn wracked his brains for answers. Who the hell was this guy? He'd studied Burma's military and government, but neither was intact enough to have current intelligence units reporting. They'd been ruled by the British when the Japanese came, but since then everything had gone to hell in a handbasket.

Then it hit him, "Opium," he said.

Dachen smiled. His teeth that remained were dark and ragged. "Ah, the wonderful poppy plant. Do you partake?"

Shawn shook his head slowly. "No. I didn't realize a viable operation was still possible, given the war."

"The wonderful thing about opium is its addictive power. It will always be sought after, even by the most tyrannical and militaristic government officials, for there is always a craving. Always a need to fulfill that craving."

"It's my understanding that the British were in charge of opium production."

"True, but since the Japanese invaded, things have changed."

"You've taken over the process."

"The invaders aren't stupid. They know the value of the poppy as well as the British."

Shawn nodded. "But you still own a slice." He rubbed his chin. This could get dicey. "You want more control, no doubt."

Dachen stared for a long minute. He finally said, "This is none of your concern. Suffice it to say, I know what goes on in my country."

"You're planning ahead for when the war ends."

"Like I said, this is none of your concern. Now, would you like our help or not?"

"Yes, of course, but what's the price?"

Dachen smiled. "I never knew Americans could be so cynical. We share a common enemy. Isn't that enough?"

"Yes, I suppose it is. So, you'll help us?"

"Yes. I know where the general is and I know his schedule, at least enough for your intentions."

Shawn glanced at the others. It was good news, but he still had reservations about trusting an opium dealer. "Will you give us a moment to discuss things?"

Dachen held his hands out as though presenting the room. "Of course. But know that we have already risked much by letting you in here. The sympathizers will insist that they saw you. The Japanese will search, especially with the general in the area."

"Thank you. We'll just need a few minutes."

Dachen and the others moved out of the room. The OSS men huddled closer. Shawn asked, "So, what do you think?"

Guthrie shrugged. "He sounds sincere, but he's a drug lord. He'd lie to his own mother."

JoJo added, "Yes, but the only thing we need to figure out is how helping us might impact his bottom line."

Shawn raised an eyebrow. "Explain."

"If he's in deep with the Nips—financially deep—he'll betray us."

"He could've already done that," Guthrie said.

"True, but he may be fishing for the whole operation. He knows we're not alone. They might be out looking for the others as we speak."

Shawn said, "I think he's smarter than he looks. He can see the writing on the wall. Even if he's in deep with the Japs, he knows they're on their way out. Getting in good with Americans? That'd go a long way once this thing's over."

JoJo said, "This was a British colony before the war. Americans might not be that important to him."

Shawn said, "Maybe, but we're close with the Brits. I think he wants to play for the winning side, not necessarily the winning team."

Guthrie leaned in close. He looked hard at Shawn. "What's your gut tell you?"

Shawn had been exploring his gut feeling all morning. He said, "I wouldn't trust him with a loved one, but I trust him in this situation. I think he knows where the general is, and I think he'll be happy to see him gone."

JoJo raised a finger. "Then why wouldn't he just do it himself?"

Shawn answered. "I don't think he likes getting involved in the war. He only cares about profits and power. Since the Brits left, he's probably getting a real nice feel for both with the Japs. He doesn't want to risk that in the short term. It's a win-win, he'll gain notoriety in the resistance and he'll gain points with the allies. All he has to do is point us in the right direction."

"Perhaps we should ask him for more than that? If he has skin in the game, he might be less likely to betray us," JoJo mused.

Shawn snapped his fingers. "Weapons. We'll ask him for weapons." He looked from one to the other. Both nodded back. Shawn stood up straight and looked around the room. "Okay, it's settled then."

∼

SHAWN SAT on bench and stared out the window of the two story building. The street bustled with people, a mix of civilians and Japanese soldiers. Troop trucks and smaller military vehicles honked their horns as they barely slowed for people on foot. The Burmese simply moved aside, their heads bowed.

The building across the street towered four stories tall. It wasn't the tallest in town, but certainly the nicest. It had been one of three building they'd identified as the likely target building when they'd scanned the area from the overlook.

Shawn leaned forward and glanced out the window toward the foothills where he hoped the other OSS men watched and waited. It must be murder for them, not knowing what was happening in town. Their eyes must be glued to the binoculars, looking for any sign of them, but he doubted they could have seen any of them.

They would've almost certainly noticed the increased patrols brought on by the sympathizers alerting the Japanese to their possible presence. They'd busted down doors and searched all over the city, but Dachen's men were always at least two steps ahead of them. They found nothing they weren't supposed to find.

Shawn hefted the scoped Arisaka rifle. Dachen had given it to him. If the Japanese found it, it couldn't get back to him. It was just a stolen weapon. He scanned the street through the scope. He used scoped rifles before, but never a Japanese design. Dachen assured him it was perfectly calibrated for the distance it might be used for, but they'd only use the rifle as a last resort. The goal was a silent kill in the dead of night, preferably by knife.

He looked over his shoulder to where Guthrie and JoJo slumbered. He watched their slow breathing, knowing if he simply whispered their names, they'd wake up instantly, ready for action. It was how they were trained, and the past few years had only deepened their deadly habits. Would he ever be able to return to a normal life? Did he want to? He didn't know the answer. He pushed it out of his mind.

He hadn't spotted the general yet. Dachen assured him he was inside the building across the street. He'd seen plenty of women go in and out, some escorted by high-ranking officers. Two guards stood outside. They rotated every four hours. They took their jobs seriously. Dachen explained all entrances were similarly guarded. When Shawn pressed how he intended to get them inside, he deferred and told him to trust him. It grated on Shawn and perhaps that was the point. Dachen liked to play games.

An official black sedan with a general's flags pulled up to the front door. The guards both stiffened and held their rifles straight up and down. An officer came out the back passenger side door. He hustled to the front door, ignoring the guard's salutes. Shawn immediately hated him.

The doorman opened the door and he went inside quickly. Shawn used the scope to scan the entrance. Would the general be coming out? It looked that way.

Shawn whispered and Guthrie and JoJo were at his side a minute later. Shawn pointed at the front door. "Something's happening."

Five minutes passed. Finally, the front door opened again and out strolled the general. Along with the officer from the sedan walking behind a respectable distance, two women hung on each side of the general. Their painted faces shone in the afternoon light. He ignored the ramrod straight guards. The sedan's driver hustled to the passenger side door and opened it, then stood aside. He wore white gloves and an immaculate uniform.

The general let the ladies enter first. He smacked the last one's ass as she bent over, then he entered the sedan. The driver closed the door. The officer entered the front passenger side door. He opened it himself. The sedan shot away and disappeared around the corner.

"I coulda shot him and ended it."

"Yeah, and we'd be dead by now," JoJo said.

Shawn smiled. "Which is why I didn't do it."

Guthrie said, "So, now what? Looks like our boy's going out on the town."

As if in answer, a knock on the door made them all turn. The sequence of knocks was correct and they relaxed, but only slightly. The young man who they'd met with Dachen stepped in, followed by Dachen himself and Rogan behind him. Rogan had cleaned up and was barely recognizable, save for his crushed nose and heavy scarring.

Dachen stepped to the side of the window and pulled the curtain back slightly. "You saw the general, no doubt?"

Shawn answered, "Yeah, we saw him."

"Good. He will be out for at least five hours. We must use this time wisely."

"Okay. So what's the plan?"

"You Americans—so impatient."

Shawn let it roll off, but Dachen was getting on his nerves.

Dachen said, "The good general will visit a restaurant and then an opium bar. It is only a few blocks away. He and his escorts will have a lovely time, but the general will have too much opium and will need to return here with the women."

Shawn looked skeptical. He exchanged glances with the others. Dachen held up his hands. "Both girls work for me, as does the opium bar owner, of course. The general will get a heavy dose. When he returns, he will be barely coherent. You will be inside waiting for him. It will be easy."

"And just how you planning on getting us inside?"

"The hotel has cook crews, which will be on shift change right before the general comes back. He has a habit of ordering food at all hours, so the staff must be ready. One of you will be on that staff."

Shawn raised his hand. "That'll be me."

Both JoJo and Guthrie objected, but Shawn stopped them before they could finish. "I'm lead on this. It's my call."

Dachen smiled. "Good, then it's settled. My men will give you a uniform and take you to the entry point when it's time. He looked at his watch. 10:30PM, will suffice."

"How will I get to his room?"

"The room is on the fourth floor." He stepped to the window and pulled the curtain back slightly. He pointed to an ornate corner window. "That is the general's room. How you get in is your business."

"You could've told us that earlier. We might've shot him through the window and been done with it by now."

Dachen looked appalled. "You would not have survived such a brash move. I only gave you the sniper rifle as a sign of goodwill and trust. I didn't expect you to use it. As we discussed, it is only as a final measure when everything else has failed." He smiled, "But it won't fail."

Shawn glanced at the rifle leaning against the wall. He wondered if they had messed with the bullets. He'd check later and reload it if possible, although the only ammo he had came from Dachen and his men.

Rogan cut his eyes away from Shawn as he looked at him. He got the feeling he wasn't completely happy with the situation, but had to go along. *Interesting.*

Shawn smiled. "Okay, it sounds like you've thought of everything. We'll wait here until you come for us."

Dachen's smile broadened. "Good, good. I'm glad you decided to trust me. I foresee a growing relationship between us and the Americans. We are world building," he said with a grand gesture. "It is truly wonderful." He shook hands with each of them. Shawn couldn't help but notice the young man standing behind Dachen scowl as they left them alone again.

Shawn waited a few minutes before he crept to the door and listened for a full five more minutes. He crept back to the others. They put their heads together and Shawn whispered. "What d'ya think?"

JoJo said, "I think it stinks."

Guthrie agreed, "Like a dead cow left in the sun too long."

"I agree," Shawn said. "I think he'll get me in okay, but after that, I think he's gonna turn on us—or at the very least, simply turn his back on us. I'll bet the girls aren't as docile as they seem."

Shawn opened the breech in the Arisaka and removed the bullet. He inspected it closely. He hefted it in his hands. "Feels a little light."

He flicked it to JoJo, who caught it out of the air. "Yeah," he handed it to Guthrie. He hefted it, then pulled his knife and cut the end off. "No gunpowder," he stated flatly.

Shawn said, "The rest of the ammo has probably been tampered with, too." He tapped the pistol still tucked into his waistband. "We know these work."

"So, what do we do?" JoJo asked.

Shawn smiled. "Our boy thinks he's got it all figured out, but he's never dealt with the OSS. Remember hitting the marines back at Shangri-La?" He directed the question at JoJo because Guthrie hadn't been there, but he'd been through the same training style and would be familiar with the tactic.

JoJo grinned and rubbed his hands together as though warming them beside a fire. "Do the unexpected."

"Exactly."

～

THEY SPENT the rest of the day watching the house and planning. They heard men at the door a few times, obviously eavesdropping. Each time, they talked about the operation as though it was all going to Dachen's plan.

The sun set and the streets settled down a little. The civilian traffic lightened noticeably and Shawn wondered if it was due to a curfew, or if they'd gotten wind that Dachen and his men would be operating in the area. The Japanese patrols had lessened, their futile search for the renegade OSS men moving out to the outskirts of town where Dachen's network had led them by the nose.

"I've gotta hand it to the son of a bitch. He really has his fingers on the pulse of this town."

JoJo agreed. "He's gonna be a force to be reckoned with somewhere down the line. Ambitious son of a gun."

Two hours before Dachen's men were due to come retrieve him, the OSS men silently jammed the door shut with every heavy item they could move into place. They did it as quietly as possible, avoiding scraping the furniture along the floor. Satisfied, they went to the window.

Shawn scribbled a note and left it in the breech of the sniper rifle. He peered out the window and looked down at the dark street below. It was two stories, not a fall that would kill, but it wouldn't feel good. He stepped onto the thin wooden windowsill. He spotted the handhold above his head. With one last look at the ground, he stood and lunged for the ledge. His fingers dug into the overhanging roof and he hung there a moment before Guthrie stabilized his feet.

Guthrie kneeled on the ledge. When he was settled, he cupped Shawn's foot in his hands, creating a somewhat stable platform for him. Shawn pulled with his arms and pushed with his legs. If not for JoJo holding Guthrie's belt, he would've fallen to the ground.

Shawn vaulted onto the roof and took in the scene. He half expected to find one of Dachen's men waiting there, but the roof was empty, except for a few barrels.

He scanned the street. No one seemed to notice him. He lay on his belly and looked over the roof edge. JoJo balanced below him, Guthrie stabilizing him from inside the room.

Shawn gave him a thumbs up signal then moved aside. JoJo was about the same height as Shawn, so would need help from Guthrie, who was taller by a few inches.

JoJo leaped up and grasped the roof edge. Guthrie helped him the same way he'd helped Shawn. Now it was Guthrie's turn. Shawn and JoJo lingered on the edge ready to help haul him up if he needed it, but it Guthrie's extra few inches allowed him an easier time. His feet pressed into the wall and he vaulted himself up. Shawn and JoJo clutched his pants and hauled him the rest of the way to the top.

They checked themselves, making sure each still had the pistol and the knife. With one last glance down to the street, they made their way to the other side of the building. There was an old dilapidated door, which looked like it was made for dwarves. They hoped to find something more accommodating along the outside of the building.

They found no easy way down. They went to the corner where there were more ledges sticking out from the wall, mostly made of stone. They chose the darkest alleyway, and Shawn went over the side first. He made it easily and the others followed soon after. The alley was empty of people, but they disrupted a clutch of sorry looking cats. They hissed and scattered into the night.

They moved through the alley until they came to a street. It wasn't the main thoroughfare, but it still had some foot traffic. A few folks stood in dark doorways, smoking cigarettes. There was nothing for it, they couldn't avoid them.

They walked on the darker side and moved as though they belonged there. They huddled close and muttered as though a group of friends in deep discussion. They didn't want to be disturbed, particularly with the recent memory of discovery the night before. They hoped the night would shroud them enough to throw off any prying eyes.

They made it two more blocks without anyone giving them notice. The sounds coming from the main road, a block north, pulled them that way. Dachen said the opium bar was close to the bordello hotel. They slowed as they approached the brighter street. Thankfully, wartime kept the lights to a minimum. The Allies didn't bomb Burmese towns often, but it happened occasionally.

Shawn approached the corner slowly, making sure his face was well hidden in the darkness and beneath his hat. A car whizzed past, the dimmed out headlights momentarily blinding him. He saw a few options that could be the opium bar. He didn't know the name and doubted it would have much fanfare at the entrance.

He searched until he finally saw what he was looking for. The sedan was parked a half a block away, tucked into an alley across from them. He could just see the black front end sticking into the light cast from the Main Street. The driver probably enjoyed a dark recess to better keep out of sight and perhaps grab a nap. Soldiers were the same everywhere—few missed out on the opportunity for shuteye.

He faded from the corner and whispered to the others, "The car's across the road about a half a block." He pointed, "See it?"

They both looked and nodded. JoJo said, "It's perfect."

Guthrie lingered at the corner. He finally pulled back. "I don't see any Japs keeping watch. They're probably guarding the opium bar."

"Just like we figured," Shawn said.

Shawn pulled out his wristwatch and checked the time. "We still have an hour before they come for us. Let's get this over with."

Shawn left the cover of the dark alley and turned right onto the Main Street. He kept the shadows as much as possible and made a point not to look at the sedan as he passed in front of it across the street. JoJo followed then Guthrie a few minutes later.

Shawn crossed the street after half a block. No one seemed to take any notice of him. He acted naturally, but it was all he could do not to check his backside.

He made it to a storefront entrance only twenty yards from the alleyway entrance. He stepped into the dark entrance and hunched. He hoped he looked like a person seeking a stoop to sit upon and rest his feet for a while.

He saw JoJo out of the corner of his eye. He moved slower, allowing

Guthrie time to catch up. By the time JoJo reached Shawn, Guthrie would only be a few steps behind.

The street held a few civilians and even a few Japanese officers and soldiers, but no one seemed to pay any attention to them or the general's sedan.

Shawn pulled the pistol from his pants and checked the action carefully. He stepped out, just in front of JoJo and Guthrie. They walked with purpose straight at the dark sedan.

When they were only feet from the driver's open window, Shawn went to his haunches and met the startled gaze of the driver. Shawn pushed the pistol into his face and in Japanese said, "Don't move or you die."

Guthrie stayed on this side and JoJo went around to the other. They entered the passenger side doors. Shawn waited until they had the driver held securely, making sure his hands were on the steering wheel where they could see them. Then Shawn went around and entered the front seat. They locked the doors.

The driver shook with fear. Beads of sweat formed on his forehead. He looked young, but he'd been chosen for not only his driving skills but also his soldiering skills—that was the safe assumption.

Shawn held the muzzle low, aimed at his guts. "You cooperate, you live. If not, I'll shoot you in the balls first, then your guts." To emphasize his point, he pushed the muzzle into the young man's groin hard. The soldier winced and shook even more. Shawn smelled urine, but couldn't see well enough in the darkness to confirm. "You'll be fine. Just do exactly as we say." The soldier gave a quick nod, but he was clearly terrified. He might not function when the time came.

He played a hunch. "We just want to talk with your boss. We're with Dachen." That helped a little. He saw some recognition in his face, as though he'd overheard conversations, perhaps even recent conversations. "Okay?" The driver nodded again, but this time, he seemed more relaxed.

In Burmese now, Shawn spoke with the others just to put the driver's mind at ease that he was who he said he was. "He'll do what we say. We don't need to hurt him." If the driver understood, which he doubted seriously, his mind would be put even more at ease.

In Japanese again, he said, "When the general calls for you, do as you normally do. If you fail, your balls are history." The driver closed his eyes as though feeling the pain already. He nodded.

They waited for nearly an hour before the radio squawked and a voice, which Shawn imagined must be the general's assistant, barked, "Bring the car, quickly."

The driver stiffened as though a jolt of electricity went through his body. "Easy now. Just do your job and you'll live to see your balls intact." Shawn wasn't totally sure if he had the syntax down correctly, but the young man seemed to understand the gist. He was actually enjoying himself.

The driver's shaky hand turned the engine over. He pressed too hard on the accelerator and the engine roared. Shawn pressed the barrel into his crotch, the message clear. The driver got control of himself and put the car into gear with a grind.

The car lurched into the street. The kid hadn't even looked for other traffic. "Don't be careless," Shawn said sharply. The driver took a deep breath and blew it out slowly. "There you go, that's better."

He kept the barrel trained on him but glanced into the back seat. JoJo and Guthrie had pressed themselves into the far corner of the spacious seats. They'd need to get the general in quickly. Shawn would have to deal with the officer somehow.

The opium bar came up quickly. The general and his entourage stood on the corner. The general used the women to help balance. He was clearly out of sorts. The lesser officer looked worried and he waved to the driver to hurry when he saw the sedan approach.

Shawn pressed the barrel into his crotch again. "Nice and easy." He sank beneath the dashboard as they approached, but he kept his eyes on the driver and the gun in his crotch.

The car slowed and turned toward the curb. Shawn felt it crunch into the sidewalk, which was only a wood ledge covering a ditch full of sewage. The jolt nearly made him pull the trigger, and he could see the panic in the driver's eyes. The sedan lurched to a stop.

The driver put it in neutral. He didn't move at first and Shawn knew why—he'd pissed his pants and it would be obvious once he left the car to assist the general with his door.

"Go," Shawn hissed at him.

The driver opened his door and stepped out. He hesitated for a moment, then looked at Shawn, still crouching low and out of sight. He bolted, screaming at the top of his lungs, "The enemy, the enemy!"

Shawn figured it would happen that way. He hoped it would. He didn't relish killing the kid, but he would've if he hadn't done his job.

Almost in the same instant, Guthrie pushed the back door open and JoJo leapt out. He punched the closest woman in the face and her head snapped back and she dropped off the general's arm. He swung behind the general like a striking viper. He delivered a punishing blow to the second woman's kidney. She yelped and dropped away. He shoved the general into the back seat and into Guthrie's waiting arms. Then he drew the knife and went after the officer.

The officer realized something was wrong. He clutched at his holstered pistol when JoJo's knife sliced across his neck, nearly decapitating him. JoJo swung back into the sedan and shut the door. By that time, Shawn was at the wheel. He pushed his foot down and the powerful sedan fishtailed down the street, gaining speed quickly.

Shawn saw the fleeing driver sprinting along the side of the road. He considered veering into him, but he couldn't risk damaging the engine. He supposed the boy would be shot for his part in the general's capture, anyway. A small part of him revolted at the callous thought.

He sped down the street. The lane was mostly empty at this time of night. Those that were out leaped out of the way. The general stars flapping in the wind warned everyone to stay back.

He took a few turns, but stayed on course toward the foothills and their salvation. He wondered if Calligan was watching him. It would be difficult at night, but he'd soon know of their arrival.

Shawn kept pushing the vehicle and glancing in the rearview mirror. He'd passed a few parked troop trucks, but he didn't see any troops. He thought they were home free, but as he took the final turn and saw the street he planned to leave on, he cursed, "Shit! Roadblock."

Guthrie and JoJo both looked up from the general whose head lolled back and forth, clearly higher than a kite. He murmured incoherently, having no understanding of his circumstance. Shawn slowed. "They might let us through once they see the stars."

JoJo grinned, "Maybe they'll salute us."

Shawn had the pistol ready in his lap. He pulled his hat as low as he could pull it and still be able to see. The bored-looking guard came out from a small building. When he saw the stars, he stiffened and halted in place. He stared into the windshield. Shawn said, "Push the general where he can see him."

JoJo and Guthrie pushed him forward. The guard barked something at another guard standing off to the other side. Shawn watched as the gate lifted and both soldiers snapped to attention and saluted.

Shawn pulled forward and when he was abreast of the nearest guard, he smiled and saluted back. The soldier didn't move, but his face changed to confusion. But he held his stiff salute.

Shawn sped up, following the road for a few hundred yards, then turned off onto a dirt track. The sedan bounced harshly and the general grunted and groaned, but otherwise kept quiet.

Shawn finally pulled off the goat track when he couldn't go any farther. "This is it. Everybody out!"

"What about him?" Guthrie asked.

The plan had been to kill him. JoJo said, "I'll do it. I've never killed a general before."

"Wait. Let's take him with us."

"What? He can barely walk," JoJo protested.

"I wanna see the look on Calligan's face."

They hesitated for only a moment before they broke into grins and agreed. They stepped from the sedan, the general between JoJo and Guthrie, while Shawn led the way into the darkness.

They could hear growing commotion from the town, whistles, and even what sounded like police sirens. They had to get out of there quick or they wouldn't get out at all.

They'd only moved a few hundred yards when he heard the familiar night bird call. He went to a knee and made the call back. A moment later, they were surrounded by Kachin. Didi stepped out only feet from his left side. If he had ill intent, he could've easily killed him before Shawn even knew he was there. *Sneaky little bastard.*

They soon united with the other OSS men. Calligan stepped out and looked them up and down. "What the hell've you been up to down there?"

Shawn stepped aside and showed off the general swaying between JoJo and Guthrie. "We brought you an early Christmas present."

Calligan pushed his hat back and spit. "Well, I'll be goddamned. You coulda just got me a card."

19

Mindoro Island, Philippines
February 12, 1945

Corporal Clyde Cooper knew something was up. The camp they'd occupied for the past month and a half hadn't felt this energetic since they heard they were getting another turkey dinner on New Year's Eve.

Officers congregated inside buildings with tightly secured doors and windows, and guards with serious scowls watched the doors like attack dogs.

Clyde wandered the grounds, looking for any more clues. Mindoro Island had been deemed secure a few days after their harrowing fight on the northwestern tip of the island. Since then, the regiment had been lounging.

The nearby airstrip was busy with incoming and outgoing aircraft, but now, instead of fighters and bombers, the only aircraft parked there were C-47s from the 317th Troop Carrier Group. Clyde had gleaned that information from one of the crew members. He didn't know much else, but it was obvious that an aerial assault was in the offing.

Clyde found his squad in the barracks. They lay on or sat on the cots, mostly reading old magazines and barely held together paperbacks, which most of them had read a couple of times already.

Private Gutiérrez looked over the top of his magazine. "There you are. Quartermaster delivered mail." He pointed to Clyde's cot, where two letters sat unopened.

Clyde's heart rate increased, as it always did when he received mail. It was usually from Abby. He scooped them up. The first one was from Abby, the second from his parents. He stuffed the letter from his parents into his back pocket and brought Abby's to his nose. He inhaled deeply. He might have imagined it, but he thought he could smell her perfume.

He hustled out of the barracks and sat against his favorite palm tree. It had a crook at the base, which was perfect for sitting. He'd sat in it enough to make it shiny on top.

He looked at the return address; still in Virginia. He carefully opened the letter, despite his growing excitement. He read slowly at first, savoring every word.

My Dearest husband,

The holidays have finally passed. I've never missed you more. The holidays are the worst. I can't imagine how hard it must be for you. It's just not the same without you here. I spent Christmas morning with friends, and baby Cora. She is such a ray of light during this dark period. I can't wait for you to meet her, and I can't wait until we have one of our own . . . several perhaps? I miss you every second. What a day it will be when you step off that ship and return to me. I can picture it so clearly, like it's destined to happen. Please come home to me, my love.

In past letters I alluded to some trouble I had earlier with one of my flights. I told you I had to put the airplane down and landed emergently. I wasn't completely honest with you, I'm afraid. I didn't want you to worry, and I wasn't ready to tell you everything. After all, you have so much to worry about already without me adding to the burden. But I feel it's important for you to know the truth. I had to bail out and I spent a long week alone in the wilderness before my fellow pilots finally found me. I was so scared, but thinking of you helped me come through. Now you're not the only one in the family who has jumped out of an airplane!

The incident was terrifying, but it also taught me a lot about myself. I survived. I found water, food and shelter. I also faced some demons which I didn't really know I had. I told you before about my friend Trish Watkins passing away. I was in the room when she died and I felt guilty. If I hadn't been there, she'd still be alive. It ate me up inside. But during that week in the forest, she came to me. I know it sounds outlandish, but she did. She helped me. She came to me when I thought about giving up. She led me to a place where I could survive until help finally arrived. I know how it sounds, crazy, but the experience changed me for the better. I guess I see things more clearly now and the one thing that I see more clearly than ever is us. We are so good together and I can't wait for you to come home to me.

I know I said it in my last letter, but I'll say it again; Merry Christmas and Happy New Year, even though it feels so hollow knowing this terrible war has carried into another year.

Don't worry about me, darling. The flight incident was a fluke. It won't happen again. I haven't flown in a long while now. I'm afraid you'll have to wait for all the details when you come home.

Please stay safe my love and know I love you and will always be here for you.
Your loving wife,
Abby
December 27th, 1944
P.S.
I visited your friend Gil Hicks again. He's doing fine. He's a good man, I can see why you get along with him so well.

CLYDE READ the letter a few more times. He tried to imagine Abby in the forest alone for a week. His first reaction was fear, then anger. Why did she insist on this dangerous job? He thought about what she'd said about her friend Trish. He supposed she must've been addled from lack of food and water. He remembered how Private Butler had hallucinated when he suffered from dehydration and heatstroke back in Australia. That hallucination ended in a good officer's near death.

He took a deep breath and blew it out slowly. She was fine and it wouldn't happen again, she'd said so herself. He wondered how much longer the WASP program could last. He'd read somewhere that it was already dead, but she hadn't mentioned that in her letter. He supposed it was inevitable. Flying aircraft was a man's job, and now that more and more were back from the war, it just made sense. How would that impact Abby? She loved flying, that much was clear.

Gutiérrez trotted over to where he sat. "I figured I'd find you here."

"What's wrong?"

"Nothing. Huss just told us we've got a new mission and you're not gonna believe where we're going."

Clyde sprang off the palm tree and stood before Gutiérrez. "Well, spill it."

He leaned in close as though it was a state secret. "It's still hush-hush, but we're taking back Corregidor."

Clyde's belly twisted in that odd sensation of both excitement and fear. Corregidor—The Rock—the key to Manila and the rest of the Philippines.

"Holy shit!" He looked at Abby's letter. She was so sure he'd make it back home, almost as though she'd divined it. His hand shook slightly. Corregidor would be a hard nut to crack. The only target he could think of that'd be worse would be Japan itself. The place was like a fortress. Gutiérrez trotted off and Clyde said under his breath, "I hope you're right, my love."

~

CLYDE SAT in the stiflingly hot building which the guards had been guarding with such intensity. A replica of Corregidor Island sat on a sand table. He'd seen it on maps before. He'd been interested because his brother Frank had fought on it way back in 1942, and he wanted to know more. He remembered how it looked uncannily like a tadpole. It was relatively small, full of cliffs, fortifications, and jungle-covered hills and impenetrable ravines choked with thick brush. How ironic that he'd be taking back the island his brother had been taken prisoner all those years before.

The replica had been intricately done. It showed the wider and higher points further west and the lower points, along with Malinta Hill further east. The tail of the tadpole pointed toward Manila Bay and the head pointed out to The South China Sea. Buildings dotted the replica, the most notable a large building on the head of the tadpole which was labeled "officer's quarters." Just west of that building, a large letter A had been painted. In the narrower region near a few more buildings and, oddly enough, a swimming pool and golf course, the letter B.

Lieutenant Bursk looked around the room at his NCOs. He was Second Platoon's new CO. He'd replaced Lieutenant Palinsky, who'd died just a few miles from where they stood. Bursk was a veteran from another airborne unit and seemed to know what he was doing, which was a relief considering where he'd be leading them.

Bursk cleared his throat. "Gentleman, this is Corregidor Island, our target. As you can see, it's not much to look at and it looks even worse than this mockup. Since mid-January, the Fifth Air Force has dropped nearly three hundred *tons* of explosives on the place. With that much firepower, I'm surprised the island hasn't sunk," he snickered, but when no one else joined him, he continued. "The island might be the most heavily photographed island in the world."

He pointed to the various black and white photographs pinned up around the room, showing some of the recent bomb damage. The whole island looked like one big bomb crater.

"Reconnaissance flights haven't seen much enemy activity. Sixth Army G2 doesn't think it's heavily fortified." His eyes hardened. "But we know all about those kinds of assessments. The fact is, they're guessing. There are tunnels everywhere. The Japs could be hiding an entire division in there and we wouldn't know about it, so expect heavy resistance."

He smacked the letter A. "This is one of our primary drop sites. This whole area is called Topside. This large building here labeled officer's quarters is blown to shit, but still standing, even with the recent pounding. The first troopers will land here. It's essential we take and hold Topside. As you can see, it's the high ground and is the key to the whole operation. The second site is here at B. This is an old golf course, but don't get your hopes up, it's only nine holes and nothing over a par 2. In other words, it's not much of a landing site. Neither is what I'd call optimum."

He pointed near the tail, near Malinta Hill. "This is obviously a better landing zone, but the Nips would have us sighted from Topside, so we're going Topside. Now, that brings me to our leg friends in the 34th Infantry. A few hours after we take Topside, an amphibious force will land here at Bottomside, at Black Beach. They'll be exposed, but by then, we should have the Japs shitting themselves around Topside. They'll be too busy trying to figure this whole thing out to worry about the 34th boys."

He took a long slurp of water. "Now, as you can see, these drop sites are small, and there will be wind. We don't know how much, of course, but it's always windy there. They're predicting fifteen mile per hour winds on jump day, which will be the 16th and 17th at 0830 hours. The number crunchers have determined that our C-47s won't be over the drop sites for longer than six seconds. So, they'll fly at 400 feet and only drop sticks of eight men at a time. They'll make another pass and drop the next stick. Anyone leftover and they'll make a third pass." There was grumbling and private conversations. "I know, I know. That's a long time to be over an enemy-held island in a slow flying C-47, but that's just how it's gotta be this time. Once the first batch is delivered, the flyboys will come back here and pick up the next load." He grinned and pointed at his chest, "We'll be landing at site B right next to the swimming pool and golf course, so bring your bathing suits." He laughed at his own joke again, then continued. "Our objective is to put fire on any Nips making a move on the beachhead and to cut their communications capabilities." He leaned back and crossed his arms.

Clyde stroked his chin and considered everything. It would be hairy, to say the least. The cliffs to the south of drop site B scared the hell out of him. They were far too close for comfort. One gust of wind or a mis-drop would put them over the cliffs and into the sea.

Bursk continued. "The flyboys are going to pound the crap out of them all night and right up until we jump. The Navy boys'll be sending high explosive greeting cards, too. We can call on them for pinpoint support if we need it. That goes for air support, too. MacArthur himself is highly interested in this operation. As most of you know, he had to abandon Corregidor back in '42, and that hasn't sat right in his craw ever since, so we have the full support of Sixth Army as well as the Navy and Air corps. They really want to kick the Japs off this rock in the worst way."

Despite the obvious danger, Clyde felt excitement growing in the room.

The men had missed out on a few recent combat drops around Manila, which they thought they should've gotten. They'd gone to the less experienced 11th Airborne, but this would be the ultimate drop of the entire war, European or Pacific. The 503rd would make history.

Clyde's chest swelled with pride. The fact that they hadn't done any practice drops told him how confident their commanders were in the troops. Give them a mission and send them on their way. They'd truly become America's elite warriors. He thought of Abby back in the states. She'd be so proud of him.

Bursk clapped his hands together. "I want you men in here whenever you have a spare moment studying this table. When we jump in two days, I want you ready. Understood?"

"Yes, sir," the room erupted in unison.

~

Mindoro, Philippines
February 16th, 1945

CLYDE SAT NEXT to Sergeant Huss on the tarmac. It was finally here, go day. The past two days had been a whirlwind of activity. As assistant squad leader, Clyde had too many duties to count. Now that was all finished. He took a deep breath and blew it out slowly. He'd done everything he could to prepare himself and the men for today. He'd even written one last letter to Abby.

They'd been up well before dawn. As usual, before a combat drop, the cooks went out of their way with a huge breakfast with everything they could imagine. But as usual, he could hardly eat any of it. He forced what he could, but his nerves unsettled his stomach.

He checked the time for the thousandth time. The jump-off hour was quickly approaching. The flight from Mindoro to Corregidor was relatively short, about an hour. They'd fly in threes and arrive over the target at 0830, so they'd take off at 0700, form up for thirty minutes, then head north to the Rock, Corregidor.

Now that he had nothing to do but wait, his thoughts turned to his brother, Frank. He didn't know the details, but he knew Frank had been at Corregidor when General Wainwright surrendered. Accounts from men like his brother who'd escaped from Japanese POW camps had filtered through the ranks after the military released the information to the public just a few months before. A forced march under brutal conditions had killed many prisoners. Stories of dehydrated and exhausted men falling and either being run through with bayonets or simply run over by trucks abounded. The descriptions enraged him and every other paratrooper.

Now, just a month short of three years later, he would jump onto that same island where it all began and take it back. Three years of war. Three years of hard fighting to get to this point. It felt good, but also daunting.

He wished he could talk to Frank and let him know what he was about to do, but even his parents didn't know where he was now. The latest letter had no new information. It galled Clyde. His brother had suffered enough. Why the hell wasn't he back home?

The line of C-47s suddenly came to life as one engine at a time turned over and coughed white smoke. Soon, the roar stopped all conversation. The time was quickly approaching. He took another deep breath and blew it out slowly.

Huss said, "Alright, here we go."

Lieutenant Bursk walked to each man and helped him stand. When he came to Clyde, like he'd done with everyone else, he offered his hand like a handshake and hefted him to his feet. Clyde felt the hundred pounds of weight hit his shoulders. The familiar feel of tight straps digging into his crotch made him feel right at home.

"You ready, Corporal?"

"Yes sir. More than ready."

"Good man." He stepped in front of Huss and gave him a hand up. After saying a few words to him, Bursk looked down the line. Clyde thought he might say a few words to the group, but the engine noise was too much, so instead, he simply turned to face their aircraft. Clyde decided he liked him.

Clyde checked his gear one last time, making sure nothing had shifted or loosened. He adjusted the Thompson submachine gun tucked vertically along his back, the belly band keeping it firmly in place. He went through a mental checklist. Ten, twenty round magazines, two fragmentation grenades, and two white phosphorous grenades, his trench knife, utility knife, rations, and finally the Mae West preserver in case he missed the island and landed in the sea. He chuckled to himself. If he didn't have everything by now, it was too late anyway.

He looked down the line at the other paratroopers. His stick was chock full of veterans. Good men, every one of them. He'd trusted them with his life before and he'd do so again today. Despite the danger, he couldn't think of anywhere else he'd rather be right now.

A signal and Lieutenant Bursk barked, his voice just loud enough over the din of so many engines, "Okay, men. This is it. Advance to your aircraft! Good luck, I'll see you on The Rock! Geronimo!"

Clyde felt an exhilaration rise and he yelled "Geronimo!" along with everyone else. Then he ambled toward the open door of the C-47. The crew chief helped each man through. Clyde made his way to his seat. Even now, after so many jumps, he felt the confined space pressing in. The smell of fuel and body odor only got worse the longer they sat there, but it didn't diminish his excitement.

Soon, the door shut and the aircraft taxied slowly. He shut his eyes to keep the dust from the other propellers from getting into his eyes.

Sooner than expected, the pilot pushed the throttles; the engines roared and the airframe shuddered. The release always felt exhilarating, and even more so now. The shaking and bouncing changed to smooth as the aircraft left the ground and rose into the air. Clyde adjusted his chinstrap and settled in for the ride.

The rest of Third Squad surrounded him. He wished Gil could be there, too. He'd be ecstatic. Maybe he'd see him again someday and tell him all about it. He'd be jealous, but he'd be one of the few who'd understand once he got home. *If I make it home.*

He shut that line of thinking down quickly. He eyed Second Platoon's Platoon Sergeant Plumly. He'd be their acting jumpmaster and would go out last. Lieutenant Bursk was in the aircraft in front of theirs. If all went as planned, Clyde and Third Squad would be some of the first men down on landing site B, near the swimming pool and the married NCO housing. He smiled, remembering what Bursk said about bringing a swimming suit.

The planes climbed, then circled while the rest of the C-47s climbed to join them. It didn't take long before they straightened out and headed for their target. Everything seemed to be happening faster than normal. It usually slowed down. Maybe he was getting used to this stuff. Now all he had to do was wait to jump.

No one talked. A few men smoked cigarettes. The thought made his stomach turn. He enjoyed a smoke as much as the next man, but not before a jump. For some reason, his belly didn't like that. He refused when Gutiérrez offered him one.

An hour passed, just enough time for the hard seats to become uncomfortable. Men adjusted themselves, searching for that evasive comfortable spot.

The red light beside Plumly lit up. Plumly barked and held up his hand, "Five minutes!"

This was all happening. Hadn't they just gotten into the airplane minutes before? Best to quit thinking and just go with the flow. Do what they'd trained him to do. If he made it, great. If not, well, he'd had a good run. That's just the way it was out here. Men died—or they didn't. There was no rhyme or reason that he could discern. So why worry?

Plumly yelled, "Stand up! Equipment check! Hook up!" They'd done it so often, it was all automatic.

Clyde caught his first glimpse of the Rock. He could see smoke and a dirty white landscape pockmarked with countless bomb craters. The place looked like a desolate wasteland with a bad case of acne.

"Stand in the door!"

Clyde was three men back. Sergeant Huss would have the honor of going out first.

The light turned green. "Go! Go! Go!"

They'd pressed the need for speed out the door. It was crucial for this jump in particular, since the landing zone was especially short. They expected men out the door every half second for a scant six seconds. He went out the door, still touching Gutiérrez, but when the static line pulled his chute, plenty of space separated him.

He checked his canopy, everything looked good. Then he checked the ground and his mind changed. The wind pulled him fast toward the damned cliffs and gullies on the west side. He pulled hard on his risers, hoping to arrest his sideways drift, but the wind was too strong. He had to change his plan, or he'd land in the scrub and trees in the gully. He aimed for a ridge of rock a couple hundred feet away from the Wheeler Battery.

He didn't have much time in the air. He released the risers and braced for a hard landing. His body slammed onto the rocky ledge. His legs collapsed and he did his best to PLF, but pain shot through his body and he saw flashes of lightning and his ears rang, but he was down and alive. The hard part was over.

It took a moment for him to get his wits. He did his customary inventory of ailments and found a few problems that would cause him trouble, no doubt. His right ankle screamed the loudest.

A strong gust of wind filled the parachute and dragged him across sharp rocks. He felt them scraping across his back and buttocks painfully. He rolled onto his belly and the silk snagged on rocks and scrub brush. On his knees now, he pulled until he had enough slack to unlatch from the harness. He threw the Mae West off and shrugged out of the harness. He didn't bother trying to recover the rest of the parachute. They'd been told to leave everything and get into the fight as soon as possible. Even if he'd wanted to roll his chute, it was tangled, torn, and hung up in ratty brush and sharp rocks.

He brought his Thompson off his back shoulder and checked it over. Thankfully, it still seemed to be in working order. He loaded a magazine and pulled the top bolt—ready for action. He saw another parachute fluttering in the wind only twenty yards from him. He put pressure on his right ankle and nearly fell over. He stifled an agonized cry. *Damn.* He gingerly made his way along the little clearing toward where the other trooper should be. The pain coming from his ankle made beads of sweat form on his brow, but he kept going.

He saw Gutiérrez thrashing, dangling over a short cliff, hopelessly tangled. "You okay, Guti?" he called.

"That you, Cooper?"

"Yeah, it's me, buddy. Looks like you can use a hand."

"Hell yes. I think Butler's down here, too. Fucking wind blew us way off course."

"No shit. Hang tight, I'll cut you loose." Clyde moved carefully over the rocks. Every time he put pressure on his right foot, shots of pain ran up his leg. He glanced toward Topside to see if any enemy soldiers might've noticed them and might be lining them up in their sights, but it was all clear for now.

He pulled his razor sharp trench knife from his left ankle sheath and cut a few shroud lines. Gutiérrez called out, "Careful, Coop. I don't wanna drop into the gully."

"Well, then grab onto something."

Gutiérrez struggled and finally faced the rock he hung against. Clyde stopped cutting until he seemed secure. "You good? Got a good hold of something?"

"Yeah, yeah. Go ahead. Cut away."

Clyde sliced through the lines until Gutiérrez was free. The parachute silk fluttered behind him but quickly caught on the low scrub brush. Clyde placed his Thompson on the rocks, crawled on his belly and reached down for his friend. "Give me your hand."

Gutiérrez squinted up at him. His nose had a nasty gash and blood dripped from it, but he looked alright otherwise. Clyde stretched and their hands clasped. "Gotcha," Clyde said.

He hauled back and Gutiérrez made it off the precarious ledge and onto the top with Clyde. They both lay on their backs breathing hard from the effort.

A distant voice called from the gulley, "Hey, who is that?"

Clyde poked his head over the edge. He saw more shredded parachute silk and endless tangles of riser lines. "That you, Butler?"

"Cooper? Yeah, it's me. I'm way the hell down here."

"Are you hurt?"

"I think I'm all right. Took a good knock to the head. I might've passed out, but I think I'm okay."

Clyde pushed to his feet, being careful to keep the weight off his right ankle. Gutiérrez pulled his carbine from his back and swiped at the blood he felt dripping from his nose to his chin. He rubbed the blood on his pants, but otherwise ignored it. He noticed Clyde limping along. "You okay, Coop?"

"I twisted my ankle real bad, but I'll live. Let's get Butler out of there."

"Hey, Cooper," Gutiérrez called.

Clyde looked over at him. Gutiérrez had a shit-eating grin on his face. Overhead, C-47s circled and dropped more paratroopers in blossoming bursts of white and black.

"What?"

"Welcome to Corregidor."

20

Butler found his way from the gully and up to the rocky slope, where Clyde and Gutiérrez waited.

Clyde noticed a dent in the side of Butler's helmet. "You sure you're okay?" he asked, paying close attention to his pupils. They looked normal, but he must've hit hard to dent the steel pot so deeply.

"Yeah, I feel fine now."

Clyde said, "You see anyone else down there?" Butler shook his head. Clyde continued, "I didn't see anyone else nearby. Let's get Topside and get in the war. I think Wheeler battery is just up there. The landing site's just a few hundred yards further on. We'll meet up at the rally point."

He took a step and nearly fell over, but he caught himself. Gutiérrez stepped to his side. "You wanna lean on me?"

"Nah, it's loosening up a little. I'll be alright." He gritted his teeth and hobbled along. Every step hurt, but he did his best to put it out of his mind. It felt a little better, although it throbbed inside his boot and he wondered if it was more than a simple sprain.

They moved up the slope. A few rifle shots and the incessant roar of aircraft overhead kept them focused. Barrages from destroyers and cruisers hammered the beach where the 34th would land.

After a few hundred yards, Clyde stopped to catch his breath and give his ankle a breather. He looked out over the ocean. The destroyers and cruisers cut large white swaths through the ocean, and smaller PT boats zipped around closer to shore. The PT boats promised to pick up any wayward paratroopers that drifted out over the sea. Landing in the ocean would be even more terrifying than landing where he had, but at least it would be softer.

Between the cruisers, destroyers and the PT boats, a couple large LVIs and LVMs churned. The LVIs carried the infantry and the LVMs carried the tanks and heavy weapons crews. Soon the 34th Infantry would assault Black Beach on Bottomside. It was up to the paratroopers to keep the enemy occupied until the two forces could link up.

Butler and Gutiérrez stopped to wait for Clyde. Clyde waved them forward. "I'll be fine, keep going. I'll catch up." They nodded and moved off. Clyde cursed to himself. He'd seen plenty of sprained ankles and even breaks, but it hadn't happened to him yet. *Guess I was due.*

He hobbled along, using the Thompson as a makeshift crutch. He tried to keep up as best he could, but the others were soon out of sight as they crested a hill. If he remembered correctly, Wheeler Battery was just ahead. He recalled the reconnaissance photos. It might hold enemy units. He grit his teeth and pushed himself harder. He didn't want the others to hit trouble without him by their sides.

He crested the ledge and saw Butler and Gutiérrez crouched behind boulders only a few yards ahead. Beyond them, he saw the gun battery. Flat concrete with iron works sticking up was all that was left of the actual gun emplacement, but that's not what caught his attention. A small car was parked nearby. He didn't see anyone, but they had to be close. It didn't look abandoned.

He hunkered between them, momentarily forgetting his throbbing ankle. He whispered, "See anyone?"

Gutiérrez shook his head, "No, but they've gotta be close."

Clyde glanced up the hill toward the rally point. The battery was the furthest western tip of the landing zone, but he saw no parachutes fluttering nearby.

"Okay, let's move up, carefully."

Without a word, Butler and Gutiérrez moved forward while Clyde

watched for any movement, his Thompson at the ready. They found cover
and waved Clyde forward. He didn't move as quickly or as gracefully, but he
soon crouched beside them again. They moved forward again. Clyde kept
the muzzle aimed at the car, which was only thirty yards away now.

Butler suddenly froze. Gutiérrez noticed and stopped, too. Clyde
scanned the area, but didn't see what had caught their attention. He stayed
put until Butler signaled that he'd spotted the enemy. Clyde's mouth went
dry as dust.

Gutiérrez motioned him forward. Clyde moved up, being extra careful
not to make a sound, although the circling aircraft and the occasional crash
of naval guns engaging unseen targets helped cover any missteps.

He finally made it to them. Butler pointed, never taking his eyes off the
gun battery. Clyde raised his head until he saw four figures standing on the
other side of the battery. They must be the occupants of the car. Two of
them scanned the sea with binoculars, clearly watching the amphibious
landing party at their doorstep, while the other two held submachine guns
and watched their surroundings. They had to be a contingent of officers
come to take a closer look. *Ballsy sons of bitches*. Clyde studied the situation
for only a few seconds. It was obvious what he had to do.

The group of Japanese weren't looking in their direction, firmly focused
on the sea and the circling C-47s discharging paratroopers. Any moment,
they'd realize their danger and bolt. Clyde wanted to prevent that.

"Let's take 'em," he hissed.

That's all the direction the others needed. They sprinted from cover,
running straight at the hapless enemy. Clyde did his best to keep up, but
the best he could do was keep them covered if something else popped up.
He veered toward the vehicle. The least he could do was to prevent their
escape.

Gutiérrez and Butler made it to within thirty yards before one soldier
noticed them and called out a warning. The paratroopers went to their
knees, brought their carbines to their shoulders and fired in quick succes-
sion. Bullets smacked into bodies and two soldiers fell immediately, but the
other two dove out of the way as bullets whizzed and ricocheted off the
rocks.

Clyde made it to the car and propped his Thompson on the roof, aiming toward the action. Gutiérrez ran forward while Butler peppered the area with covering fire. The pop of the carbine carried on the wind and dust and rock chunks erupted where the enemy had disappeared. Gutiérrez sprinted and leaped over rocks and chunks of twisted metal. He dropped to a knee and fired a quick volley. Butler quickly reloaded, then ran toward the fallen soldiers.

Clyde wanted to help, but he didn't have a shot. Butler made it to Gutiérrez, and they ran to the two enemy soldiers. They pumped a few more rounds into them, then advanced. They soon dropped out of sight and Clyde heard more pops from the carbines.

He ground his teeth, desperately wanting to join them, but knowing his ankle would hold him back too much. Long minutes passed. He heard no more shots, but he heard distant yelling. Movement from the right made him shift aim. He pulled the stock tightly into his shoulder and waited. It might be one of his men, but it might not be, too.

Over the rise, a man appeared, running straight at him. The runner kept looking back as though the hounds of hell were on his heels. One arm hung down, limp and bleeding. In his other, he wielded a pistol.

Clyde centered his sights on his chest. The soldier kept right on coming. He finally focused on the car, his chance at escape. His eyes widened when he saw Clyde. Before he could bring the pistol to bear, Clyde gave him a quick burst of .45-caliber lead. The heavy rounds tore into his chest, sending a spray of fine red mist out his backside. He dropped onto his face and didn't move.

A few seconds later, Gutiérrez called from where the soldier had just come from. "Coming over the top! Hold fire."

Clyde barked back, "Come." He stepped around the car and approached the man he'd shot, never taking the smoking muzzle off the target.

Both Butler and Gutiérrez met him at the body. Gutiérrez propped his carbine on his hip like a big game hunter. "Nice shooting."

"He was already winged," Clyde noted, pointing at his blood-soaked arm.

Gutiérrez motioned behind, "Yeah, the other one's back there a bit. Butler nailed him, but this one slipped away."

Clyde sank to his haunches to take a closer look. "He's a captain."

"Well, I'll be damned," Gutiérrez exclaimed.

Butler beamed. "The one I got was a lieutenant, I think. Wonder what they're doing way out here?"

"Probably trying to figure out what the hell's happening. Wheeler Battery has a great view of the entire area," Clyde pointed out.

"Let's search the officers and get to the rally point."

Butler stalked off to search the lieutenant while Clyde searched the captain and Gutiérrez watched for any threats. Clyde found his identification, along with various other knickknacks and documents he had no idea how to read. He stuffed the documents into his pocket. He'd give it to the brass when he found them.

He pondered a photograph he found of the captain in better days. He and his wife held a baby between them while a young boy clutched the mother's side. He brushed the dirt and blood off the photo. He thought of the picture he carried of Abby. Would the day come when some heartless enemy soldier held her picture in his hand? He threw the family picture onto the dead man's bloody chest. "Sayonara, pal," he uttered.

CLYDE HOBBLED between Butler and Gutiérrez. The incessant roar of C-47s continued and parachutes continued blossoming overhead. Most hit the correct landing zones, but a few drifted out of sight. The farther they walked toward the golf course, the more discarded parachutes they encountered.

"That you Guti?" a paratrooper called from a shallow bomb crater.

Gutiérrez grinned and called back. "Yeah, it's me Cowboy. Get over here and give me a hand with the corporal."

Private Wallace and Hallon sprang from the hole and ran to them. Wallace exclaimed, "Are you hit?"

"Hell no," Clyde answered. "Twisted my ankle. We ended up on the other side of Wheeler Battery."

Hallon and Wallace took over helping Clyde. Butler bragged. "I bagged a lieutenant and Coop tagged a captain." He mimicked bringing his rifle up, "Pop, pop, pop, down he goes just like at the carnival."

Clyde gave him a sideways glance. Even though he'd come a long way since Australia, Butler still acted like a spoiled child sometimes.

Clyde asked. "Any action up here? What's the situation?"

"No Japs yet, but we've seen some machine gun nests open up on the 34th boys and even a few big guns taking potshots at our boats. The navy boys took care of them pretty quick, though."

"Where's Lieutenant Bursk?"

"At the swimming pool," Hallon said.

Clyde shook them off. "Stay in position. I can make it alright on my own."

Sergeant Huss came at the group of clustered paratroopers. "Spread out, dammit. One grenade'll take you all out."

The others spread out quickly. Huss came to Clyde's side. He glanced at his right foot, which he obviously favored. "Ankle?"

"Yeah."

"Anything to report?"

"We took out two officers and two infantrymen down by Wheeler. They were watching the landing party and we surprised 'em. They're dead, but we took some papers off the officers—a lieutenant and a captain."

"Good job," he slapped Clyde's back. "Bursk's at the pool. I'm sure the G2 guys'll wanna take a look."

Clyde looked around. The place looked like a hellscape with all the bomb craters and hollowed-out buildings. He imagined it must've been beautiful before the war. He walked with Huss. "What's the situation?"

"So far, so good. The Nips are absent, at least from Topside. A few skirmishes here and there, but just unorganized groups of twos and threes. I suspect that'll change come nightfall. The 34th should come ashore any second now." He pointed to the edge overlooking the sea and Bottomside. "We have good visuals and can hit anything the Japs throw at the beachhead from here. Machine guns placed there and there, .50 cals." Clyde hobbled along, doing his best to mask the pain. "You'll need to get that looked at, but right now, I need you on the line."

"It's no problem. I think it's just twisted," Huss raised an eyebrow as though he knew the truth, or at least suspected.

The further they walked, the more paratroopers, until it almost felt crowded. The shelling continued, and a group of A-20 bombers made a pass on Malinta Hill. The explosions sent geysers of dirt and smoke skyward.

"Not much left to bomb," Clyde commented.

"The Nips have gotta be somewhere."

They made it to the swimming pool. It had long ago emptied of water, but Clyde imagined how nice it must've been. Beyond it stood the remnants of the married NCO quarters. He tried to imagine Sergeant Huss basking in the sun alongside the pool and couldn't. Huss'd probably still wear the scowl that seemed imprinted on his face permanently.

Huss led him into the ruins beyond the pool. They both braced when they saw Lieutenant Bursk speaking with Captain Stallsworthy, the C.O. of Able company.

Bursk noticed them and waved them inside. Inside was a relative term, as the buildings no longer had rooftops. Bursk gave them a once over. "You found Corporal Cooper," Bursk commented.

"Yes, sir. He and Butler and Gutiérrez landed long and just joined us. They took out some officers and have some intel to pass along."

Stallsworthy broke away from the maps he perused. "What kind of intel?"

Clyde stepped forward and handed all the documents they pulled off the dead Japanese officers. "We killed two officers, a lieutenant and a captain. We pulled this off them."

Bursk took it, then handed it to Stallsworthy after he took a quick look. Stallsworthy went through each sheet of paper. When he came to the Captain's ID, he looked at the picture for a long time. "I think you bagged their commander, corporal. If I'm not mistaken, this is Captain Tarakagi. He's, or he was in command of this garrison." Clyde's mouth dropped open. He didn't expect that. "Where'd you say he was?"

"He and three others were down at Wheeler Battery, sir. They watched the amphibious assault. There was a car down there, too. That's what first tipped us off."

Stallsworthy nodded, taking it all in. He pointed to Huss. "Take your squad down there and bring that car back if you can. If not, bring every speck of intel you find in there."

"Yes, sir. Right away." He stepped out. Clyde turned to join him, but Stallsworthy stopped him. "You're injured, corporal. You've earned a rest. Doc's set up a temporary infirmary up the way a little. Get that ankle looked at."

Clyde protested, "It's just a sprain, sir."

"Bullshit. I can see it swelling through your damned jump boots. That's an order, corporal."

Clyde ground his teeth, but said, "Yes, sir."

"Oh, and Cooper? Good job, you just cut the head off the Jap's leadership."

"Thank you, sir."

"Dismissed."

~

CLYDE SAT ON A ROCK, or more accurately, a shattered piece of the NCO quarters. Medics scurried around, treating wounded paratroopers. Most had suffered from broken bones and or twisted joints. Clyde couldn't take his eyes off the two rows of bodies covered in tarpaulins. For meeting only light resistance from the Japanese, the first wave of troopers had taken a heavy toll, mostly from hard landings into structures and rocks. A few had parachute malfunctions, too.

A medic finally came to his aid. He looked Clyde up and down, then hunched and lifted Clyde's right foot gingerly. "This all, or is there more?"

"That's all. The brass ordered me to come here."

The medic didn't take his eyes off the bulging boot. "It's likely broken."

"Nah, it's just a sprain."

The medic sounded exasperated. "I'm a paratrooper medic. Leave the diagnosing to me, corporal. I've seen hundreds of these."

"I'm gonna have to take your boot off to treat it."

The thought made Clyde nauseous. It was the last thing he wanted to do. "If you do that, I'll never get my boot back on, right?"

"That's right. We can splint it and get you to the boat once we link up with the 34th."

Clyde shook his way out of the medic's grasp. "I followed orders by reporting here, but now I'm leaving. I ain't going barefoot while the Nips try to retake what they lost."

The medic stepped aside. "Keep it elevated whenever you have a moment. That'll keep the swelling down." He handed him a few aspirins. "Take these. It'll help with the pain." Clyde gave him a surprised look. He expected some kind of pushback. The medic shrugged. "You're at least the tenth guy that's done the same thing."

Clyde grinned. "Thanks, doc."

"I didn't do nothin'." He quickly made his way to the next paratrooper, a man holding a massively swollen wrist and hand.

Clyde hobbled to the door and picked up his Thompson. He'd have to avoid Captain Stallsworthy, but that wouldn't be a problem. He'd be the furthest thing from his mind by now. He had a company to run.

Clyde stepped out of the ruins and into the direct sunlight. Wind still whipped across the island, but the temperature was pleasant enough. For the first time, he noticed the only aircraft circling overhead were fighters and bombers. He didn't see a single C-47. They'd be heading back for the second load of paratroopers by now. It was up to them to hold Topside until the rest of the battalion dropped in later that day.

A cluster of troopers huddled in a massive bomb crater just beyond the bone-dry swimming pool. Parachutes waved in the wind, some in the pool itself. Boxes of ammunition had been stacked at the far end. Clyde remembered the large pallet in the middle of the C-47 he'd rode in. He supposed one of those boxes could've come from the same aircraft. He checked his ammunition and realized he'd lost a few grenades. He restocked himself.

A sergeant in the bomb crater noticed him and called out. "Hey trooper, what unit you with?"

Clyde thought he recognized him from First Platoon, but he couldn't be sure. "Second Platoon, Able Company."

He pointed downslope. "Down there."

Clyde nodded. "Yeah, I know. I'm heading there now."

"Well then, get going."

Clyde swallowed the remark he wanted to make and said instead, "Hup, sergeant." He limped along, hoping the NCO didn't ask any more questions.

A scream from a dozen voices rose from beyond the temporary infirmary where he'd just been. He'd heard that yell plenty of times on other battlefields, and it twisted his stomach into knots. He turned while dropping to a knee, his ankle suddenly unimportant.

From around the far corner of the NCO quarters, a group of fifteen Japanese soldiers charged straight at the clustered group in the bomb crater. Clyde aimed and pulled the top bolt on the Thompson back. The enemy soldiers fired from their hips as they ran. Bullets whizzed and ricocheted off rocks. The troopers in the crater moved to the front lip and took aim.

The enemy soldiers hadn't noticed him yet. He rose above a chunk of twisted debris, aimed, and fired off a long burst. His bullets tore into their right flank, dropping three men immediately and making others dive for cover. A few seconds later, the men in the crater opened fire.

Clyde quickly reloaded. By the time he came back up with the Thompson at his shoulder, most of the twenty men were already down, but a few diehards continued their suicidal charge. He fired a short burst, dropping another man.

Bullets slammed into the debris he crouched behind, making him duck. A flurry of bullets whined past where his head had been. He pulled the grenade he'd just restocked. He threw it as far as he could, then held his helmet and waited for the blast. The grenade blew with a muted thump. He rolled to the corner of the debris and poked his head out. He saw the smoke from the grenade rising amongst more dead bodies. The troopers from the crater poured more lead into the area, but the enemy soldiers were down.

Clyde kept his muzzle on the spot and watched for movement. He shifted his aim behind, seeing movement from the NCO quarters. He hoped none of his bullets had ricocheted that way and hurt any friendlies.

A medic poked his head out of one of the gaping doorways of the makeshift infirmary. He held a carbine to his shoulder, but he didn't aim at the pile of enemy soldiers, but at the corner where they'd come from. He fired off a quick volley and the wall erupted in dust and rock chips. Clyde didn't see any enemy soldiers lurking, but the medic must have seen something he couldn't.

If the enemy rushed them, the medics would have a tough time repelling them. Clyde got to his feet. His ankle screamed at him, but he did his best to ignore the pain. He hobbled his way back toward the ruins. He kept an eye on the pile of Japanese bodies. He was about to fire a burst into the closest of them just to make sure, when more Japanese soldiers came around the corner, this time angling for the infirmary.

The medic went to a knee and unloaded his carbine. Men fell, but most kept coming. The medic pulled back into cover. A few more yards and the enemy would make the ruins and be much harder to root out. He thought of all the wounded men laying defenseless on stretchers. The Japanese would use their bayonets on them for sure.

Clyde took careful aim. He pulled the trigger, keeping his bursts short and controlled. The heavy slugs tore into the lead man and he dropped. The six others leaped into windowless windows and were inside. Clyde held his fire, fearful of hitting wounded paratroopers.

He yelled in frustrated anguish and ran as fast as his ankle would allow. He made it to the wall where the medic had been. He heard shots and shouting. Some were angry, some petrified, some in Japanese, some in English. He went inside. The muzzle of his Thompson led the way.

A shape darted past an open hole in the wall. He recognized an enemy uniform. He ran to the hole and leaned in. The back of the soldier was only feet away. He had his bayonet held high and it dripped with blood. Clyde pulled the trigger and four bullets ripped into the enemy's back and hurled him onto his face. His rifle skidded away.

Clyde stepped the rest of the way through the hole, looking for more targets. A wounded paratrooper stared at him through glazed eyes. He clutched a fresh wound in his belly. His mouth gaped as blood oozed out the side and he coughed, then let out a long last breath and died.

More shots and more yelling from deeper inside pushed him forward. He reloaded without thinking about it, letting his nearly spent magazine clatter to the ground. He didn't have time to stow it; he wanted to prevent any more wounded from dying. He wanted to kill the bastards.

The distinctive pops of carbines drew him into another room. Smoke wafted heavily as two medics and two walking wounded troopers fired into an adjacent room. A Japanese soldier's body slumped across the threshold, bleeding from multiple gunshot wounds. Japanese voices screamed from the room.

"What you got?" Clyde yelled.

One of the wounded men looked his way. "At least three of them went in there."

Clyde pulled a grenade off his harness. "Any friendlies inside?"

The harried medic answered, "Nope. Only Japs."

"Fire in the hole!" Clyde yelled, then tossed the grenade. It bounced off the back wall with a metal clank, then exploded. Smoke and dust spilled out over the dead enemy soldier. Clyde pulled another and threw it in, too. The second crash brought part of the roofing down on their heads.

Clyde waited a few seconds to let the dust settle, then stepped over the body and into the room. He fired from the hip, sweeping the room with short bursts, but there was no need. When the dust finally settled, he saw only mangled bodies tangled in death.

He stepped back out. The others looked at him with wide eyes. It reminded him of the way his men had looked at him way back in New Guinea, when he'd shot the enemy soldier in the side of the head at point blank range. He didn't like it much.

"That all of them?" No one spoke, just continued to stare at him as though he were a murderer. "Well?" he barked it this time.

A private with a head wound snapped out of it first. "That's all of 'em, corporal. You—you got 'em all."

Clyde looked from one to another. *Why they looking at me that way?* They were supposed to kill the enemy. *That's why we're here, dammit.* "I'll send someone to help you. I've gotta get back to my men."

"Sure thing, corporal," the medic said.

Clyde hobbled his way back across the swimming pool area and onto what they called the golf course. It looked nothing like a golf course, and he had a hard time imagining what it had once looked like.

The troopers from the bomb crater sifted through the dead Japanese bodies in the rubble, going through their personal effects. They didn't pay any attention to him as he passed on his way to his squad.

By the time he made it to the edge overlooking Bottomside and found his squad, his ankle felt as though it had been lit on fire. After reporting to Huss, he sidled into a hole beside Gutiérrez, Butler, and Oliver.

"Where the hell've you been?" Oliver asked him in his heavy New York accent.

"None of your business. What'd I miss?"

Oliver pointed toward the sea. "The 34th landed and they're pushing in."

Clyde had to adjust his position to see the view. He gave a low whistle. Far below, the LVIs disgorged troops directly onto the beach. From here, they looked like incredibly disorganized ants. Tanks churned to shore in twos and threes as they emerged from the bellies of the big LVM transports. One tank, a few hundred yards up the beach, burned mightily, sending black smoke into the sky.

Gutiérrez said, "That one hit a mine or something. You've missed most of it. They put up a pretty good resistance at first." He pointed to an area around Malinta Hill. "They had dug in machine guns and a few bigger guns in there, but the Navy and flyboys took care of them about a half hour ago. Been pretty smooth since."

Oliver punched his arm. "If you hadn't been slacking back at the infirmary, you woulda seen the whole thing."

"Yeah, guess so."

21

Clyde sat in the bottom of the foxhole and desperately tried to sleep. He had his ankle propped up on an ammo box. It didn't stop the awful pain, but it helped the swelling. He needed to sleep, but whenever he drifted off, some night noise would pull him back and his ankle would scream all over again.

The noises on Corregidor were unlike other islands he'd fought on. The place had been so heavily bombed he doubted any wildlife remained, so any noises were mostly man-made. Wrenching metal and collapsing concrete walls were common. The sounds of naval vessels off the coast mixed with the sounds of more troops and equipment landing on the beachhead grew louder with each shift in the wind, which had slackened with the darkness, but not disappeared.

He'd heard rumors that the 3rd Battalion slated to come in on C-47s in the morning might make an amphibious landing instead, because of the unpredictable wind. He remembered how it had pushed him off the landing site that morning. Despite the fear and his broken ankle, he would still rather drop in by parachute than walk off a boat, as they'd done on Mindoro. They were paratroopers, by God.

He sat up and rubbed the ankle through the boot, gingerly. He had no illusions now about whether he'd broken it. Now it was just a matter of how badly. But he refused to leave the line. He'd seen men with gunshots stay on the line—he just had a simple bone break. He could push through the pain if he had to. He'd proven that at the infirmary. That felt like a bad dream now.

It had happened far from their position, and he doubted anyone in his squad, or platoon for that matter, even knew he was involved. The action hadn't gone unnoticed. He'd heard troopers discussing it. The enemy numbers swelled from twenty men to over one hundred, but he hadn't corrected them. It was over. He'd done his duty—end of story.

He gave up on sleep. He found a position where he could watch the beachhead next to his squad leader.

Huss looked him up and down. "Can't sleep?"

"Nope. I can take over if you wanna catch a few winks."

"I doubt I could sleep either."

They both watched the black shapes of ships down by the beach. More ships patrolled back and forth on the open ocean, their white wakes clearly visible even at night. The smaller wakes denoted PT boats. They sped along much closer to shore. Occasionally, thick strands of tracer rounds shot out from them in a spectacular light show. They took it all in.

"Quite a view," Clyde said.

"Yeah. I wonder what the folks back home would think of this?" Huss mused.

Clyde thought of Abby. This was the last place he'd ever want her to be, but if she were here, he had no doubt she'd be mesmerized. Clyde said, "There's a whole slew of reporters here. They're taking pictures of everything, so I guess they'll get a look that way."

"One of those crazy bastards asked me how I felt right after I landed. I'd barely gotten unhooked."

"What'd you say?"

"Nothin'. I ignored them and went about my business."

"Hell, you coulda been famous, sergeant."

"I don't wanna be famous. Besides, the son of a bitch was blocking my way."

"Gotta respect them, though."

"I do? Why's that?"

"Can you imagine jumping into this shit with just a camera or a pencil and notepad? I can't."

"I guess I'd never thought of it that way. I wonder what the Nips would do if they captured one of 'em?"

"They kill unarmed medics. What d'you think they'd do with 'em besides kill them?"

"I dunno. You're right I guess. Just seems strange to see reporters walking around everywhere asking for interviews while dodging Jap bullets. It's probably unheard of for the Japs. Probably think they were some kind of spies."

They watched the beachhead in silence. A flurry of rifle fire erupted to the rear a couple of times, and flares from mortar crews erupted overhead twice, but there wasn't any real action in their sector.

Clyde's eyes drooped and he finally fell asleep sitting upright. He didn't dream, but he slept soundly. He woke to the sound of a naval barrage.

He wiped the drool off his arm and the side of his face. The stars overhead had shifted, so he knew he'd slept at least a few hours. Huss slept in the bottom of the hole. For a moment he thought he'd fallen asleep on guard duty, but their rotation had passed onto the next man.

He adjusted himself and immediately regretted it. His ankle sent a shock of pain up his leg that made him gasp. He broke out in a cold, clammy sweat and nausea swept over him. For the first time since breaking it, he worried about long-term damage. Perhaps he should let the doc put a splint on it. But that would certainly take him out of the fight for good. The 34th and 503rd would likely link up once the 3rd Battalion dropped in that morning. Once that happened, they would send all the wounded to the waiting hospital ships.

In the wee hours of the night, he wondered if he'd done enough. Perhaps he should take himself out of the fight. Did his wound earn him a trip home? The war might end before he healed enough to return to the fight. He doubted that and felt shame at the thought. But he also felt a twinge of something he hadn't felt in a very long time—hope. For the first time in a long time, he saw a way out of this that didn't include a body bag or a missing limb. He may see Abby again, after all.

The thought terrified him as much as buoyed him. Perhaps he'd survived this long because he figured he was already dead. He shook his head at the absurdity of it all. He had stayed alive only because he was already as good as dead? Changing that outlook, having hope instead of darkness, might make him care enough to get himself killed. He could hardly keep it straight in his head.

Abby would never understand such a crazy way of thinking. No one back home would. Only those who'd seen death close up and personal, seen the randomness of who lived and who died, would understand. Suddenly he realized it might be easier staying here beside men who understood him than facing the uncertainty of going home. It was so unfair to Abby, but there was truth to it. Everyone talked constantly about the day they'd earn the right to go home, but the reality might not be as cherry-perfect as they thought.

$\sim$

THE DAWN BROKE and the rising sun lit up the clouds in a beautiful tapestry of orange, red, and yellow. The first roar of naval gunfire rumbled and huge billows of smoke rolled out from the distant ships. Shells as big as small vehicles arced through the morning skies and slammed into the area around Malinta Hill in great explosions. Clyde felt the explosions deep in his chest. How many tons of shells could this island withstand before it finally succumbed and simply sank into the South China Sea?

The beachhead below pulsed with constant motion as troops and tanks pushed inland. So far, enemy positions were scant, and easily overcome by the massive push of firepower up the beach. The intelligence boys had estimated less than a thousand enemy soldiers garrisoned on the island, and for once, they might be correct.

The naval guns fell silent and small arms fire from the beachhead continued. Occasionally, a tank fired a round and the shell screeched before slamming into some unseen target with a muted thunderclap.

Lieutenant Bursk passed behind them, making sure everyone was in position and ready. He raised his voice, "Keep sharp, men. We don't know what the Nips have in store today."

Clyde understood his concern. The paratroopers held most of the important positions on Topside, but the deep ravines leading up to Topside and most of Bottomside could still hold Japanese. If the enemy fired on the next batch of descending paratroopers, it could turn bad for them.

Bursk lingered behind Clyde's back. He said, "By the way, Corporal, that Captain you and your men killed yesterday was probably in overall command of this garrison. The intelligence boys think you cut off the head of the snake, just like we suspected."

Clyde said, "I'm glad we could help, sir."

"Oh, and another thing. A medic told me that a corporal from Second Platoon with a gimpy right ankle helped them out of a tight jam yesterday. Said he saved their bacon. You wouldn't happen to know anything about that, would you, son?"

The rest of the squad looked at Clyde, waiting for his reply. Clyde finally said, "Uh, no sir." Bursk raised an eyebrow and Clyde reconsidered his answer. "Well, I guess I was there, sir. But I wasn't the only one."

"Well, when this shit's over, I'm putting you in for a medal."

Clyde's face turned hot and he forgot about the pain in his ankle for a few seconds. He didn't know what to say. "I—I just did my job, sir."

Bursk squeezed his shoulder and nodded. "Well, keep up the good work, trooper."

"Yes, sir."

Bursk left them, and it didn't take long before the questions started. "What happened? Why didn't you say anything? How many more you'd get? Can I get your autograph? What's it like to be famous?" They slapped him around and accused him of making the whole thing up just for the glory. It was all in good fun, but it made him uncomfortable and he couldn't wait for it to end.

When things finally calmed down, Huss said, "You got anything else you wanna tell your squad leader?" Clyde shook his head. "You're making me look bad, corporal. I should know this stuff. When Bursk brought it up earlier, I had no idea what he was talking about. I looked like an idiot."

"I didn't think it was important."

Huss might've wanted to reply, but the air filled with a low hum and all eyes went to the skies overhead. Men pointed and Clyde saw dots in the distance growing slowly into aircraft. Soon, the distinct outlines of C-47s filled the air. A hail of hurrahs lifted from the men all around as the first parachutes blossomed over Topside at drop site A, then drop site B.

The first batch of paratroopers descended around the barracks, the landing zone just out of sight from the golf course. A smattering of small arms fire reached up for the C-47s in lazy spurts of tracer fire, but none of it seemed concentrated or particularly accurate, and none of it was near their area.

Bursk made his rounds across the line again. "Keep close watch on the ravines. The next drop'll come to our position and I don't want any of our guys hit on the way down."

Huss said, "Yes, sir."

Soon enough, the transports wheeled overhead. Just like the day before, they made three passes before the next airplanes dropped the next stick of paratroopers. The wind wasn't as bad today, and so far, most of them landed where they intended. Clyde heard grunts and cursing as men landed and rolled. Even a perfect landing wasn't pain free in his experience, and The Rock was anything but soft.

A string of heavy machine gun fire erupted out of the trees in the ravine directly below Second Platoon. The rounds stitched the underside of a transport only four hundred feet over the deck. They could hear the impacts like hammer blows on steel. The C-47 shuddered, but kept on course and soon passed out of the enemy machine gunner's line of sight. Smoke billowed from the right engine and the propeller on that side sputtered to a stop as the pilots shut it down. Instead of dropping the last few paratroopers, it turned back for home, still trailing smoke.

Third Squad watched helplessly as another transport wheeled over the area and once again, tracer fire reached from the ravine like an angry hive of bees. But the pilots dipped and weaved and avoided the gunfire. Seconds later, paratroopers dropped out the back and floated toward them.

Bursk barked orders. "We need to silence that gun! First and third squads move up and see if you can find the son of a bitch."

Oliver exchanged an exasperated look with Clyde, as though saying, "Us again?"

Huss waved them forward. "You heard him, let's go."

Clyde readied himself and was about to push out of the foxhole, but Huss said, "Not you, hero. You're wounded. Stay put and cover us."

Clyde could hardly believe his ears. He stared at Huss's back. "I'm fine, sergeant."

"That's an order, corporal," Huss replied without looking back.

Clyde gripped his submachine gun until his hands hurt. "Dammit," he cursed to himself. He watched his squad move forward to the edge overlooking the ravine. The mass of scrub brush and stout trees reached up from the ravine and poked over the horizon. Despite the incessant bombing, the ravine's plant life remained relatively untouched. They were too deep for the bombs to have much effect. The thick undergrowth would make it difficult terrain to fight through, but it could hide an entire division of enemy soldiers.

The men were now nearly out of sight. His ankle throbbed, adding to his foul mood. He desperately wanted to be with them, but he'd just slow them down. "I'm deadweight," he muttered.

He split his time between watching the ledge and the circling C-47s. More and more paratroopers landed near the swimming pool and NCO quarters. Most landed where intended, but a few drifted toward the edges of Topside and a few even drifted into the ravines. He didn't think they'd have an easy time.

Long minutes passed before another transport came in along the flight path, which would take them over the ravine where the enemy fire came from. He had heard no fire from his squad-mates, nor any more enemy machine gun fire, but no targets had presented themselves until now.

The transport finished its slow turn and lined up on the drop zone. He could see a paratrooper leaning out the side door. That would be the jump master. Machine gun fire erupted from the trees. He heard return fire almost immediately, small arms and even the crash of grenades. The grenadiers must be using their rifle grenades, firing from the ledge. The machine gun fire cut off abruptly and the transport continued onto the drop unmolested.

The intensity of the small arms fire increased. They were really laying into them. Had they found a large group of enemy, or just the machine gun crew? He wanted to leap out of the hole and find out, but his ankle screamed at him when he placed pressure on the foot. He'd have to be content where he was.

He heard Bursk yell an order. "Second Squad, move up."

Clyde could see Bursk with the radio to his ear. He must be speaking with the NCOs, and they'd just called for reinforcements. That couldn't be good. Instead of sitting on his ass, he moved closer to the only remaining squad. Maybe he could hear what was going on down there better.

Bursk barked into the radio, "I understand, heavy resistance. Can you hold? Can you hold?" he repeated. He slammed the radio down and cursed, "Dammit!"

The volume of fire grew and it wasn't just friendly fire. The distinctive woodpecker sound of a Nambu machine gun dominated the crescendo. Clyde cringed. He hated those damned things. He'd been on the receiving end of them too often. His men were in trouble, but he couldn't do anything about it. Clyde watched the backs of the Second Squad troopers as they moved to the ledge overlooking the ravine.

Bursk yelled at the remaining men. "Get ready! They're pulling back and the Nips are right on their tails."

Clyde's heart raced. He checked and rechecked his weapon. He moved in staggering steps back to his old position. He was the only man there and it felt lonely and exposed, even though he had good cover. The firefight raged just out of sight.

He glanced down at Bottomside and the expanding beachhead. Heavy smoke rose from multiple Sherman tanks. They'd been hit either by mines or anti-tank rounds. He steeled himself. With or without leadership, the enemy wasn't ready to call it quits just yet.

Finally, he spotted shapes coming from the ravine. He squinted over his sights before he saw American uniforms. He pulled off and watched as they performed a classic break contact maneuver. A few men would hustle back while others hunkered and fired rounds to keep the enemies' heads down, then the first group would stop and do the same for the others, leapfrogging their way back to the lines.

Once everyone was out of the ravine, Second Squad stayed back to cover the rest as they ran. Oliver and Gutiérrez slid into the hole beside Clyde. Both men breathed like overworked freight trains. The rest of the

squad filtered in on either side. Sweat poured off their faces and they struggled to find the canteens they'd left behind. Oliver drained his in one go.

"What the hell's going on?" Clyde asked.

Oliver threw the empty canteen on the ground. Between heaving gasps,
he said, "Whole shitload of Japs in there. The ravine's full of 'em."

The covering squad hustled toward them. They ran much faster than
the others, as though men were right on their heels. Clyde pulled his stock
tight to his shoulder, but saw nothing but scrambling paratroopers.

Once they slid into cover, Bursk barked orders, "Put some mortars on
them!"

Clyde lifted his head, trying to see who Bursk was talking about. By
now, the others had recovered and had taken up firing positions on both
sides of him. He felt better having them back, even if they might be
overrun.

Mortar tubes thumped and rounds arced overhead gracefully, then
disappeared over the ledge and into the ravine. The muted explosions
sounded pitifully ineffective. Debris and smoke rose from the ravine, but he
still didn't see any enemy soldiers.

"How many are there?" Clyde asked, feeling very much out of the loop.

Huss didn't take his eyes from his sights. "Too damned many to count."

Another transport floated overhead and more paratroopers dropped
out the back. Enemy fire from the ravine suddenly erupted, their targets the
helpless paratroopers. Clyde watched one man unstrap his Thompson and
fire a long burst into the ravine as he descended. He landed hard and lost
his grip on the weapon.

"Here they come!" Huss yelled.

He finally saw movement. Japanese soldiers surged over the side,
running straight at them, their weapons leveled. He ignored the smack and
whine of bullets all around him. He kept his muzzle firmly placed on the
chest of the nearest man.

Bursk finally ordered, "Open fire! Fire at will!"

Clyde squeezed the trigger and sent out a short burst. His target staggered and dropped out of sight. He barely had to move the barrel to find the
next target. He squeezed off more rounds, but the soldier dodged out of the
way and fired a shot from his hip. Clyde kept on him and sprayed a long

burst. His internal counter told him it was time to reload. He dropped below the lip of the hole. "Reloading!" he yelled. He quickly swapped out magazines and rose again.

Smoke and carnage dominated the area as troopers put up a thick wall of lead. Japanese soldiers dropped with screams of agony, but more and more surged over the edge. They leaped over their fallen comrades, screaming and firing wildly. Clyde wondered if they had enough ammo to stop them.

He chose his targets carefully. He fired three-round bursts into men, not watching the results as much as simply punching tickets on a train. His thoughts boiled down to one thing; killing as many as possible before they killed him. He focused on one section. Any man that came into it caught his bullets. His vision tunneled as he concentrated on the grisly task they had trained him for.

Finally, he ran out of targets. He swept side to side over the mass of dead and dying enemy soldiers, but found no more threats. His muzzle smoked and glowed red-hot. How many times had he reloaded? He could only recall the first time, but the pile of spent shell casings and the empty magazines told the tale. He'd been on automatic pilot.

"Cease fire!" Bursk barked.

The shooting died off quickly. The smell of burnt gunpowder mixed with the iron scent of blood. Clyde looked up and down the line. No one clutched wounds or called out for a medic.

Gutiérrez pushed his helmet back off his forehead as he looked out over the carnage. The disgust grew on his face. "What the hell's the matter with them? What makes them charge into certain death?"

Oliver shook his head. "Crazy sons of bitches, you know that."

Huss moved behind them, checking on the men. Clyde knew he should get a head count and an ammunition check, but he couldn't take his eyes off the carnage. He marveled at the state of absolute focus he'd slipped into during the attack. Killing had almost become like a normal job, one he and every other paratrooper seemed to excel at. He'd become a professional killer and felt no remorse.

It hadn't always been like that. He'd been terrified the first time he'd seen combat. He thought he might just curl into a quivering ball at the bottom of the foxhole. He'd been terrified this time, too, but it was far more manageable. He wondered if half the fear back then had just been the mystery of what it was like and how he'd react. Now that he knew, it wasn't quite as terrifying.

His hands shook and the familiar nausea overtook him. He understood this phase, too. The aftereffects of a massive dose of adrenaline. It would pass soon enough and hopefully he'd keep his breakfast down until then. *What have I become?*

He tried to picture Abby and couldn't. In a panic, he clutched at his front pocket where he kept her picture. He finally pulled it out and concentrated on her lovely face, but he hardly recognized her. The picture he'd spent countless hours staring at now seemed like it could've been an anonymous photo from a magazine.

He dropped it from his shaky hands. It landed on the pile of spent hot shell casings and singed the edges. He pulled himself out of the hole. He distantly felt his ankle, but he ignored it. He walked to the nearest body. He stood over him and stared at the dead eyes gazing into the clear blue sky. His face held a pained expression. Would he take the pain with him to the afterlife? He went to the next man. His torso torn by heavy bullets.

Distantly, he heard Huss call out to him. "What the hell're you doing, Cooper? Get back here."

He weaved between bodies until he came to a soldier propped against another dead body. The soldier could've been taking a nap, but his leg had been torn off at the knee and a mass of bloody meat shimmered in the sunshine where the stump met the dirt. Blood still pulsed and he realized he still lived.

More voices behind him made him turn. Gutiérrez and Oliver trotted toward him, their faces masks of concern and even anger.

Clyde pointed, "This one's still alive," he said it as though reporting the weather. A simple, somewhat interesting fact.

Both Gutiérrez's and Oliver's eyes grew wide and Oliver yelled, "Watch out! He's . . ." Clyde turned back to the soldier and saw the hatred in his eyes a moment before the world flashed in bright light, then went dark.

22

Northern Philippines
December 1944

Frank and Grinning Bear watched the Port of Calaya from the safety of the thick jungle. Since the debacle with the ammunition trucks and the village massacre, they'd laid low. Nearly a month had passed since the Japanese garrison troops swept the tiny island from one end to the next. Gustav and Frank had ordered the resistance fighters to fade into the woodwork until they called on them again.

The Japanese had taken their revenge on anyone they suspected to be involved in the heist and later the killing of the Japanese patrol. The Japanese killed a few officials outright and kept others in holding cells for weeks. They had released most of those, but they still carried their scars. Despite being tortured, no one had given up the location of the HQ across the channel, but they'd abandoned it anyway, just in case. Frank missed the little island and the small thatch hut he and Constance had shared.

Grinning Bear pointed out to sea at a dim outline of a ship in the distance. This far away, it was impossible to tell if it was friendly or not. More and more, they'd proven to be friendly, as they often fired seemingly random volleys onto the tiny enemy occupied island—almost as an afterthought as they passed by.

Frank said, "Hope the son of a bitch doesn't send any high explosives our way this time."

Grinning Bear pulled Gustav's powerful binoculars out of his pack and glassed the ship. "Looks like one of our cruisers."

"We've seen more and more friendly ships over the weeks. I wonder when they'll invade?" Frank asked.

"They won't invade this tiny island."

"I'm not talking about here. I'm talking about Luzon and Manila."

"Maybe they already have," Grinning Bear murmured.

"We should ask Gustav to turn his damned radio back on."

"He won't do it. You know how he is. He follows orders to the letter. Neil's been pestering him about it, too."

"Maybe we should sneak in there and do it ourselves."

Grinning Bear handed the binos off to Frank. "Didn't I tell you? He didn't just turn it off, he dismantled it and buried the pieces across the island. He's the only one who knows where."

Frank spit. "What the hell'd he do that for?" But he knew the answer. When the Japanese swept the island, the chances of the radio being found increased and his orders were clear: don't let the radio end up in enemy hands no matter what. So Gustav simply followed orders. But now they had no idea what was going on in the rest of the world. The Japanese had confiscated all civilian radios years before. Neil had tried unsuccessfully to create a receiver out of knickknacks, but he could never find a battery with enough charge left to make it work.

"Why the hell are we even watching this damned port? The Japs barely use it anymore and we can't report it if they did." He sighed heavily. "I wanna get off this island and get back home."

Grinning Bear looked at him hard, then took the binoculars back from him.

Frank said, "What? Don't you?"

Grinning Bear took a moment to consider his answer. "Of course I wanna go home, but the job's not done."

"You don't think we've done enough? I don't wanna die out here for nothing because some navy slob decided to take target practice on the island." He gestured out to the passing cruiser. "We could signal him and maybe they'd check it out. We could use a mirror."

"Or maybe the Japs would check it out." He swung the binoculars from the sea to the row of buildings along the rocky beach where the small contingent of Japanese soldiers lived.

"Since the sweep, they've kept mostly to themselves. They know the score, too. This place is like a tinderbox. One false move and this whole place'll come down on them," Frank mused. "We should just leave it the Filipinos. It wouldn't take them long, and they'd relish the opportunity."

"What about Connie?"

Frank shook his head. "I dunno. More and more I get the feeling she's just using me to make the others jealous. She likes being the leader's woman, gives her status among her peers, but I don't really feel the passion anymore. I still see her making eyes at Antonio. I think she might be going behind my back."

"Ah, jealousy."

Frank shrugged it away. "I'm not jealous. Not really. I guess that tells you everything you need to know about the relationship. I just don't care anymore."

"Well, you come from two different worlds. Are you gonna break things off?"

Frank looked at his old friend with a sideways glance. He normally clammed up when this sort of discussion started. "I dunno. Why, you wanna give her a try?"

Grinning Bear shook his head hard. "Of course not. My mother was right. All you white men are crazy."

Frank pointed out to sea. "Look, there's a bunch more ships out there, or am I seeing things?"

Grinning Bear focused the binoculars back on them. He scanned back and forth, then gave a low whistle. "You're right. And they're steaming straight at us."

∾

FRANK WATCHED the American convoy approach the island from a hill overlooking the small harbor. He could hardly believe his eyes. He kept expecting them to turn south and head toward Luzon, but they kept coming straight for them.

Grinning Bear had gone to alert Gustav, who would alert the Filipino resistance. If the Americans planned to invade their tiny island, they could help.

The Japanese near the port had noticed the convoy's approach soon after Frank and Grinning Bear had. They scrambled around the beach and port, looking like ants from his vantage point. Through the binoculars, he watched an officer directing the soldiers as they manned hidden defensive positions. He noted two machine guns and some kind of heavy cannon tucked into the jungle. He wished he could relay that information to the invasion force, but he had no way of doing so. He wondered if Gustav's handlers were desperately trying to get a hold of him. He'd never know.

The ships remained out to sea a good distance. Before long, two speedy PT boats approached the port, making random zigzags as they came. Frank watched them through the binoculars. They were soon in range of the machine guns and certainly the big gun on the beach. They turned away, only a hundred yards off the coastline. Frank felt helpless. If the Filipinos were with him, they could've mounted an attack on the enemy positions.

One of the PT boats opened fire, sending .50 caliber rounds and 20mm cannon rounds into the huts, flying Japanese flags. The heavy rounds tore the nearest hut apart. The dry thatch smoked, then flames erupted. But the huts were empty. Frank had seen the Japanese leave them a few hours before.

The Japanese cannon opened fire, the sound made Frank jump. He held his breath, hoping the round missed the streaking PT boat. The round exploded in the PT boat's wake some thirty yards off the stern. The machine guns opened fire a moment later. Tracer rounds reached out like fingers at the boats, but failed to connect.

Frank glassed the Japanese positions. The officer screamed and waved his arms, obviously not happy with their performance. The PT boats raced away and the machine guns stopped firing, but a pall of white smoke marked their positions perfectly.

Five minutes later, the American cruisers opened fire. Frank hugged the ground as the rounds covered the distance in scant seconds. The ground shook as explosions rocked the island. He kept his head down and held on. If they fired a long round, he'd be pulverized. Three more salvos rocked the enemy positions.

When it stopped, he raised his head. The scene had changed dramatically. Where the defensive units had stood, now only smoking craters remained. He saw the cannon tilted on its side, the barrel bent. Bodies littered the ground around the cannon and the machine gun positions, which looked to have simply evaporated. Nothing moved but smoke and fire.

Another salvo came in, this time targeting the buildings. Frank ducked and covered his head. When he looked again, the parts of the huts were scattered around the beach like children's toys. The smoke from the naval guns obscured the ships, but out of the smoke emerged a fleet of smaller boats churning toward the beach.

Frank could hardly contain himself. Rescue was finally happening. The nightmare that had been his life for the past few years was about to end. He couldn't tear himself away from the perch, but he knew friendly fire might hit him if he stayed. He took one last look at the smoking ruins from the naval fire and the approaching boats full of American infantrymen. He could just make out the tops of their helmets.

He heard shouts from enemy voices. He slowed and moved back into the jungle. The garrison troops were obviously reacting to the incoming assault. He glimpsed their greenish uniforms through the trees as they trotted along the path, heading for the beach. They'd most likely die in the next few minutes.

He waited for them to pass. He held his rifle and once he figured they were out of earshot, he pulled the bolt and loaded more rounds. He hadn't had the need for a loaded weapon in quite some time.

He trotted along an adjacent path toward a tiny village that a couple resistance fighters called home. They must've heard the naval fire, and they'd be itching to get into the fight. Sure enough, the tiny village bustled with action. Men and women darted around, most armed with rifles they'd stolen from the Japanese.

Frank held up his hand and waved at the nearest man. "Ernesto," he called.

The middle-aged man's eyes lit up when he saw him. In his stilted English, he said, "Frank. They here. They here."

"I know. I saw them bomb the harbor beach. Americans are landing."

More men and women gathered around him. These weren't the core resistance fighters that he and Grinning Bear had trained, but they were eager for direction. He raised his voice. "The Americans are coming. I saw them myself. They'll be landing at the harbor any minute now. Japs are running that way." A loud yell of approval and hand pumping greeted the news.

"We help kill Japs," Ernesto said.

Frank knew the American infantrymen would have little trouble with the Japanese garrison troops. This island was a backwater and the quality of the troops reflected that. Their inept shooting at the PT boats only helped to confirm that. They should sit back and let things pan out the way they inevitably would, but he saw the excitement in their eyes. They'd been on the wrong end of Japanese aggression for years. They wanted revenge, and they waited for him to give the order.

"Yes," he finally said. "We can help. Gather weapons and ammo and we'll ambush any Japs that try to reinforce the beach."

Another yell of approval went up. Frank felt a heavy knot in his stomach. There was no need for any more of them to die. If even a single Filipino did, he'd feel responsible. But they were beyond being practical. They wanted blood. At least he'd have some semblance of control this way. He wished Grinning Bear and Gustav would arrive with the main force.

Minutes later, they gathered around him. He nodded his approval. They looked ready. He waved them to follow. He went back the way he'd come. Small arms fire erupted from the direction of the harbor. Everyone slowed and smiles crept across their faces.

Frank took them to the path where he'd seen the other Japanese just an hour before. He hunkered and watched the trail for a few minutes. Would the threat come from inland or from the beach? Perhaps the enemy would use the path to retreat, in which case he'd be facing the wrong way.

He motioned them closer, then said, "They might come from there," he pointed, "Or there. Keep alert. Don't fire on your brothers and sisters, or any Americans."

Frank took his position in the middle of them. He secretly hoped nothing would happen. Most of these men and women weren't trained. Pulling off a successful ambush wasn't easy, even with highly trained troops. He should take them back to the village and wait it out, but their eagerness and willingness to fight kept him there. He hoped he wasn't making a huge mistake.

The intensity of gunfire from the direction of the beach suddenly increased. On top of rifles and machine guns, he heard explosions and assumed they were grenades or possibly mortars. He looked both ways, trying to decide where he should focus his attention.

He hissed to Ernesto, who crouched nearby. "This way. Watch this way." He turned his body to look toward the beach. The enemy would take this path as they retreated. The rest of the Filipinos took the cue and positioned themselves accordingly.

A few short minutes passed. The small arms fire continued. It seemed to come closer. He thought about moving them back. The last thing he wanted was to exchange fire with Americans.

His heart leaped into his throat when he saw first one enemy soldier, then another sprinting down the path away from the advancing Americans. More appeared until he counted ten.

Rifles went to shoulders, but the Filipinos held their fire. Each second brought the fleeing soldiers closer. Frank had his rifle up and tracking the second man in the line. He applied pressure to the trigger, but before he fired, another rifle further up the line fired first.

A flurry of shots erupted from the Filipinos. Japanese soldiers dropped, but more dove out of the line of fire, unscathed. Frank's target was one of those divers. He tracked where he'd gone and fired into the underbrush. He worked the bolt action quickly and fired again and again.

Return fire whizzed through the trees, and he dropped flat onto his belly. He could see the path from his low position. Puffs of smoke from enemy rifles filled the path. He centered his sights on movement, fired, and heard a scream. He fired into the spot twice more before he had to reload.

Enemy soldiers sprang to their feet and made a mad dash across the path and into the deeper jungle on Frank's left flank. One went down when Ernesto shot him through the side of the head. The rest disappeared. The Filipinos kept firing at them until Frank yelled, "Cease fire! Stop shooting!"

The fire kept up sporadically, then finally stopped. A stunned silence filled the air, then the Filipino's voices rose into triumphant calls, taunts, and even laughter. They whooped and pumped their weapons over their heads like conquering heroes. Frank couldn't keep from laughing as they danced around like crazy people. The villagers had finally gotten revenge.

"Americans coming out," a voice called.

The Filipinos kept dancing, but Frank stepped forward and cupped his hands. "Come on out, you gorgeous sons of bitches!"

From up the path, he saw an American GI dressed in a brand new uniform. His helmet had mesh over the top, but that didn't diminish the shine beneath. He held an M1 Garand and a bemused look on his face. More followed, their hard faces scanned the surrounding jungles for more enemy. Frank waved. The GI waved back, but moved cautiously forward. The Filipinos saw him at that moment and they descended on him like adoring fans meeting a sports hero. Frank just watched. It was the happiest sight he'd ever seen.

Grinning Bear slapped his hand onto his shoulder. "There you are," he said. "Did we miss the party?"

Frank hugged his dearest friend. Grinning Bear hugged him back just as hard. "Yeah, you did. But better late than never." They parted and watched the Filipinos and Americans. Frank clutched Grinning Bear's shoulder. "We made it, Larry. We really made it!"

The American soldier with the shiny new uniform pushed his way through the mass of fawning Filipinos until he stood in front of them with a bemused smile. "Where the hell'd you two come from?"

Frank fought the urge to hug him. He extended a hand instead. "I'm— I'm Corporal Frank Cooper, 21st Infantry Division at your service."

Grinning Bear extended his hand to the stunned GI. "And I'm Private First Class Larry Grinning Bear of the 4th Marine Regiment."

The soldier looked them up and down. They wore raggedy civilian clothes and looked anything but soldiers or marines. "The 21st? The 4th Marines? You mean from Bataan?"

Both of them puffed out their chests. "That's us," Frank said.

"Yep," Grinning Bear said.

"Well, I'll be damned. Come on, my CO's gonna wanna meet you two."

"Wait, where's Gustav and Neil?" Frank asked.

"You mean there's more?" the soldier asked.

"Valentine Gustav. He's a coast watcher, or at least he was," Frank said. "And another American GI."

Grinning Bear said, "They'll be along. Gustav was gathering up more Filipinos."

"You'll have to forgive him. He's a German national," Frank said.

The soldier tilted his helmet back on his forehead. "German? Will wonders never cease?"

~

FRANK, Grinning Bear, and Neil sat on the beach eating chocolate bars one after the other. After meeting the CO, Captain Hurz and telling him the condensed version of how they got there, he gave them new sets of dungarees, fed them and treated them as well as they could at an active beachhead.

Soldiers hustled around, stealing glances at the three Americans who'd appeared as if by magic from the jungle. Word got around quickly, but they gave them their space.

They watched the ships unload supplies and men onto the beach. They hadn't seen so much equipment and materiel in one place in their lives.

"Look how quick they are," Frank said. "It seems like a different army from the one I remember in '41."

"I suppose everything's changed," Grinning Bear said. "War has a tendency to do that."

"The mother of invention and all that?"

"Exactly."

"It's like we've been frozen for a few years and they thawed us out."

Gustav approached. He saw them and waved. They stood to greet him. "How'd that go?" Frank asked.

"Hurz is a good man. He comes from the same area as my grandparents."

"I guess it's a good sign that you're not in handcuffs."

"No handcuffs. In fact, he was told to keep an eye out for me."

That caught Frank's attention. "Really? But not us?"

Gustav shrugged. "I only know what he told me."

"So what now?" Frank asked. "I mean, will you stay here or what?"

"I think not. The world has changed. I need to be a part of that now."

"Germany? I'm not sure that's such a good idea." Neil said.

"This war will end. When it does, I will do what I can to help rebuild. What about you?"

Frank exchanged a glance with Grinning Bear. "It's a long boat ride home for us, I hope."

Gustav said, "Yes, I should hope so."

"I can't wait to tell my family. They must be worried sick," Frank said.

"Yes, my mother will be relieved," Grinning Bear added.

"I wonder if my girl's still waiting for me?" Neil mused.

Frank felt his eyes grow heavy. All the food made him want to curl up and sleep. "I'm gonna find a place to get some shuteye."

They said their goodbyes to Gustav, then found a shady spot on the beach out of the way from the hustle and bustle of the micro-beachhead. Frank fell asleep within seconds.

He woke up a few hours later. The sun had dipped from high noon on its way to the sea. Grinning Bear still snored softly by his side. Neil's imprint remained in the sand, but he wasn't there. Frank stood and stretched. He hadn't felt this good in a long time, as though a great weight had been lifted from his shoulders.

The beachhead had a more relaxed tone. He noticed a group of Japanese soldiers in a makeshift pen with a few GIs guarding them. They hadn't been there when they'd laid down.

He walked to them and stared. They had their heads down and sat cross-legged. They looked young and almost relieved. He addressed a guard. "Where'd these guys come from?"

The soldier looked him up and down suspiciously, not recognizing them. "They surrendered. They're the last of them. At least that's what the brass thinks."

Frank marveled. The small Japanese garrison had run this island for years and now, in a matter of hours, they'd been vanquished. They didn't look like much. "Any officers?" he asked.

The guard shook his head. "Nah, they found a few, but they were dead. Suicide. Wish they'd just done that a few years ago."

"You can say that again," Frank murmured.

"What outfit you with?" the GI asked.

"It's a long story," he said as he walked away.

~

FRANK AND GRINNING Bear stood on the deck watching the island they'd called home for the past few months grow smaller and smaller. Neil had gone below to sleep.

"Well, I guess we're finally getting out of here, Larry."

"Yep. Guess so. Say, whatever happened with Connie? I've barely seen her."

"I have. The night of the liberation, she and Antonio were inseparable. Didn't even look in my direction."

"Damn, I'm sorry to hear that."

"Don't be. It wasn't what I thought it was. She'll be happy with Antonio. It wouldn't work out for us, anyway. She can't come with us. I'm just grateful for the time we had together."

"Hmm. Just seems kinda harsh, ignoring you like that."

"She's young. It's fine. Better this way. Say, you ever think of your gal back on the other island? What was her name?"

Grinning Bear smiled. "Sometimes. Seems like a thousand years ago now. That poor girl."

"What d'you mean? What's wrong with her?"

"She'll never find as good a lover as me on that tiny island. I ruined her."

Frank clutched the rail and laughed from his belly. Soon Grinning Bear joined him. They laughed uncontrollably for long minutes. Navy personnel glanced at them as though they'd lost their minds. Perhaps they had, they had a right to.

23

Burma
February 1945

Shawn Cooper watched the town of Lashio from the high ridges. He tried
to find the streets and even the buildings he, JoJo, and Guthrie had used
during their mission the month before, which ended with the capture of
the general, but everything looked different now. The town had withstood
weeks of artillery and aerial bombardments. Half the buildings had burned
to the ground and stood as husks. He wondered what had become of
Dachen and his band of opium dealers. He suspected they were down there
somewhere, just waiting for their opportunity. Those types of people lived
while innocent civilians died in war.

Lieutenant Umberland stood nearby, glassing the town with his own set
of binoculars. He let them dangle and said, "Well, that's it then. The first
trucks should come along any day now."

Shawn gazed in the general direction where the Ledo road would
finally intersect with the old Burma road connecting Allied supplies to
China. "Does that mean the Japs are finished?"

"They're in full retreat, but they've set up on the far side of the

Irrawaddy river. They'll be tough to kick out of there, but the Brits and Chinese are fixing to do just that."

"So what's that mean for us? Are we done here?"

"Hardly. It's all political now. Since our operations have run so intricately through the Burmese countryside, we'll be acting as liaisons between negotiating parties."

"Negotiating what?"

"Burma wants independence and the Brits will go along with it. So, we'll be tasked with helping that transition in any way we can, but it's still all a bit murky."

Shawn shook his head. "I'm not sure I wanna be involved in something like that."

Umberland looked at him sharply. "What are you saying?"

Shawn tilted the baseball hat he still wore from his pilot friend. It reminded him every day of the cruelty of the Japanese. "I guess I'm saying I don't wanna be a political pawn. If the job's done, I guess I'm saying I wanna go home."

"Not so fast. The Japs aren't licked just yet. They still hold Mandalay."

Shawn had seen the maps. The battle lines were distinct now, with large forces opposing one another across rivers like the massive Irrawaddy. Cities like Mandalay and Meiktila were under siege by sizeable forces of Chinese, Indian, and British. Divisions stacked against divisions. The days of guerrilla fighting seemed to be over.

"It just seems like we're no longer needed in our prior roles."

"Yes, like I said, it's political now. They still need us. It's just a different job now. I'll be happy to move on from all the killing."

Shawn looked him in the eye. He knew he should feel the same, but he wasn't sure he did. He and Umberland had been through a lot together. He respected him immensely, but it seemed their paths might diverge. "I hear you, but . . . will you excuse me, sir?"

Umberland nodded and went back to scanning the ruins of Lashio. "Sure thing."

Shawn wandered the camp. Bellevue men greeted him and he recognized Kachin Rangers from Henry Calligan's gang. He bee-lined it to where he knew he'd find him.

Calligan swung languidly in a hammock strung between two stout tree trunks. Shawn stood beside him and Calligan pulled his hat back from his eyes and squinted up at him. "That you, Shawn?"

"Yeah, it's me," Shawn sighed.

Calligan said, "Uh oh. I know that tone." He sat on the edge of the hammock. "What's on your mind?"

"I was just talking with Umberland about the war and our role in it."

Calligan nodded sagely, as though he knew what this would be about, but he didn't say anything.

Shawn asked, "I was just wondering what you think of the whole thing?"

"By the whole thing, you mean the war?"

"I mean our new role as political liaisons for the Burmese."

Calligan grunted. "Oh, yes. Well, I suppose this war was bound to end at some point."

"As crazy as it sounds," he took off the baseball cap and spun it in his hand, "I'm not sure I'm ready for it to be over."

"You haven't had your fill of killing?" Calligan asked.

Shawn shrugged, but didn't answer. He knew how it sounded.

Calligan said, "When I first met you, I didn't think you'd last more'n a couple of months."

That surprised Shawn. "You thought I'd be killed? Really?"

"Not killed, no. I didn't think you'd be able to hack it. Your face when you first saw Didi take that Jap trophy . . ." He grinned and shook his head. "It horrified and disgusted you. I thought to myself, this guy's too kind-hearted to make it out here." He packed his pipe from a pouch of tobacco. "And I was right. You were too good for this place. But that Shawn Cooper died. I saw him die, bit by bit. I helped kill him."

Shawn nodded. "I guess I have changed."

"No. You died. You're not simply changed. You killed off Shawn Cooper and replaced him with you. A different Shawn Cooper altogether."

"I guess that's true. I had to adapt or go crazy. So what's your point?"

"You and me are cut from the same cloth. We're more at home in the jungle slitting throats than in suits negotiating terms of a treaty."

"Exactly. So where does that leave us?"

"Right where we're sitting. The old Shawn Cooper is dead and buried, I'm afraid. He can't be resurrected, but the new Shawn Cooper's alive and well."

Shawn didn't follow, so he asked, "So, will you leave the OSS? Head home? Become a hitman or something?" He laughed weakly and Calligan didn't smile.

Calligan lit the pipe and puffed until it burned. He let the smoke tumble out of his mouth and nose. "This war's changed the good ole U. S. of A. We're a leading world power now, no question about it. As much as the government won't like to admit it, they need men like us, violent men, just as much as they need men like Umberland and Burbank for all that political bullshit. They need men who know how to kill and aren't afraid to do it. And don't think they didn't notice how you brought in that Nip general. You're on a list somewhere."

"I don't follow. You think they'll need us here for more guerrilla stuff?"

"Maybe not here, but somewhere. What d'you think'll happen to the OSS when the war ends? To the *men* in the OSS? They created this organization out of thin air. Spent millions of taxpayer dollars to make it happen. You really think they'll just throw it all away once the war's over?"

"I guess I didn't really think about it. Makes sense to keep it going, I guess. But with the war over, what's the target? What's our mission?"

"Time will tell. But just like here, we won't be in the headlines," he pointed the tip of the pipe at him, "But we'll be plenty busy."

24

Maxwell Air Force Base
November 1944

Abby Cooper stood beside the sleek P-51 Mustang and marveled at the beautiful lines. She couldn't believe it was the last time she'd ever step into the cockpit again.

The government had picked December 7th, 1944 as the final day of the WASP program, but Abby had volunteered to leave the program early. It broke her heart, but she thought it would be much worse if she held on until the bitter end. Their fate had been decided and it was best to move on.

She strode to the flight ops building. The tone inside was somber, as it had been for the past few weeks, but there were even fewer WASP personnel than normal today. No one met her gaze as she strolled through.

She understood why they were shutting down the program. More and more male pilots were coming home from Europe and the South Pacific and they wanted their jobs back, but the bitterness came with the way the female pilots were being treated—like second-class citizens. The papers were full of stories and editorials implying that Jacqueline Cochran, the woman responsible for forming the WASPs, had somehow manipulated General Arnold. It infuriated Abby and every other person associated with the program. They'd answered the call when their country asked, and now they were being treated as though they were some kind of nasty harpies.

She saw Mandy Flannigan drinking a coffee and reading the paper at a table in the otherwise empty cafeteria. She sat next to her. "Well, I guess that's it, then."

Mandy carefully folded the paper and stuffed it beneath the coffee cup. "Are you gonna miss it?"

"Of course. What can I possibly do that'll match flying one of those?" She thumbed toward the P-51, shining in the sunshine.

"Having a litter of children?" Mandy teased.

"I want nothing more, but even that won't be as exciting as this has been. It just feels so wrong to be ending it like this. I mean, none of us went into it for glory or accolades, but I didn't think we'd be ridiculed for it."

Mandy waved her hand like swatting an annoying fly away. "Oh, that's just all the political horseshit flying around. Don't pay any attention to what you read in the papers. I don't think people really feel that way when it comes right down to it. I think everyone just wants things to get back to normal as soon as possible, and having women flying fighters around the country doesn't match that perception. No one can ever take away what we did for this country."

"Yeah, I hope you're right. It just seems so abrupt. I mean, we worked *so* hard to get here and with the stroke of some politician's pen, it's over just like that," she snapped her fingers.

Mandy stood and draped an arm over Abby's shoulder. "Come on, I'll buy you a drink."

Abby gripped Mandy's hand and walked with her. "You know I don't drink anymore."

"Then I'll buy you an ice-cold soda." They walked through flight ops arm in arm.

Abby glanced around at the pictures on the walls, some old, some new —smiling male pilots alongside smiling female pilots. "I'm gonna miss this place."

"Me, too." Mandy said and she pushed open the door. Once outside, she clapped her hands. "Oh shoot, I forgot something in the hangar. Come on, it'll only take a second."

"Okay," Abby said.

They moved across the tarmac toward the nearest hangar. Abby glanced up at a training flight circling the airfield, a student pilot performing touch and go landings. How many countless times had she done that? It reminded her of her time back at Avenger Field, where even now WASP trainees still struggled to earn their wings.

"I'm glad they're allowing the final WASP class the opportunity to graduate."

Mandy pursed her lips but nodded her agreement. "I guess it's better than just disbanding them in the middle of the program. But it's also kind of cruel. They'll never put their newfound skills to use, at least not the way they've been trained."

"Are you still going to try to fly for the Airlines?"

Mandy nodded, although her smile didn't travel to her eyes. "Yes, but I think I have a better chance of flying combat missions over Germany."

"Well, you've always been a pioneer, Mandy. Maybe you'll be the one that paves the way for everyone else."

Mandy stopped at the door to the hangar. She sighed heavily. "Thanks for saying that." She hugged her. "But it seems like an uphill climb. It sounds exhausting. Maybe I'll find a man and settle down. Maybe raise a family like everyone else." Abby couldn't keep from laughing. Mandy placed her hands on her hips and said, "What's so damned funny?"

"I just can't imagine it, that's all. I mean, it's all I ever really wanted, but I just can't see you being happy. I see you up there in the clouds, not changing dirty diapers and hanging laundry on clotheslines."

Mandy laughed, too. "I know," she said. She grasped the door handle. "Now enough of that." She swung the door open and stepped into the cavernous, darkened hangar. "I left something on the other side. Walk with me." She closed the door behind them, sending them into utter darkness.

Abby clutched her arm. "Where's the light switch?"

The lights suddenly blazed and a crowd of women screamed, "Surprise!"

Abby nearly jumped out of her coveralls. Balloons and confetti fell from some kind of contraption over her head and rained down on them. Loud honking and buzzes from various party toys filled the room with noise. Music suddenly blared full blast from a record player.

The crowd surrounded Abby and soon she was engulfed in hugs from fellow pilots, mechanics, and even airport personnel. They thrust a drink into her hand and she gulped it down despite her recent abstinence. There was a time and place for everything, and now was the time to celebrate with the best friends she'd likely ever have.

The longer the celebration lasted, the more it felt like something much bigger than just her retirement party. This was a celebration of their accomplishments over the past two years. This wasn't just for her.

Two drinks later, Abby's head spun. She hadn't drunk alcohol in a few weeks and she could really feel it. Mandy slung her arm around her and dragged her to the far corner of the hangar where a stage had been set up, complete with a podium and microphone. She hoped they didn't expect her to give a speech. She almost pulled away, but Mandy gripped her tightly. "Relax, this is something else."

"Something else? What do you mean?"

"Just watch."

A tall, slender woman walked onto the stage, and Abby's mouth hung open. "Is that Jackie Cochran?" she asked.

Mandy shushed her as the founder of the WASP program tapped the microphone to get everyone's attention. The group of women quieted and pushed toward the stage until they all stared in rapt attention.

"Ladies, it is a great honor to be among you today. I wish it was on better terms. As you know, General Arnold's proposed Bill to give us military status was narrowly defeated. Our organization is ending, but that doesn't diminish our contributions one bit. The war isn't over, of course, but the government doesn't feel they need our contribution any longer. It's sad, but there's no need to dwell on such things. You should always be proud of what you did for your country in its hours of need. No matter what happens in your life from here on, you can always look back on this time with pride."

She stepped away from the microphone for a moment to compose herself. Then she continued. "Besides being here for our fellow pilot, Abby Brooks on her final day as a WASP . . ." A raucous cheer rose to the rafters.

Abby blushed heavily. Jacqueline continued. "We are also here to start a new tradition, a new organization." The room quieted. Jacqueline held up a colorful patch, which everyone recognized as the Fifinella gremlin designed by Walt Disney himself for them to wear on the sleeves of their flight suits. "Our organization is dissolving into the annals of history, but that doesn't mean we have to fade away from each other. This new organization will work to keep members informed of WASP news and happenings, and, more importantly, give us a reason to get together as a group. I give to you, The Order of the Fifinella!"

An eruption of cheers ensued. The music started again and someone thrust another drink into Abby's hand.

25

Virginia
Late February, 1945

Abby Cooper went to the mailbox and peaked inside. She always felt a flutter of both excitement and fear whenever she did so. Would she get another letter from her beloved Clyde, or something else she didn't even want to fathom?

His unit had dropped onto Corregidor Island in the Philippines just a few weeks before. She'd read it in the papers. He hadn't mentioned any upcoming operations in his most recent letters, which didn't surprise her. He didn't want her to worry, and he couldn't tell her much, anyway.

Since hearing about Corregidor, she'd scoured the news for any scrap of information. The parachute operation had been well documented for once, but none of the pictures showed her man, or mentioned his name. She'd been worried sick since mid-month. She didn't have the WASP job to keep her mind occupied anymore.

She pulled out the mail, and her heart soared. Right on top was a letter from Clyde. She closed her eyes and silently thanked God. She quickly pawed through the others. The last piece of mail nearly made her legs buckle. It was the letter she'd been dreading. A drab envelope from the US Army.

Her hand trembled as she compared the postmarks of Clyde's letter and that on the government letter. She fell to her knees. The date on Clyde's letter was earlier than the one from the government. She nearly vomited.

She forced herself to her feet and staggered to the small deck in front of her bungalow, never taking her eyes off the two letters in her trembling hands. The rest of the post lay scattered at the base of the mailbox stand, where it had fallen from her hands. The cool March air cut through her light clothing like a scythe, but she couldn't make it past the deck and into the cozy bungalow. She sat heavily on the top step. The world beyond the porch simply ceased.

Which one to open first? She wouldn't be able to read Clyde's letter until she knew what the other one said. She could barely open it. Her hands shook too much. Tears blurred her vision. Perhaps it wasn't bad news at all, perhaps it was happy news about his imminent return. If it was the worst, they would've sent a priest, not a letter.

She pulled the contents and held it as steadily as she could manage. The block-typed words seemed cold. She could hardly read it through her bleary eyes.

Dear Mrs. Abigail Cooper, we regret to inform you . . .

Her heart nearly stopped. She felt as though a dozen knives pushed into her chest. She suddenly forgot how to breathe.

. . . that your husband, Corporal Clyde Cooper, was wounded in action . . .

Her heart started again, she gasped in a deep breath, and her tears dotted the page. She could barely read the rest, but she pushed on. He'd been wounded in action on Corregidor Island. She remembered it was the same island where Clyde's brother Frank had been taken prisoner years before.

A neighbor walked along the sidewalk. She saw the scattered post, and Abby on the porch crying while holding a letter. Such scenes were tragically common. The neighbor approached her. "Are—are you okay, dear?"

Abby looked up from the letter. She could hardly see the woman through her tears. She swiped them away. She felt drained from the roller coaster of emotions.

Abby held up the government letter. "It's from the military. It's about my husband, Clyde. He's—he's . . ." she couldn't get the rest out and her tears dropped steadily. The woman sat beside her and wrapped her arms around her shaking shoulders. Abby finally said, "He's wounded, but—but he's alive."

The older woman rocked her side to side and gently stroked the top of her head. "Oh, thank heavens for that. When I saw you, I thought the worst. So many destroyed lives."

Abby pulled away slightly and wiped her tears. She recognized the woman but didn't know her name. "He's alive. He's alive and he's coming home. He's finally coming home." She shook her head and smiled. "I can't believe it's finally happening. He's been gone *so* long—a lifetime."

"Oh dear, I'm so glad. I'm so sorry he's hurt, but I'm glad he's coming home."

Abby took a deep breath and blew it out quickly. She held up the other letter. "This is from him. It's postmarked earlier than this one. He wrote it before he was wounded. I—I thought it might be the last time I'd ever hear from him."

The woman grasped her necklace. "Oh my word, what are the chances of them arriving the same day? I can only imagine what you must've felt. Do—do you need me to stay awhile?"

Abby smiled at her and touched her shoulder. "You are so kind, but no. I'll be fine. Thank you so much for doing what you did. It means a lot."

"It was nothing, really. This war has been so awful. I'm proud of your husband . . . and you. Such a terrible thing to have to go through. Please, let me help you inside."

Abby stood and the woman made sure she didn't fall. They went to the door and Abby went inside. The woman stood at the threshold. She said, "I'll collect the rest of your mail for you. You go read your husband's letter."

Abby sat on the loveseat and looked at the picture of Clyde on the mantle. Did his wounds mar his handsome face? It didn't matter if he looked like a monster. She'd love him just as deeply as ever. She heard the woman at the door and the mail came through the mail slot. She marveled at the woman's kindness. She didn't even know her name.

~

NOW THAT SHE could see and think more clearly, she read the letter from the government more carefully. Clyde's wounds were severe enough to warrant a medical discharge from the Army, the same way that Gil's had. She remembered Gil's scarred face, missing eyeball, and his body still full of shrapnel. What would Clyde look like?

The letter didn't go into specifics, but her eye lingered on the word severe. Had he lost a limb? All his limbs? Was he conscious? She had no idea, and not knowing was agony.

The wounds were severe enough that he'd convalesce in Hawaii for the next few weeks. Could she use her connections in the WASP community to hop a flight to Hawaii? Why didn't they send him the rest of the way to the west coast, where she could take care of him and help him heal? She suddenly felt helpless and angry all at once.

She put the government letter down and opened Clyde's letter. She read it, then read it again, savoring every word. He had dated it February the 14th, just a few days before the Corregidor drop happened. It must've been one of the last things he'd done before he went into combat.

He hinted that he'd be doing something extraordinary and that she shouldn't expect letters over the next few weeks. He talked about how scared he was to hear about her incident in the forest. He asked about the WASP program. He'd heard it was shutting down and wondered how she felt about that. She didn't know why she hadn't told him she'd quit the job way back in November. She supposed she didn't want him to feel sorry for her—he had enough to worry about.

She folded the letter and put it reverently back into the envelope, which had traveled from the ends of the earth all the way to her mailbox. It never ceased to amaze her whenever she bothered to consider such things. *All the marvels of the modern world, yet we still kill one another in blood-thirsty rampages.*

She picked up the phone and the operator connected her to her old airbase operations center. "Hello, Marianne, It's me Abby. Yes, Abby Cooper. I was wondering if that cross-country flight offer was still on the table? Yes? Oh, excellent. I'd like to leave as soon as possible."

Once off the phone, she checked the dates on the calendar hanging in the kitchen. She only had a few days to pack her East Coast life up and move back to the West Coast. She'd have just enough time.

A feeling of dread overtook her as she remembered the one task she had yet to do, which she'd been putting off these past few months. It wasn't that she was avoiding him, but she hadn't gone out of her way to see him, either. She'd seen him on and off at social events, particularly around Christmas, but they'd never been alone together. She needed to confront Sal Sarducci and find out not only what happened in Seattle with her father, but also confront him about Clyde's training accident incidents and her father's involvement.

Anger flooded through her, and she briefly forgot about her wounded husband steaming his way toward Hawaii.

∽

ABBY SAT on the park bench where Sal had asked to meet her. She was right on time, and he was late. The cooler spring days had her dressed warmly, but the sun peaked through and she closed her eyes and lifted her face to the warmth. It felt good. She sensed a presence and a shadow passed in front of the sun, blocking the warmth.

"Hello, Abby," Sal said.

She opened her eyes and Sal stood there as though waiting for a hug. She had no intention of hugging him, but then he motioned to the bench and asked, "May I sit?"

"Yes, of course."

He sat down and gazed at the park view. "Beautiful this time of year."

"Yes, it is, but I didn't bring you out here to talk about the view. I need to talk to you, Sal."

Sal nodded and rubbed his hands together. "I figured this day would come. It's been so busy lately that I wondered if it ever would. I'm glad you got in touch."

"So you know what this is about?"

"I assume you want to talk about your father and my visit to Seattle."

"Yes, that's part of it."

He raised his chin, and the scar he carried across his jaw showed up prominently in the sunlight. "What's the other part?" he asked.

"We'll get to that in a bit, but first I need to know how it went with my father. What happened?"

"Well, it didn't go well. Do you remember that new security man, Hastings?" Abby nodded and he continued. "Well, he met me armed, and took me to see your father. He had other security men, all armed. When I brought up going to the police with the diary and turning ourselves in, Victor had his men beat me up."

"What?"

Sal nodded, remembering Hastings's insane eyes after Sal hit him with the brick-laden briefcase. "I've had worse. I had a briefcase with a fake diary inside. I wanted to see how your father reacted once he thought he had the diary in his hands. He told me he was going to burn it for both our sakes." Abby's eyes dropped to the ground, and Sal continued. "He never intends to turn himself in, Abby."

"Even after . . . ?"

"Even after I told him you demanded it if he ever wanted you to speak with him again," Sal finished for her. "He's changed, for the worse. I'm worried about him. Hastings is a cruel man and I'm afraid of what he might do." He rubbed his hands as though wondering if he should continue.

Abby said, "What else happened?"

"Your father locked me in a room for a week while he figured out what to do with me. I'm sure Hastings tried to convince him to kill me, but . . ."

"You really think he wants to kill you?"

Sal took in a deep breath and blew it out slowly. He leaned closer and said, "I haven't told anyone this, not even Beatrice." Abby focused on him. Did he want her promised silence? She wouldn't give it to him. She didn't owe him anything. He finally said, "Hastings tried to kill me in a bookstore. He cornered me and put a gun on me. He tried to force me into a bathroom to muffle the shot, but the store owner got in the way." Sal shook his head as though trying to forget a terrible memory. "There was a fight. He killed the shopkeeper and I got away."

Abby could scarcely believe her ears. It sounded like something from a crime novel. "He—he murdered someone?"

"Yes, and I couldn't do anything to stop it. He's a trained killer. I barely escaped with my life."

"Did you call the police?"

Sal shook his head, never taking his eyes off the ground. "He used my gun. He meant it to look like a suicide, I guess, but now it just looks like I killed the shopkeeper and skipped town."

"Are they searching for you? The police, I mean?"

"I don't think so. I think Hastings is keeping it in case he needs it later. I'm sure Hastings will turn me in if I make any kind of trouble."

"But you didn't do it."

"Doesn't matter. My gun, my fingerprints are on the gun, and on the shop door, and someone probably remembers me leaving the store in a hurry. All he has to do is phone in an anonymous tip."

Abby didn't know what to say. This Hastings fellow was certainly crafty. "Does, does he know where you live? What about Beatrice and Cora? They should leave immediately."

Sal looked her in the eye. "I'd move them if I thought they were in danger, but I'm positive that they don't know where we are."

"How do you know? They could be there right now, they could . . ."

"Because Hastings sent someone to deal with us in Texas right after we left. It came up when I was with your father. Hastings sent some men to our old address."

"Oh my God," Abby said. "What if you'd still been there? What if they'd found Beatrice and Cora?"

"They didn't. That didn't happen. But it makes me angry—more angry than I've ever been."

"What will you do?"

"I don't know. Nothing for now. I have to think of Beatrice and Cora's safety."

"And Bea doesn't know?" Sal shook his head. Abby continued. "But you can't live in fear the rest of your life. You have to do something. And that poor man at the shop."

"I know. It tears me up. I can't get his face out of my head. He was in the wrong place at the wrong time."

"Hastings has to pay for what he's done."

Sal looked truly pained. "I know. I've been wracking my brain for a solution all these months, but if I show up in Seattle, he'll contact the police and I'll be arrested."

They both sat in silence on the park bench for a few minutes. A few folks walked along the dirt path, but the change in the weather seemed to have kept most folks home.

Sal finally asked with some trepidation in his voice, "So, what was the other thing you needed to talk about?"

Abby thought about the conversation she'd had with Gil Hicks in the hospital. She considered not bringing it up. Sal had been through a lot lately, but anger flushed through her and she felt her ears warm. She deserved to know.

She scooted away a little and faced him as much as she could on the park bench. "I spoke with one of Clyde's best friends, Gil Hicks, from the Army. He's in the hospital here. He was wounded and sent here for eye surgery."

Sal nodded, but looked somewhat bemused. He obviously didn't know where this was going.

Abby continued. "His real last name is Trambolini."

Sal reared back and his mouth gaped open. "I think I remember him. I met him the day he—the day he held you at gunpoint. Gil Hicks, I'd forgotten that was the name he used."

Abby steeled herself for what she was about to say. "He told me a few things." She smoothed her slacks with nervous energy. "First, there were a series of accidents when Clyde was in airborne training. Gil thinks my father is responsible for those." She scrutinized his reaction. The color in Sal's face faded, and he looked at the ground as though he'd been dreading this. "So it's true?"

Sal closed his eyes and nodded. "Yes, it's true," he whispered.

She couldn't keep a tear from forming in the corner of her eye. She hated herself for it and swiped it away quickly.

Sal reached for her, "Abby, it's . . ."

She sprang to her feet and hissed, "Don't touch me." She leveled a finger at his face. "Father didn't have connections in the Army back then, Sal, but—but you do. Don't you? You set the whole thing up, didn't you?"

He sighed and his shoulders slumped into himself. She saw tears in the corner of his eyes. She'd never seen him cry. Didn't think it was possible. "Yes, Abby. I put your father in contact with an old friend of mine. I helped set that part of it up."

She could barely contain herself. She wanted to claw his eyes out. She screamed at him. "He nearly died, Sal! They sabotaged his parachute—it didn't open! You did that!"

Sal stood up abruptly. People at the park stared and a few shuttled their children away. "I just put your father in touch. I had nothing to do with it after that. I give you my word. I didn't know he'd go that far."

"Is that supposed to make me feel better? It doesn't. You betrayed me. You betrayed Clyde. You betrayed our friendship, Sal. How could you?"

Sal grabbed her shoulders and gripped her. "Abby, listen to me. I didn't know. In fact, I don't think your father knew it would go that far, either. He didn't want Clyde dead, just brought down a few notches. He wanted him to fail, so you'd see him for what he thinks Clyde is—weak."

She glared at him, but didn't shake loose from his iron grip. Her voice turned icy. "Take your hands off me, Sal."

He released her as though she were actually made of ice. He said, "I wanted to tell you, but after the journal, I thought it would be too much for you to forgive."

She nodded and she felt a deep sadness. "It is, Sal. It is too much."

He sat down heavily on the park bench and put his face in hands. "I never wanted any of this to happen. I've only ever wanted you to . . ."

"To what, Sal?"

"You're like a daughter to me. Victor did what he did to protect you, and I guess I went along with it because I wanted to protect you, too."

"By nearly getting my husband killed?" she huffed. "What else aren't you telling me, Sal? What other dark secrets do you have waiting in the shadows?"

His eyes snapped up and she nearly took a step back. She'd never seen such hurt in his eyes, but also something else she couldn't quite put her finger on. The moment stretched and she waited for him to divulge something truly catastrophic, but he shook his head and his eyes returned to normal. "Nothing. I only hope you can forgive me someday, Abigail."

She crossed her arms and glared at him. She thought he had more secrets to tell, but whatever they were, they weren't coming out now. Maybe never.

Abby finally got control enough to continue. "Gil said something else that day." Sal raised his bloodshot eyes expectantly. She said, "He thinks his father is gunning for my father."

Sal's demeanor changed like a light switch and his eyes turned hard once again, just the way she always remembered them. "How sure is he?"

"Very sure. He's been in contact with his father and he's convinced he's planning something. He wants to stop it, because of his friendship with Clyde and I. He doesn't want anything to happen to our family."

"Can he do it? Stop it, I mean?"

Abby thought about their conversation. Despite Gil being next in line to take over the business, she didn't feel like he had much say at the moment. "I don't think so."

Sal said, "I'm going to hop a train and head west."

"What? What about Beatrice and Cora? You can't just leave them, and what about the police and that awful man, Hastings? If you try anything, he'll just turn you in. You said so yourself."

Sal took a moment to gather his thoughts. He stared toward the horizon, then snapped his fingers. "It all makes sense now."

"What makes sense?"

"Hastings is tied in with Julius Trambolini. When I was a *guest* of your father, he found out that Hastings had sent men to find me in Texas. He was angry about it and he wanted to speak with those men, but he told me that Hastings was evasive. He obviously didn't want Victor to speak with them."

"So what? I don't follow."

"They must've been Trambolini men. Victor would've recognized them for who they were and known Hastings had dealings with the Trambolinis. It all makes sense. Trambolini is using Hastings to get closer to your father. He's probably working for him."

"To what end?"

"Well, if Gil is correct, to kill him."

Abby felt a lump form in her throat. She hated her father at the moment, but she didn't want him dead. He was still her father. She said, "You have to stop it, Sal."

"I know. I'll leave today."

Abby shook her head. "No, tomorrow."

"But the sooner I leave, the sooner I get there. It's a long trip."

"The government agreed to shuttle WASP pilots wherever they need to go after they left the program. Apparently, they're attempting to unruffle our feathers over canceling the program. But that's neither here nor there. I'll insist you be on that flight with me. We'll be in Seattle much quicker if we fly."

His eyes hardened. "Okay, but before we go, I need to talk to your friend Gil."

26

Brooks Industries
Seattle
Late February, 1945

Victor Brooks stood overlooking the factory floor from his office. The machines and workers flowed in perfect precision. Production numbers had only increased since updating some systems. The factory could produce stunning numbers quicker and more efficiently than ever before, which only added to his bottom line.

Everything was going great, but he still had a nagging feeling in the back of his mind that he couldn't shake. It had been there ever since his old security man, Sal Sarducci, visited him a few months before. At the behest of his daughter Abigail, Sal had urged him to face his criminal past so she'd forgive him and include him in her life. The notion seemed ridiculous. What he'd chosen to do was a business decision. It wasn't personal, although he knew that wasn't quite true. Trask Industries had always been a thorn in his side. Since the arson, they'd simply faded away, which was fine with him.

But that wasn't what nagged him. No, Trask got what he deserved, but Abigail? She was a different matter. Despite the callous facade he strived to maintain for his employees and anyone else in his life, he had a soft spot for Abigail. Would she really cut him out of her life? If she did, she'd cut herself off from his money. No one could be that simple.

True, she'd been on her own these past few years, but that was temporary while her husband was away at war. Once he returned, Clyde would certainly change her mind. He didn't like Clyde, but he wasn't a fool. No one in their right mind would throw away such a fortune out of misguided principles. But why did it bother him so much?

He hadn't heard from Sal over these past few months. He supposed he didn't blame him; after all, he'd kept him under lock and key for a full week. Victor thought the incarceration time would scare Sal enough to drop this silly path Abigail had set him upon. Perhaps it had worked. He hadn't heard anymore nonsense about Miles's diary or the arson since.

He missed his old friend. They'd been a good team. He thought about Sal's warnings about Guy Hastings. Sal was a good judge of character and he had a healthy fear of the new man. Sal didn't trust him and certainly didn't like him, but he also thought he might be dangerous to Victor himself. Victor understood Hastings's wasn't perfect, but he was a professional. He might not be a friend, like Sal, but he did his job efficiently. Sal came from a different time. They both did. Hastings represented the new era of professionalism. He might not do things the way Sal did, but that was how progress worked.

He sighed deeply and stroked his silver mustache. Sal wasn't what bothered him—it was Abigail. What if she stuck to her guns and never spoke with him again? What if he never met his grandchildren? The thought depressed him. He pictured him and Meredith regaling Abigail's children with exorbitant gifts and exotic trips around the world. The daydream made him smile.

He marveled Meredith was in the daydream. He hadn't spoken more than a few stilted words to her for weeks now. Evenings at home with her lasted as long as it took to eat dinner—mostly silent affairs. He'd catch her staring at him sometimes, as though she wanted to say something, but she never did. Did she want a divorce? No, despite what she said, she'd be destitute without his money. She was smarter than that. She'd put up with the silence and the distance as long as she could maintain her lifestyle. *But what about Abigail?*

He pushed his rational mind aside for a moment. He considered doing what she asked. What would it look like? Could he fulfill her ridiculous demands without ending up in jail? What would happen if he confessed to the arson with his lawyer alongside him? Perhaps instead of confessing, he could frame it as a lark that got out of hand. Miles misunderstood the instructions and went too far. He never intended to burn the place down. But Sal would testify otherwise.

Sal. Perhaps he should've let Hastings kill the son of a bitch. With Sal out of the way, he could plead his case. He could say he confessed because his conscience wouldn't allow him to do otherwise. The judge would slap his hand, perhaps give him a fine and send him on his way. The hubbub would blow over quickly, and he'd have Abigail back. But would he?

She'd suspect he had something to do with Sal's death and that would be far worse. There didn't seem to be a way out unless he confessed and risked losing his business and possibly jail.

He focused on the men and women working on the production line on the factory floor. What would happen to them? They'd lose their jobs and be on the street. *It's not just my life—it's there's, too. I have to think about them.* He heard the demons guffaw in his head.

He provided those people with their livelihoods—hundreds of them. It didn't matter if he cared for every one of them on a personal level or not; they fed their families because of him.

He sat at his desk and opened a folder. He had work to do—work that only he could do. But the itch in the back of his mind didn't go away. His daughter wouldn't let him go.

~

VICTOR PORED over spreadsheets and numbers. He felt a headache coming on, something he'd never had to deal with until recently. He jumped when the buzzer on his desk buzzed. He suppressed the urge to yell at his secretary. He took a calming breath before answering the blinking light. "Yes, what is it, Hildreth?"

"Sorry to disturb you, sir, but your wife is here to see you."

Victor stared at the small intercom as though it had somehow garbled the message. "Meredith?"

"Uh, yes, sir. Your wife, Meredith. Shall I send her in?"

"Of course, yes."

The door opened quickly, as though Meredith had her hand on the door handle when Hildreth buzzed her in.

Victor stood, suddenly unsure of where to place his hands. "Meredith? What's wrong? Has something happened?" She took the office space in and he realized she'd never once visited him here.

She smiled for an instant, then said, "Nothing bad. In fact, it's wonderful news." She stammered, "Well—well, good and bad, I suppose."

"Is Abigail alright?"

Meredith stared at him hard, as though the question was completely unexpected. "Yes, as far as I know. Yes. This isn't about her . . . well, that's not entirely true either."

He felt the old anger climbing into his throat. "Quit being so evasive. Out with it, woman." He regretted it as soon as he said it. Nothing made her clam up as much as demands. But instead of clamming up, she turned sideways and extended her hand to him. "Come on. We have a dinner date."

"What? No, I still have work to do. It's only . . ." he looked at the clock and saw it was already six thirty in the evening. "Oh, it's later than I thought." He stood and looked out over the workers. Second shift already. Hours had slipped past without him noticing. "Dear me." He took his coat off the rack and as he put it on, he raised his voice to Hildreth. "Go home, Hildy. I didn't realize the late hour."

She smiled and quickly stood. She grasped her purse as though she'd been ready to leave for hours now and only waited to be released. "Thank you, sir. Have a lovely evening out." She nodded to Meredith. "So lovely to finally meet you, ma'am."

"You too, Hildreth. Sorry to be so brusque with you."

She blushed and stole a glance at Victor. "You weren't. It's no problem."

"I'll lock up. See you tomorrow," Victor said.

Hildreth smiled demurely. "Um, it's Saturday tomorrow, sir."

"Ah, so it is."

Hildreth left in a hurry, putting her coat on to battle the rainy winter day outside, which had long since slipped into darkness. Meredith said, "I hope you're paying her well."

Victor scowled at her. "I'm paying her the going rate, I suppose. Now, what's this all about?"

Meredith shook her head and he couldn't decide if it was over Hildreth's pay, or his question. "You'll just have to wait and see. Come on, the car's out front."

Victor thought about raising a stink, but he stifled the urge. He actually felt a little giddy. His estranged wife, who looked and smelled marvelous at the moment, had a surprise for him. Perhaps she'd heard of a new restaurant opening and she wanted to try it with him. But she had done nothing like this since their early days of marriage. He couldn't imagine what it could be, but he'd go along for now. He only hoped she didn't plan on humiliating him.

She strode to a sedan parked across the main entrance driveway. He wondered why Hastings wasn't waiting in his normal spot, and why the sedan instead of the Rolls? Perhaps it was having engine trouble.

Meredith went to the driver's door, opened it, and slid in behind the wheel. He stopped dead in his tracks. She reached across and rolled down the window. "Are you going to stand there in the rain or get in the car?"

The rain felt cold on his shoulders. He hustled to the car and got in the back. He slid in, setting his briefcase and hat on the seat. "What in blazes are you doing, Meredith? You're driving? Where's Hastings?"

"Yes, I'm driving. I quite enjoy it. Hastings can pound sand."

He'd never heard her speak with such brusque language. And driving? He was going to keep his mouth shut and see what happened tonight, but this was almost too much. "I will not sit here and be . . ."

She stepped on the gas and the sedan shot away from the curb with squealing tires. It forced him into the seat, stifling his protests. When he got himself back together, he said, "Meredith, what is going on? Have you lost your mind?"

"No, Victor. We're going to have dinner with the Coopers'"

Victor wracked his brains, searching for any families named Cooper. He came up empty. "You can't mean . . .*those* Coopers?"

"Our daughter's in-laws, yes. They invited us to dinner. They have news."

"News? Couldn't they simply call or send a letter like most sane people?"

Meredith looked at him through the rearview mirror. She seemed to enjoy his discomfort. "It'll be good for you to reconnect with them. They're grand people."

"You've been seeing them? I mean, since the *wedding?*" he said the last word as though it were rancid on his tongue.

"Yes. Ceecee and I have become good friends, and you'll like Sidney. He works nearly as hard as you do."

"I doubt that," he murmured to himself.

"It's neither here nor there. We're having dinner with them and that's final."

He sat back. It felt odd being driven around by his wife, but he had to admit she seemed to know what she was doing behind the wheel. "When did you learn to drive?"

"Sal taught me ages ago. Honestly, you should try it. It's exhilarating."

The mention of Sal made him scowl. He still didn't have a solution for how to deal with him or Abigail. It drove him crazy.

Meredith drove deeper and deeper into the city until they stopped in front of a quaint neighborhood. The houses were small and the walls nearly butted up against each other, leaving only narrow walkways between them, but the gated front yards were well kept for the most part, and the lights spilling from the windows looked warm and inviting.

"I would've felt safer if Hastings were with us in a neighborhood like this."

She waved the comment away with a flick of her hand. "He's more dangerous than anyone you'll find here." She stepped out and when he didn't step out right away, she stuck her head back inside. "I'm not opening your door for you, Victor." She pointed. "It's the silver lever right there."

"I know how to operate the damned door," he blustered. But he realized he hadn't actually done it himself in years.

He stood beside her. He had to admit, she looked fabulous. She might be annoying, but she still looked as beautiful as the day he'd met her all those years before. She strung her arm through his and he thrilled at the contact, but he didn't let it show. They walked the short distance to the modest front door, but he wanted the moment to last much longer.

She knocked and he heard clomping footsteps from within. The door opened onto a brightly lit foyer and living room. The smell of fresh-baked bread and garlic wafted over him and he salivated despite himself. The man at the door held a smoking pipe. He looked vaguely familiar and Victor remembered his name was Sidney. He smiled at Meredith, but that didn't last when he eyed Victor. "Welcome," he uttered as he thrust his hand out to Victor.

Victor shook and it felt like shaking hands with one of his production line workers. He caught a hint of fish smell. He remembered Sidney worked on the docks in Seattle's fish market.

"Thank you," Victor forced himself to say with a thin smile.

Cecelia Cooper burst from the kitchen with her arms spread wide. For a terrified instant, Victor thought she meant to hug him, but she bypassed him and went straight for Meredith. They hugged like long-lost sisters, swaying back and forth.

She finally broke away and extended her hand to him. He attempted to take it lightly, as was custom, but she grasped his hand almost as hard as Sidney had. "I haven't seen you since the kid's joyous wedding day. Bless me, but you look like you could use a good meal." He thought she might poke him in the ribs to feel his bones. She blurted, "Well, don't just stand there in the cold, come in, come in." She pushed Sidney aside and draped her arm over Meredith. "Step aside Sid. Let 'em in."

Sidney squished against the wall, saying something under his breath. He rolled his eyes at Victor as the women passed. Victor wanted to smile back, but caught himself in time. He wouldn't lower himself to their base behavior.

∼

AFTER A HALF AN HOUR of excruciatingly stilted conversation with Sidney Cooper, which mostly orbited around the state of things around the fish market, Cecelia called them into the dining room for dinner.

The dining room table filled half the room. The table could expand to fill the entire space when the need arose. The chair backs nearly knocked into the walls, and Victor had to come to his chair from the side. It wasn't the opulence he was used to at home, but he certainly appreciated the smells wafting from the trays of food steaming on the table. He hoped he didn't get food poisoning.

"Sit, sit," Cecelia insisted.

Victor noticed the two empty chairs off to the side and thought of Clyde and the other brother. He couldn't remember the oldest boy's name, but he remembered he'd been taken prisoner early in the war. Despite the military service pictures of both boys prominently displayed on the mantle in the living room, Sidney had avoided the subject of the war entirely.

Victor gazed over at Meredith, who gave him a wan smile. He sat and put his napkin on his lap. His empty plate sat in front of him and he supposed he'd have to serve himself when the time came.

Sidney sat at the head of the table and Cecelia sat across from him to Victor's left. Sidney extended his hand first to Meredith, then to Victor. Meredith joined hands with Cecelia and he did so as well on the other side. Prayer had never been a part of their dinner routine, but he didn't abhor the idea.

Sidney said a simple prayer, which ended quickly. Victor glanced at Meredith, deciding he'd take his cues from her. He felt out of place and foolish. Perhaps he should just leave, but he was hungry now and couldn't bring himself to do it.

The food passed hand to hand and he took moderate portions as was proper. He couldn't remember the last time he'd eaten ham. They normally ate steak or chicken, but the sauce smelled divine, as did the entire meal.

When everyone had full plates, he took a bite and nearly swooned. He'd eaten at the finest restaurants and, indeed the chef at the estate was world class, but none of them had anything on Cecelia Cooper's fare. As he mopped up every last bit of food, he wondered what in the world her secret could be? It was simple food, but there was something about it that really hit the mark. Cecelia beamed at his obvious enjoyment, and he even caught Meredith smiling at him.

Satisfied, he leaned back in his chair. Sidney and Cecelia exchanged glances and Victor remembered why they were there; the news. He supposed it couldn't be too dire, or they would've come right out with it as they arrived.

Sidney raised his chin. "We've heard from our boys." He smiled and pushed his plate away from himself. "I suppose they aren't boys anymore." He leveled his gaze first at Meredith, then at Victor. "Clyde was wounded in some place called Corregidor. Wounded badly." Meredith gasped and touched her necklace. Sidney continued. "He's gonna be fine, but he has a lot of rehabilitation ahead of him. He's been in Hawaii the past week for surgery, but they're flying him here in two days. He'll be in Samaritan Hospital for a few months."

Meredith exclaimed, "That's great news! He'll be so close. Does Abby know? She must know."

"Yes, Abby's coming home, too."

Meredith gave a chirp of joy and Victor couldn't keep the smile off his face. He knew he must look like a simple dolt, but he couldn't help himself. He didn't think such news would affect him so. Was he simply happy to have his daughter home, or was it more than that? She'd be getting her beloved husband back after all this time, and that would make her truly happy, and somehow that made him happy.

His mood darkened slightly when he remembered what she thought of him. He had to hear of her imminent return from the Coopers instead of his own daughter. Despite the good news, she still wouldn't let him back into her life unless he met her ridiculous demands.

Meredith asked with some trepidation in her voice, "And your other boy, Frank?"

"He's coming home, too."

Victor clapped his hands loudly. He knew Frank had somehow escaped the Japanese, but somehow he never thought he'd actually survive and make it home. It seemed impossible. Everyone stared at the loud clap. He said, "That's great news. When will he arrive?"

"Not for a while. Four months at the earliest."

Meredith gasped. "Why so long?"

"They tell us his health needs monitoring. He's suffered from various tropical ailments while he was a captive," Sidney said.

Cecelia wiped tears from her eyes and blurted, "But he'll be coming home to us. After so many years, they'll both be home again. We can finally be a family again." She looked directly at Victor and said, "Won't it be wonderful to be a family again?"

He nodded woodenly and Meredith gave him a concerned look. He wondered if she knew of Abigail's terms. They'd become closer recently, but when would have they discussed it? Perhaps he should tell her she might dissuade Abigail from her stalwart path.

Cecelia kept up the joyous tirade. "It won't be long before Abby and Clyde have children." She clasped her thick hands together and nearly squealed in delight. "Grand children! Can you imagine? I can't wait!" She reached out and clutched Meredith's hand.

Meredith giggled in delight. Victor hadn't heard such a thing from her in years. It dug deep into his soul and at that moment, he wanted nothing more than to be a part of it. He pictured himself and Meredith bouncing grandchildren on their knees as they beamed at one another. He decided he'd do whatever he needed to do to make that fantasy a reality.

～

GUY HASTINGS WORKED the leather upholstery, covering the steering wheel of the Rolls Royce with his hands. He sat in the back parking lot where he normally picked up his boss, but he wasn't there yet. It wasn't unusual for him to work late, but he'd never seen him work *this* late, especially on a Friday night. On this night of all nights, he needed to be on time. Dangerous men waited for his call.

He checked his watch one more time, then drove to the front of the building. The factory lights leaked from the corners of the doorways and out the top of the windows as the night shift workers toiled away on the production line. He couldn't see Victor's office from outside. He shut the car off and walked across the driveway.

The main front door leading to the office spaces was locked. That was unusual unless Victor had already left. Had a day worker inadvertently locked things up as they left? Perhaps that dolt, Hildreth.

He went to the side door where the factory workers entered. It was unlocked, as usual. He stepped in and had to squint in the bright lights. The sounds of machinery surrounded him, and the smells of oil and sweat mixed in the air. He could go upstairs and try to access the office suites from here, but those doors might also be locked. He stepped out onto the main floor, ignoring the curious glances from the workers whose pale faces reminded him of zombies. Victor's office windows were dark. He cursed to himself. When had he left? Did he suspect something? He doubted that very much. He'd been thorough. *Where the hell are you?*

He needed to make a call. He went to the night foreman's office on the first floor beneath the main offices. He rapped on the door and the foreman's gruff voice said, "Come in."

Hastings pushed the door open, and the foreman's scowl deepened. "Who the hell're you?"

Hastings wanted to throttle the insolent bastard. Didn't he know a superior when he met one? "I'm head of security for Mr. Brooks. I need to use your phone." He stepped to the desk and stood beside the foreman expectantly.

The foreman stood up to his full height. He towered over Hastings, and his arms were twice the size of the security man's. He looked like he could bench press an elephant. "I've never seen you before. Show me some ID or get the hell outta here."

Hastings struck, punching him in the throat with three stiff fingers. The foreman clutched his neck and stuck out his tongue as he tried to catch a breath. He staggered backward and fell hard over his own chair, still gasping for breath.

Hastings stepped to the phone and lifted it off the cradle. He needed privacy. "Get out. I need the room."

The foreman's breath came back in ragged gasps as he picked himself off the floor. The wheezes made him sound as though he had a severe case of asthma. "The hell you say," the foreman croaked. He swung a meaty fist, which would've crushed Hasting's jaw if he hadn't ducked out of the way.

Hastings used the phone as a bludgeon and punched him in the nose, flattening it in a spray of blood. "I don't have time for this," he said as he pushed the big man out the door. He slammed the door and locked the bolt.

He wiped the blood off the phone, then dialed a memorized number. He could hardly hear the voice on the other end answer over the foreman's banging fists. "Yes?"

"Something's happened. Delay until Monday."

There was a long pause, and he could almost feel the anger coming through the phone. "Understood," then a click and a dial tone.

27

Victor and Meredith left the Cooper household around midnight. He hadn't stayed up this late for years. He'd never had an occasion to, but the dinner had been delightful and he enjoyed talking with the Coopers about the possible future they'd share. He didn't know if it was the wine or the good food, but he didn't want the evening to end.

They said their goodbyes and they made their way to the sedan. Meredith held the keys. He'd almost forgotten that she had driven them here. He briefly wondered what had become of Hastings. How long had he sat in the back lot waiting for his boss in the Rolls? It didn't matter. Like Meredith said, he could pound sand.

She went around to the driver's side. He hesitated for a moment, then slid into the front passenger seat beside her. She stared at him for a few long moments, then started the car. "Well, this is much nicer, Victor."

She pulled onto the street. He watched the city lights flash by. Even at this late hour, people still hustled and bustled on the sidewalks. More and more vehicles were on the roads, too. "It looks different from the front seat." He realized it sounded ridiculous.

"Yes," she said and she smiled at him. "So, what do you think of the news? I can't believe the kids are finally coming home."

"I think it's wonderful. I—I can't wait, but . . ." He looked down at his well-manicured hands.

"But, what?"

"Abigail has made it clear that she won't let me into her life until . . ." He didn't know how to proceed. He wrung his hands and stared out the window. He didn't want to ruin the evening by getting into all this.

Meredith slowed the car, reached her hand across, and squeezed his hand. "I know about the journal, Victor. I know about the arson."

Her hand felt warm and soft, but her words cut into him like cold steel. He didn't know what to say. His mouth opened and closed like a gaping fish out of water. He felt a fool and anger grew in his belly. "I—I don't . . ." He was going to say he did what he had to do, but it didn't feel right. That was the old Victor. But admitting it was a mistake, admitting anything having to do with bettering the business he built from the ground up felt wrong, too.

She kept her hand on his. "You made a mistake, Victor. What you do now is what matters."

"She won't let me into her life unless I turn myself into the law." He said it with as much earnestness as possible, as though Abigail was the one being unreasonable, but it felt weak and wrong on his lips.

Meredith continued rubbing his hands. He didn't want that to end. "I could go to jail," he said softly.

"Yes, but then you'd have your daughter and son-in-law back forever. We could have a life together. We could spoil grandchildren together."

"I'd be a convicted felon. The business would surely die."

"What's more important to you? The business or your family? Really, that's the only thing you need to decide, Victor. It's as simple as that."

He looked at her hand stroking his. He'd missed her touch. He didn't remember the last time they'd had a real conversation like this. He remembered why he fell in love with her all those years before. She was obviously a natural beauty, but also whip-sharp smart. He took in a deep breath and blew it out slowly. What happened in the next few minutes would alter the path of his life forever. He felt the heaviness of the decision deep in his bones. "I want my family back," he finally said.

They'd made it to the outskirts of town. Meredith didn't say a word, but she pulled onto a secluded side street and parked. She shut the engine off and faced him in the bucket seat. She leaned forward and Victor felt the heat coming off her body like she'd just returned from a sauna. Their lips met gently at first, but the kiss grew in intensity as an old passion long doused came back to life in a flood of fiery heat.

~

VICTOR WOKE on Saturday morning in his own bed feeling refreshed, despite sleeping only a few hours. He stared at the ceiling for nearly a minute before he turned his head to see if what he remembered from the night before was real or imagined. He was terrified he'd dreamed the whole thing, but he hadn't. Meredith lay on her side, facing him. Her mop of lustrous hair spread out over the pillow and he could smell her perfume and soap. She breathed softly in and out; the air moved a piece of her hair back and forth across her closed eyes. She looked even more gorgeous in her disheveled state than she had the night before. He couldn't take his eyes off her. He couldn't remember the last time he'd made love to his wife— years. *What a fool I've been.*

The make-out session in the car seemed like a dream now. He hadn't done something like that since his school days. Their rekindled passion only grew from there. They barely made it to the bed before they were in each other's arms again. How could've he lived so long without her touch? He'd been depriving himself and he hadn't even realized what he'd been missing. Now he couldn't imagine anything else. They had a lot of catching up to do.

Her eyes flickered open, and she took a moment to focus on him. She smiled and stroked his face with her soft hand. "Victor Brooks, hello. It's been a long time."

He pressed his hand to hers. "Hello Meredith Brooks, yes it has. Too long."

She leaned forward and put her lips to his forehead. He closed his eyes and savored her soft lips. How could he have forgotten those soft lips? She pushed herself out of bed and he marveled at her naked body as she shimmied to the bathroom. She glanced over her shoulder and grinned when she caught him looking. "Eyes front, Mr. Brooks."

He laughed and sat up in bed. *How long has it been since I laughed out of pure joy rather than spite?* He gazed out the window, seeing a grey Seattle day. Despite the dreary weather, the day seemed rife with opportunity. He threw back the covers and walked to the window. He opened the curtains all the way and looked out over the estate. He'd forgotten how beautiful the grounds were.

He heard the shower start in the bathroom. Meredith hadn't used that bathroom or that shower in years. She normally slept in her own room and used her own bathroom and shower. But all that had changed now. He wrapped a bathrobe around himself and went out to the hallway. Across from his room, a full coffee service had been laid out, including three different newspapers. Everything was the same as it always had been, but somehow the sameness had disappeared overnight. Everything felt new.

After he took his coffee and read all three newspapers, he dressed and left the bedroom. Meredith had long since finished her shower and had gone to her room to dress for the day. Victor had nothing planned, but he wanted to spend as much time with Meredith as possible that weekend. But for all he knew, she might already have plans.

Hastings stood at the bottom of the stairs as though on guard duty. It irked Victor. He seemed to be a relic from his past.

Hastings greeted him. "Good morning, sir." Victor lifted his chin but didn't otherwise acknowledge him. He stepped past him and Hastings walked beside him. "You gave me quite a scare yesterday. I thought perhaps something had happened."

Victor glared at him. He didn't like him walking by his side like an equal and certainly didn't like his day-to-day goings on being questioned by him. "Meredith picked me up. Nothing happened to me. Quit being so paranoid."

Hasting's mouth tightened into a thin line. "It's my job to be paranoid . . . sir," he added the sir almost as an afterthought.

Victor stopped and faced the smaller man. "Why don't you take the rest of the weekend off, Mr. Hastings. Surely there's something you'd rather be doing."

Hastings looked truly baffled. "A day off, sir?"

"Yes. I insist. Take the rest of the weekend off. I'll see you on Monday."

"Sir, has something happened? What's going on?"

"Nothing has happened. You're an employee and I'm insisting you take the weekend off. Now go."

Hastings didn't follow him the rest of the way to the breakfast table. Mr. Hanniger stepped forward and held his hand toward the front door. "This way, Mr. Hastings. I'll show you out." Victor gave a thankful nod to Mr. Hanniger.

Victor's heart skipped a beat when he saw Meredith sitting at the breakfast table, sipping coffee. She brightened the room with her smile. They normally sat at the ends of the table, as far apart as possible, but Victor pulled the chair out beside her. The staff adjusted things quickly. "Thank you," he said to Edith, one of the newer staff members.

"Certainly, sir," she answered.

"From now on, we'll be eating in closer proximity. Perhaps we can shorten the table once breakfast is finished."

Edith beamed a bright smile. "Certainly, sir. That'll be no problem."

Victor sat, and Meredith leaned forward and planted a kiss on his cheek. "That'll be nice, darling."

"Yes, it will." He spread his napkin across his lap. Soon, breakfast was served and he savored eggs, bacon, and French toast with globs of butter and maple syrup. He didn't remember breakfast ever tasting this good. He rarely ate more than a piece of toast during the week and even during the weekend, he rarely ate more than a few bites of similar fare.

When he finished, he pushed the plate back, dabbed mouth and placed his napkin on the table. "What would you think if I terminate Mr. Hasting's employment?"

Meredith dabbed the sides of her mouth daintily. He'd never asked her about such things before, but she didn't seem too put out by the question. "I would be in favor of that. There's something about him that seems a little off."

"Yes, Sal said the same thing."

"Well, he's an excellent judge of character."

"Do you think Sal would ever come back if I asked him to? I mean, now that things have changed."

She gave him a long, hard stare. He wondered if he'd said something wrong. She finally said, "Have things changed? I mean, *truly* changed." He stroked his mustache and she continued, but in a lower voice. "I mean, last night was wonderful, but it was just one night. Will you really do as Abigail asked? Will you jeopardize your business and your freedom?"

Anger flashed. Did she doubt his backbone? But she was right. Could she really trust that he'd truly changed? Would he if the roles were reversed?

He pointed to the empty plate. "I've had this breakfast every Saturday for the past twenty years, but it has *never* tasted as good as it did this morning. I understand your trepidation—I truly do—but things feel different now. I feel changed to my core. I really do."

She sighed heavily and closed her eyes as though it was the most beautiful thing she'd ever heard. She said, "Sal has a new life now. He has a new family, but I know he'd be thrilled to visit occasionally."

"Yes, well, I suppose he's earned his retirement working for the likes of me for so long." He clapped his hands, then rubbed them together as though about to dig into a succulent dessert dish. "Now, what do we have planned for the rest of the weekend?"

28

Seattle
Monday, February 26, 1945

Victor Brooks accepted his coat from Mr. Hanniger standing at the door. "Thank you," he uttered. He had a lot on his mind this morning. He'd talked things over with Meredith extensively over the weekend. They'd agreed the best way to proceed was to confer with his lawyer before going to the police. He was willing to face justice, but he wanted to be smart about it. No need to expose himself to more liability than he deserved.

Hastings leaned on the hood of the Rolls Royce, smoking a cigarette. When he saw Victor, he put the cigarette out and held the door open for him. "Good morning, sir."

Victor looked up at him and gave him a quick smile. He'd deal with him after he'd met with his lawyer. One problem at a time. "Good morning."

He slid into the back and watched Hastings walk to the driver's seat. Hastings slid in and adjusted the mirror so his dark eyes could see his boss. "Traffic should be light this morning. I'll have you to the office quickly."

"I'm not going to the office. Take me to my lawyer's office. You know it?"

Hastings glared for a second, making Victor momentarily uncomfortable. Perhaps he should get it over with and terminate his employment now. Mr. Hanniger could certainly drive him. He smiled. *Meredith could, for that matter.* Or perhaps he should take Meredith's advice and take up driving again. But no, he had too much on his mind already.

"Yes, sir. I know it." He pulled into the long driveway leading to the road. He gripped the steering wheel as though kneading dough. Victor couldn't help but notice his agitation. Simple schedule changes seemed to throw the man off his game. It didn't matter, he'd be out of his life by this time tomorrow.

He normally read the paper on his way to work, but today he gazed out the window. Thick clouds overhead threatened rain, but so far it had held off. The road glistened with rain from the day before. Large puddles dotted the road, but the heavy Rolls powered through them as if they weren't there.

The Rolls would likely be one of the first things he'd need to sell off. Meredith assured him they'd be okay, but what did she know? She didn't know their finances like he did. How would she feel if they had to sell the estate? She loved that house. Would she still think they'd made the right decision if she had to move into one of those postage stamp–sized homes in the Coopers' neighborhood? Her closet had more square footage.

He chewed his inner lip and stroked his mustache, watching the trees flash by outside. There had to be another way. Did he really have to give up everything he'd struggled so hard to build?

Then it hit him. He could talk with Trask personally and work something beneficial out with him. He could admit his guilt to him, and they could go into business together. To ease Trask's anger, he'd make an offer he'd be a fool to refuse. He'd take a big hit financially and Brooks Industries would never look the same, but it wouldn't ruin him and he'd stay out of jail. Surely, that would appease his daughter. Bancroft, his Vice President would be livid. He loathed Trask even more than he did, but it wasn't Bancroft's decision. He'd go along or he'd retire.

He slapped his knee. Why hadn't he thought about this before now? Should he turn around and discuss it with Meredith? No, he was his own man. He'd decide. Even with the new plan, he'd still like to run it by his lawyer, though. They could write something up today.

He watched Hastings pass the street to his lawyer's downtown office. "You missed it."

Hastings's dark eyes caught his in the mirror. "Sorry?"

Victor raised his voice. "You missed the turn. My lawyer, remember?"

"Ah, yes. There's construction. It's a mess. I know a way around it."

Victor leaned back. He didn't recall any construction projects. They had put most on hold for the war effort. "Construction?"

"A sink hole, sir. They're filling it in."

Hastings still drove along the route to the office, moving farther and farther from the law office. His route made little sense. He held his tongue for a few blocks, but he finally said, "This isn't right. You're still heading north and we need to head east."

Hastings didn't answer, just kept driving. He turned off the familiar route to the office, but instead of turning right toward the law office, he turned left.

"Where the hell are you going?" He leaned forward so he'd be sure to hear him. "Hastings! Where are you going?"

Hastings sped up but didn't answer. The powerful Rolls shot down the empty road. The buildings here were older and industrial. He'd looked at real estate in this area, but crime rates and maintenance costs deterred him. He didn't see a single car or pedestrian. The area seemed deserted. Fear lanced through him. Something was very wrong. "What is this?" he demanded.

Hastings finally deigned to answer. "I'm taking you to see my boss."

Victor sputtered, "Your—I'm your boss." Hastings's smile dripped with malice.

Victor clutched the door handle but their speed was too great. He'd break something and probably die if he leaped out, but it might be better than wherever this was going. He pulled the handle but lost his grip and fell onto the floor when Hastings slammed on the brakes, sending the large vehicle into a skid. He expertly kept them on the road, and they finally lurched to a stop in the middle of the street.

When Victor picked himself up off the floor, he froze. Hastings aimed a pistol at his head. "You're not going anywhere, Vic."

He felt only anger now. He'd finally figured out a workable plan and now this. "What the hell's the matter with you? Who are you working for?"

Three black sedans pulled out from side streets. Two parked at angles in front and one behind, blocking the Rolls completely. Victor's anger changed to fear when he saw Julius Trambolini himself step out alongside a troop of heavily armed thugs.

Victor gathered himself. Hastings chuckled like a deranged hyena. Victor ignored him and stepped out of the Rolls. Hastings stepped out, too, his pistol steadily aimed at his chest.

Victor raised his hands. He walked toward the overweight Mafia boss. "Julius, what's this all about? I thought we had an agreement."

Julius stepped closer and his black-suited men matched him step for step. Each held a Tommy gun with drum magazines attached. Their grins oozed violence. Julius was dressed in a dark, nondescript business suit. "Hello Victor. I know we discussed an agreement, but I just couldn't let it go. You killed my favorite nephew. I can't let that stand. It's all about family, my friend. You can understand that, can't you?"

"So, you're going to kill me? That doesn't seem very profitable. If you kill me, everything stops. No more payments."

"I considered killing your wife or your daughter, but they don't seem to like you much anyway, so it might not have meant as much to you as my nephew did to me. And as far as payments go? I'm in an excellent position to fold your business into mine." He pointed toward Hastings. "I think a new management style might be in order."

Victor glared at Hastings. "This dolt couldn't run a lemonade stand. I was going to fire him today, in fact. And besides, you'll never have my business."

Julius pulled out a cigarette and one of his men lit it for him with the snap of a Zippo. He whispered something to the man. The thug motioned at the lead sedan and the back door opened. A man dressed in a tan suit stepped out and Victor recognized him instantly. "Bancroft?"

Phillip Bancroft lifted his chin and the folds jiggled. "Hello Victor. Sorry, but they made me an offer I simply couldn't refuse."

"Phillip, you can't do this, you . . ." but Victor realized if they killed him,

Bancroft would be the leading shareholder and become the de facto president. His own VP and Julius Trambolini had outplayed him.

"I can assure you it's nothing personal, Victor. As you always say, it's just business," Bancroft said.

Julius stepped forward. He had a shiny pistol in his hand. Hastings took a step back from Victor, but kept his pistol leveled at his chest. "Here you go, boss. Hand-delivered, just like you wanted."

Julius ignored him and the other Trambolini men scowled at him with outright disdain. No one liked a traitor. Julius raised the pistol and aimed it at Victor's face. His hand didn't waver. "Good bye, Victor Brooks. Nice doing business with you."

Victor gazed at the muzzle and Julius Trambolini's dark eyes just beyond. He saw no mercy there. He closed his eyes and dropped his arms to his side. He pictured Meredith and Abigail at his side, beaming up at him proudly the way they used to so long ago.

~

SAL STEPPED out of the cab and quickly paid the cabbie. "You sure this is the right address?" the cabbie asked.

"I'm sure," Sal said, as he hefted the suitcase out of the back seat.

The cabbie took the money and muttered, "None of my business." The cabbie turned the cab around, nearly squealing the tires in his haste to leave.

Sal took in the wet, deserted streets. The cabbie dropped him off a half block up from the actual address Gil Hicks had given him. Something bad was definitely happening. Even in this part of town, there was normally some traffic. But it was deserted—more like abandoned. It felt unnatural, and the hairs on the back of his neck stood on end.

He trotted along the sidewalk as fast as prudence allowed. He didn't want to stumble upon anyone, but he also felt the pressing urgency. As soon as he and Abigail landed at the airfield on the outskirts of Seattle, he'd called his old friend Mr. Hanniger. Hanniger told him the news he feared hearing; Victor had already left with Guy Hastings as his driver. Sal chided himself for not calling earlier, but he wanted to get on the flight and the one stop they made to refuel didn't have a phone, so he called him as soon as he landed. But was he too late?

He ran faster, throwing caution to the wind. If they saw him, it might not matter anyway. He'd only get one shot at this. He eyed the dilapidated buildings on either side of the road. They were mostly industrial warehouse-style buildings without windows to prop a rifle out of a window.

His breath grew short, and his legs burned. He hadn't kept his physical fitness level up since leaving the employ of Victor Brooks and he felt it with every step.

He turned a corner and nearly tripped when he saw a cluster of cars only sixty yards away. He threw himself to the ground, hoping the sound of the suitcase hitting the pavement didn't attract unwanted attention. He stayed low and hustled to an old bus stop awning. It would not provide suitable cover in a firefight, but it would hide him for the time being.

He glanced through a slit in the side and saw a group of heavily armed men advancing toward a single man with his hands up. Victor Brooks, his oldest friend, was in a heap of trouble.

Sal opened the suitcase and went to work assembling the rifle he'd brought from Virginia. He forced himself not to look at the developing scene. He heard voices and hoped they kept chatting until he completed his task. His hands seemed to be as thick as fenceposts. He forced himself to calm down and concentrate on each movement. It had been a long time since he'd put the rifle together.

He finally finished. He inserted a round and pushed the bolt into place. He went to a knee and rested the rifle barrel on the metal handrail, then put his eye to the sights. A shot rang out and he flinched. Where Victor had stood, he only saw a large man holding a smoking pistol. He recognized Julius Trambolini, Gil's father. He felt sick to his stomach. The body at the mobster's feet didn't move and even from here, he could see the blood running out of his skull. They'd gunned down his oldest friend in cold blood. Rage filled him.

He centered the sights on the big man. His finger went to the trigger. It would be an easy shot from this distance, but he didn't pull the trigger. Something stopped him. A promise he'd made to Gil Hicks. Gil had given him the address in exchange for his word that he wouldn't harm his father, no matter what. He nearly did anyway, consequences be damned, but then he saw another man kneel next to the body of his friend and spit in his shattered face.

Sal rested his sights on Guy Hastings. He was just as much responsible for Victor's death as anyone else, not to mention the hapless bookstore owner. He breathed out slowly, then pulled the trigger. The bullet entered Hasting's temple and blew the side of his head off in a splash of blood and brain. His body tilted into Victor's.

The mafioso men dropped to their knees, bringing their submachine guns up. A few hustled Mr. Trambolini out of harm's way. Sal dropped to his belly. They hadn't seen him, although they'd notice the plume of smoke from the rifle shot soon enough.

He backed as far away as he could get before the structure could no longer hide him, then he darted for the corner. Automatic weapons fire erupted, and the buzz and snap of near misses made him run faster. He dove behind the corner and pressed his back to the wall. He could feel the bullet impacts. He'd left the suitcase on the street along with the extra rifle rounds. It wouldn't have been a fair fight, anyway.

He heard footsteps and yelling, followed by more automatic weapons fire. They'd be at the corner before he could run far enough to find cover and they'd shoot him in the back as he ran. He dropped the useless rifle and pulled his pistol. He hadn't practiced with the newly purchased weapon, but he figured he was close enough to get a few of the bastards before he went down. He centered the muzzle on the corner and waited.

He heard squealing tires and for a moment wondered if they'd bugged out. Then he heard more automatic fire, but the corner didn't explode in brick and mortar dust. The burp of the machine gun came from the other direction. He heard cursing in both Italian and English.

Sal risked a peek around the corner. He saw the mafia men scrambling to find cover. Bullets kicked up chips of concrete and thunked into car metal. Down the street a familiar sedan sped his way, sans the front windshield. Mr. Hanniger steered with one hand and spurted lead in controlled bursts at the fleeing Trambolinis, with the other.

Sal scooped up the rifle and stepped out into the street, waving at Hanniger. Hanniger kept sending shots downrange but angled toward Sal.

At the last instant, he slammed the brakes and the sedan skidded and with a deft jerk of the wheel; the car spun until it faced the other direction. A thick cloud of smoke filled the street, obscuring the sedan.

Sal ran through it as fast as he could make himself run. He jumped into the sedan's back seat. "Go! Go! Go!" he yelled.

Mr. Hanniger passed him the Tommy gun. "Here you go," he said, as though delivering morning coffee. Sal took the submachine gun and leaned out the back window. He sent a few more spurts down the street, but the smoke from the skidding tires was too thick to know if he'd hit anything.

He sat back onto the seat and smacked Hanniger's shoulder. "You saved my bacon back there."

Hanniger sped along the empty street. He eyed Sal in the rearview mirror. "Where's Mr. Brooks?"

Sal felt a lump in his throat as he remembered the body. "He's dead. They shot him in cold blood."

Hanniger gripped the steering wheel and stared straight ahead. "Damn," he said.

"It was Trambolini, just like I figured," Sal stated flatly. Hanniger slowed as he turned and entered a more populated area. Sal said, "I shot that sick little shit, Hastings, though. He's dead."

Hanniger didn't respond. He stayed off the main streets as much as possible. The missing front windshield might attract attention. He finally said, "What now? What about Trambolini?"

Sal pushed his hand through his hair and said, "I made a promise that I wouldn't harm Julius. I could easily have shot him dead, but I shot Hastings instead. He's gotta know I had him dead to rights. I doubt he'll miss Hastings too much."

"So, we're done?"

"I think so," Sal said.

29

Samaritan Hospital
Seattle
March 1, 1945

Abby put her hand on the door to Clyde's room. It felt cold and sterile, just like the whole hospital. She shut her eyes and said a silent prayer. She opened her eyes and pushed the door open slowly, unsure of what she would see, but determined to smile, no matter what.

A bedside light was on, giving the room a warm glow. She smelled antiseptic and stale breath. There was only one bed in the room and thin curtains surrounded it.

She stepped into the room, barely able to breathe. Her Clyde was in there somewhere and, for some reason, it terrified her. What if he didn't want her anymore? What if he turned her away?

She took a cautious step toward the foot of the bed. The doctor said he'd be tired. Perhaps he was sleeping. She heard a stirring from beyond the curtain, then a raspy voice. "Abby? Abby, is that you?"

She threw caution to the wind. She couldn't stop herself. She thrust the curtain back and there he was, staring at her with those gorgeous eyes and that thick wavy hair. She sucked in a breath and fell into him. "Clyde, my Clyde. It's really you." She held his face and took him in.

He grinned, just the way she remembered. "Careful," he said.

She reared back. "Your wounds. I'm so sorry, I forgot. But I can't believe you're really here. You're finally home," she gasped and kissed him on the forehead, her tears splashed onto his face, mixing with his own tears.

"Oh, Abby," he said. "Oh, Abby, I've missed you so," he said. "I thought of you every day."

She touched his face and he cupped hers, wiping her tears with his thumbs. He shook his head, marveling at her face as though he'd never seen it before. "You're even more beautiful than I remember, Abby. How can that be? You're an angel."

"I'm your angel, my darling. I'm all yours, forever and always."

He pursed his lips and nodded. "I know Abby. I've always known."

She put her head gently on his chest. She could hear his heartbeat. It sounded strong and steady. He stroked her hair and kissed the top of her head gently. She'd never been happier a day in her life. Nothing else mattered anymore. She'd lost her father, but gained back her husband. "You came back to me. I knew you would. I don't know how, but I knew you would." She looked at him through tear-blurred eyes. "I've missed you, my love. I love you, Clyde Cooper."

"I love you, too, Abby Cooper."

She placed her lips on his and they kissed, and the world faded away.

～

Brooks Estate
Seattle
September 20, 1945

CLYDE SAT on the bench with Abby by his side. The leaves had turned from vibrant green to yellow, red, and orange. The warm September sun filtered through the leaves in bright shafts of light. It would be one of the last nice days before the winter rains set in. He planned on enjoying every minute.

Meredith sat across from them, sipping iced tea. She had a faraway look in her eyes that reminded him of what she'd so recently lost. He had despised Victor Brooks, and he didn't sound as though he'd improved much since he'd left the states so long ago, but he could see the hurt of loss in her eyes. Even after all the bitterness, she still loved him.

Victor's murder had created quite a stir. The police suspected a mafia-style hit, but with no one coming forward, the police had very little to go on. His body had been found with his security man by his side, both shot by different weapons.

Clyde had never met him, but Abby abhorred the security man. She hadn't trusted him. The whole thing was a mess that he didn't want to be involved with. All he wanted to do was be with Abby.

She had mended her relationship with her mother and Clyde had to admit, Meredith seemed like a much different person than the woman he'd known before the war. Just the fact that she was outside with them and not complaining was proof enough. When she'd visited him in the hospital, she seemed genuinely happy to see him.

Mr. Hanniger stood nearby, ready to refill their glasses. He looked exactly the same, although he seemed to smile more often now.

A car turned into the long lane. Abby stood up abruptly. "They're here. They're finally here."

She jumped up and down like a pogo stick and Clyde stood and put his hand on her arm. He whispered in her ear, "Take it easy, now."

She smiled at him knowingly and stopped jumping. She squeezed his hand and gave him a secretive smile. "I'm just so excited. It's been ages. I can't wait for you to meet them."

The car pulled into the roundabout and parked. Abby could hardly contain herself. She ran to the door as Beatrice sprang out and yelled, "Abby Cooper!"

Right behind her, a little girl with floppy curls going in every direction hit the ground running. She passed her mama and squealed as Abby lifted Cora to the sky and swung her around.

Clyde limped his way to them, seeing the old security man, Sal Sarducci, step from the driver's side. Sal leaned on the door and smiled at the reunion. Clyde wasn't sure he'd ever seen the man smile in his entire life. He always had the feeling he wanted to bury him alive, but now he looked harmless and even possibly endearing.

Meredith settled in beside Clyde, and she strung her arm through his. He didn't need the help, but he appreciated the gesture none the less. She waved at Sal. "Hello, Sal."

He called back, "Hello, Meredith." Sal shut the door and went to stand beside Beatrice.

The toddler arched away from Abby's grasp toward Sal. Abby reluctantly let her go to him, then hugged Beatrice fiercely. They squealed and rocked back and forth. Abby finally pulled away and pointed at Clyde. "Beatrice Malinsky, I'd like you to meet my husband, Clyde Cooper." As she said it, she wrapped her arm through his so mother and daughter surrounded him.

Clyde separated from Meredith and took her hand. Beatrice beamed and blushed. "I've heard so much about you. I feel like I already know you. Welcome home." She winked at Abby. "So handsome," she whispered.

He nodded his thanks. "I feel I know you, too. It's great to finally meet you."

She gestured toward Sal, and he went to her side. Cora leaned into both of them. Beatrice said, "But you introduced me incorrectly, Abby." She extended her left hand and a wedding ring caught the September sun. "I'm Beatrice *Sarducci* now."

Abby released her grip on Clyde and the women screamed nonsense and jumped around before hugging each other. Sal watched bemusedly. Cora wanted to be involved with the squealing women, so Sal put her down. She hopped at their feet, trying to imitate them.

Clyde shook Sal's hand. Sal said, "Welcome home, Clyde." Clyde felt the earnestness in his grip. The scar on his cheek reminded him of his service during the First World War. They had fought on different continents and different eras, but they understood one another perfectly.

Clyde looked him in the eye and said, "Thank you. It's good to be home."

"How are you adjusting?"

Clyde cut his eyes at the still occupied women. "I'm doing alright. I—I still have nightmares, though."

Sal nodded sagely. "That'll get better."

"Will they ever go away?"

"No," he stated flatly.

They retired back to the lawn. The staff brought out more iced tea and Mr. Hanniger held a plate of treats. Cora went up to Mr. Hanniger and tugged on his pant leg. He peered down at her from on high, then lowered the plate of food. She stole a pastry, screamed and darted away. Laughter rolled across the lawn. Clyde smiled at the sweet scene, but laughter wasn't something that came easily for him anymore.

Another car entered the driveway. Clyde recognized his parents beat up old truck. He didn't know they'd be coming tonight. He glanced at Meredith, who gave him a knowing smile.

He raised his glass of iced tea. "Thanks for inviting them. I coulda brought them over if I'd of known."

She smiled, "It was kind of a last-minute thing."

He nodded and watched the truck come trundling down the tree-lined street. He was glad they'd be there for the big announcement. It would save him a trip tomorrow.

He saw his dad driving and his mom beside him, but there was a third person near the window. He stood abruptly and dropped his iced tea. Everyone turned and saw his slack face as he watched the truck approach. He took off as fast as his injured body would allow.

Abby yelled, "Clyde!"

Meredith said, "it's okay, Abby, let him go."

Clyde stopped in front of the driveway and the truck ground to a halt. A cloud of dust engulfed it and the side door opened with a rusty squeak. From the dust, a familiar figure emerged. Clyde gasped, "Frank!" He went to him and stopped just short, to be sure. He looked him up and down, as though he might not be real. "It's really you."

"It's me, little brother."

The brothers hugged fiercely, and Clyde felt that all was finally right with the world.

~

Seattle, WA
January 5, 1946

CLYDE GAZED at the framed picture on his desk of Abby and the baby daughter she held in her arms. The baby wasn't even two months old yet, and she seemed to grow as you watched.

He leaned back in his comfortable chair and looked around the plush office. He lifted the plague, which faced out to anyone entering the office. He polished it with his shirttail and read it out loud, "Clyde Cooper, Trask and Brooks Industries, Vice President." It had a nice ring to it.

He checked his watch and realized he'd be late unless he left right now. He and Abby were having dinner at Sal and Beatrice's house tonight. She was probably already on her way.

He locked the door behind him and strolled past Sal's office. He put his ear to the door and listened in. He could hear papers shuffling. He knocked. "You're going to be late, El Presidente," he teased.

Sal raised his voice. "Come in."

Clyde opened the door. No matter how often he saw Sal sitting at the large desk, he never got used to it. He did an excellent job running the place, but his body just didn't seem to fit, no matter how large the desk or room.

Sal hung up the phone. "That was your mother-in-law."

"Oh? And what's on her mind?"

"She's sending the final paperwork through for the merger. Trask is now a full partner in more than just the name."

"So, have you decided to stay on? I'm sure Trask would love to have you. He knows all about your extracurricular activities. He could use someone like you."

"These past few months have been a living hell. I can't wait to get out from behind this desk. I'm not cut out for it. And as far as extracurriculars, I'm done with that work, too. I enjoyed being retired just fine. Besides, I need more time with Beatrice to give Cora a little brother or sister."

Clyde checked over his shoulder for anyone that might be close by. "You're a crude son of a bitch, you know that?"

"What can I say?"

Clyde closed the door and stood in front of the desk. "So about those extra curriculars . . . is everything good?"

Sal crossed his arms, and his muscles rippled. "Yes. Absolutely. Once I explained to him that he'd lost the Trambolinis' support, Bancroft signed his shares over to Meredith."

"And no pushback from the Trambolinis?"

"No, not since you and Gil chatted with them. Julius knows I coulda killed him. He respects our position. I think he just wants to move on from the whole thing."

"Gil assured me of the same thing, but you never know with the rest of the crew. Gil's still only second in command."

"How's he dealing with his wounds? He seemed pretty messed up last time I saw him."

Clyde grinned. "Are you kidding? He's going through women like a hot knife through butter."

Sal clapped his hands. "Good for him."

"But I think his current girlfriend might be different."

"Yeah? What makes you say that?"

"He's gone out with her more than twice and he looks at her differently than the others. She's tough, and I think he likes that."

"Just like Abby?"

"Yeah, maybe so." He turned to leave, then spun back when he remembered something else. "By the way, I hope you don't mind. My cousin's in town. I invited him to dinner. My brother, too. Neither of us have seen him since before the war."

Sal stood and leaned on the desk. "We can cancel. It's no problem if you wanna spend the night with your long-lost cousin."

"We might go out after, but no. He'll enjoy meeting you and the family."

"I look forward to it. What's he doing now?"

"He was in Burma with some shady unit he doesn't tell me much about in his letters. He was in the airborne just like me, but ended up in Burma somehow. I don't know much more, other than his current job has some-thing to do with his past job."

"He's a spook? A spy?"

Clyde pointed at him. "Bingo. That sounds right."

"Well, your brother's always welcome and your cousin, too." Clyde took a step toward the door. Sal said, "Are you leaving baby Patricia with your parents?"

"They wish. No, little Trish will join us for dinner."

Tark's Ticks
Tark's Ticks Series, Book 1

A desperate and bloody defense in the early days of WWII.

Hours after the fateful attack on Pearl Harbor, the Imperial Japanese Army invades Luzon. The allies retreat to the Bataan Peninsula and the ensuing bloody battle sets the tone for the entirety of the war in the Pacific.

Far from home and abandoned, the brave GIs and Filipinos fight the Japanese to a standstill. Long months of bloody combat take their toll on both sides, however. The Japanese have reserves...the allies don't.

Sergeant Tarkington and the soldiers of the 1st platoon are put to the ultimate test. With dwindling supplies and constant harassment from the battle-hardened Japanese, the GIs must adapt and become a cohesive fighting unit if they hope to survive.

Get your copy today at
severnriverbooks.com

AFTERWORD

Writing this series has been an incredibly arduous, yet rewarding, experience. I never thought there would be so many different storylines diverging in so many different directions. Bringing everything together in this final book proved difficult. I sometimes thought it was an impossible task, but the characters always showed me the way . . . eventually. Thank you for taking a chance with the series. It has been a success because of you, dear reader.

AUTHOR'S NOTE

The fictional character Clyde Cooper was injured early in the battle for Corregidor Island, but the battle actually lasted for ten days. The Japanese lost their communications and their commander early in the fighting, so they never were able to mount a coordinated attack against the paratroopers, even though they greatly outnumbered them.

The retaking of Corregidor Island attracted a lot of attention from the press. Many pictures and videos exist showing the actual drop. It makes for some great viewing. I highly recommend it. You get a proper sense of just how dangerous the drop zones were on the rock-strewn island.

Corregidor wasn't the final battle for the 503rd Parachute Infantry Regiment. They spent the last five months of the war fighting a costly battle on Negros Island in the Philippines, where their unique skills as paratroopers were wasted.

The fictional character Shawn Cooper worked for the OSS and captured a Japanese General in Burma, but that never happened.

The OSS had many important jobs but were most valuable for their intelligence-gathering abilities. After the war ended, the shadowy organization disbanded, but eventually transitioned into the CIA. I think Shawn would fit right into the coming cold war.

The WASP program was deemed a complete success. It freed up many male pilots from stateside duty so they could serve overseas. General Henry "Hap" Arnold pushed for the women to be inducted into the military so they could receive the same benefits as their male counterparts, but the bill didn't pass in congress. President Carter signed Public Law 95-202 in November 1977, which granted former WASP pilots partial veteran status.

ABOUT THE AUTHOR

Chris Glatte graduated from the University of Oregon with a BA in English Literature and worked as a river guide/kayak instructor for a decade before training as an Echocardiographer. He worked in the medical field for over 20 years, and now writes full time. Chris is the author of multiple historical fiction thriller series, including A Time to Serve and Tark's Ticks, a set of popular WWII novels. He lives in Southern Oregon with his wife, two boys, and ever-present Labrador, Hoover. When he's not writing or reading, Chris can be found playing in the outdoors—usually on a river or mountain.

From Chris:

I respond to all email correspondence.
Drop me a line, I'd love to hear from you!
chrisglatte@severnriverbooks.com

Sign up for Chris Glatte's reader list at
severnriverbooks.com

Printed in the United States
by Baker & Taylor Publisher Services